"Here," he said in that husky voice of his.

He held her by the shoulders and made her stand up straight. "Are you too cold?"

Her face, her hands, her feet—yes. But other parts of her?

CJ pushed the hood back for her. The rush of air around the back of her neck made her shiver. "A little," she said, but anything else she wanted to add died on her tongue when he reached up and began to pull the zipper of her suit down.

He was unwrapping her. Slowly.

Oh, yeah—some parts of her were beginning to burn. She wanted to shift her feet to take some of the pressure off her center, but she didn't want to break the spell of this exact moment.

"You never did tell me the other way of warming someone up." She was surprised to hear her own voice come out deeper—more sultry.

Because she wanted this. Not the story, not her ratings—the man.

Rich Ranch is part of the Beau

RICH RANCHER
FOR CHRISTMAS

BY
SARAH M. ANDERSON

MILLS & BOON

First Published in Great Britain 2016
By Mills & Boon, an imprint of HarperCollins*Publishers*
1 London Bridge Street, London, SE1 9GF

© 2016 Sarah M Anderson

ISBN: 978-0-263-91889-2

51-1216

Our policy is to use papers that are natural, renewable and recyclable products and made from wood grown in sustainable forests. The logging and manufacturing processes conform to the legal environmental regulations of the country of origin.

Printed and bound in Spain
by CPI, Barcelona

Sarah M. Anderson may live east of the Mississippi River, but her heart lies out west on the Great Plains. Sarah's book *A Man of Privilege* won an *RT Book Reviews* 2012 Reviewers' Choice Best Book Award. *The Nanny Plan* was a 2016 RITA® Finalist.

Sarah spends her days having conversations with imaginary cowboys and billionaires. Find out more about Sarah's heroes at www.sarahmanderson.com and sign up for the new-release newsletter at www.eepurl.com/nv39b.

To my mom, Carolyn, who insisted I take
touch-typing in high school instead of welding.
You were right. But then, you usually are!

One

An old-fashioned bell chimed as Natalie Baker shoved the door open at Firestone Grain and Feed. Oh, the amount of dirt on that thing—she hoped it hadn't ruined her expensive skirt. Except for the pine boughs and holly that hung in the windows, the entire store looked like it had been rolled through a pasture. She was a long way from downtown Denver.

"Help you?" a man wearing suspenders over a flannel shirt asked from behind the counter. His eyes widened as he took in her five-inch heels and her legs. By the time his gaze had worked its way back up to her perfectly contoured face and professional blow-out, his mouth had flopped open, too. The only thing missing was a stick of grass hanging out of his lips.

"Hello," Natalie said in her best television voice. "I could use a little help."

"You lost?" He looked her over again and she had to wonder if he'd ever had a woman in heels in this feed store before. God knew she wouldn't be here if there were any other option. "You look lost. I can get you back to Denver. Take a left out of the parking lot and—"

She managed an innocent blush and then looked up at him through her lashes. His eyebrows rose. *Excellent*. He was a malleable kind of man.

"Actually," she began, practically purring, "I'm looking for someone. I was hoping you might know him?"

The old man's chest puffed up with pride. *Perfect*.

She *was* looking for someone—that part was the truth. Her information was that Isabel Santino had married a local rancher by the name of Patrick Wesley in the small ranching town of Firestone, Colorado. It had taken Natalie months to track down the marriage certificate in the county courthouses.

That's how long it had been since the Beaumont bastards had revealed themselves to the public, back in September. Zeb Richards was the oldest of Hardwick Beaumont's illegitimate children. Through a great deal of underhanded dealings that were rumored to be possibly illegal and definitely unethical, he had taken control of the Beaumont Brewery. When Richards had done so, he had had another one of Hardwick's bastard sons, Daniel Lee, standing next to him. The two brothers now ran the brewery and, according to their last quarterly statement, their market share was up eight percent.

But there was more to the story than that. Richards had slipped up at a press conference when Natalie had flashed her very best smile at him and he had admitted that there was a third bastard out there. She hadn't been able to get any more information out of him, but that had been enough.

The Beaumont bastards were big, big news. Natalie's show, *A Good Morning with Natalie Baker*, had been milking the Beaumont family drama for months. It'd been easy, for a while. Zeb Richards had taken over the brewery and then had gotten the brewmaster pregnant. Apparently, he had fallen in love with Casey Johnson— or, at least, they were putting on an exceptionally good public face. They had mostly been seen at the playoffs and the World Series—and at their wedding, of course. That alone had fueled a twelve-percent ratings jump throughout the fall.

But it was December now. Richards and his new wife were old news and would stay that way until she had her baby. That was a good six months off and Natalie's ratings couldn't coast that long.

She had tried to dig into Daniel Lee's past, but that had proved nearly impossible. It was as if he'd been erased from the public system. No one knew anything about him other than he'd started running political campaigns a few years ago, but even then, she couldn't find anything. He was reputed to play hard and dirty—just like a Beaumont, she figured—but any question Natalie had asked about Lee had been met with a blank stare and a shrug.

That left her with one option and one option only: the mysterious third Beaumont bastard. Which presented its own special set of challenges because no one knew anything about the man except that he existed.

Natalie needed this story because she needed her show. Without it, what did she have?

"Well now, I know just about everyone around these

parts. I'm sure I can help you out," the old man said. "Who are you looking for?"

"I believe his name is Carlos Julián Santino? He also might go by Wesley." She batted her eyelashes at the old man. "Do you know where I might be able to find him?"

The old man's grin cracked and he looked significantly less welcoming. "Who?" he asked after a long moment.

That long moment told her things. Specifically, it told her that this feed store owner knew exactly who she was talking about—but he wasn't about to give it away. *Interesting.* She was getting closer.

"His mother's name was Isabel? She might go by Isabella."

"Sorry, missy, but I don't know anyone by those names."

"Are you sure?" She fluttered her eyelashes at him. "I can make it worth your while."

The old man's cheeks shot red. "Can't help you," he grunted, retreating a step. "Do you need any cat food? Dog food? Horse feed? Salt licks?"

Dammit. She was getting closer, she could feel it—but she had overplayed her hand.

An insidious voice whispered in the back of her head—*you can't do this.* Natalie tried to push that voice away, but it was persistent. It always was.

She needed to find Carlos Julián Santino. *A Good Morning* was everything she had and she couldn't let a little something like the lack of exclusive celebrity gossip be the final thing to take her down.

Still, she wasn't going to find out anything else in this feed store. Maybe there was a café or a diner in town. She'd only started here because, as far as she could tell,

Patrick Wesley owned a ranch where his family raised beef cattle and surely, cattle ate…something. She wasn't even sure if the Isabel Santino who had married Patrick Wesley was the same Isabel Santino listed on the birth certificate from the Swedish Medical Center in Denver. There was no mention of any child in the marriage certificate and, try as she might, Natalie had been unable to turn up any adoption record between Patrick Wesley and Carlos Julián Santino.

So she could still be wrong. But given the feed store owner's reaction? She didn't think she was.

She slipped one of her business cards out of her coat pocket and forced her most winning smile back onto her face, as if she weren't grossly disappointed. "Well, if you hear anything, why don't you give me a call?" She pushed the card across the counter.

The man did not reach out and pick up the card, so Natalie left it in the dust. She turned to go…only to find herself directly in the sights of a tall, dark and extremely handsome cowboy.

"Oh!" She put a fluttering hand to her chest, playing up her delicate sensibilities to the hilt. "I didn't see you there."

The cowboy's face was in dark shadows under the brim of his black hat, but she could tell he was watching her. Had he been there the entire time? It would be easier to flirt with him if he hadn't seen her flirting with the old man.

Of course, it would be easier to flirt with this cowboy, period. Even though he was wearing a thick sheepskin coat, she could tell his shoulders were broad. He didn't look like a man pretending to be a cowboy—he looked like a man who worked with his hands day in and day out. What kind of muscles were underneath that coat?

"Who are you looking for?" he asked, his voice deep and low and carrying just a hint of menace.

A delicious shiver went through her that had nothing to do with the cold. Her gaze dropped to where his hands rested on his hips. Dear God, look at those hands. Massive and rough-looking—a working man's hands. Not smooth and polished and manicured. Not perfect. But *real*. How would those hands feel on her skin? Her body tensed at the thought of his fingers tracing a line down her chest, circling her nipples…

Oh, she could have a lot of fun with a cowboy like him. If she hadn't had an audience, she might've told him that she was looking for *him*.

But she did have an audience. And a lead to chase. So she put on her most sultry smile. "Have you ever heard of Isabel Santino or Carlos Santino?"

His reaction to these names was so subtle she almost missed it, but a muscle ticked in his jaw. He tilted his head back—not far enough that she could see his eyes, but far enough she knew he was looking her up and down. She rolled her shoulders forward and popped out a hip—her Marilyn Monroe pose. It was usually *very* effective.

Today must not be her day, though. Not even the best that Marilyn had to offer got anything out of this cowboy. He might look like a fantasy come to life, but he clearly wasn't going to play along. "Wilmer's right—I've never heard of either of those people, certainly not here. And this is a small town."

"What about Wesley?"

She saw that muscle in his jaw twitch again. "Pat

Wesley? Sure, everybody knows Pat." He tilted his head down again, hiding the rest of his face in shadows. "He's not here, though."

All the smiling was beginning to make her cheeks tight. "Where is he?"

She had couched the question in a sultry tone but the corner of the cowboy's mouth twitched up—was he laughing at her?

He leaned an elbow against a stack of feedbags. He wasn't her type—but there was something so gritty about this cowboy that she couldn't look away. "Why do you want to know? Pat's just a rancher. Keeps to himself—lived here his whole life. Not much to tell, really."

This cowboy was not following the script. He wasn't taking her seriously and he wasn't falling under her spell. Most importantly, he wasn't giving her anything she could use. Quiet ranchers who kept to themselves did not make for good headlines.

"Do you know if he has an adopted son?" She knew that Carlos Julián Santino would be thirty-four years old. She didn't know how old this cowboy was—there was no way to tell, with his face in the shadows like it was.

There was that twitching in his jaw again. But he said, "Ma'am, I assure you he does not."

What if she were wrong? *Of course you're wrong*, the voice in the back of her head scolded her.

It was ridiculous for her to have thought she could find the one man nobody else could. *She* was ridiculous, pinning all her hopes and dreams for ratings gold, for fame and fortune, onto the Beaumonts and their various and sundry bastards.

She swallowed down the bitter disappointment. Unexpectedly, the cowboy tilted his head to one side, letting a little light spill across his features. It was a damn shame he wasn't more helpful—or more interested—because he was simply gorgeous. He had a strong jaw with a healthy two-week stubble coming in that made her want to stroke his face and other things. What color were his eyes?

No, she shouldn't be thinking about this guy's eyes. She should be focused on her end goal—finding the lost Beaumont bastard. What would his eyes be like? Dark? Or light? Zeb Richards's eyes were a bright green—which really stood out on a black man. She didn't know if Carlos Santino's eyes would be light or dark.

Still, she wanted to see what this cowboy's eyes looked like. Would they tell her something that his body wasn't? If she could get a good look at his eyes, would she see wariness—or want?

He tilted his head back down, throwing his face completely in shadows again. *Crap*. This was not her lucky day. This man was immune to her charms and she couldn't stand in a feed store all day. She might not be very smart, but even she knew when to cut her losses. She pulled out another card and offered it to the cowboy. "If you find out anything, I can make it worth your while."

He didn't take the card. "I'm sure you can, Ms. Baker." He stepped toward her and Natalie tensed. He knew who she was? Was he a viewer? A fan? Or was he one of those anonymous internet trolls who made her skin crawl even as she craved their attention?

Because when they were insulting her, at least they were paying attention. She was *someone*, even if she was someone they despised.

But he stepped around her, careful to cut a wide enough berth that there was no accidental touching. Instead, he went to the counter and leaned against it, his entire body angled toward Wilmer.

The body language was clear. It was them against her.

She did what she always did when she felt insecure— she took up as much space as she could. She straightened her shoulders and shot another one of her best smiles at the two men.

She said, "Gentlemen," even though it was pretty clear that was a loosely applied term at best. And then, head held high, she walked out of the Firestone Grain and Feed and contemplated her next move.

"What the heck was that all about?" Wilmer asked, scratching the back of his head.

CJ Wesley kept an eye on the woman through the grimy windows of the feed store. She stood on the front step, no doubt plotting where to look for him next. Jesus, Natalie Baker was even more gorgeous in real life than she was on television. And in that outfit?

He knew what she was wearing was part of her act. No sane human would drive out to the windswept northern hills of Colorado in December in a skin-tight black skirt that, with black lace overlaying a black silk lining, looked exactly as warm as a bathing suit. Between the skirt and the sky-high heels—he was damn impressed at how she walked in them—her legs were what men wrote poetry about.

CJ cleared his throat. He wasn't a poet and he wasn't interested in Natalie Baker. As he watched, she stepped carefully down the stairs and moved toward a red convertible—a Mustang. Was there any car less appropriate for December in Colorado than that one?

Then again, everything about Natalie Baker was inappropriate, from her amazing cleavage to her fake smiles to her terrifying questions.

"No idea," CJ lied.

"She's one of those TV people," Wilmer said, and CJ had to wonder if Wilmer had just figured that out. He was many things, but Wilmer was not a morning-chat-show guy. If anyone paid even the slightest attention to the morning shows, they'd recognize Natalie Baker immediately. She kept her finger firmly on the pulse of the Denver social scene. If a sports star cheated on his wife, an actress fell in love or, say, a billionaire fathered a bunch of illegitimate children, Natalie Baker was there.

Which meant she was *here*.

Of course, CJ knew Natalie Baker was a beautiful woman. Her face smiled out at him in high definition every morning. But in real life, she'd not only been more beautiful, but also more…delicate, too. Although that could have just been the juxtaposition of her expensive clothes and perfect makeup with the grime of the feed store.

Wilmer waited until her car was out of sight before speaking again. "What do TV people want with your dad?"

"Don't have a clue," CJ lied again. Because he knew. He knew exactly why Natalie Baker was here. It had very little to do with his father, Patrick Wesley.

It had everything to do with Hardwick Beaumont.

CJ shook his head, hoping Wilmer would read it as confusion. "Dad's not even here," he reminded Wilmer because CJ knew one thing: all the gossip in this town ran through Wilmer. The Firestone Diner was almost as bad, but Wilmer Higgins at the Firestone Grain and Feed was officially worse. CJ had to get out in front of this and make sure Wilmer had his version of events before anyone started looking around too hard. "You know that man's never done a scandalous thing in his life."

It helped that Pat Wesley had lived in Firestone for all of his fifty-six years. Everyone thought they knew everything about him and not a damn bit of it was scandalous. He was the third generation of Wesleys to raise beef cattle on his land—CJ was the fourth. As far as this town was concerned, the most outrageous thing Patrick Wesley had ever done was marry a woman named Bell that he'd met while he was in the army instead of the girl who'd been his high-school sweetheart. But that had been thirty-three years ago, and since then?

CJ knew exactly how dull his dad was. It was not a bad thing. Patrick Wesley was a good man and a good father, but his idea of a wild Friday night was driving to the next town over to eat at Cracker Barrel and even then, he'd be home by eight and snoring in his recliner by eight thirty. Safe? Yes. Reliable? Absolutely.

Newsworthy? Not a shot in hell.

CJ didn't know what made him madder about the sudden appearance of the gorgeous Natalie Baker asking questions—that the people he'd grown up with might one day figure out he wasn't actually Pat's son or that, once they found out, they might treat Pat and Bell Wesley differently.

He knew who Natalie was, of course. She was hard to miss. Her beautiful face was on his screen every morning at seven thirty. CJ didn't actually like her show—it was too much gossip and innuendo about celebrities.

But she also seemed to be the first to know anything about the Beaumonts. It wasn't like CJ religiously followed them. Hell, he didn't even like their beer. But he liked to stay informed. And that meant he caught *A Good Morning with Natalie Baker* most days.

Besides, it wasn't like he was watching it for her. He wasn't. Yes, she was beautiful on screen and, okay, she was stunning in real life. That had nothing to do with anything. He preferred that station's morning weatherman to the other options, that was all. So watching her show was just a matter of convenience, really.

"I know," Wilmer said, snapping his suspenders. "It just don't make a lick of sense. I mean, you weren't adopted."

CJ forced himself to smile. "That's what they tell me," he said in a joking tone. It was a relief when Wilmer chuckled. "Clearly, they have the wrong Wesley." Wilmer nodded and CJ took advantage of the pause to ask about the latest supplements for his horses. Wilmer enjoyed gossip, but he wasn't about to miss out on a chance to sell a feed supplement.

CJ didn't actually want the supplement but it was a small price to pay for distracting Wilmer from one Ms. Natalie Baker. He finished up his regular order with a sample of the new supplement and headed out to his truck.

He was going to have to tell his mother. She had lived in fear of the day when the Beaumonts would come for him. He had heard all the stories and, for years now, had followed all the headlines. He knew Hardwick Beaumont was dead and the idea didn't bother him even a little. He couldn't even bring himself to think of the man as his father—not even his birth father. Hardwick had been nothing more than a sperm donor. Patrick Wesley was his father in every sense of the word. He knew it, his parents knew it and the state of Colorado knew it. End of discussion.

God, this was going to upset his mother. She had relaxed after Hardwick's death—although by then, CJ had been twenty-one and a man in his own right. But Bell Wesley had lived in fear that Hardwick Beaumont would come for her son for so long that worrying about it was a reflexive habit she couldn't break. It was one of the reasons why his parents wintered in Arizona now. The Denver TV stations were saturated with Beaumont Brewery Christmas commercials this time of year and it always upset her. And his dad hated it when his mom was upset.

CJ always missed them at Christmas, but otherwise, he was glad to have the place to himself. And when they came back from wintering in Arizona, they were happy and relaxed and everything went smoothly.

This year, he was even gladder they were in Arizona. If Natalie Baker had found his mother and started asking questions, Mom might've had a nervous breakdown.

He drove slowly through town, keeping his eyes peeled. It was impossible to miss her Mustang parked in front of the diner.

Damn it all. He knew deep in his heart that he had not seen the last of that woman. Isabel might've gone by Bell and they might've downplayed her being Hispanic, but it was a damn short leap from Carlos Julián to CJ.

It was only a matter of time until he was outed as one of the Beaumont bastards.

Two

There were many things Natalie wasn't—talented, pretty, likable, smart—but no one could say she wasn't persistent. Even her father would have to grudgingly admit that she didn't give up when the going got tough. It was maybe the only valuable lesson he'd ever taught her.

She shivered in her car, cranking the heat up a little more—not that it made a difference. The winds were blowing out of what she assumed was the north with a howling ferocity and there was no way her trusty Mustang was going to keep the chill at bay.

She'd spent the better part of the last three weeks visiting Firestone, making friends with the locals and trying to weasel out more information about Patrick Wesley and his family. It had not been easy. For starters, the coffee at the diner was awful and no one in this town had ever heard of a latte. More than that, it felt like the town had closed ranks. Just like that handsome cowboy and the feed store owner had.

Natalie was an outsider and they weren't going to allow her in.

Still, she had just enough celebrity cachet to razzle-dazzle some of the locals. She was famous enough and pretty enough and she knew how to use those assets like laser-guided weapons. She had spent weeks flirting and smiling and cooing and touching the shoulders of men who probably knew better but were flattered by a young woman paying attention to them.

Maybe they did know better. Because it hadn't been one of the old geezers who'd finally slipped up. It had been a younger man, in his late twenties and full of swagger. He'd been the only real threat to her. The old guys never would've followed up on her flirtations, which was why it was safe to make them. But this guy had seen her as someone he could use just as much as she could use him.

He had finally given her what she wanted, after she had made some vague promises that maybe the next time he was in Denver, he should look her up. It turned out that Pat Wesley—who appeared to be some sort of saint, according to the locals—*did* have a son. That in and of itself wasn't so unusual.

But his son's name was CJ.

Carlos Julián Santino *had* to be CJ Wesley. There was simply no other alternative.

She rubbed her arms over her coat, trying to keep the blood circulating through some of her body. She had been sitting outside of the house on Wesley land for half an hour and she wasn't sure how much longer she could take it. It was *freezing*.

She kept going over the questions she'd ask this Wesley guy. Maybe it was the mind-numbing cold, though, because her thoughts kept drifting back to the second person she'd talked to—the tall, dark cowboy in the feed store.

Despite the amount of time she'd spent in Firestone over the last three weeks, she hadn't seen him again. Not that she'd been looking—she hadn't. He'd made his position clear. He would not help her and she couldn't afford to waste time on a dead end.

But that hadn't stopped her from thinking of him. It was hard not to—not when she peeled that heavy sheepskin coat off his body and threw his hat to the side in her dreams. She'd spent weeks waking up frustrated and achy, all because of one cowboy with an attitude problem.

What had his eyes looked like? Did he watch her show? Did he ever wonder what she was like?

While she mused, she kept scrolling through Twitter. Her last tweet—a tease about tomorrow's big reveal of a "major star" on *A Good Morning*—had only gotten four retweets. She clicked over to Instagram and saw that the cross post had gotten no replies.

Tightness took hold of her chest that had nothing to do with the cold. It'd been like this for weeks now—her reach falling, her interactions dropping off a cliff. If no one paid attention to her, she wouldn't matter. At least if they were mad at her, they were paying attention. But once the attention stopped…

Her phone pinged—a text from her producer, Steve. Anything yet?

Natalie forced herself to breathe once, and then twice. Working on it, she texted back.

The latest numbers are in—you're falling behind. If you can't pull this out, I'm giving your slot to Kevin.

The tightness in her chest squeezed so hard she had trouble breathing. There was no way she could wait until the next Beaumont baby was born—she needed Carlos Julián Santino or CJ Wesley or whatever name he went by and she needed him *now*. She could not lose her spot to Kevin Durante. Kevin had great hair and that was it. He was dumber than a post, lousy in bed and, unfortunately, was exactly the sort of benign golden boy that did well on morning television. She'd rather cut off her toe than give her spot to Kevin.

No worries! she texted back. I'll be in touch.

There was an agonizingly long pause before Steve replied. You better be right about this, Baker.

I won't let you down! she texted back, hoping that sounded far more confident than she felt.

Steve was running out of patience with her. If she lost ground to *Denver This Morning*, then she'd be out of a job, out of broadcasting, out of the public eye. Steve's job security rested entirely on beating *Denver This Morning* in the ratings. She knew damn good and well he wouldn't go down with her ship. He would replace her in a heartbeat if it came to that. With Kevin.

So, she continued to sit in the freezing cold outside of the Wesley house, waiting. The house was dark and she had knocked on every visible door when she'd arrived. She was as confident as she could be without breaking and entering that no one was home.

Okay, she bargained with herself, she would tough it out for ten minutes and if no one showed up she would head back to the diner. The coffee might be god-awful, but it was hot. And maybe that grumpy cowboy would show up.

She spent the next ten minutes toggling between Twitter, Instagram and Facebook, trying to fight the growing sense of panic at the lack of likes and hearts and favorites and retweets. Clearly, her last posts hadn't been shocking enough. Feeling desperate, she posted: Rumor has it that Matthew Beaumont and his child-star bride Whitney Wildz are expecting—but is the baby really his?

She felt a pang of guilt at the lie before she reminded herself that the Beaumonts were a public entity and this was how the game was played. Besides, if anyone could handle the heat, it was PR genius Matthew Beaumont. Really, the Beaumonts should be thanking her. She helped them sell beer, after all.

The guilt successfully contained, she posted and cross-posted the rumor. As the comments added up and the retweets accumulated, the tightness in her chest loosened. This was better. She had a therapist once tell her that her need for approval was unhealthy and she should accept herself for who she was. Natalie had accepted that she was not going back to that therapist ever again.

Still, she was freezing. She put down her phone and went to put her car into Reverse when she saw it—a vaguely familiar pickup truck rolling up behind her. *Oh, thank God*—she was in no mood to die of frostbite out in the middle of nowhere.

Well, well, *well*. If it wasn't a particularly familiar-looking tall, dark, handsome cowboy climbing out of that pickup truck. She should've known. The cowboy in the black hat from the feed store was none other than Carlos Julián Santino Beaumont Wesley. That muscle twitch in his jaw—that was his tell. She had been so close to the truth—why hadn't she seen it?

Her heart did a funny little skip at the sight of him and honestly, she wasn't sure if that was because he was the man she'd been searching for to secure her job for the foreseeable future or...

Or if she was just glad to see him.

That was ridiculous. She wasn't glad to see him and he sure as hell wasn't glad to see her—even at this distance, his scowl was ferocious. She waited until he had shut the door of his truck before she opened her own door. She unfolded her legs slowly, letting her skirt ride up a little so he could catch a glimpse of her thigh as she stood. "We meet again."

A whole lot more than his jaw was twitching. "What the hell are you doing here?"

He was pissed, but she refused to cower. "I believe I've been looking for you, Mr. Santino. Or should I say, Mr. Beaumont?"

She was pushing her luck and she knew it. He was practically vibrating with rage and no amount of bare leg was going to appease him. If only she'd guessed that the man she was looking for was the cowboy from the feed store, she would've at least put on long pants because that cowboy had not been interested in her body. And, by all accounts, he still wasn't.

"My name is Wesley," he said through gritted teeth.

"Sure, we can play it that way. CJ Wesley, right?"

With shivering fingers, she pulled out her phone and opened up the camera app.

The next thing she knew, she was staring at her empty hand. She blinked and looked up just in time to see Wesley pocketing her phone. "Hey! Give that back!"

"No," he said, and almost smiled. "I don't think I'm going to. You're on private property, Ms. Baker. You're about two steps away from flat-out stalking me. You've been working your way through the population of Firestone for the last three weeks trying to get out here. I'm trying to think of a good reason why I shouldn't call Jim Bob and have you arrested for stalking, trespassing, and—" His gaze swept over her body. "And sheer stupidity. Did you even look at the weather before you drove out here today? Don't you know there's supposed to be a blizzard that hits tonight? And you're out here in what—a pair of heels and a skirt? You're lucky you're not dead of exposure already."

She stared at him and, for a moment, forgot to arrange herself in the most seductive way possible. The first part of what he said—the trespassing and stalking—wasn't so surprising. She'd had people angry at her before.

But the part about the blizzard and exposure? He was mad at her—perhaps justifiably—but it had almost sounded like he was concerned about her. "Our meteorologist said it wasn't going to hit until tomorrow."

"Get in your car," he said sharply.

The force of his words backed her up a bit. Although it could have been the wind. "What? No! You're crazy if you think I'm going anywhere without my phone."

Unexpectedly, he jerked his head up and looked at the sky. Dark, she realized. His eyes were a deeper color—hazel? Maybe light brown. Not the light green of so many of the Beaumonts. The shadow from the brim of his hat had to have been the reason why she hadn't seen the Beaumont in his face in the feed store. Every Beaumont man had the same jawline. CJ Wesley was no exception.

She was beginning to shake, the wind was that vicious. She eyed his heavy sheepskin coat with jealousy. "Look," she began, "I'm sure there's something—"

"Ms. Baker," he interrupted, "get in your car and start driving. That storm isn't going to hit tomorrow. It's coming. Now." As he spoke, he reached back into the bed of his truck and pulled out several grocery bags. "And I'm not giving you your phone back. I'll take a hatchet to it before I let you take pictures of me and splash them all over God's green earth. My life is not for sale." He looked up at the sky and grimaced. "City slickers," he mumbled, she thought.

He brushed past her, moving too fast for her to grab him and get her phone out of his pocket. He set down the groceries on the porch and fumbled with his keys.

She just stood there, gaping at him. "I am *not* leaving without my phone." Her life was on that phone— her connection to the world. If she didn't have it…well, she didn't have anything.

He stopped as he got the door open and turned back to her. "You leave right now or you won't be leaving at all." He pointed at the sky behind her.

Reluctantly, Natalie turned her face into the wind. It was so bitingly strong that it was hard to keep her eyes open. Finally, she saw what he was talking about. It wasn't just the gray sky that had washed the colors out of the landscape—it was a huge gray cloud. Suddenly, she could tell that it was moving—quickly. The cloud was bearing down on them, erasing the landscape underneath it. It was a living, moving thing—a wall of swirling white. She hadn't noticed because she'd been too busy looking at her phone and then at him. There weren't many buildings around here to use as landmarks, but it was clear now that the storm was almost upon her and that she was *screwed*.

For the first time that day, she felt real fear. Not just the everyday anxiety that she struggled with all the time—no, this was a true, burning fear. Storms in Denver could be a weather event—but there were snowplows and twenty-four-hour pharmacies. There were snow shovels and sidewalks, and sooner rather than later, she would be able to get out and move around her city.

But now she was in the middle of nowhere with a blizzard about to hit. This wasn't the makings of a white Christmas. And given that she was already half-frozen, it wouldn't take much to finish her off.

She didn't know how long she stood there, staring at the cloud wall. Time seemed to slow down the faster the storm moved. Then, suddenly, she was in the wall of snow and wind. She tried to scream, but the wind tore her cries out of her throat and threw them away. Her first instinct was to curl into a ball and shield her nearly bare legs, but dimly, in the back of her mind, she knew she needed to move. Standing still meant death. Not the slow death of a ratings slide. A real, irreversible, not-coming-back-from-it death.

She stumbled to one side, but the wind pushed her back. Her car! She looked around but couldn't even see the Mustang. There was nothing but gray and stinging snowflakes and blisteringly cold wind.

Then, unexpectedly, she felt something warm and solid at her back. Arms closed around her waist and physically lifted her into the air. *Wesley.* Her first instinct was to struggle—but the fact that he was warm overrode everything else. She let him carry her, trusting that he knew where he was and where he was going. After what seemed like an hour but was probably only a minute or two, a dark shape loomed out of the snow—the house. He carried her up steps and thrust her through the door, where she promptly tripped over the groceries. She landed with a thud on her bottom, dazed and freezing and wet.

She looked up and saw Wesley struggling to get the door shut. He put his shoulder into it and slammed it against the wind, and instantly, she felt at least ten degrees warmer.

"Thank you," she said. Well, she tried to say it. Her teeth were chattering so hard what came out sounded more like a keyboard clicking.

Wesley loomed over her, his hands on his hips. At some point, he'd lost his hat, which meant that for the first time, she had a really good look at his face. His hair was a deep brown and his face was tanned. He had snowflakes stuck to his two-week beard. She couldn't stop shivering, but he just stood there like an immovable boulder.

An *angry* immovable boulder.

She didn't like the way he was looking at her, as if he could see exactly how worthless she felt. So, still shaking so hard that she could barely get her feet under her, she stood. It was then she realized she'd lost one of her shoes. Dammit, those had been Dolce & Gabbana.

"Thank you," she said again. It came out less clicky this time. "I'll just warm up and then I'll go." She swallowed. "I'd like my phone back, please, but I promise I won't take any pictures of you." It hurt to make that promise because her producer was expecting results and without them…

CJ Wesley had just saved her life. He obviously didn't like her, but he'd still dragged her into his house. And for that, she was grateful.

"You don't get it, do you?"

She could be grateful and still be irritated at the tone in his voice, right? "Get what?"

"The convertible of yours? It's not four-wheel drive, is it?"

"No…"

He sighed heavily and looked toward the ceiling. "I send you back out in this, assuming you can even get to your car before you freeze to death in that getup," he said, waving a dismissive hand at her outfit, "you won't make it off the property. You'll drive off the road, get stuck in a ditch and freeze to death before nightfall." He leveled a hard gaze at her and all of her self-defense mechanisms failed her. She shrank back. "You're stuck here, Ms. Baker. You're stuck here with me for the duration."

Three

"*What?*"

CJ had to stop himself from stepping forward and brushing the snowflakes from her eyelashes. She was an ice princess right now, the White Witch of Winter. If he wasn't careful, she just might bewitch him. "You're not going anywhere."

She shuddered again and this time, he didn't think it was entirely from the cold. Now what? Maybe he should have just left her out there, since he couldn't seem to get rid of her any other way.

But even as he thought it, he felt guilty. That was not the Wesley way and he knew it. So now, it appeared he would be spending the next several days—possibly even Christmas—with Natalie Baker. The one woman who had not only figured out he was related to Hardwick Beaumont, but also wanted to use that knowledge for...for what? Ratings?

"I could…" She looked out the front window. CJ looked with her. It was a solid mass of gray. It could've been fog, except for the small particles of snow and ice pinging off the window.

"No, you can't. I'm not going to let you freeze to death out there." He gritted his teeth. How was he going to keep her out of his business if she were physically stuck in his house?

How was he going to keep his hands off of her if she were stuck in his house?

Hell, he'd already failed at that. He'd picked her up and all but slung her over his shoulder like he was a caveman, dragging her back to his cave. Her body had been cold, yes—but also soft and light and…

"You're probably freezing," he went on, trying to stay in the present.

Because the present was a wet woman who was criminally underdressed. He needed to get her warmed up before she caught her death. And given the way the wind was howling out there, he didn't have a lot of time. "You better take a hot shower while we still have power. And if there's anyone you need to call to let them know you're all right, you should do that now." She opened her mouth but he cut her off. "You can use my house phone."

He wanted her to move, or at least do something—but she didn't. Instead she looked at him with a mixture of confusion and anxiety. "Are you being nice to me?"

"No," he answered quickly, even though it was a lie and they both knew it. "But I don't want your death on my hands."

That statement sobered her up. "Oh."

She sounded small and vulnerable and dammit, that

pulled at something inside of him. But he wasn't going to listen to that something because he liked to think he wasn't an idiot. And only an idiot would fall for whatever Natalie Baker was trying to pull over him. She'd spent weeks hunting for him and she'd already tried to use her fabulous body as an enticement on more than one occasion. For all he knew, she had decided raw sexuality wouldn't work and instead was making a play for his heartstrings.

It wasn't going to work. He was immune to all the vulnerability she was projecting right now. "Who do you need to call?"

He wouldn't have thought it possible, but she seemed to get even smaller. "Well, I guess..." There was a long pause. "Well..." she said again, blinking furiously. "No one."

He stared at her. "You're probably going to be here for Christmas, you realize that, right?" Surely, there had to be someone who would miss her. She was a famous TV personality. He'd recognized her the moment she set foot in the feed store. Someone as beautiful and talented as Natalie Baker... Even if she didn't have close family, she had to have friends.

She shook her head. Then she tried to smile. "I'm not going to lie, the shower sounds great. I don't think I've ever been this cold."

He eyed her clothes again. She kicked out of her other shoe, and suddenly, she barely came up to his shoulder. She had nothing on her legs but a tight, short skirt underneath a peacoat in a wild fuchsia color. He couldn't decide if she was oblivious or just stupid about the weather. Or if she'd planned it this way—planned on getting herself trapped out here with him.

Either way, he was willing to get her some dry clothes. That skirt wasn't going to keep her warm even if he got his fireplace cranked up. "All right. But," he said before she could make a move deeper into his house, "these are the rules. I hold on to your phone for as long as you're here and you stay out of my life. Otherwise, it's a hell of a long walk to town in this weather."

He wouldn't really kick her out—but she didn't need to know that.

For a second, a sign of toughness flashed over her face and he thought she was going to argue. But just then, the wind rattled the door and the color—what little of it she'd managed to regain—drained from her face. She nodded, looking almost innocent. "Understood. I'm sorry that I'm intruding upon your Christmas."

He rolled his eyes. "Are you?"

It wasn't a nice thing to say—thereby proving her wrong. He wasn't being all that nice to her. Which bothered him, even though it shouldn't. It especially bothered him when she had the nerve to look so... defeated. Sure, maybe that was the wet clothes and the straggly hair—and the mascara that had started to slide. The woman before him right now was anything but polished.

Before his guilt could get the better of him, he said, "This way."

This was a mistake because someone like Natalie Baker—he didn't even know what to call her. A journalist? A reporter? A talking head? Well, whatever she was, he knew that he wouldn't be able to keep her out of his life, not if they were going to be stranded here for four or five days. Sooner or later, she'd stumble upon something he didn't want her to see. His baby book or the awkward photo from eighth grade when he accidentally cut his hair into a mullet while trying to be fashionable.

He hoped she'd take a *long* shower so he could do a sweep of the house and hide as much of his life as he could.

He passed the thermostat and cranked it up. It might get warm in the house, but with the way that wind was blowing, they would lose power sooner rather than later. If he hadn't been busy arguing with her, he could've gotten the generator going already. As it was, he'd have to wait until the snow stopped. And who knew when that would be.

Besides, when he glanced back at her, she had her arms wrapped around herself as she trailed after him. Her lips were blue—actually, all of her looked blue. *Crap.* He really did need to get her warmed up.

He led her back to the guest room, which had the advantage of being the room with the least amount of family pictures. As long as they had power, he'd leave her in this room. If he could, he'd lock her in it—but he knew that would only make matters worse. He could see the headline now—Long-Lost Beaumont Bastard Locks Beloved Celebrity in Guest Room.

No, thank you.

The guest room had an attached bathroom. "We're probably going to lose power in the next half hour, so plan accordingly." He thought she nodded—it was hard to tell, because she was shaking so hard.

God, what a mess. He went into the bathroom and turned on the hot water. "Make sure you stay in there until you've returned to a normal temperature."

The other alternative to get her body temperature

back up was to strip them both down and crawl under the covers with her.

He looked at her legs again. Long and, when not borderline frostbitten, probably tanned. The kind of legs that would wrap around him and—

Whoa.

He slammed the brakes on that line of thought something quick. There would be no nudity, no cuddling and absolutely *no* sex. What he had to do right now, as steam curled out of the bathroom and she shrugged out of her fuchsia coat to reveal a thin silk blouse that was soaked at the cuffs and collar, was remember that every single thing he said and did from this point on was as good as public. He wouldn't touch her and, what's more, he wouldn't allow her to touch him. End of discussion.

"I'll bring in some better clothes for you," he said as he headed out of the room. Because if he had a look at her walking around in that tight skirt and that sheer blouse for the next three or four days…

He was a strong man. But even he wasn't sure he was *that* strong. Not if she was going to look all soft and vulnerable as well as sexy.

"Thank you," she said again in that delicate voice.

No, he wasn't going to think of her as vulnerable. Or delicate. It was probably just an act designed to get him to open up to her.

He hurried to his parents' room and dug out some appropriate clothing—long underwear, jeans, shirts and sweaters and socks. His mom was a little shorter and a lot curvier than Natalie Baker, but her things should fit. Better than anything of his, anyway. She'd swim in one of his sweaters.

He knocked on the guest room door and, when no

one replied, he cracked it open. Good. The bathroom door was closed and he heard splashing. She was in the shower, then. Standing nude under the hot water, maybe even running the soap over her body, her bare breasts, her...

He hoped she'd locked that damn door. He laid the clothes out on the bed and almost scooped up her things to take them down to the laundry room to dry. But then he caught sight of the lacy bra and matching panties—pale pink, like a confection that she'd worn on her body—and he drew back his hand as if he'd been burned. Okay, so now he was going to *not* think about her body wearing those things. And he also had to *not* think about her *not* wearing those things.

Oh, God. This was a disaster in the making.

He forced his thoughts away from the woman steaming up the shower. He had practical things that he needed to get done. It was obvious she had no idea how to ride out a blizzard, which meant it was up to him to keep them both from freezing to death.

He made sure that every other door on the second floor was shut, then he hurried downstairs, pausing to snag the family photos off the wall. He shoved those into the coat closet. Luckily, he'd laid a fire in the fireplace before he'd gone to town this morning, so all he had to do was light it. Once it was going, he went to the kitchen. He had a roast in a slow cooker, but he turned on the gas oven anyway, just to build up the heat in the house. Once the power went, the wind would sap any warmth from this room in a matter of minutes. And if he just left it on, he wouldn't have to worry about lighting it with a match later.

He scrubbed a couple of potatoes and put them in the

oven and then, after a moment of internal debate, dug an apple pie out of the freezer and put it in the oven, too.

Every fall, his mom went into a frenzy of cooking and baking. CJ had long ago figured out that it was her way of coping with the guilt of leaving her only son alone during the holidays. He had an entire deep freeze full of casseroles and cobblers and meals in bags that all he had to do was heat up in the oven or the slow cooker. Pretty much the only thing she didn't leave him was pizza and beer, which was why he'd headed to the store this morning after sending his hired hands home for the storm and cutting his chores short. If he was going to be snowed in for Christmas, he wanted a couple of pizzas to round out the menu.

Then he did another sweep of the downstairs. He pulled more photos from the wall and the mantel over the fireplace. These he carried back to the office—that had a door he could lock. If he could, he'd put the entire house in that room and bolt the door shut.

The parlor was where most of the photo albums were—it had a door, but not a lock. Well, he'd just have to keep her out of it. Much as he didn't like it, he would have to stick to Natalie Baker like glue.

Finally, with dinner underway and as much of his life hidden as he could hide, he headed back up the stairs. Just as he reached the top, she opened her door and stepped out into the hall.

CJ's breath caught in his throat. Gone was the too-polished, too-perfect celebrity. And in her place…

She'd pulled her hair into a low tail at the side. Her face was free of makeup, but somehow she looked even prettier. Softer, definitely.

That softness was dangerous. So was any question

he was asking himself right now about whether or not she'd put the lacy pink panties back on.

So he did his best to focus on anything but that. "Better?" he asked in a gruff voice, but he didn't need to ask because he could tell. The color had come back into her cheeks—a natural blush instead of an artfully applied one. Her hair was fair—more blond than it looked on-screen. Without the heavy layer of eye makeup, her eyes seemed wider, more crystal blue.

Bad. This was *bad*.

"Yes, thank you." Even her voice sounded different now. True, she was no longer shivering with cold, but when she was on television, talking to the camera and interviewing stars, her voice had a certain cadence to it, low and husky. That was gone now.

CJ realized with a start that he might be looking at the real Natalie Baker. And he couldn't do that. If he started thinking of her as a real person instead of a talking head, then he might get lost in those blue eyes.

Luckily, the storm saved him from himself. With a pop, all the lights went out. Natalie didn't scream, but he heard her gasp in alarm.

"It's all right," he said, coming the rest of the way to get her. The hall was darker than normal because he'd shut the doors. "It's okay. I'm right here." He reached out to touch her—just to give her a reassuring pat on the shoulder. But when he did so, she latched onto his forearm with a tight, fearful grip.

He sucked in air and fought the sudden urge to wrap his arms around her and keep her safe. Dammit, she was getting to him.

"Sorry," she said, loosening her grip—but not letting

him go. "I guess I'm a little jumpy. I'm not normally this poorly prepared."

CJ didn't think he could believe she'd gotten stranded by accident. But whether or not her presence here had been planned didn't change things, at least not for the next few days.

Suddenly, he was aware that they were standing in a mostly dark hallway, touching. He withdrew his hand. "We should grab the pillows and things."

She jerked her head up in surprise. "What?"

"I've got a fire going downstairs in the living room. Once the snow stops, I'll go outside and get the generator started, but until then we should stay in front of the fire." He didn't tell her that he had a fireplace in his room and that there was another one in his parents' room. This wasn't his first blizzard.

He wasn't letting her sleep in his parents' bed—or his. Absolutely no sharing of beds.

He felt her exhale, the warmth of her breath around him. Almost without being aware of it, he started to lean toward her. "Is that so you can keep an eye on me?"

There wasn't any point in lying. Besides, lying did not come naturally to him. Perhaps Hardwick Beaumont had been good at it, but Patrick Wesley was honest to a fault. The only thing he had ever lied about was CJ's mother and CJ. In fact, CJ was sure that Pat had told the lie so many times about marrying Bell on leave and having CJ arrive before he'd been honorably discharged that both his parents believed it, heart and soul.

CJ wanted to believe it, too—because Pat *was* his father. CJ resented the fact that the ghost of Hardwick Beaumont hung over him—always had, always would. And he resented this woman for bringing Hardwick

Beaumont's ghost with her. Yes, the anger felt good. He was going to hold on to that anger for as long as he could. She might be prettier in real life, and that softness about her might call to him, but he was furious at her and that was *that*.

He walked back into the guest room and stripped the blankets and pillows off the bed. "Here," he said, shoving them at her. Then he went to his own room and did the same. There. Now they didn't have a reason to come back upstairs for the next several days.

Wordlessly, he led the way back downstairs to the living room. The fire had taken and the room was bathed in a warm, crackling glow.

He dropped his bedding on the couch and went to work rearranging the room. The coffee table went to the far side under the windows, where it would be darkest and coldest. He pulled the couch forward so it faced the fire and then dragged the recliners over so they boxed in the heat on each side. He laid a blanket over the coffee table so that drafts wouldn't come in underneath it. And then he made a pallet on the floor. "You can take the couch."

Her eyes widened and CJ knew she understood him perfectly. He would sleep on the floor, directly in front of her, to keep her from sneaking off in the night and snooping.

She hesitated. "You've done this before."

He wasn't sure how he was going to talk to her without revealing things. Well, the trick was to reveal as little as possible. "I have. This is not my first blizzard. But I'm gathering that it's your first time." The moment the words left his mouth, he winced. That was an unfortunate double entendre.

But, gracefully, she ignored his poor choice of words. She fluffed her pillows and shot him a sheepish grin. "I suppose that was obvious. It's different in Denver." She folded her blankets, making a sort of sleeping bag on top of the couch. Then she straightened, her hands on her hips. He got the feeling she was judging her work—and finding it lacking. "I didn't plan this," she said softly. "I'm not... I'm not always a good person. But I want you to know that I didn't come out here with the intent of making you rescue me." She didn't look at him as she said this. Instead, she kept her head down.

If that were the truth—and that was a big *if*—he wondered how much the admission cost her. "Might as well make the best of it. I prefer not to spend the next few days being miserable. It's the Christmas season— good will toward all men *and* women."

She glanced at him, but quickly dropped her eyes again. Her mouth curved down in a way that CJ recognized—it was the kind of smile his mother made when she was trying not to cry.

He didn't want Natalie Baker to cry. She hadn't cried when she'd been half-frozen. Why would she do so now? Finally, after several painful seconds, she whispered, "Peace on earth?"

That was the truce. "Can't promise you a silent night, though—that wind's not going to stop." Her smile was more real this time and somehow it made him feel better. What was wrong with him? It was enough that he had saved her from freezing to death. It was not his responsibility to make her happy. End of discussion.

However, that didn't stop him from adding "Dinner should be ready. We can fill our plates and sit in front of the fire."

She followed him into the kitchen. The house had always had a gas stove and this was exactly the reason why. CJ got a burner lit and put the kettle on.

"We have some instant coffee and a lot of tea." He left out the part about how his mom vastly preferred tea to anything else. Those were the kinds of details he had to keep to himself. He went on, "There's a roast in the slow cooker and potatoes and apple pie in the oven." He lifted the lid and the smell of pot roast filled the air.

"Oh, my God—that smells heavenly," Natalie said. She stepped up next to him and inhaled the fragrant steam.

They worked in silence, assembling the meal. He got down two big bowls and showed her where the tea and the instant coffee were located. He carved the roast and filled their bowls with meat, vegetables and gravy. The kettle whistled and she moved to turn it off.

He was not going to think about how effortlessly she moved around his kitchen. She did not belong here and the fact that he was having to remind himself of this fact approximately once every two-point-four seconds was yet another bad sign. At this point, he wasn't sure he'd recognize a good sign if it bit him on the butt.

It was only when he settled onto the couch with his feet stretched toward the fire that she spoke again. "This is wonderful," she said as she gracefully folded herself into a cross-legged posture on the couch—a solid four feet away from where he sat.

He appreciated that she wasn't starting with another line of questioning—even if she was just trying to soften him up, he was glad there was no full-on assault. That didn't mean he was going to not ask his own questions, however. "How come you don't have anyone waiting for you?"

She didn't answer for a long time—which was understandable, because she was devouring the pot roast. CJ did the same. They ate in silence until she set her bowl to the side. "I could ask the same of you—you're here all alone and Christmas is coming. You don't even have any Christmas decorations up." She looked around his living room. It seemed more barren than normal, with all the pictures gone. "But I won't ask," she said quickly before CJ could remind her of the rules.

He didn't miss the way she avoided answering his question. He glanced up—no ring on her finger. He didn't think she ever wore one—but it was entirely possible that, if she had a ring, she just didn't wear it while she was on TV.

She tucked her hands under her legs. "So, what are we supposed to talk about? I'm not allowed to ask you questions about yourself and so far, I haven't felt comfortable answering any of your questions."

He shrugged. "We don't have to talk about anything. I don't have a problem with silence."

"Oh." Her chin dipped and her shoulders rounded. But then she straightened. "Okay."

He gritted his teeth. At any point, she could stop looking vulnerable and that would be just fine by him. "I don't want to be your lead story. I would rather not talk than have everything I say be twisted around and rebroadcast for mass consumption."

She sighed in resignation, but she didn't drop her gaze this time. "I think it's pretty safe to say that I'm off the clock. Anything we talk about would be off the record."

Like he was going to take her word for *that*. "Patrick Wesley is my father. That's the end of this discussion. I will not allow my personal life to be monetized for someone else's gain."

Besides, outside his parents and apparently Hardwick Beaumont, there was only one other person who knew that Patrick Wesley was not his birth father. CJ had been in love in college—or he thought he had. Really, he had been young and stupid and full of lust and he'd confused all of that with love. But he thought he'd had what his parents had found so he'd told his girlfriend about Hardwick Beaumont being a sperm donor because if he were going to propose to a woman, he wanted her to know the truth about him. He didn't want to spend the rest of his life hiding behind the Wesley name.

He had never forgotten the look on Cindy's face when he'd told her that actually, he was sort of related to the Beaumonts. Her eyes had gone wide and her cheeks had flushed as he'd sat there, waiting for her to say... something. He hadn't been sure what he'd wanted her to say—that it didn't matter, maybe, or that she was sorry his mom was paranoid about the Beaumonts. *Something*. Hardwick Beaumont had still been alive then, although CJ had been twenty-one and beyond his reach.

Cindy hadn't done any of that. After a few moments of stunned silence, she had started to talk about how *wonderful* this was. He was a Beaumont—and the Beaumonts were rich. Why, just think of the wedding that they could have on the Beaumonts' dime! And after the wedding, they could take their proper place in the Beaumont family—and get their proper cut of the Beaumont fortune and on and on and *on*.

That was the moment he realized he'd made a mistake. Panicking, he tried to write the whole thing off as a joke. Of course he wasn't a Beaumont—look at him. The Beaumonts were all sandy and blond—he was brown. It was just… Wishful thinking. Because he'd been bored with being a rancher's son.

He was never sure if Cindy had believed him or not. She'd been pretty mad at him for "teasing" her with all that money. The breakup that followed had been mutual. She wasn't going to get her dream wedding with the bill footed by the Beaumonts and he…

Well, he had learned to keep his mouth shut.

Besides, it had always been easy to ignore the two fundamental lies that made up his life—that Pat Wesley was his father and that his parents had married quietly a year before Pat had brought Bell home with him. It'd been an easy lie to tell—Pat had been finishing up a tour of duty in the army and they told everyone that he and Bell had met and married in secret while he was home on leave. That was why he'd shown up with a wife and a six-month-old that no one else had known about. And because Pat Wesley was an honest, upstanding citizen, everyone had gone along with it.

CJ's mother was brown and Pat Wesley was light. Pat was tall and broad, just like CJ. The fact was, CJ looked like their son. There had never been a question.

The Beaumonts had no bearing on CJ's life. He would've been perfectly happy if he'd never heard the Beaumont name for the rest of his life.

But now he was sitting across from someone who knew—or thought she knew. Which was bad enough. But what made it worse was that she was looking to capitalize on the knowledge.

She was staring at him, this Natalie Baker. "What do you want me to call you?" she asked.

"My name is CJ Wesley. You can call me CJ."

She held out her hand. "Hi. I'm Natalie."

He hesitated, but when he touched her, palm to palm, a jolt of something traveled between them. He might've thought it was static electricity, but it hit him in all the wrong places. His pulse quickened and warmth—warmth that had nothing to do with the roaring fire only a few feet from them—started at the base of his neck and worked its way down his body.

Oh, no—he knew what this was. *Attraction*. If he wasn't careful, it might blow into something even more difficult to contain—*lust*.

He jerked his hand from hers. "Natalie." Quickly, he got to his feet and gathered up the dishes. "I'll get the pie."

Four

Natalie sat on the couch, trying to make sense of what had happened.

It didn't look like that was a thing that could be done because the longer she stared into the fire, the less she knew about what was going on.

That wasn't entirely true. Once she had thawed out in the shower, her brain worked just fine. She just didn't quite grasp how, in the last two hours, she had gone from being Natalie Baker, host of *A Good Morning with Natalie Baker*, to being a human popsicle, to being…

To being CJ Wesley's unofficial guest.

She felt naked. That feeling had nothing to do with the three separate layers of clothing she was wearing. It had everything to do with the way that man looked at her, his face no longer hidden in the shadows—with

the way he asked her why she didn't have anyone waiting for her.

Because she didn't. She could try to lie and say that
her producer, Steve, would notice her absence but…it
was almost Christmas. They'd been filming segments
ahead of schedule and planning to strategically reuse
old clips so the crew could have some time off.

She didn't have a single person who would miss her
over the next five days. It wasn't like that was a shocking revelation. She'd known damn good and well that it
would be yet another Christmas spent alone. She didn't
celebrate the holiday. Why would she? The day was
nothing but the worst of bad memories.

But somehow, telling CJ that had been… Well, it'd
been painful. It had been acknowledging that she was
completely alone.

She was more or less completely at CJ's mercy. And
he didn't even like her.

But he wasn't taking advantage of the situation. Anyone else would've looked at her half-frozen and seen
an opportunity—but not him. Instead, he had clothed
her and now he was feeding her. He had gone out of his
way to make sure she was comfortable.

He was being entirely too decent. She hadn't realized that people like him existed.

Oh, sure—she knew there were still good humans
in the world, the ones who ran soup kitchens and read
books during story time at the library. But they didn't
come into her world. No, everyone she dealt with wanted
something. She didn't know how to talk to someone if
it wasn't a negotiation.

And CJ Wesley had made it abundantly clear that
he didn't want to negotiate. She didn't have anything

he wanted and he wasn't interested in giving up anything to her.

They had reached an impasse. In less than two hours.

Awareness prickled over her skin the moment he entered the room, even though he was padding around silently in thick sheepskin-lined moccasins. There was something about the way the air changed around him. For all of his decency and grudging niceness, CJ Wesley was a powerful force to be reckoned with.

"Good," he said as he crossed in front of her and sat back down on the couch, then handed her a plate overflowing with what looked like the best apple pie she'd ever seen.

She wasn't sure what he was calling *good*—the pie or the fact that she hadn't wandered off to unearth his family secrets.

"Thank you," she said. "You don't have to serve me."

There—the muscle in his jaw twitched just as he said, "It's no problem. I'm happy to do it."

She twisted her lips to one side, trying not to smile at him. "You're lying. But I appreciate it anyway."

He paused, a forkful of pie halfway to his mouth. "I'm not lying." The twitch was harder to see this time, because he was sliding his fork into his mouth.

But she saw it anyway.

"You have a tell. Did you know that?"

He avoided answering her for several long minutes, so she dug in to the pie. Sweet merciful heavens, it was even better than it smelled. Homemade and warm, the apples perfectly spiced and the crust flaky. The roast had been excellent—but this?

Maybe she had died in the snow. She'd frozen to death and this was actually heaven. Curled up on the couch with a sexy, grouchy cowboy and the best apple pie in the world.

"This is fabulous," she all but moaned around her third forkful.

"Thanks, my—" He bit off the word. "Thanks," he said again.

She surreptitiously glanced at his hand—no ring, no tan line, either. Aside from the clothes she was wearing—which were baggy and not exactly in the height of fashion—there were no other signs of women in this house. At least not since she'd taken her shower. She was pretty sure there had been pictures on the wall and now there weren't. But she had been too cold to study them when she'd originally walked through the house.

No, CJ didn't have a wife. Which meant that this pie had probably been made by his mom. The very woman that Natalie had been stalking through court records for months.

It was equally obvious that he was absolutely not going to acknowledge his mother's existence.

Natalie Baker, morning television host, would have pressed for details. But the pie was too good and the fire was too warm and she just didn't want to. If CJ were right, she would have several days to work on him. But not right now. Her stomach was full and she was feeling warm and drowsy—well, parts of her were. Other parts of her were way too attuned to the man sitting three feet away from her.

"I don't have a tell," he said suddenly.

"Yes, you do." She shot him a little smile—it didn't even feel forced. She was teasing him and there was something about it that felt okay. Like she could tease him just a little and he wouldn't throw her out.

He was trying to look mean. "No, I don't." She lifted her eyebrows and, still grinning at him, nodded sympathetically. He held her gaze for a moment and then slumped back against the couch. "What is it?"

She sat her plate to the side and leaned forward. When she lifted her hand toward his face, he tensed. "Easy," she told him as his eyes widened—and darkened. "I'm just going to show you this." She laid the tips of her fingers against the muscle of his jaw. "Call this an...experiment, if you will."

The edge of his beard pricked the pads of her fingers and the question that she had been going to ask—are you Hardwick Beaumont's son?—died on her lips. She knew what would happen. He would shut down on her or tell her to stop talking or get off the couch. She didn't want that to happen.

So her mind spun for a question that he wouldn't want to answer truthfully but wouldn't be the end of the conversation, either. "Did your mom make the pie?"

The muscle under her fingertips moved. "No."

"Did you feel that?" She gave his cheek a gentle pat. "Right here. Every time you tell a lie, a muscle twitches."

"I don't believe you." But he hadn't pushed her hand away. Instead, he sat still as a stone—a boulder. But not the angry, immovable boulder he'd been earlier. There was something cautious about him now.

She pulled her fingers away—but only to pick up his hand and push his palm against the side of his face. "Pay attention," she told him and was more than amused when he sat up straighter. She didn't pull her palm away as she held his hand to his face. "Do you watch my show?"

"Yes. Sometimes." Then he said, "I didn't feel anything."

"Were you being honest?" Because suddenly, that seemed very important. Obviously, she knew that he knew who she was. He had known from the very first.

"Yes."

"Okay," she told him. "So you can see that nothing happened when you told the truth." She tilted her head to one side and his eyes widened. *What?* She hadn't done anything. She needed another question. A safe question. "Did you lie to me in the feed store about who Pat Wesley was?"

"No," he answered quickly. Then his eyes widened. "Crap."

Reluctantly, she let her hand drop. "See? That's your tell."

He was rubbing the side of his face. "I would deny everything, but I get the feeling you would know immediately."

She laughed. Not a coquettish giggle, but an honest laugh. "I bet you were a Boy Scout and everything, weren't you?"

"I don't have to answer that." But instead of sounding irritated, one corner of his mouth curved up into a small, blink-and-you-miss-it smile. All she could do was stare at him as the firelight played over his face. He was so handsome it was almost unfair. It certainly overruled every one of her self-preservation instincts.

She did not normally go for rough-and-tumble men. Mostly because they had very little to offer her, beyond occasionally great sex.

But CJ Wesley was something else entirely. Rough and grouchy, but with a core of human decency that was more surprising than anything else—and all wrapped up in muscles. Suddenly, she knew that if he turned that smile on full power and aimed it directly at her, she wasn't going to make it.

This was *terrible*, she realized with a start. She was actually starting to like him. Sexual attraction was one thing, but this? This was something else entirely.

Quickly, she reminded herself of the stakes. He was just being nice to her because… Because it was better to keep your enemies closer than your friends and there was no mistaking the fact that she was his enemy. If she made the mistake of confusing niceness with affection, then she really *was* stupid.

Besides, he was not interested. But the moment that thought occurred to her, she wished she'd asked "Are you attracted to me?" instead of the question about the pie. Because what would he have said?

His gaze slid toward her. "I'm not the only one with a tell, you know."

She highly doubted that. She was experienced in bending the truth—which was a nice way of saying she had learned to lie through her teeth. "Nice try, but I don't think that's going to work."

He turned his entire body to her, propping up one of his legs on the couch. The distance between them got smaller. "You don't think so?"

She arranged her face into a mask of casualness. "I know so. Don't forget who I am."

He stared at her for a long moment. The back of Natalie's neck began to prickle and she was terribly afraid she was about to blush.

"I haven't forgotten," he said and he sounded so serious about it.

"I'm very important," she reminded him because that was the sort of thing she *had* to say.

His eyes widened. "There."

"What?"

"The way you swallowed. That's your tell."

It was suddenly a little more difficult to breathe, but she couldn't let him know that. Instead, she looked at him doubtfully. "First off, you didn't even ask me a question—ergo, how can you tell if I was lying? And second off, how do you know I didn't just have a bit of apple pie stuck in my throat?"

He notched an eyebrow at her and angled his body toward hers. In all reality, there probably was still a solid two and a half feet between them. But that's not what it felt like. The air seemed to crackle. Or it could have been the fire. "All right, I'll ask a question. Are you seeing anyone?"

She considered lying, but she didn't. "No."

He tilted his head to one side as he appraised her. "Why won't anyone miss you?"

Somehow, she wasn't surprised that was the question he went with. She was pulling her punches because it seemed like the polite thing for a semi-involuntary guest to do—but he had no such social obligations.

"People will miss me," she told him. "Trust me, people pay attention to me."

He smirked. It was not a reassuring gesture. "You don't even know you did it, do you? You swallowed. You pause and then you swallow and then you tell a bold-faced lie." With that, he turned back to the fire.

She should let it go. He was getting uncomfortably close to some basic truths about her and she didn't want him to. But she couldn't help it. "People do pay attention to me, you know? I'm something of a celebrity."

To her horror, he hitched up a hip and pulled her phone out of his pocket. He didn't have her password—there was no way in hell she was going to give it to him—but the Twitter notifications were rolling over the screen. "Yes, I see that. What did you tweet to get—" He paused, his eyes popping wide. "Do you know what these people are saying?"

She couldn't watch him read all the horrible, terrible things people were saying about her, so she closed her eyes. "Probably. But they pay attention to me."

He looked at her like she was absolutely nuts. And here, in the warm safety of the Wesley family home, it did seem a bit crazy. "You can't seriously want them to say— Good Lord, is that even legal?" He glanced at her, looking more worried by the second. "This isn't right. People shouldn't say— Oh, that's just disgusting."

The embarrassment was too much. She lunged at him, trying to grab her phone. He easily held it out of reach, damn his long arms. Instead, all she accomplished was lurching into the side of his shoulder.

"Put it away," she said, her cheeks burning. "Just… put it away."

He glanced at the screen one more time before he pushed the button at the top. The phone powered down until it was blissfully, safely black. "You should save your battery, anyway." But he didn't give her the phone. Instead, he slid it back into his pocket. "Do I want to know what you said that garnered such evil replies?" His face hardened. "Was it about me?"

"No."

He looked at her for a long time. "Was it about a Beaumont?"

This time, she noticed it. She swallowed just before she opened her mouth. So she shut her mouth a second time. He was studying her way too closely—like he could see beneath her TV personality, beneath the aura of untouchability that she cultivated. He could see *into* her and she was suddenly terrified he would realize there was nothing really there.

"So, that's a yes, then."

She didn't know what to say, so she said nothing. If he could hide behind silence, so could she.

The moments stretched into minutes and the minutes kept right on stretching as they sat there, a few feet separating them, both watching the fire. She didn't know what time it was. It was near total darkness outside. The shadows played over the corners of the room and once again, she felt small.

The longer she sat there, the more she realized something—aside from her father, who accused her of lying with every other breath, no one had ever noticed that she had a tell before. She was creative with reality on a daily basis and aside from the people on social media, no one ever called her on it. Certainly not to her face. No one had ever pressed her for the truth before. Not even her father, who never believed a single word she said.

Why was that? She was afraid to look too closely for the answer.

Unexpectedly, CJ asked, "Why?"

He didn't expand on that. He didn't have to.

"It's my job. It's how the game is played." People like Matthew Beaumont understood that. People like CJ Wesley? They didn't understand it at all.

"It's a lousy game, if you don't mind me saying so."

Almost against her will, she smiled. There was something so…gentlemanly about him. She wasn't sure she'd ever met a man she could call a gentleman. "It's not all bad," she said, willing herself to believe that was the truth.

The moment stretched again and then he stood up so abruptly that she jolted in her seat. "I'll bring in more wood from the mudroom. Don't move."

"I won't." She owed him that much. She had made a promise and, for once in her life, she was going to keep it. As long as she was a guest in his house, she would not pry.

She felt the air shift and a cold draft blew through the living room before CJ walked back in, his arms overflowing with logs. He carried them as if they weighed nothing at all and when he crouched down in front of the fire, she got a good look at his ass. As he messed around with the fire, she studied his body. Lord, he was built. Okay, so maybe she was starting to like him. A gruff cowboy who was also a gentleman? A man with rough hands who liked apple pie?

They were stuck here for several days. She knew one way to pass the time.

He stood and dusted off his hands before turning back to her. Her breath caught in her throat as he looked down at her, backlit by the fire. *Strong*—that was the word that bubbled up through the building lust in her mind. He was strong and safe and confident. What would he be like? Was he the kind of gentleman who would put her first or was he like all the other guys—quick, selfish. *Lousy.* God, she was so tired of having lousy sex and then feeling nothing but…hollow after.

Maybe it would be different with him. She wanted it to be—more than that, she wanted *him* to be different. A thought flitted through her mind—maybe *she* could be different with him.

She pushed herself off the couch and stepped onto his pallet.

His hands dropped to his sides and he straightened. "What are you doing?"

She stepped into him and touched his cheek, right where his muscles would twitch. He was warm and solid and Natalie knew he could pick her up and carry her anywhere he wanted to. "Thanking you," she said, wrapping her other arm around his waist and molding herself to his body.

Just the contact of her breasts to his chest—never mind how many layers of clothes were in the way—was enough to make her knees weaken. Her nipples tightened and she exhaled in anticipation. She could be someone else while she was stranded with him. Someone *better.* Someone who got what she wanted. He was hot and hard and she wanted to rip the shirt off of him and test each and every single muscle. What other parts of him twitched?

She lifted herself on her tiptoes, close enough for her cheek to brush over his beard before he put his hands on her hips and forcibly pushed her away. "Don't," he said, his voice thick with strain.

His hands were still on her hips—but now there was a solid foot of space between them. She blinked up at him. "Why not? You're being wonderful and I—"

"For God's sake, Natalie—*don't*." Now he sounded angry at her. "You don't owe me anything and I don't owe you anything and…and…" He let go of her and instead of sinking to the floor, he pushed her back. She stood there for a moment, confused.

He wanted her, she realized. He didn't like her, but he wanted her.

She could work with that. "CJ," she began in what she thought was a sultry voice.

His eyes snapped up and he glared at her.

She faltered. "Don't you...don't you want me?"

He jerked his head to the side and quickly stepped around her. "This is not happening." She blinked at him as he kicked off his moccasins, his back to her. "Go to sleep, Natalie. And don't try that again."

"Why not? Am I that—"

"There is absolutely nothing that's going to happen between us. You know it. I know it. I'm not having any part of my life made public and there's no guarantee that anything I say or do with you won't wind up on television." He finally turned to face her, his eyes narrow and his shoulders bunched up under his sweater. "It's bedtime. Go to sleep." There was a hard edge to his voice that made her chest tight.

"Oh. Okay. I..." She swallowed. "All right."

She stepped around him, careful not to touch him, and laid down on the couch. But sleep didn't come.

Instead, she stared into the fire and replayed all the ways she'd made a complete and total fool of herself in the last twelve hours. In the last lifetime.

Just as she finally started to drift, she realized something—when she'd asked him if he wanted her, he'd turned away.

He'd hidden his tell.

Five

He was going to regret this.

That was nothing new. CJ already regretted the moment Natalie Baker had walked off his television screen and into his life. But, as he stared down at her sleeping form, he knew he was going to regret what he was about to do more than anything else.

Even more than he regretted pushing her away last night.

To be honest, only parts of him regretted that. He knew that keeping a hard wall between him and the woman out to expose him as one of the lost Beaumont bastards was the only thing to do.

But try telling that to his erection.

So what he needed to do now—which he was going to regret, also—was keep them both busy. Idle hands were the devil's workshop, after all. He couldn't take any more sitting around and talking to her and he especially couldn't give her another chance to press her body against his and look up into his eyes and...

A very hard wall. "Natalie."

She was dead asleep. The vulnerability that called to him yesterday? It was magnified a hundred times right now. In sleep, she didn't just look soft and vulnerable— she looked innocent. Without the calculating shift to her eyes and the hardened jaw tight and ready for battle, she was a completely different woman. Sweet, even.

"Natalie. Wake up."

Her brow creased, so he knew she heard him. But still, her eyes didn't open.

He sat on his heels in front of her and held a cup of coffee directly under her nose. But he didn't touch her. He didn't dare brush the strands of hair that had come loose from her ponytail away from her cheek and he didn't dare stroke his thumb over her cheek to coax her awake. If he touched her, he might be lost.

"Wake up," he repeated and he blew on the coffee so the steam hit her in the face.

"What time is it?" she asked without opening her eyes.

"Six thirty." Then he waited for her reaction to this. He wasn't quite sure what he expected.

She stretched like a cat in a sunbeam and pushed herself into a sitting position. "That late?" She blinked at him, tilting her head from side to side. "Wow."

He stared at her and offered up the coffee. "Is that a joke?"

She took the cup in her hand. "I normally get up at four thirty every morning. I'm at the studio by five thirty for hair and makeup and to prepare for the show." She took a sip and CJ forced himself to look somewhere else—anywhere else, except for where her lips were touching the edge of the cup.

Those lips had almost touched his last night. All he'd had to do was turn his head ever so slightly and...

"I get up at four in the summer," he told her for no reason at all—except because he was trying not to stare at her. "I don't meet too many people who get up that early who aren't ranchers."

She cupped the coffee in her hands and sighed with what sounded like happiness. When she lifted her gaze to his, it took everything he had not to lean forward and kiss the taste of coffee off her lips. "Are you saying that we might actually have something in common?"

He stood, putting some distance between them. *No kissing. End of discussion.* "We have things to do today. We need to get moving."

She stared up at him as if he had suddenly started speaking French. Of course, someone like her probably did speak French. He was fluent in Spanish—not that he was going to tell her that. "We...do?" She looked around, her head moving slowly. She was not fully awake yet. "Did the snowstorm end?"

"No. It's still going. I think the wind has died down a bit, but there's probably about eighteen inches outside. We'll have over two feet before it's done."

Something in her face shifted. Was it fear? Resignation? She'd tried to seduce him last night. Was the thought of being trapped here for another few days that unpleasant to her? "What are we going to do?"

He stepped back and threw another log on the fire. "I was thinking about it. Last night you asked me what we were going to talk about and I made a decision." Flames licked along the new wood and then caught. "We're not going to talk about the past and there's no point in talking about the future. So what we're going to do is focus on the now." He peeked back over his shoulder to see that she was looking at him, utter confusion written all over her face. "It's Christmas, Natalie. And I think we need a little Christmas."

Her eyes brightened. "Right this very minute?"

"Yes," he said, feeling a smile take hold of his face. "We need a little Christmas. But the same rules apply. You won't ask me about anything and I won't tell you. Also, you should know—if I can get my snowmobile out, I'm going to town on Christmas Eve. There's a big party there every year and this year I'm Santa. The roads in town might be cleared, so you can have someone come get you." The twinkle in her eyes faded. "You can get your car later."

She dropped her gaze to the coffee cup and took a slow, steady breath. "You really don't look very much like Santa."

"Looks aren't everything." Before she could respond to that, he clapped his hands. "Normally, I'd already have decorated some by now but things have been a little…different this year." As in, he had been busy trying to keep Natalie Baker from finding out who he was—and failing somewhat spectacularly. The thought of his father's two great lies suddenly being exposed hadn't exactly put CJ in the holiday mood.

Even though the room was still a washed-out gray, he could see the color in her cheeks deepen. She was the thing that was different this year—there was no getting around that obvious fact—but he still felt bad reminding her of it. "Come on."

* * *

"Hold the light," he told her. It'd taken twenty minutes to get breakfast squared away, but now they were downstairs, poking around in the bins of decorations.

When his mom had been here for Christmas, every square inch of the house had been decorated until the entire place was red, green and shimmery silver. Bell Wesley loved shining tinsel and, even though Dad hated the stuff, he let her go wild. Claimed that what made his wife happy made him happy. Therefore, the house had always been completely decorated from the Day of the Dead until January first. They had storage containers stacked four high and three wide for all of the holiday decorations.

CJ wouldn't get all of them out. First off, he didn't really want to drag out all of the Mexican decorations. The papel picado—the colored paper cut in lace patterns—and the ornaments of tiny piñatas and sombreros would be dead giveaways. But things like his mother's manger scenes and Virgin Mary ornaments—those were fine. "Can you shed a little light over here?"

Natalie adjusted the beam. "This is a lot," she said in amazement. "Is this all Christmas?"

"Maybe seventy percent of it." He began pulling the appropriate bins—each labeled with tags like Manger, Lights and Wreaths—and setting them to the side. He stopped in front of a bin labeled CJ's Handmade Ornaments. Crap, he'd forgotten about that one. If they weren't talking about the past, he didn't want to pull out the collection of ornaments he had been making for his mother, one per year, every year for the last thirty-two years. The early ones were nothing more than little handprints in clay or scribbled paper trees with yarn strung through the top.

He hadn't even given her this year's ornament before they left—a wooden star he'd cut on his drill press. It sat out in the barn, finished except for some sanding and maybe another coat of lacquer.

He must've stared at that bin too long because when he finally moved to pull it off the shelf, Natalie stepped forward and put her hand on his shoulder. "You don't have to," she said in a soft voice.

He tensed. Even through all the layers of clothing, he could feel the warmth from her touch, just like he'd felt last night. "Don't have to do what?"

"That." The beam of the flashlight bounced off the bin. "You don't have to show me those."

He turned to stare at her, although there wasn't much to see in the basement. "Don't you want to know?"

She swallowed, then appeared to catch herself. Her mouth twisted off into a half frown. "I do," she said, looking frustrated, "but I don't."

CJ stared at her. He had no hopes of ever understanding her, none whatsoever, but still, times like these, when she almost made sense... And then didn't.

She rolled her eyes. "It's called plausible deniability, CJ. If you don't show me the ornaments, I don't have to ask about them and you don't have to lie. Then, if anyone asks me if I've seen any of CJ's homemade Christmas memories, I can say *no*, I did not."

See, that was a prime example of her making sense and no sense at the same time. He understood what she was saying... But the fact that the woman who had stalked him for three weeks was the one saying it? *That* didn't make any sense. "You're not going to pry?"

This time, he didn't see her swallow at all. "I gave you my word I wouldn't."

Abruptly, she turned off the flashlight. CJ tensed, but she didn't make another pass at him. Instead, she leaned down and picked up one of the bins. "This basement is cold," she said, hauling the bin up the stairs.

He was never going to understand women. Specifically, this woman. Because everything she had just said was completely at odds with everything she had said prior to this. Was this some sort of persuasion technique he wasn't familiar with? Reverse psychology, maybe? Was she hoping that, by telling him she didn't want him to share secrets, he would be more likely to start blabbing?

He'd never much been one for psychology. So, as dangerous as it might be, he was going to take her at face value. She wanted plausible deniability? Fine. He would give her all the plausible deniability she could handle.

It took everything Natalie had not to ask questions. Because obviously, some of these decorations had been in his family for years. Decades, even. The manger scene that he arranged on the mantel over the fireplace? It was so old that the baby Jesus's face had been rubbed off and one of the donkeys was missing a leg.

The sleigh bells CJ told her to hang on the front doorknob—which was freezing cold—looked even older than the manger. But the silk poinsettia arrangement that she set in the middle of the big dining room table, that was newer.

Then he pulled out one of those things that she'd never known the name for—it was shaped like a Christmas tree but it had candles and a little propeller at the top. If you lit the candles, the heat turned the propeller. It was like a Christmas tree crossed with a helicopter. She had always wanted one and had once, when she was a little girl, asked Santa for one.

Her parents had told her Santa wasn't real but Natalie had held out hope that maybe, just maybe, Santa existed and that she'd been a good girl. She'd tried so hard, hoping that if she could just act right, everything would be good. Or, at the very least, Santa would bring her a present, one that said she was worth something special.

Foolish childhood delusions. And she'd gotten so upset when her special Christmas toy hadn't appeared that she'd cried. And that was when her mother had walked out because Natalie had ruined Christmas for everyone.

Still, it was exciting to see a Christmas helicopter in person, Natalie thought, dragging herself back to the present. CJ had said it himself—the past didn't matter. Not today.

And since CJ seemed to have a lot of candles, maybe they could light it up and she could watch the wheels spin. "I always wanted one of these when I was a kid," she said, stacking the layers on top of each other. "Where do you want it?"

"Here," CJ said, pointing to a side table. "You didn't have one?"

"No." Carefully, she set the assembled whirly thing on the table. "I hope we'll be able to light it. I always wanted to see one in action."

She could feel CJ looking at her. He did that often. Maybe too often. Was he thinking about the way she'd thrown herself at him last night? Was he regretting saving her life and bringing her into his home? She was trying so hard not to make him regret it.

"Yes?" she asked as she turned to face him. There it was again, the look that told her he was trying to figure her out.

"I think we got that thing when I was a kid," he offered. But even as he said it, he looked mad at her again. "What kinds of decorations did you have growing up?"

"Oh." She turned back to the bin and pulled out a bag full of beautiful, hand-tied bows made of lustrous, sheer ribbons. Someone had put a lot of love into those bows—the same love that went into the apple pie, she'd bet. "Where would you like these?"

She felt him step closer a moment before he touched her hand. "Do you celebrate Christmas?" When she didn't answer right away, he added, "One of my best friends from college is Jewish. Hanukkah, the eight nights, the candles—it's all really interesting," he added, as if he were trying to make her feel better for not having Christmas.

"We aren't Jewish." Being Jewish would give her a reason to avoid Christmas, but it wouldn't have made those years of miserable holiday seasons any more bearable. "I've seen pictures," she said, helpless to stop the words that were inexplicably rolling off of her tongue. He was sharing so much with her that it suddenly felt wrong not to share anything with him. "Back when my mom was still with us, there's a picture of me and her and Dad all sitting in front of the tree with ornaments and lights and presents and *everything*."

Unexpectedly, her throat closed up. She had that picture in a box under her bed. The one time the Baker family had been happy—and she was too young to remember it. Instead of memories, all she had was a picture. "So I know we used to celebrate it."

The words hung in the quiet room and mortification swamped her. It was the truth—but that didn't make it sound any less sad.

She dug in the bin again and turned up a pair of snow globes. "Where do you want these?" she asked, ignoring the way her voice cracked.

"I'm sorry you lost your mom," he said gruffly.

This whole situation was so ridiculous that she couldn't help but laugh. "She's not dead. At least, I don't think she is. She just…left me. Us," she quickly amended.

But she hadn't been quick enough. "Natalie."

Damn it all, she should have lied. She made the executive decision that the snow globes belonged on opposite sides of the mantel. "What do you think?" Before he could answer, she dug back into the bin and came out with two cut-tin candleholders. With a lit candle inside, they would throw the shadows of trees and stars and snowflakes onto the walls. "These are perfect. We're already using candles," she said brightly.

"Natalie," he said again, this time with more force.

But she couldn't stop. She couldn't think about what she had just said out loud. She had never once admitted to anyone that her mother had left her because she'd ruined Christmas—or that her father had never celebrated the holiday after that.

As far as Natalie knew, Julie Baker had never seen either her daughter or her husband again. Now that she was an adult, Natalie knew her father had been a major factor in Mom's departure. The man was impossible to please and harder to live with.

But that realization had come later. Natalie had spent *years* with her mother's parting words ringing in her ears.

She focused all of her energy on the bins of decorations. The next thing she pulled out was plastic mistletoe with a bell hanging out of the bottom. "Where should I hang—"

"Natalie." CJ grabbed her by the shoulders and spun her around.

"What?" She looked into his eyes—*hazel, definitely hazel in this light*—and realized there was nowhere to hide. He could see her.

It was terrifying.

"Your mother left you?"

Natalie hated that prickling at the corner of her eyes, so she ignored it. "It's not a big deal." Too late, she realized she had swallowed. Hell, if she were going to lie, she might as well go big. "It's fine," she assured him, forcing a big sunny smile to her face.

"And after she left, you didn't celebrate Christmas?"

"Oh, sure we did. In…" She swallowed. "In our own way."

His mouth twisted. "You're not a very good liar, you know?"

His comment was so ridiculous she didn't know what to do—except laugh. "Actually, I am," she told him. "I can't remember the last time I was this honest." With someone else *or* with herself. That realization made her laugh even harder.

He did not laugh with her. "Is this a trick?" he asked, but his voice wasn't angry. Neither were his eyes. He was staring at her with such intensity that it made her want to squirm. If anyone else had looked at her like he did, she would know that sooner rather than later, they would wind up back at her place, naked and panting.

But CJ Wesley wasn't like anyone else.

"A trick?" It took a few moments for her to make sense of what he'd just said. Then it hit her.

He thought this entire thing—the damsel in distress, not having anyone to call for Christmas, even her hysteria—was an act.

Her giggles died in the back of her throat. Is that how he saw her?

She deserved that, she knew. If anyone else had accused her of playing mind games, she would've smiled softly and said something outrageous—something to prove them right while still maintaining what little dignity she had left. Dignity she didn't have right now. For once, she wished that she'd kept her big mouth shut.

"It's all right," she said and was horrified to hear her voice crack. "I mean, come on—I'm nothing but a whiny, spoiled-rotten little brat, right?" The words spilled out of her before she could stop. "I ruin everything. I always have."

She didn't know what she expected him to do with this—because she was, in fact, ruining both his Christmas and his life—but suddenly, she was crushed against his chest. His arms enveloped her—he was so strong and sure of who he was and what he was doing.

She tried to hold back because she didn't deserve this hug. His anger, his mockery, his criticism—yes. Not this tenderness.

But he didn't let her go.

"It's okay," he whispered, low and close to her ear

and damn it all, she sank into his warmth. He smelled of wood and smoke, of warmth and safety. She was safe in his arms and if she couldn't blink fast enough to erase the prickling in her eyes, well, that was okay, too.

She shouldn't want this—the way his arms felt around her waist, the way her face fit against the crook of his neck. She shouldn't want the way his hands were rubbing up and down her back, relaxing her and pushing her closer to him—closer than she'd been last night. But he wasn't taking anything. Instead, he was offering comfort—the comfort of his body, of *him*.

Comfort was perilously close to pity and she didn't want his pity. She didn't want him thinking she needed him at all. She was Natalie Baker and that meant something. She took care of herself. She had for years.

Still, it was several minutes before she could bring herself to push away from him. "Are you always this damn decent?" she asked, rubbing her cheeks with the cuff of her sleeve.

A long moment passed where he wasn't touching her and he wasn't talking. Finally, when she could barely take another second of it, he said, "Just doing what anyone would do for a friend."

"That's just it," she snapped at him. She was angry now. In theory, she was supposed to be breaking down CJ Wesley—and the opposite was happening. She was starting to like him and if that happened, she might as well kiss her morning show goodbye. "No one is this good and decent and kind and nice, don't you see that? No one is." He made a motion toward her, but she backed away. Her legs touched the couch and she sat with an undignified *thump*. "You are not normal and we're not friends."

The words weren't very insulting and they did exactly zero damage to him. "I don't think you're whiny and I'm not sure that you're such a spoiled brat," he said gently. She cringed to hear the words spoken aloud again. "I think you're…"

"What?" she demanded. If she made him mad, he wouldn't pity her. "Delusional? Scheming? Conniving—that's a good one. One of my favorites."

He shook his head. "I think you're lonely."

She had to laugh—*had* to. Because she could absolutely not sit here and cry. "Really, CJ—me?" She scoffed as best she could. "Please. Do you know what my market share is in morning television ratings?" As if that had anything to do with loneliness. "And what about you?" she quickly added because she didn't want him to expound upon this flash of insight. "Why the hell aren't you married? Because you should be. You are gorgeous and decent and well-off and you don't play games. Why don't you have a wife and kids? Or even a husband and some kids?"

Now it was his turn to blink at her. But he didn't cuss her out or tell her to go to hell. "You know why."

She did? Really, she didn't know that much about him except…

Except she was sure that his father was Hardwick Beaumont.

"So?" she asked in confusion. "It's not like you've got a third nipple or a vestigial tail—right?"

The corner of his mouth twitched—an almost smile. "You mean, something useless and left over from the past that has no impact on my life anymore, but that people still find fascinating?"

"That is the definition of *vestigial*." It was such a relief to be off the topic of her that she kept going. This was as close as he'd come to admitting the truth about his birth father. But they weren't actually discussing the Beaumonts. They were maintaining the aura of plausible deniability. Somehow that made it okay. She hoped, anyway. "But I don't see why that would keep you from being with someone."

He winced. "Let's just say that having a vestigial organ—that's important to some people. And you never know which people it's going to be important to, so you don't tell anyone about this *organ*." Her gaze dipped down to a different organ, but before she could wonder about *that*, he turned to face the fire. "And then let's say that you fall in love—or you think you do. And you're convinced that this person you've fallen in love with doesn't care about vestigial organs. You're convinced that this person can see past that imperfection. So you tell them about it and it turns out it matters." His voice dropped. "It matters a lot."

She regarded him for a long moment as she thought over his disclosure. Unexpectedly, shame hit her low and hard. He was right. It was important—if it weren't, she wouldn't be here. And if things had gone according to plan, she would have been telling everyone else in the broadcast market that it mattered more than anything else they might hear on another channel.

She felt ill. "But if this vestigial organ was so important to some people, why did they keep quiet once they found out about it? Because if it was important to them, they wouldn't keep it to themselves. Trust me on that one."

That was how she made her living—people knew something they weren't supposed to and they just couldn't keep their mouths shut. More than that, though, they were looking to capitalize on their knowledge. Knowing something that other people didn't know was exciting. Knowing you could get paid for it was *power.*

He adjusted the angle of one of the snow globes on the mantel. "You lie, of course. You tell them it was a practical joke, that you were just pulling their leg. You laugh it off. And then, a few weeks after that, you break up with them." He glanced over his shoulder at her. "They never figured it out, because they never noticed that you had a tell. And then you decide not to tell anyone else."

For some reason, that bit about the tell made her smile. But it didn't last. Because no one else had ever figured out her tell, either. All those people watching her and following her online every day—and none of them had seen that simple truth. Not like CJ had.

She looked him over again. Years of not telling anyone? They weren't that far away from Denver— an hour, maybe. The Beaumonts and their soap-opera lives would be unavoidable. And he said *she* was lonely.

"She couldn't tell? Because I can. I can see the vestigial organ in you."

He turned to face her head-on again. "My dad—"

"Pat?"

He nodded, politely ignoring her interruption. "He's six-two. He's a little bit Scot and more than a little Irish. Eyes that aren't quite blue, aren't quite green. When he was a kid, he was strawberry-blond—although his hair's darkened and now he's a light-brown kind of guy."

"You look like him." True, he could've been describing Hardwick Beaumont—but that would explain why no one would have seen the Beaumont in him if he also looked like Patrick Wesley.

"I look like both my parents." It was such a simple statement—and nothing twitched in any of his muscles.

A new feeling—unfamiliar—blew up faster than a winter storm. Guilt. Because she knew what was going to happen next.

Oh, sure—maybe for the rest of the Christmas holiday things would be quiet. But after that?

"I'm so sorry, CJ."

His brow wrinkled. "For what?"

"For finding you."

CJ exhaled heavily and came over to the couch. He slumped down in it, a couple of feet still between them. But it wasn't uncomfortable, that space. "You're not ruining my Christmas," he told her. "So stop worrying about it."

"But…"

He shook his head. "Natalie, I told you—we're dealing with the present today." Never mind the fact that they hadn't actually been doing that at all, beyond thinking about where to put the snow globes. "The future isn't going anywhere and I'll deal with it when the time comes."

So he understood, then. She had found him, after all. She'd spent weeks asking questions about Carlos Julián and Isabel Santino, about Beaumont's bastard son. She had made the connection and in doing so, she'd paved the way for others to make the same connection, too.

And he knew it.

"Why aren't you madder at me?" She stared at him, but he kept his gaze on the fire. "You should be furious, you know." He should've left her in the snow. It probably wouldn't have solved anything in the long run, but she deserved his anger.

She wasn't going to get it. That much was already clear, and it became clearer when he just shrugged. "I don't know," he said in an amused tone, as if he couldn't believe he wasn't more upset with her, too. "Maybe..." He glanced at her and forced an awkward smile. For a moment, she thought he was going to finish that statement.

But then he stood and nudged a nearly empty bin with his toe. "We should get this mess cleaned up and then I'll see if I can get out to the generator."

They finished decorating and carried the empty bins back downstairs. The whole time, Natalie tried to figure out why he wasn't raging at her. She hadn't exactly destroyed his life—but she had upended it, at the very least. She'd had people threaten to do all sorts of horrible things to her for far less than this.

But if they were threatening her or talking about how stupid she was, at least she knew they were paying attention. That was how the world worked.

Or it had, before she had met CJ Wesley. Finally, someone who should be legitimately angry with her, someone who had plenty of opportunity to exact revenge, and what had he done?

Saved her life. Kept her safe and warm. Made sure she was comfortable and fed. Hell, he'd even let her celebrate Christmas with him. He had offered her the simple reassurance of a hug when she'd let down her guard and accidentally thought about her childhood.

And all he asked in return was that she not pry. There had been no threats, no physical or sexual intimidation. Just kindness.

She wished she'd never found him.

Six

"How much do you think we got?" He and Natalie were standing by the big picture window, staring at a world muffled by white.

"Two and a half feet, maybe a little more. That," he said, pointing toward a tiny mound just a little higher than the rest of the snow, "is your car."

"Wow," Natalie said, sounding awestruck.

He snorted. She'd be lucky if she got her car back before March, CJ thought as he watched the moon finally appear out from behind the last straggling clouds. Suddenly the world was bathed in a bright, crystal white.

"It's so peaceful out here." She crossed her arms and shivered.

They were far from the fire, but neither of them moved away from the window. He fought the urge to wrap his arm around her shoulders and pull her closer.

"You say that now, but that's just because the cabin fever hasn't hit yet."

She gave him a sideways glance. "Is that going to be a problem?"

Hell, yes it was going to be a problem. It was a problem already. They'd killed an afternoon decorating the living room. Even then, they hadn't managed to stick to the here and now. Instead, he'd held her and she'd asked about third nipples. What the hell would happen tomorrow?

Would they get bored? Boredom couldn't be good.

He knew the cure for cabin fever—it would be to peel her out of all of those clothes, curl his body around hers and spend hours getting lost in her.

And he couldn't do it. He wanted to, though. It was probably a normal thing for two consenting adults who were attracted to each other and stranded together during a Christmas blizzard to spend some time working through sexual frustration, right?

But that wasn't the only reason why he wanted to pull her into his arms. Part of it was the devastated look on her face when he had said she was lonely. He actually wasn't sure if she was or wasn't. But saying it out loud made him realize something.

He was lonely. Aside from Cindy back in college, he hadn't told anyone about being a Beaumont—because he hadn't given himself the chance to do that. He had kept to himself for years.

Long, lonely years. All because he didn't trust another person with the truth. He assumed that whoever he told would react much the way Cindy had—with shock, quickly followed by greed.

But Natalie? He hadn't even had to tell her—she'd

figured it out. She knew the truth—and it *was* true. There was no point in lying about it because she would be able to tell.

She knew that Hardwick Beaumont was his father and...

It wasn't like she didn't care. She wouldn't have gotten this far if she didn't care. But she wasn't acting like he was her personal bank account and she was hell-bent on making a withdrawal. Instead, she had apologized. And he had no reason to believe it wasn't a sincere apology.

He still didn't want to be a featured segment on her show. But today she'd made him realize how damnably exhausting it was to keep other people's secrets and he didn't want to do that anymore, either. Hell, he didn't know what he wanted.

So he focused on the present. "Tomorrow, when the sun's out, I'll get the generator going. If I can get to the barn, I'll be able to get the snowmobile out. We can go for a ride after I feed my horses."

She beamed up at him and damn if it didn't make him feel warm inside. "Really?"

"Yep." He'd have to take her with him. No matter what she promised and no matter how sincerely she apologized, he couldn't leave her alone in his house.

But it would also be fun. He loved the snowmobile and this was perfect weather for it. He'd take her out and show her the ranch—a perfect, pristine white version of his ranch, that was—and then he'd take her over to where there were some wild holly bushes. They'd need to get a tree, so he'd better pack a rope and...

It had been thirteen years since he'd almost asked Cindy to marry him. It'd been four years since his parents started going south for the winter, testing out retirement and avoiding things like blizzards and Beaumonts.

He was startled to realize that this was the first time he'd had company for Christmas in his adult life. But that wasn't as startling as it was to realize how much he had missed having someone to talk to. Yeah, he talked to his parents, but this was different.

She leaned into him, shoulder to shoulder. "You know, I don't think I've taken a day off in... Well, can't remember when. This has been—okay, maybe not a vacation," she said with a rueful smile. "This has been nice."

"Better than being miserable," he agreed. "We'll have fun tomorrow."

She didn't pull away from him. Instead, they stood next to each other, watching the moonlight sparkle over the landscape.

It was so tempting to think that the rest of the world didn't exist anymore. She wasn't a television personality and he wasn't going to have to walk into town dressed as Santa Claus in less than three days and wonder if everyone looked at him and saw a Beaumont instead of a Wesley. Right now, it was just him and her, the quiet and the snow.

He was struck with the oddest urge to keep it this way. He wanted to stay in the present. This time was a gift, in its own way, and he wanted to make the most of it.

Without really making a conscious choice, he slid his arm around her shoulders and hugged her tight. "If I get the generator going tomorrow, we can watch movies. What's your favorite Christmas movie?"

Unexpectedly, it took her a long time to answer. "I've

never really celebrated like this before. I tend to skip Christmas. For obvious reasons," she added with a sigh.

Not for the first time, he wondered about what she had said about herself—a whiny, spoiled brat who ruined everything. There was a certain measure of truth to the fact that she had upset his life—but he wouldn't go so far as to say that she'd ruined it.

It wasn't the sort of thing a person said about herself. It was, however, the sort of thing someone might say to a little girl, and that little girl might believe it.

"We've got time," he said, giving her a squeeze. She rested her head on his chest. "We can watch as many as you want."

Another shiver passed through her. "Hot cocoa?" he asked. He didn't understand his strange urge to take care of her but he was tired of fighting against it. He would regret it...eventually. But right now? He was just going to go with it.

She looked up at him, her eyes wide and sparkling with humor. "Only if you have marshmallows."

"What kind of man do you take me for? Of course I have marshmallows."

Together, they turned toward the kitchen. He didn't let go of her and she didn't pull away from him and that was okay. The more time he spent with her, the harder it was to see the morning television host who traded in gossip and innuendo.

Instead, she was just a woman. Natalie. Complicated and messy—yes. No one here would argue with that.

But, when she wasn't trying to be a morning television host, she was also soft and vulnerable, the kind of woman who could find happiness in marshmallows.

He was being an idiot. This was nothing more than

a delusion. A pleasant one, but a delusion all the same. There was no guarantee that anything they said or did wouldn't wind up on her show.

But he hadn't expected this feeling of freedom. She already knew the truth. He didn't have to keep hiding it from her. He could just be himself. Well, maybe not entirely himself.

What a mess.

In the kitchen, he got out the Ovaltine and the marshmallows while she put the kettle back on. "Ovaltine?" she asked, not even bothering to hide her amusement. "You're really just a big kid, aren't you?"

He dug around in the pantry until he came up with the bottle of peppermint schnapps. "I didn't drink it spiked when I was a kid."

Her eyes widened and she stared at him and he remembered last night, when she'd made a move. Was she thinking about that again? Because he was. He'd been trying not to think about the way her body melted into his last night, the way her fingers had felt stroking over his cheek—but he'd been failing most of the day.

Would she try again? Would she press her breasts against his chest and run her fingers through his hair? Until he had no choice but to kiss her, long and hard and deep?

The more important question was, would he let her? Was he so hard up that he would ignore all logic and common sense and let himself get lost in her body?

He would. His gaze dropped to her mouth and she ran her tongue over her lower lip and he knew that, without reservation, he wouldn't be strong enough to push her away.

They doctored up their cocoa and carried it into the

living room. "Here," he said, handing her his mug as he threw a few more logs on the fire. When he turned back around, she was sitting in the middle of the couch, watching him with those eyes of hers.

If he were smart, he'd get his mug back and sit on the floor. He'd maintain a modicum of distance between them.

But he must not be as smart as he thought he was because instead, he sat down next to her and put his arm around her, drawing her close. She gave him his mug and rested her head on his shoulder. In a comfortable silence, they sipped their cocoa and watched the flames dance.

"What would you be doing if I weren't here?" she asked.

"This. Except alone."

"You really don't have anyone?"

He took a long swig of his cocoa, letting the schnapps burn on its way down. "I have my parents, but it's not the same. They're snowbirds now and I won't see them until March."

"I haven't talked to my dad since last Christmas," she admitted. "I try once a year but...it's not worth it."

"It must be rough during the holidays."

She shrugged and burrowed deeper against his chest. He rested his head on the top of hers. Everything about this was a mistake but, God help him, he wasn't going to get off this couch anytime soon. "I stay busy. Really, Christmas is just another day."

That was possibly the saddest thing she had said yet. "Christmas is one of the best days of the year—and I'll prove it to you. Assuming we can get out, I'm supposed to be Santa in two days at the Christmas Eve party in

Firestone. And you," he said, giving her a tight squeeze, "are going to be Santa's little helper."

Which was yet another piece of evidence that he had lost his mind. If he could get her to Firestone, someone was supposed to come get her. He didn't know who but that wasn't his problem. He would get her to town, someone would retrieve her and at some point when he could plow out his drive, he would get her car back to her. That had been the plan.

But it wasn't the plan anymore. He had to show her that Christmas was more than just another day. It was a time of hope and renewal. It was a time of change.

And since everything had already changed and would continue to change, he might as well spread the joy around and hope for the best.

Deep in the back of his mind, he knew his days of anonymity were numbered. She asked too many questions—questions other people would keep asking. But maybe he could...

Hell, he didn't know. Maybe he could get out in front of it? But he wasn't even sure how to do that. He could contact Zeb Richards. Or even Chadwick Beaumont. They were both his half brothers. CJ had to let them know what was coming and maybe they'd have the public relations know-how to spin the impact in a positive direction for everyone involved.

Natalie looked up at him. "You'd let me help you hand out presents?"

"It's better to give than receive. It restores your faith in humanity."

She looked at him for a long time, as if she couldn't believe what she was seeing. He felt the same way. Away from cameras and relatives and townsfolk, he was starting to realize that Natalie Baker was someone he could like quite a bit.

She nuzzled back into his side. "Do you ever talk to them?"

He didn't have to ask who *them* were. "No."

"When Zeb Richards got married, we all wondered if you would show up. Everyone was there."

He knew. That wedding had been the focus of weeks worth of coverage on *A Good Morning with Natalie Baker.* "I saw."

He had gotten an email inviting him, but he hadn't wanted to go public. Months ago, Zeb had contacted him and asked him to come to dinner. Looking back, CJ now knew that was the beginning of the end. Zeb had found him and their other illegitimate half brother, Daniel, and like an older brother, Zeb had invited both of them to join him at the Beaumont Brewery as they took it back.

But CJ wasn't interested in Zeb's version of revenge. Beaumonts weren't to be trusted, so he had walked away.

He remembered something now. Zeb had given a press conference where he'd talked about the brewery being back in Beaumont hands. Natalie had covered it. In fact, she had been the one to get the final piece of information out of Zeb that no one else had—that there was a third bastard out there somewhere.

She was nothing if not tenacious.

"What will you do, now that you know?" He would have to face whatever was coming head-on—but he didn't want this to be a runaway train that plowed him down.

"My ratings are slipping. My job is on the line and I

don't know how to do anything else," she told him in a small voice. "I told my producer I would find you and if I don't, he'll pull me off the air." He could feel her curling into a ball, getting smaller. He drank the rest of his cocoa, set his cup to the side and wrapped both arms around her. "I don't know what I am if I'm not Natalie Baker."

He lifted her up and settled her onto his lap. He shouldn't want to comfort her because she was going to ruin everything. No, that wasn't right. She was going to *change* everything and that was a different thing entirely.

But, as he ran his hand up and down her back, he wondered if maybe it wasn't time for a change.

"I still don't want to be your headline. I'm not some celebrity you can package and resell. This is my life. I'm Bell and Pat Wesley's son."

"You're a good man, CJ." Which was no kind of answer. She wrapped her arms around his waist and held on and CJ thought maybe he didn't really need an answer. Not right now.

"I think you're a good woman, too. When you're not trying so hard to be someone else."

They sat there for a long time. CJ's eyes grew heavy as the fire mesmerized him and the warmth of her body sank deep into his bones.

Just as he was about to slip off to sleep, he thought he heard her whisper, "No, I'm not."

Seven

"Natalie."

Natalie moaned, burrowing deeper into the warmth that surrounded her. Was it bright out? It seemed bright. She squeezed her eyes closed even tighter. She didn't want to wake up.

"Natalie," the voice repeated again. This time, she was aware that the voice was low and very close to her ear.

CJ. That was his voice. And those arms around her waist? Those were CJ's arms. He was warm and comfortable and safe and she didn't ever want to get up.

Wait a minute. CJ's arms were around her? And that warm, solid chest she was nestling against—that was CJ's chest?

Oh, hell. What had she done? She tried to think. Had they had sex? She couldn't recall. And that seemed a shame because if she were going to have sex with CJ, she wanted to remember it.

Something stroked over her forehead. "Why are you frowning?" And then something else touched her right where she undoubtedly had a divot. Something warm but wet.

His lips.

Oh, *hell*.

"I hate to wake you, but we need to get up," he said gently, his lips moving against her skin.

Without moving, she tried to take stock. Her cheek was pressed against a sweater and her hand was resting on the same. Slowly, she wiggled her toes—her socks were still on. Were they fully clothed?

She bit the bullet. "Is there any way to make this not awkward?"

"Why would this be awkward?"

At that, she cracked open an eye and stared up at him. He leaned back enough that he could look at her—but there was very little space between them. She realized her head was resting on his arm and his hand was stroking her hair. "Last night, we..."

"Yes?"

Her cheeks began to heat. "What did we do?"

This close, that half smile was even more dangerous because all she would have to do to taste it would be to tilt his head down and press her lips against his. "We had cocoa in front of the fire. I might have been a little heavy with the peppermint schnapps, because we fell asleep."

Now she had both eyes open. She could see the distinctive flecks of green and brown in his. At a distance, they were hazel. But this close? She could see the two different parts that made one whole. "And that's it?"

It was his turn to wrinkle his brow. "Yeah."

She couldn't believe it. This had to be a first. Any other time she had been incapacitated and alone with a man, she'd woken up in various states of undress and she never could remember if she'd said yes or no. It hadn't mattered anyway. When she woke up with a man's arms around her and the taste of him in her mouth, it'd always been proof that someone had wanted her and that was the most important thing. More important than the hollow feeling she always had as she pulled on her clothes and did the walk of shame.

CJ was out-and-out frowning at her now. "I think you hang out with the wrong kind of people." That was all he said about it, but it was enough. He understood what she hadn't said.

She couldn't look at him and see confusion and maybe a little bit of anger. So she buried her face against his chest. "Do we have to get up?"

"Only if you want heat and hot water," he teased. "It's going to be a beautiful day. We could actually leave the living room."

She took the change of topic and ran with it. "Even the kitchen, too?"

He chuckled. The sound came straight out of his chest and surrounded her. "You crazy dreamer, you. Come on," he said more insistently. "I have big plans for you today and tomorrow's Christmas Eve." With that, he leaned down and gave her a firm kiss on the forehead. But before she could kiss him back he forcibly sat her upright and all but rolled her off the couch. "Get moving!"

He was just too damn decent. It wasn't healthy and it wasn't normal, she thought as she splashed cold water on her face in the bathroom. Anyone else would have pressed their advantage. She'd already come on to him once. She liked him. He was gorgeous as sin—but not a sinner. If he started kissing her, she wouldn't have stopped him, regardless of how tipsy she might or might not have been.

But it also seemed as if maybe he liked her, too. He hadn't at first—that much had been obvious. But the longer they were trapped in this house together, the more relaxed he became. The more comfortable he became, the more he touched her—but not in a pushy way. She remembered the feeling of his arm around her shoulders as they stared out at the moonlit snowscape and how easy it had been curling up next to him and sipping the spiked hot chocolate on the couch. It had been warm and comfortable and safe. She hadn't had to be someone else to keep his interest.

And now he had big plans for her, and tomorrow night if they could make it to town on a snowmobile, he was going to be Santa for some sort of town party.

Did she want to stay for this party? Because originally, he'd wanted someone to pick her up in town and take her far, far away. She wouldn't get her car until the road was clear and she had no idea when that was going to happen.

But who was going to come get her? Steve, her producer? Kevin? He would rather see her freeze to death so he could have her time slot. She doubted that a car service would come this far north to fetch her.

The fact was, she had nowhere to go and no one waiting for her. The second fact was that the sooner she went back to Denver, back to her sleek apartment with black furniture and white walls and white carpeting—and not a single Christmas decoration in sight—the sooner she would be faced with another Christmas alone. She'd have to psych herself up to make her annual call to her father to wish him a merry Christmas and hope against hope that this time, he'd do the same.

And the sooner she would have to face Steve and make some sort of decision about the third lost Beaumont bastard.

Could she really do that to CJ? Could she drag him kicking and screaming into the public eye and subject him to the same sort of trolling that she dealt with every day? He didn't deserve it and he didn't want it. He was too good of a man to throw to the wolves because he wouldn't defend himself. He was too damn polite to survive in her world. She knew it and she thought he knew it, too.

She couldn't hide out here forever, though—tempting as the idea was. She had obligations and sooner or later, she was going to have to decide.

Was CJ her story? Or was he something else?

Later, she decided. She would choose later.

By the time she got out of the bathroom, CJ had grown three whole sizes. He was wearing a full-body snowsuit thing with a hood that made him look like a tan Abominable Snowman. "Good heavens. I suppose that crime against fashion is warm?"

He laughed. "You're more than welcome to brave the snow in that cute little coat of yours." He held out another snowsuit.

With an exaggerated sigh, she took it from him. "After you went to all that trouble to keep me from freezing to death once, I'd hate to undo your hard work." The suit weighed a ton in her arms. "Good heavens," she repeated, lugging the whole thing over to the couch.

"It's about sixteen degrees outside. I don't want you to freeze," he said. "Then I'd have to warm you up again."

Her head shot up. It wasn't so much what he said but the way he said it. The low timbre to his voice made her feel things in places hidden by far more than a snowsuit.

"I didn't think there was any hot water left," she said carefully.

"There are other ways to warm a body up."

Heat flooded her as she stared up at him. He shouldn't be that sexy—not in that hideous snowsuit. But the way he looked at her, like he wanted to unwrap her for Christmas...

She let her gaze drift over his body—the body that had been in her arms just a few short minutes ago. "Like how?"

Because maybe she wanted to be unwrapped. Maybe she wanted him to peel every single one of the seven thousand layers of clothing off and lay her out in front of that fire. The only thing that was missing was a tree dripping in lights—but she could be his present and he could be hers. Outside of the white-elephant exchange at work every year, she hadn't had a present to unwrap in...well, in a very long time.

The muscle in his jaw twitched. "Shoveling snow will keep you plenty warm."

"Oh." She cleared her throat and focused on shoving her legs into the massive snowsuit. "Is that what we're doing?"

"For starters. The snowmobile can go up to forty miles an hour. That's a wind chill you don't mess around with."

He held out something that looked like a stocking

cap, but when Natalie took it, she felt neoprene instead. "I didn't realize we were going to be robbing banks today," she joked as she yanked it down over her hair.

"With a face like yours, you could get away with robbing banks." As he said it, CJ stepped into her. He tucked a few loose strands under the mask and tugged it down until it was in the right position. "No one would think someone as beautiful as you would be capable of it. They'd be falling all over themselves to give you money."

It didn't seem possible, but he was entirely serious. His gaze was fastened on hers as his fingers stroked over the few inches of exposed skin on her cheeks. Then he was pulling the hood of the snowsuit over her ski mask and wrapping a scarf around the whole thing. "There," he said with satisfaction as he stepped back to look at her. "You probably can't put your arms down."

Natalie gave it a try and discovered she could—but only a little. She was beginning to sweat. She could safely say she had never had on this many layers before and she had lived almost her entire life in Denver. She wanted to go outside and see how weatherproof she was, but at the same time, she couldn't quite pull herself away from CJ's gaze.

"Is there something wrong?" It was hard not to feel insecure about her looks when there was only a third of her face showing. No doubt, she looked lumpy and bumpy and the exact opposite of glamorous.

The way CJ was looking at her, though... There was a light in his eyes that hadn't been there yesterday and she didn't think it was solely due to the sunlight flooding the big house. "Nope," he said, turning away and pulling his own ski mask over his head. "Let's go see how bad it is."

It was pretty bad. They had to go out the front door because there was a five-foot-tall drift blocking the kitchen door. Even then, they still had to shovel their way off of the porch. Walking through this much snow was, hands down, the most intense cardio workout Natalie had ever had. It was like slogging through mud, only colder. If she hadn't had CJ by her side, she might've panicked because how the hell was she ever going to leave? Even if she wasn't sure she wanted to leave, she would have to go home at one point or another. But her car was nothing but a lump in the snow and the cold was so biting she could feel it slipping under the neoprene face mask.

She could be out here until spring. And the thing was, she had no idea if that thought terrified her or not.

She didn't have time to figure it out, either, because all of a sudden, a snowball hit her in the arm. She whipped her head around to see CJ in the process of patting another ball of snow into a sphere.

"Oh, no, you don't," she yelled, dropping her shovel and scooping up snow. She launched it at him before she even got it into a ball. It hit him in the chest and disintegrated with a *pfft*.

"Hey," he hollered—but he was laughing.

They lobbed snowballs at each other—Natalie missed more often than not, but CJ had a good arm. Of course he did. He'd probably been having snowball fights and playing catch in the backyard with his dad for years. She hadn't. She never even had a house with a yard. There was something so sweet about a snowball fight—sweeter still, that CJ went to great efforts not to hit her in the face.

She was having fun. Honest-to-goodness fun. It was such a foreign concept she almost didn't recognize it. Laughing, they made their way back to the side of the house, where CJ called a truce.

The generator was housed in a small shed less than five feet from the back door. For a moment, Natalie felt guilty. If he hadn't had to drag her woefully unprepared behind into his house and keep her from freezing to death, he would've been able to get the generator started already. But once the storm had hit, there was no getting out here.

"Can you work on digging out the back door while I get into the shed?" CJ asked cautiously, as if he didn't believe she knew how to move snow from one place to another.

"Sure." The air bit at her lungs and her nose was probably going to be permanently red after this, but beyond that, she was plenty warm. She had to trudge back and grab her shovel from where she had dropped it during the snowball fight. Then she got to work.

She did spinning classes and Zumba and she ran— but nothing prepared her for shoveling five feet of snow. It was an intensive, full-body workout because the snow was a little wet. Which was good for snowballs, but made for heavy shoveling. Finally, she got the door cleared and then began working on meeting up where CJ had dug out the shed. He'd already disappeared inside of it and in a few minutes, she heard a whirring sound.

She knew she should be thrilled that the power was back on. She could use a hot shower like nobody's business. But that also meant that, if she and CJ didn't have to stay in front of the fireplace for warmth, they could sleep in separate bedrooms. They wouldn't have a good excuse to sit in front of the fire and lean against each other and drink spiked cocoa. They could go back to being more like themselves.

The thought saddened her. But then she remembered that he had promised her Christmas movies once they got their chores done today.

CJ emerged from the little shed and whistled in approval. "Great job. You ready to get to the barn? I need to feed my horses. They're probably starved. Then we can get the snowmobile out."

Natalie nodded and they began trudging the hundred feet to the barn. The barn was cold, but not freezing. CJ showed her where the grain was and told her how many scoops to put in each bucket. The horses pawed at the doors and CJ spoke to them in low, steady voices.

"It's going to be a while, boys," he told them as he carried hay and filled water buckets. He didn't even make fun of her when she jumped as one horse sniffed at her. "You ever been around horses before?"

"No—I suppose that's obvious. I really am just a city girl."

He could've made her feel stupid for not knowing what to do—but he didn't. Instead, he gave her a reassuring grin and said, "You're doing a great job." And again, that was one of those things that could've been a load of bull—but coming from him, seemed one hundred percent sincere.

They worked in the barn for almost an hour. CJ had six different horses and he spent time with each one of them. He clearly cared for his animals, which just confirmed that this was who he was as a person. He wasn't acting all nice to her just because he wanted something from her. He simply *was* this nice.

Again, guilt pinched her. Because if she made him her story to save her job, all this would change for him.

She tried to tell herself that it wouldn't last forever, him being a hot news item. Sure, he might be in for a long winter, but sooner or later, something would happen and CJ would no longer be the focus of the public's attention. Perhaps someone would know something about Daniel Lee and there was always the upcoming birth of Zeb Richards's baby to look forward to. Or one of the younger legitimate Beaumonts could do something crazy. *Something* would happen, she told herself, and CJ would fade away from the public's awareness. Her ratings would be secure and her show would be safe.

And after that…

"Ready?" CJ asked. At some point, he had pushed his hood and ski mask down. Even bundled up like a snowman, he was too handsome.

"Yes." She had to be.

At the far end of the barn was a bigger door and next to that, a room where three different snowmobiles sat. It took some work, but CJ got the biggest one out of the barn and up onto the top of the snow. It was unfortunate that he was wearing just as many layers as she was because she would've loved to have seen all those muscles in action.

Maybe this summer, she thought. But even as the thought occurred to her, she pushed it aside. She wouldn't be back. CJ wouldn't want her out here. This time, just the two of them, was a special time. Once they went back to their separate rooms, their separate lives, the magic of the moment would be shattered and they'd never get it back again.

She'd never wake up in his arms again, warm and comfy. She'd never go to sleep with him again, either—knowing that she could trust him completely.

God, what was wrong with her? She didn't want these melancholy thoughts. She didn't want the sensation of guilt. She didn't want to know that something was wrong and have to do it anyway. But she couldn't see another way to save the life she'd made for herself.

She ruined everything, after all.

"Here we go," CJ said, infectious enthusiasm in his voice. Even though she was conflicted about what she wanted to happen with him, she smiled as he helped her up onto the back of the snowmobile and took his place in front. "Now you hang on real tight," he said before he gunned the engine.

Natalie just had time to get her arms around his waist when the snowmobile lurched forward, picked up speed and then began to fly. She buried her face against his back to protect the exposed skin but even then, she couldn't resist peeking out as the pure white landscape zipped by them.

The snowmobile was much louder than she had anticipated and she wished it could've been quiet so she could have heard the wilderness around them. As they went past, birds skittered out of trees and she thought she saw a rabbit or two ducking for cover. But this wasn't that different from them being in the living room. They were alone in this pristine world and Natalie liked it far more than she should.

He slowed and pointed to dark moving shapes in the distance. "My herd," he shouted back at her.

"Do we need to feed them?" she yelled, remembering how hungry the horses had been.

He shook his head. "I laid out extra hay. They'll have to dig for it, though. But they'll be all right."

Then they roared on for a while until suddenly, CJ eased to a stop in front of some snow-covered lumps. "Here," he said loudly—Natalie's ears were ringing from the ride.

"Here what?" As far she could tell, they were in the middle of nowhere. But she slid off the snowmobile and waited.

CJ trudged over to the lumps. He kicked at them until the snow went flying. Natalie gasped. The deep green leaves and bright red berries stood out against the white snow. "Holly?"

CJ nodded and produced a knife from somewhere. He cut off several large branches and gave them to her to hold. Then he trudged a little farther back to a slightly larger looking lump. Again, he knocked off more snow, revealing some evergreens. He cut long boughs and handed them to Natalie as well. "One more thing," he said, motioning for her to set the foliage down on the back of the snowmobile. Then he held out his hand and she took it.

Together, they trudged deeper into the woods. The snow hadn't drifted as high under the cover of the trees. Instead of being indistinguishable lumps of white, the shrubs and trees were instead dusted with a thick coating of snow. She stopped as a pair of cardinals settled onto a branch of a nearby pine tree like two ornaments hung just so.

CJ followed her gaze and saw the birds. He took a step back so their shoulders were touching again and let her watch for a few minutes as the birds hopped from limb to snow-covered limb. Nature had decorated the tree for them. It was the most perfect thing she'd ever seen.

When the birds finally fluttered off, Natalie turned to CJ and said, "I never knew it could be this beautiful."

He stared down at her, a mysterious smile on his face. "Neither did I."

She didn't think he was talking about the birds. She dropped her gaze, embarrassed. Then CJ took her hand again. They moved on a little farther until he stopped and pointed at a cute little tree. "What do you think?"

"It's lovely." And it was. About six feet tall, the little pine tree had a nearly perfect cone shape and thick branches covered in snow.

"Then it's yours." She was surprised when CJ produced a small saw out of a different pocket.

"Really?"

"It *is* Christmas," he said, getting down on his hands and knees and sawing through the trunk. "And what's Christmas without a tree?"

A mix of strange emotions fluttered through her. She couldn't remember the last time she'd had a Christmas tree—just that one in that picture, when they were still a happy family.

But CJ was going to give her real tree—a real Christmas. One she could remember.

When the tree fell to the ground, he stood up and looked at her. "Are you crying?"

Natalie sniffed, swiping at her eyes with the back of her thick work gloves. "No," she lied and she didn't even care if he saw her tell.

CJ looked at her for a moment longer. "Good," he said in that gentle voice of his. "I wouldn't want your face to freeze on the way back."

She didn't want that, either. "How are we going to get the tree back? I can't hold it and hold on to you, too."

He cocked an eyebrow at her and grabbed the trunk of the tree. "I have my ways," he promised. Slowly they began walking toward the snowmobile.

Once they made it back, he produced some rope from yet another mysterious pocket. In short order, CJ had tied the tree onto the back of the snowmobile. He had enough rope left over to bundle the boughs of holly and pine together. Natalie tucked the bundle under one arm and with the other she held tight to his waist. Then they were screaming across the countryside toward his home.

When they got back into the house, it was noticeably warmer. She struggled to get the thick gloves off her hands and the hood off her head. "I'd hate to see it really cold out here," she mumbled, trying to kick off a boot.

The next thing she knew, CJ was in front of her. "Here," he said in that husky voice of his. He held her by the shoulders and made her stand up straight. "Are you too cold?"

Her face, her hands, her feet—yes. But other parts of her?

CJ pushed down the hood and pulled the mask over her head. The rush of air around the back of her neck made her shiver. "A little," she said, but anything else she wanted to add died on her tongue when he reached up and began to pull the zipper of her suit.

He was unwrapping her. *Slowly. Oh, yeah*—some parts of her were beginning to burn. She wanted to shift her feet to take some of the pressure off of her center, but she didn't want to break the spell.

"You never did tell me the other way of warming someone up." She was surprised to hear her own voice come out sultry.

Because she wanted this. Not the story, not her ratings—the man. She wanted CJ selfishly, all for herself. She didn't want to share him.

He pushed the snowsuit down her shoulders and then he stepped even closer, skimming his hands over her waist and her hips, shoving the warm, heavy suit down her legs. "If someone is too cold," he said as his hands kept right on skimming. He fell to his knees and lifted her left leg up. "Then the best way to warm them up is with body heat."

She'd seen enough movies to know what he was talking about—two people with as little clothing as possible tucked under blankets.

She swallowed and said in her most innocent voice, "How do you do that?"

But he didn't see her tell because he was pulling the suit off of one foot and then the other. Then, slowly, he climbed to his feet. His pupils were so black she almost couldn't see the brown or the green in his eyes and he was breathing hard. But he didn't say anything. He just stared at her.

She couldn't take it. She reached for his zipper and said, "Maybe you should show me."

But before she could get him unwrapped, he grabbed her hands. "The water heater should have caught up by now. You go first."

She bit back the disappointment. What was wrong? She wanted him. He wanted her. The last few days had been as close to perfect as she was capable of imagining. So why wasn't he giving in?

Then a new thought occurred to her. The shower she'd been in had been more than big enough for two people. Water and soap and hands everywhere—that would warm her up. Hell, just thinking about it was making her hot. "You could join—"

He cut her off. "I'll get the tree set up," he said as he turned away. "Go on." It was not a request. It was an order.

She opened her mouth to ask what she'd done wrong. Why didn't he want her? Was it just because of her morning show or was it something else?

That insidious voice in the back of her head whispered, *Of course he doesn't want you. No one does.*

But she didn't want to listen to that voice. Not today, when things had been so perfect and there was the promise of decorating Christmas trees and movies and…something more. Something wonderful.

"Go on," CJ repeated, motioning with his chin toward the stairs.

She didn't answer for a long, long moment—but finally, common sense won out. "Thanks. A shower would be perfect right now." It was only after she said it that she saw he was staring at her throat.

Crap.

Eight

For the second time in three days, CJ was forcing himself not to think about Natalie Baker naked in his shower. And if he thought it had gone poorly the first time, it was an absolute flipping disaster today.

Because the woman in his shower today seemed like a completely different woman from the one he'd dragged into this house a few days ago. Instead of belligerent and cocky and hell-bent on using her beautiful body as a weapon, the Natalie he'd come to know was someone else entirely. Soft and vulnerable and easy to be around. Someone who didn't mind shoveling a lot of snow and could see the beauty in a pair of songbirds in a tree.

It could still be a trick, he told himself as he dug out the tree stand and got the tree set up. All of this sweetness could be part of her larger plan to weasel information out of him.

That's not what his gut told him, though, and up until this point in his life, his gut had been a fairly reliable indicator of who to trust and who to avoid.

And what was he thinking? Unzipping her snowsuit for her? Peeling it off of her body like he had a right to touch her? Because he didn't. He *couldn't*.

Okay, when she looked up at him with those beautiful blue eyes like he was this rare specimen just because he did something any decent man would do—yeah, that hit him midchest. And, sure, when he'd woken up this morning with her body curling into his, all warm and soft and sleepy, it'd hit him in other places.

He shouldn't have kissed her on the forehead this morning. He shouldn't have helped her out of her things this afternoon. And at no point did discussing getting naked and under the covers for "warmth" become a good idea.

Because that's what she was right now. Naked. In the guest room. In the shower. Hot water sluicing over her bare back, her breasts, as she ran the soap over the pointed tips—

He cleared his throat and adjusted his pants. He had crap to do. He had to focus. There was the coming revelation that he was the third Beaumont bastard heir. There was the Firestone Christmas party tomorrow night. There was a tree that needed tinsel, dammit.

He would have to call Zeb, he decided as he headed down to the basement—without a flashlight this time—and grabbed one of the bins of ornaments. The man owed him a favor. After all, it was Zeb's fault that anyone knew about CJ in the first place. The least his half brother could do was offer some sort of PR backup. CJ would call Zeb and somehow get Natalie back to Denver. And after that...

After that, it was back to a long, cold, dark winter out on the ranch. He'd tend to his horses and try to keep his cattle from freezing to death and watch a lot of movies and drink a lot of beer.

Alone. His thoughts drifted back upstairs, where Natalie was no doubt drying off and putting on fresh clothes. Was it selfish of him to wish that she could stay here for a little while longer? Maybe through the New Year? He might be able to plow the drive, but towing her car out of that drift without ripping the axle off of it would be next to impossible without a major warm-up. And she wouldn't want to leave without her car, right?

She could stay, he decided. It really wouldn't be that bad. He could help her get more comfortable around the horses, show her other parts of the ranch—tomorrow, he really did have to go check on the cattle. And then, after they'd done the day's chores, they could...

He dropped his head and jammed his hands onto his hips. He didn't want the images—Natalie in his arms, naked and bare to him. He wanted to stroke his fingers over her skin and see how her body reacted. Would her nipples tighten with his touch? What kind of noises would she make if he touched her?

This whole day had been an exercise in painful lust. It wasn't right that a woman could make a snowsuit and ski mask look sexy, but she did. Standing out there in the woods this afternoon, watching that pair of cardinals coo and sing to each other—she had been the most beautiful woman he had ever seen. And the look on her face when he cut down the Christmas tree for her?

She pulled at something in him and it was getting harder and harder to resist.

First things first. Tomorrow night was Christmas Eve and he was pretty sure that, barring another weather disaster, he would be able to make the trek into Firestone for the annual Christmas party. While she was still upstairs, he made his phone calls. Everything was still a go—it might be a lot of horse-drawn sleighs and snowmobiles, but they were going to have a parade for the kids, come hell or high water.

Then, quickly, he left a message for Zeb and Daniel. "Natalie Baker has found me. I'm not sure what she's going to do. I'm trying to convince her that I'm not a story, but just in case, be ready." He wished he could tell them what to be ready for, specifically, but he had no idea.

Then, knowing he was running out of time, he pulled her phone out of his back pocket. He'd kept it with him at all times for the last several days. It was tempting to turn it on—almost too tempting. She had said that no one would miss her for Christmas and he wasn't sure if he believed that. If he turned on her phone, would there be notifications from someone who was thinking of her? A father, a boyfriend—any friend? Or would it be more of those horrible tweets and notifications? No one should have to put up with that.

That was what he was afraid of, he realized. It wasn't just that people would know who he was—it was that they would treat him like they treated her.

He didn't turn on her phone. He didn't want to let those trolls into his house in any way, shape or form. Instead, he slid her phone back into his pocket just as he heard her footsteps coming down the stairs.

What he saw took his breath away and he couldn't even say why. She was wearing another pair of jeans with a shirt and a sweater over it, plus thick socks. There shouldn't be anything sensual about her—but there was. It was all in her face, he realized. The way she looked at him did some mighty funny things to him. The tingling started low in his back and raced along his limbs until the only thing that would soothe it would be to pull her into his arms, just like she'd been when he woke up this morning.

"Hi," she said almost shyly.

Her gaze met his. There was something about her that glowed—something that hadn't been there the first time he'd seen her in the feed store. She didn't have that glow when she was on television. It was so hard to even see that woman when he looked at the Natalie standing before him. It didn't seem possible that they were the same person.

"Better?"

She dropped her chin and looked up at him through thick lashes. "I'm still a little chilly." As if to demonstrate this, she wrapped her arms around her waist and gave a comical little shiver.

He knew what that meant—that was an invitation. If he walked over and put his arms around her shoulders and pulled her against him, she would go willingly. Happily, even. There was a big part of him that wanted to do exactly that. He knew he had reasons why he shouldn't—although those reasons were getting harder to remember all the time.

"Come stand in front of the fire."

She notched an eyebrow at him, as if she were disappointed he hadn't taken her up on the challenge. But she did as he asked. Or started to, anyway. Because when she looked past him, she saw the tree and her whole face lit up.

"Oh," she breathed, her eyes wide with surprise and joy. "It's the most beautiful thing I've ever seen."

"Wait until we decorate it," he told her. Would it be so wrong if he kissed her? Would it be such a terrible thing if he let himself pretend, even for a little while, that reality wasn't waiting for them once the snow melted?

Could he trust her to kiss and not tell? Could he trust himself with keeping it to just a kiss?

She turned to him, her eyes luminous. He didn't think he could and he wasn't sure he wanted to. He'd kept himself apart from everyone but his family for so long that he had forgotten what it felt like to have a connection with another person. But he felt that now.

"Do we have to decorate it?" she asked. "It's so pretty just the way it is."

He couldn't help himself. He stepped in close and stroked her cheek with the back of his hand. "It is, isn't it?" But he wasn't looking at the tree when he said it.

She held his hand against her face. "You're still cold," she said, her voice barely above a whisper.

Was he? Because he didn't feel cold. All he could feel was the warmth of her skin against his. "I don't mind."

Unexpectedly, a shadow crossed her face. "Oh," she said with disappointment. Then she stepped away and looked back at the tree. "I understand."

"Understand what?" Because he hadn't meant anything by that—at least, nothing to make her shut down on him.

She walked over to the bins of ornaments and popped

the lid off one. "It's fine," she said in a voice that made it clear it was anything but.

"Natalie," he said, keeping his voice steady. "What's fine?"

She stilled. "You don't want to take a shower and leave me alone in your house. Which is fine. I mean, I wouldn't violate your privacy—but I understand that you don't want to take that risk." She pulled out a roll of colored beads. "Where would you like these?"

He stared at the back of her head. "Natalie," he said with more force this time.

She stood, but she didn't turn around. "Do you wrap these around the tree?"

He closed the distance between them and turned her around so she had no choice but to look at him. "Natalie, that's not what I meant."

She closed her eyes. "You don't owe me an explanation. I know this hasn't been how you wanted to spend your holiday and I—"

She didn't get any further than that because CJ kissed her. Roughly. Her eyes widened and she gave a little squeak that almost made him pull away. But before he could, her eyelids drifted shut as she sighed into his mouth. Her arms went around his neck and pulled him in close and then she was kissing him back. Her mouth opened and with a groan, CJ dipped his tongue into her.

God, she tasted so good—sweet and earthy, with a hint of vanilla. She was like a cookie and he wanted to nibble at her. Slowly.

But he couldn't. Dammit, he *couldn't*. There were reasons. Okay, so he couldn't exactly remember what those reasons were—not when she moaned into him like she was doing as his tongue dipped in and out of her mouth. But just because he couldn't remember them didn't mean there weren't any so, reluctantly, he forced himself to lean back. Her eyes were closed and her chest was heaving and he almost kissed her again right then and there. But then her eyelashes fluttered and she looked at him and there was a happiness to her that he hadn't expected to see. She was happy that he'd kissed her.

Doubt slithered in. Was she happy because she'd wanted him to kiss her? Or was this part of the story she was researching?

But then she touched his cheek and, with a crooked smile, said, "There. You're warmer already."

She turned to go, but CJ caught her in his arms and held her tight. "Natalie," he breathed against her skin but he didn't know what he was asking. Did he want her to kiss him? Did he want some sort of reassurance that this was real? Did he want something more?

He didn't know and it was only mildly reassuring that she didn't seem to know, either. He touched his forehead to hers but even that connection felt significant.

He hadn't had a serious relationship since college— since the last time he tried to tell someone that he was a Beaumont by birth.

The last time he had told someone about Hardwick Beaumont, it had ruined everything. But Natalie already knew about it. With each passing hour, it seemed to matter less, not more.

God, how he wanted it not to matter at all.

She was the one who broke the silence. "Go take a shower," she told him, a waver in her voice. "I won't decorate the tree without you."

He didn't want to ask this question but he asked it anyway. "What are you going to do?"

Her smile was a lot sadder. "It's been a long day. I'll probably just sit on the couch and watch the fire."

He could take her at her word because it *had* been a long day. He had gotten her up early and run her outside to shovel snow and then taken her on a ride on the snowmobile.

Or he could stay down here, forgo a shower and keep an eye on her.

He'd already kissed her. Hell, he had already made his choice. "I won't be long," he promised, stroking his fingers over her cheek. Her whole body shook with what he prayed was need.

God, he hoped he didn't regret this.

Nine

He had kissed her. *Hard.*

The kind of kiss that left a girl anxious and burning, that made sitting awkward and standing a misery. The kind of kiss that normally led to so much more than a full-body hug.

He had kissed her. And then left her alone.

Those two thoughts repeated over and over in her head as Natalie filled a coffee mug and curled up on the sofa. He had kissed her and left her alone in his house for the first time in days.

That was amazing enough. But what was even more amazing was the fact that she was doing exactly what she had told him she would. She was going to sit here and admire this beautiful tree that he had gotten for her and she was going to watch the fire dance and she was not going to pry into his life.

She didn't want him to be her story and she didn't want to share him or this time with anyone else. For someone who had lived so much of her life oversharing in an attempt to get people to look at her, it felt odd that she didn't want anyone else to know about this. But this time was hers and his. It didn't belong to anyone else.

So what was she supposed to do now? Keep hoping this semi-involuntary Christmas vacation would go on forever? That was no answer and she knew it. It was one thing to intrude on CJ's privacy and hospitality for a couple of days, but it was another thing to suggest that anything about this could become more permanent. Besides, she had a job to do—a job she loved.

At least, she *had* loved it.

Hadn't she?

She stared down at her coffee as if it held the answers. What if she hadn't loved her job? What if she actually hated it? What if putting herself on display and hoping to get noticed had secretly made her sick?

Because she was. Sick of the trolling and negativity. Sick of trying so hard to get a reaction that it stopped being about getting good reactions and started being about getting *any* reaction. She was sick of it all and she hadn't realized it until CJ had taken her phone away.

No, it was more than that. He had taken her phone away and then relentlessly treated her like a real human being. She wasn't a commodity or a collection of body parts. She was a woman and, after a kiss like that, she might even be a woman he could like. That wasn't a bad thing at all.

She didn't have relationships. So she had no idea if that were even a possibility.

She was so lost in thought that she didn't hear him

come downstairs. One moment, she was contemplating what life would be like if she just...stopped. Stopped being the Natalie Baker of *A Good Morning with Natalie Baker*, stopped tweeting and sharing. Stopped trying to get everyone's attention and instead focused on keeping one man's attention.

The next moment, CJ was standing in front of her, smiling down at her as if he were relieved to find her exactly where she'd said she'd be. His hair was damp from the shower and she had the overwhelming urge to press a kiss to the base of his neck and see what he tasted like.

But she didn't. "Are we going to decorate the tree now?"

He looked so happy. This had been building for days now, this slow thaw. What would he be like if he melted completely?

"Let me put on some Christmas music and we'll get started."

Everything about this was new and exciting. She only listened to Christmas music when she was on the air or in stores.

CJ loaded a streaming music mix, which meant they bopped from Elvis to Mariah Carey and then back to Bing Crosby. CJ knew the words to every single song and his singing voice wasn't half-bad.

They strung lights and beads and hung ornaments— some of which clearly went back to his childhood. But she didn't ask. It was enough to know that he'd had a wonderful childhood—because that much was obvious.

She thought of everything she knew about the Beaumont family—the divorces, the scandals, the rumors that people whispered. She knew a great deal about the Beaumonts—far more than was probably common knowledge. And she knew that a lot of them had not had happy childhoods. In that regard, she was more like his family than he was.

But he'd had a different life. One filled with home-made ornaments lovingly preserved and displayed every single year and Christmas carols and hot cocoa.

How would her life have been different if there'd been a little bit of hope at Christmas?

CJ was right, though—the tree undecorated was pretty, but the tree decorated? "It's stunning," she said as she felt an unexpected catch in the back of her throat.

Why hadn't she ever done this? She could've gotten a tree—even a small one, with twinkling lights and cute little ornaments that meant something to her, even if they didn't mean a single thing to anyone else. Why hadn't she celebrated Christmas before now?

Because Christmas was joy and happiness and fun. Christmas was hope and peace and she...

Did she deserve any of it?

"Christmas movies or football?" CJ asked, snapping her out of her thoughts.

She gave him a dull look, but couldn't keep the smile off of her face. "Movies," she said decisively. But then she added, "I haven't watched a lot of Christmas movies before, so you'll have to tell me what's good."

CJ popped a big bowl of popcorn and made more cocoa—he went a little lighter on the peppermint schnapps this time, but he still added some. Then they curled up on the couch and Natalie pulled the blanket over them and they started watching something called *A Christmas Story*.

"You've really never seen this before?" CJ asked as she giggled at the leg lamp.

She was trying so hard to seem normal—but clearly, she wasn't making it. Apparently, the whole world knew about the leg lamp. "I'm usually pretty busy during the holidays," she lied.

He stared at her for a long moment and she remembered that she had a tell. She was just about to say something else to cover her embarrassment when he said, "Well, I'm glad you were able to take some time off and hang out with me." Which was also not exactly the truth. "Surely you've seen some Christmas shows?"

She ignored the pity lacing the edge of that question. "Oh, yes—I remember *A Charlie Brown Christmas* and *Rudolph the Red-Nosed Reindeer* when I was a kid."

She remembered the feeling both shows had conveyed—of not belonging and wanting to so badly. And when she'd tried to watch the shows one long year after her mother had left, her dad had shattered the television screen with the remote.

How old had she been? Seven?

She pushed the unpleasant memories away and focused on the movie. And on CJ. His body was warm next to hers, and she once again found herself fighting the urge to press her breasts against his chest and kiss him. Not as thanks but because she wanted to.

And after that kiss earlier? Because he wanted her, too.

But she didn't. The kiss earlier had been damned near perfect and for the first time ever, she wondered if sex might make things...well, not worse. But more complicated. And she didn't want this to be complicated. She didn't want to kiss him and have him set her aside again.

She didn't want the rejection. And she really didn't want that hollow feeling afterwards. If she and CJ had sex, she wanted it to mean something.

She wanted to mean something to him.

So it was better not to ask the question. Besides, there was a movie on. By the time it had ended, darkness had settled back over the living room. The popcorn bowl had been set aside and the empty mugs were somewhere on the floor. They had shifted so CJ was sprawled out on his back and Natalie was lying on his chest, the blanket pulled up over both of them. He was warm and solid—and since she was *not* imagining how warm and solid he'd be without his layers on—she was tempted to close her eyes and fall asleep in his arms. Because she knew that when she woke up, he'd be there and everything would be all right.

The temptation got a lot harder to avoid when he started stroking her hair. "Have you decided what you're going to do tomorrow?" he asked as he turned off the TV with the remote and wrapped his arm around her.

He was in no hurry to get up and that made her feel better. "I can try and see if someone can come get me in town tomorrow, if you want. But I've never had a Christmas like this," she told him truthfully.

He was silent for a long time but his hand still stroked over her hair. It should have been lulling her to sleep—but it wasn't. Every inch of her skin tingled with awareness. "It might be a while before your car gets out. And I don't know what the roads between here and Denver are like."

She curled her fingers into his sweater and lifted her

chin up so she could look at him. His eyes were half-closed, but he was watching her. The hand that had been stroking her hair shifted so he was brushing a few stray strands away from her face and the other hand, which had been laying on her back, began to rub in circles that seemed to push her closer to him. Closer to his mouth. "And if I want to stay?"

"Because you want to go to the Christmas party to-morrow night?"

She shook her head.

She saw him swallow. "Because you're still gather-ing facts for your story?"

Just thinking about that made her want to cry. "No. This isn't about that."

He met her gaze with such strength that it made her quiver. What would it be like to have such conviction? "I don't want to be just a story to you."

"You're not," she promised, even as she wasn't en-tirely sure it was a promise she could keep.

He sighed and flopped his head back on the pillow, staring up at the ceiling. "But you need your story, don't you? And because my parents insisted on hiding the truth, now it's a thing. There's the small matter of the family fortune—and the family." His chest rose and fell with another heavy sigh. "I have brothers and sis-ters, but I don't want to give up my life to get them. Do you understand?"

She stared at him, trying to make sense of his words. Was he offering to—to what? Be interviewed? Even if he was, that didn't change the fact that he couldn't come out of obscurity without people noticing. That's not how this worked.

He was stuck—no way forward and no way back and

she'd been the one to back him into this corner. But then he said, "I'm tired of hiding, Natalie."

She froze. What? She didn't have anything to do with him hiding. She wasn't the one keeping him out here, alone in the darkest part of winter.

Maybe she wasn't the only problem here. For some reason, the realization made her feel light-headed as she studied his face. Not a muscle clenched in his jaw. The man didn't know how to lie. Maybe...

"I'm tired of keeping other people's secrets," he went on. "I'm tired of lies. I don't want you to lie to me. Not anymore."

"I won't." Tentatively, she touched her fingertips to his cheek, above the line of his beard. This time, he didn't grab her hand and he didn't push her away. He let her stroke her fingers over his skin, exploring him.

It wasn't until she dragged her thumb over his lower lip—the same lip that had kissed her earlier—that he stopped her. "Natalie," he said as he stilled her hand— but even then, he didn't pull it away. Instead, he pressed a kiss to her palm. "Tell me what this is about," he pleaded. "Tell me the truth."

The truth. She couldn't give him much, but she could give him that. "You're a good man," she told him. "You're a kind, hard-working, damnably decent man and I like you." He was too good for her, but she liked him anyway.

She could use everything he'd said against him. She was pretty sure that, if she tried hard enough, she could convince herself she was doing him a favor, dragging him out of the shadows and into the bright spotlight that was always fixed on the Beaumont family. He didn't want to hide anymore? Well, she could fix that for him.

But that wouldn't be fair to him and the more time she spent with him, the less she could turn him into just a story. Just some ratings. Just...

Just something less than a man. A flesh-and-blood man who was studying her closely while he held her palm to his cheek.

She liked him far more than she should.

It might wind up costing her the one thing she'd always valued most of all: her job.

"I won't, CJ," she repeated, knowing this was right. God, everything about this was right. "You're more than a story to me."

This was the point where he should tell her not to touch him, tell her that he didn't trust her. At the very least, he should pull away and tell her to go to sleep.

He did none of those things. "If you stay," he said in a low, deep voice that did things to her, "I won't be able to keep myself from doing this."

His hands slid down to her bottom and pushed her up and she let him. She wanted him to. She braced her elbows on his chest and leaned into him and this time, she kissed *him*. He tasted like cocoa and peppermint—like Christmas. And all she wanted to do was drink him in and pretend, even if only for a little while, that she was good enough for him.

She buried her fingers in his hair and pulled back only long enough to tell him "If I stay, I won't be able to keep myself from doing this, either," before she kissed him back—harder this time. She sucked his lower lip in her mouth and bit down. He groaned and yanked up the hem of her sweater. And then her shirt. And then the T-shirt she had on underneath that. But eventually, he got to her bare skin and when he touched her there, she shivered.

"Are you cold?" he murmured against her skin.

She wasn't. She was burning with the heat that started at her core and radiated out. She had on far too much clothing—and so did he.

"Maybe."

He leaned back and, cupping her face in both his hands, stared at her. "If you're cold, maybe I should warm you."

Please let me be good enough for him. "Maybe you should."

Somehow, they made it up the stairs. It wasn't easy— she was trying to yank his sweater over his head and he was doing the same. And then there were the shirts underneath. Hands and mouths were everywhere as she jerked at buttons and he slid down the zipper on her pants. There was an advantage to wearing jeans that were too big for her—they skimmed over her long-underwear-clad hips and she was able to walk out of them in the middle of the hallway.

"Which way?" she asked because she'd only been in one room up here, the impersonal guest room.

She didn't want this to be impersonal. She wanted every single thing to be deeply personal—from the way that CJ was kissing her and skimming his teeth over her neck and biting down against her skin to the way the muscles of his stomach tensed when she scraped her nails over his shoulders.

"Here—wait." CJ leaned heavily against the door and pulled the last of her shirts off over her head. His eyes fell upon her bra. "Oh, Lord," he groaned as he stared at her breasts covered in lacy pink silk.

"They're not real," she said quickly before he touched them. She'd had them done for the beauty pageant circuit. Normally, she didn't tell people that—but he had asked for the truth. So, this was her being truthful. "I had implants years ago."

It took him several moments to drag his eyes up to hers. "You must've had a very good surgeon because I never would've guessed." He dropped his gaze again and lifted his hands. But he didn't touch her. Instead his fingertips hovered above her skin. "What can you feel?"

She pressed his hands against her bra. Automatically, he cupped her and dragged his thumbs over her nipples. "I can feel that," she breathed. After she'd gotten them done, there'd been a period where things hadn't felt the same. But that had been a long time ago and the sensations had come back.

He reached around her back and undid her bra. As it slid off, she shivered because this hallway was not warm. Her nipples went rock-hard and, in response, CJ made a noise deep in the back of his throat. A noise of hunger and need. "How about this?" He teased the tips of her nipples and Natalie couldn't help arching her back and thrusting her breasts closer to him.

"Oh, *yes*." CJ hadn't made a move to open the door and drag her onto the bed. Instead, he seemed content where he was, lavishing attention on her breasts.

"How about this?" he asked, his voice straining. Lightly, *lightly* he pinched one of her nipples between his thumb and forefinger, with just the slightest pressure. "Do you like that?"

She wouldn't have thought it possible to want him even more, but in that moment, she did. To him, she was a person with wants and needs and she knew that he would take care of her. She had always known it, ever since he'd picked her up and dragged her into his house and made sure she didn't freeze to death.

"Don't stop," she pleaded.

He didn't. He took his time stroking and tugging on her breasts. When he lowered his mouth and sucked one nipple between his lips, she couldn't stand it. She moaned and whimpered and held him against her. He let his teeth nip at her until she was nearly crazed with desire.

"CJ," she begged. "I can't take much more."

But still he didn't let her go. Instead, without pulling his mouth off of her, he slid his hand down between them. She still had on panties and a pair of long underwear, but that didn't stop him. His hand dipped below the waistbands of both and moved lower, until he was stroking her sex.

"I think you can," he murmured against her skin before his teeth scraped over the top of her breast and he latched onto her nipple again.

All she could do was hold on to his shoulders and watch as he suckled her. When he hit her very center with his fingers and began to make maddening circles, she bucked against him. He looked up at her, and in that moment, she was lost. She came undone in his arms as wave after wave of pleasure threatened to knock her legs out from under her.

But she didn't need to worry because as she sagged against him, CJ caught her in his arms. "You are so beautiful when you come," he whispered, and damn if his voice didn't have a reverential tone to it.

Her mouth opened because she felt like she should say something. Normally, she did. She came up with some semi-sincere compliment on her lover's skill or she exaggerated the orgasm that she might not have had.

But *this* orgasm had been actually mind-blowing and she couldn't form words. Instead of the heavy hollowness she was used to, she felt light and shimmery. Special and wonderful.

It was so unfamiliar but already, she knew she wanted more.

She wanted all of him.

He was so hard with desire that it was now physically painful—but it had been worth it. Real or not, her breasts were fabulous. And watching her come?

That had been honest. It had been one of the most exciting things in his entire life. He had rendered her speechless and that made him feel good.

Her hand brushed over his throbbing dick and that shattered the last of his self-control.

He swept her legs out from under her and got the door to his room open. Then they were falling into bed, a tangled mass of arms and legs. He stripped her down to her panties and then down to nothing at all. He wanted to take his time—but he didn't have any more time to take. This wasn't a thinking thing. They had blown past seduction and there was no turning back.

"Oh, CJ," she whispered when she finally freed him. He sprang to full attention and when her hands closed around him, he almost lost it. Because she was stroking him and he wasn't this strong.

"Babe, now," he said, forcing himself to pull away and reach for the bedside table. The condoms were probably still good even though it'd been a while. "How do you like it?"

A look of confusion temporarily blotted out the desire on her face. He had to wonder if anyone had ever asked her that. She needed better friends.

"I liked it when you played with my breasts," she said, her eyes wide as he rolled on the condom.

"Then you can be on top." And he'd have full access to her. He'd nearly made her come just by playing with her nipples—how much would she shatter if he did that while he was making love to her?

She straddled him. There was nothing slow or gentle about either of their movements. She guided him to her opening and he tweaked her nipples as he thrust into her and it was better than good. The way she surrounded him, all warm wetness? The way she tasted in his mouth? The little noises she made as he pulled her apart so he could drive up harder? He couldn't even call it great because it was so much better than that.

He surrendered himself to her completely. Her pleasure was all his as she took him in and took him deeper. He filled his hands with her, stroking and sucking, licking and biting until she threw back her head and shuddered. He grabbed her by the hips and drove up into her, letting go as the climax tore through his body.

She collapsed down on him. They were breathing hard and a sheen of sweat covered them. "God, Natalie," he murmured as he lifted her off of him and slid her into the crook of his arm. He got rid of the condom and then pulled the covers up over them.

She was quiet and he wasn't sure if that was a good thing or not. He hoped he hadn't been too rusty for her.

"Stay with me," he said. "Stay with me for Christmas. Stay as long as you like."

She was quiet for a little while longer. "I can't. I wish I could but..."

It wasn't like her answer was a surprise or anything. Winters on the ranch were long—but they didn't last all year. And besides, eventually she'd get tired of his life. She'd want to go back to the comforts and conveniences of living in a big city instead of the isolation and hard work that went with ranching.

He accepted that. But what would happen when she left? It'd taken her less than four days to wind up in his bed. If she stayed through the New Year, how long would it take her to wind up in his heart?

Just like anything else with her, there was a risk. But apparently, it was one he was going to take, common sense be damned.

"I doubt the snow is going to melt before New Year's Eve."

She propped herself up on her elbows and stared down at him, a strange mix of emotions playing out on her face. "And you'd be okay with that?"

What kind of question was that? Especially considering that they were lying nude in each other's arms?

He rolled into her, trapping her body underneath his. Even that simple movement made him hard again because he could feel the weight of her breasts underneath him and her legs sliding around his. He began to thrust slowly, dragging his erection over the outer folds of her sex.

"I want you," he told her as he grabbed her hands and pinned them by the side of her head. "I'm tired of fighting it. I want *you*."

"I'm not good enough for you," she whispered even

as she began to writhe underneath him as he made contact with her over and over again. "I ruin everything."

"That's a lie," he told her. "Whoever told you that was lying." He let go of her long enough to fish another condom off the bedside table and roll it on. Then he positioned himself against her and, with one hard thrust, buried himself deep in her body. "You *are* good for me and I want you just the way you are."

And if he couldn't make her believe his words, by God, he was going to make her believe his actions. As he buried himself inside her, thrust after thrust, he showed her. He wanted her. Just her.

It was only later, when they were curled around each other under the covers and she was already asleep, that something occurred to him. She'd said she ruined everything—and it wasn't the first time she'd said it.

What if she hadn't been just repeating something that had been drummed into her when she'd been little?

What if she hadn't been talking about the past at all?

What if she had been telling him something about the future—*his* future?

Sleep was a long time coming.

Ten

Christmas Eve passed in a blur for Natalie. She helped feed the horses and rode the snowmobile with CJ out to different parts of his property. She got to watch him break ice on ponds for his cows. She had done a story not terribly long ago on the appeal of lumbersexuals. But watching CJ swing a sledgehammer? All of those muscles in action? *Damn.*

The day warmed up considerably. By the time they made it to the third pond, CJ had unzipped his snowsuit and had the upper part hanging around his waist while he broke ice. The snow was already beginning to melt, dripping off of trees and running in rivulets toward the ponds. Everything sparkled and was bright—but she knew what this thaw meant.

It was the beginning of the end. Once the snow melted, she wouldn't have a good reason to stay out here. Which was a shame, because they had just gotten started.

Once they made it back to the house, CJ spent a lot of time on the phone with his neighbors, making sure everything was ready for the parade and the party tonight. Then he disappeared upstairs and returned with a bright red sweatshirt and a pair of green sweatpants. He also had a more feminine-looking red top that had lace around the collar and bell sleeves. That was paired with a dark green skirt. He even had a pair of candy cane–striped tights. The last thing was a green-and-red-striped hat with a pair of elf ears attached. It was ridiculous—just looking at it made Natalie smile.

"All of this is going to be too big on you," he said, handing her the clothes. "If you put the sweats on over the snowsuit, you'll be good for the parade, and then at the party you can change into the other things. That is, if you don't mind playing my elf?" As he said that last part, the color in his face deepened. "You'll have to stand beside me and hand out presents to the kids."

She beamed at him. "I would love to be your elf," she said sincerely, trying the ears on. They felt silly—but good, too. Then something else occurred to her. "Does anyone else know I'm here?"

"I didn't tell anyone in town. I mean, I can, if you'd like—they don't have to know you've been here for days, but we could say you're the special guest of honor."

A week ago, she would've demanded just that. The honorary grand marshal or something else that would've made her the center of attention.

That wasn't what she wanted now. She could play this Christmas party and her involvement in it for ratings and self-promotion—or she could let the focus be

on Santa and the kids. She could be just an elf, handing
out presents and waving in a parade.

"Don't tell anyone," she said. "I'm just one of Santa's
helpers." Never in a million years had she thought she
would ever say anything like that.

But then again, never in a million years would a
man's smile have meant as much to her as CJ's did.
"People might recognize you," he told her. "You did
spend an awful lot of time at that diner."

She winced at the memory of wheedling and cajol-
ing information out of the locals. "There's going to be
talk, isn't there?"

But he just shrugged and pulled her into his arms
and kissed her. "I don't think it'll be a problem," he said
as she settled into his arms. "Firestone's been having
this party for forty-two years—no one wants to mess
with tradition."

She personally did not have a lot of faith in humanity. However, this was his town. All she could do at this
point was hope for the best.

Still, after a quick dinner—CJ promised there would
be food and drink at the party—Natalie suited up. She
was back in the layers again *plus* the snowsuit *plus* the
sweats. CJ helped her get the sweatshirt over her head—
and now, because she had seen *A Christmas Story*, she
understood what he meant when he asked, "Can you
put your arms down now?"

"Funny," she told him as he loaded her change of
clothes and her elf hat into a bag stuffed with pillows.

"I try," he said with a smirk. "Hold this." He gave
her his Santa beard. The plan was for them to ride the
snowmobile into town then ditch it before he put the

beard on and rode an old-fashioned sleigh down the main street of Firestone.

The stack of pillows served two purposes. One, it would make it look like the sleigh was filled with a sack of toys in the parade. But the other purpose was more practical. With a Santa suit over his snowsuit, CJ didn't need the extra padding for the parade. However, there was no way he could sit in a snowsuit inside the community center for a couple of hours without dying of heat exhaustion. So he would use the pillows for his stomach once the party started.

It was a struggle for Natalie to hold on to the sack and the beard and CJ, and even though it had been warm today, it was still a long, cold ride into town. What would have taken twenty minutes in the car took close to an hour on the snowmobile. By the time they eased into Firestone, her nose was running and her cheeks were frozen.

"This way," CJ said, parking on a snow-covered side street and helping her off the snowmobile.

"Aren't you going to take the keys?" she asked as he led her away.

He shook his head. "Everyone knows that's my vehicle. This isn't Denver, you know. Jamie!" he called out as they turned the corner. "We're here!"

Natalie stumbled to a stop. A short parade—no more than fifteen floats—stretched out along the narrow street of downtown Firestone. They came upon the rear, where an actual sleigh—with actual reindeer—waited for them. Some of the floats were on flatbed trailers that were being hauled by tractors so large they took up the entire street. There were more horse-drawn sleighs and even a couple of people dressed up like clowns on cross-country skis.

All Natalie could do was stand and stare, her mouth open. The whole thing was unreal—but in the best way possible. CJ hadn't been exaggerating. This dinky little town in the middle of nowhere put on a Christmas extravaganza every single year and it was...

It was simply the most magical thing she'd ever seen.

"Ready?" CJ had gotten his beard on while she'd patted the neck of a reindeer and suddenly, he was Santa. He *definitely* had the twinkle in his eye.

"My ears." He helped get her hood and ski mask off and then crammed the stocking cap with the attached elf ears onto her head. Then he and someone Natalie only vaguely recognized from the diner helped her up into the sleigh. The reindeer shifted nervously until CJ took the reins.

"Miss, do you think you can stand and wave?" Jamie asked as he handed the sack of pillows up to CJ.

Natalie braced her feet and her knees and gripped the back of CJ's seat. "We're about to find out," she said with a huge grin.

Jamie stepped back. "Meet you all at the community center," he called out.

The parade in front of them moved and CJ flicked the reins. Slowly, they made their public appearance as Santa Claus and his elf.

It took a block before they reached any parade watchers, but when they did, Natalie guessed that the entire town of Firestone had made it for this event. Kids bundled up in thick coats and hats and boots stood on the sidewalks, waving and shouting as CJ came into view. Clearly, the reindeer had done this before because the noise didn't seem to faze them at all. And Natalie? She managed to keep her balance and wave and smile at all of the kids.

Magical didn't begin to describe this feeling of happiness that started midchest and radiated outward. Nobody recognized her. But strangely, they didn't have to. All of her fame and notoriety mattered for exactly nothing right now. It should have been terrifying—but it wasn't. All that mattered was the way the kids clapped and cheered as CJ *ho-ho-ho-ed* his way through downtown Firestone.

Then, as quickly as it had begun, the parade was over and CJ was helping her out of the sleigh. They had parked behind a building that she assumed was the community center and a woman who looked exactly like Mrs. Claus opened the door for them. "Oh, thank goodness," she said. "Hurry! They're going to be here for hot cocoa any second."

"Doreen," CJ said, "could you show her where the ladies room is? I've got to get out of this snowsuit." With that, he hurried down the hallway.

"This way, dearie," Doreen said as she led Natalie in the opposite direction. "Thank you so much for being an elf. The children do so enjoy this."

"I'm having an amazing time," Natalie said honestly. Because she was. She hadn't believed that things like this were still possible in today's world. Childlike innocence and joy… Who knew?

As she struggled out of her layers, Natalie could hear the noise begin to rise in the building. Undoubtedly, families were flooding into the warmth and demanding hot chocolate and cookies. As she took off her elf ears and rearranged her hair so that it would be entirely hidden under the hat, a band started playing Christmas songs.

She braced herself and looked in the mirror. The candy-cane tights sealed the deal, she decided. That and the ears. Days ago, the thought of anyone seeing her dressed like this would've been horrifying. But right now it seemed like the perfect outfit. She *was* an elf.

She found Doreen in the kitchen again. "They're going to announce him in a minute," Doreen whispered. "When he comes down the hall, you can join him. The presents are arranged by size. The big flat presents are for the toddlers, the thin ones are for the middle schoolers and the heavy books are for the teenagers." Natalie must have given her a look because the older woman patted her on the arm and said, "CJ will know who gets what."

I hope so, Natalie thought as she peeked at the party. Senior citizens sat at tables and sipped punch and eggnog while kids and teenagers bopped around the postage stamp–sized dance floor. Desserts filled tables all along one wall—and people were eating them almost as fast as Doreen could carry them out.

When the song ended, the band started playing another song to introduce Santa Claus. All the kids began to cheer as the lead singer announced, "Here he is, boys and girls, all the way from the North Pole, it's the man of the hour—Santa Claus and his elf, Jingles!"

Jingles? Natalie grinned as the band dropped its volume down to a whisper and the entire room seemed to hold its breath. Natalie was no exception. She was watching the hallway, waiting for her cue.

One moment the hallway was empty. The next, there he was, *ho-ho-ho-ing* as he strode into the room. Natalie fell into step behind him as the entire room erupted into cheers. Adults and kids clapped as they headed over to a corner of the room that had been decorated with an enormous chair surrounded by piles of presents.

It was just *crazy*. She took her place next to this *throne*—the only word she could use to describe it. Some of the parents with the smallest children jockeyed to be first on Santa's lap. But CJ smiled and laughed and took time with each kid and then pointed to the book he wanted Natalie to hand over.

Through it all she smiled and giggled and nodded as Jingles. With every gift she handed over and every picture she took—because a lot of parents were handing her their cell phones so they could crowd in the picture behind CJ—she laughed. She was laughing more tonight than she had in years. And laughing was easy. It was *fun*. There was no tightness in her chest, no clawing worry about what people were thinking, what they were saying about her. Because she knew. They were coming up to her and thanking her for being a part of the night, thanking her for making the kids smile—especially the ones who were a little scared of the big man in the white beard.

Nobody knew who she was. And it was the most freeing thing she'd ever experienced. But more than that, people were nice to her for no reason. They weren't going to get anything out of it, other than a fun family evening. And the same went for her.

She hadn't thought that people could still be nice. But the entire town of Firestone was proving her wrong.

After two hours of intense Santa-ing, the community center began to empty out. Families had to get their children to bed so Santa could get to work filling stockings, and the older people had a long way to travel. CJ and Natalie weren't the only ones who'd come in on snowmobiles and it was going to be a dark trip back.

When the crowd was gone, CJ looked up at her and patted his lap. Natalie sat, grateful for the break. Happiness took a lot of effort.

"And what do you want for Christmas, little girl?" he asked, grinning widely behind his fake beard.

Natalie pretended to think about it. More than anything, she didn't want this time with him to end. "I don't suppose I could ask for another blizzard?"

Something in his eyes changed—deepened—and Natalie felt warm all over. "Here," he said, reaching underneath his seat and pulling out her—

Her phone.

She looked up at him in surprise. "You've been a very good girl," he said and then he winked at her.

She stared down at her phone. "Are you sure?" Because she'd half assumed he'd destroyed it—anything to keep her from exposing him.

And now he was giving it back to her. In one piece, even.

He didn't kiss her. It probably wouldn't do for Santa Claus to be seen cheating on Mrs. Claus with an elf. But he gave her a little squeeze. "I trust you," he said in his real voice, low and for her ears only.

Then another family approached and Natalie hopped up to get back to work. She almost didn't turn the phone on. She wouldn't have even thought about it if he hadn't given it to her.

A couple of men Natalie recognized from her time at the diner came up to CJ. "I need something to drink," she told him and he nodded and smiled as he turned his attention to his friends. She could only hope they weren't warning him about her.

As she sipped a foam cup full of cooling cocoa, she stared at her phone. The temptation to turn it on was huge. Huge. But what if she did? What would be waiting for her? All the trolling vitriol that she'd come to expect? Angry emails from her producer, Steve, demanding to know where she and her story were? For a second, she even considered that her dad might've tried to call her and wish her happy Christmas.

But worse—what if it was silence? No notifications, no messages? No…nothing?

She didn't want to see what people had been saying and she didn't want them not to have said anything at all. God, what a mess. And this was her life.

Behind her, CJ laughed with his friends. None of these people knew he was a Beaumont. It didn't matter that he wasn't famous. He was liked. That was…

That was more valuable than she'd realized it was.

A sense of peace filled her. Maybe she didn't need likes and shares. Maybe she just needed him. She looked at the silly decorations and the sugar cookies and all the smiling people who'd slogged through snow to celebrate this time with each other. With her.

She never wanted it to end.

But of course, it had to. Nothing lasted forever, not even snow in December. She'd have to go back and tell her producer…something. She still didn't know what. But when she left…

She wanted a memory. Just one to remind her of the Christmas she'd spent with a grumpy, sexy cowboy. It would be enough. More than she'd had before she'd come to this town.

As casually as she could, she turned on her phone and closed her eyes against the notifications. She opened the camera app and snapped a picture of CJ sitting on his throne. She caught him at just the right moment—his friends had moved out of the frame, but he wasn't looking at her.

She stared down at the picture. All she saw was Santa. The only parts of CJ that were visible were his eyes and she didn't think even his own mother would be able to pick him out of a Santa lineup.

But she'd know. She'd always know.

Quickly, she turned the phone back off before she lost her willpower and started tapping through to the social media apps.

When she glanced back at CJ, she caught him watching her. Guilt whispered that she should tell him she took the photo but she decided against it. It was for her and her alone. A perfect memory of a perfect Christmas.

Someone came up to her and asked for an official photo of her and CJ for the county newspaper, so she put on her big smile and went to stand by him. Everything was fine.

But through it all, she couldn't shake one nagging feeling.

She ruined everything. She always had.

Would she ruin this, too?

Eleven

CJ woke up early—he always did on Christmas. Natalie was still fast asleep. It was Christmas morning and she wasn't under the tree, but he'd gotten what he'd asked for.

He grinned at himself. There was something not quite right about Santa asking himself for a present. But he wanted Natalie. And when she had asked for more snow instead of her phone?

This probably wasn't love. The thing was, though, he wasn't one hundred percent sure that it *wasn't* love. The only other time he'd thought he'd been in love, he'd been wrong.

He watched her sleep. The ride home from the party last night had been long and cold and he didn't want to wake her.

His thoughts turned to another Christmas, one about twenty years ago. He'd been thirteen and Hardwick

Beaumont had made headlines *again* for divorcing another wife and keeping the children. CJ had always been dimly aware that Dad wasn't actually his birth father because his mother had drilled it into his head that he was never to go anywhere with anyone named Beaumont. And he was dimly aware of the story his parents told everyone about how they met—his dad had been visiting Denver on leave from his stint in the army, met his mom and fallen in love so fast that he had married her quickly before he finished his tour of duty. After his honorable discharge, Pat had returned to Denver to find his wife waiting with an infant CJ. The way the story went, it was one of those love-at-first-sight things.

But that wasn't the truth. They hadn't met while Pat was on leave—they had met after Pat's discharge. CJ had already been four months old and his mom was desperate. Her family was deeply religious and when she'd gotten pregnant with him they'd disowned her. Apparently, Hardwick Beaumont had given her some hush money, but it was starting to run out and she hadn't known what she was going to do until the handsome young soldier walked into her life.

CJ's parents had only told him the true story once, but he had never forgotten it. Even at the age of thirteen, he'd paid close attention.

It had not been love at first sight. Isabel Santino had seen a handsome young man who bore a passing resemblance to her child's father. But more than that, she had seen a handsome young man who would protect her and CJ. And Pat? His parents had died while he was in the service. He was suddenly in charge of a massive ranching operation that had been neglected for eight months. He had needed a ranch wife, basically. Isabel had applied for a job but somehow, she'd convinced Pat to marry her and give her son his name.

Pat had not formally adopted CJ until he was three. By that time, Pat and Bell Wesley had fallen in love. The adoption, more than the wedding, had been the promise to love and protect their family, until death did they part. Not that anyone had known about the adoption, of course.

At least, they hadn't until recently. There'd only been a few whispers that'd reached his ears last night during the party—a few warnings that someone was looking for him and spreading rumors that he was a Beaumont, not Pat's son. But people had been too preoccupied with the band and the spiked eggnog and CJ had managed to deflect any further questions with a simple "Yeah, I heard. I'm not worried." And he hadn't been.

As he stared down at Natalie, her face soft with sleep, he wondered what the hell was going on between them. He honestly could not figure out if he was glad that she had barged into his life or not. If she hadn't barged in, no one would ever have connected him with the Beaumont family.

But then she wouldn't be here with him now. He wouldn't be wondering if there could be something more between them. Something that looked like love.

He slipped out of bed. Out of the barn, he had the almost-finished wooden star he'd carved for his mom. He'd made up his mind—he was going to give it to Natalie instead. He meant to put one more coat of lacquer on it, but he could give it a light sanding now and put it under the tree. She hadn't told him the details of her childhood—not in so many words. But watching her last night—hell, over the last several days—had made one thing clear.

She hadn't known what Christmas truly was. And he had to wonder if anyone had ever given her a gift. A real gift, one that had meaning and hope.

She meant something to him. He didn't have the precise label for it. But he didn't need one.

As he suited up and headed out to the barn to feed his horses and sand the star, he could only hope that he meant something to her, too.

Natalie woke up alone. Even though that was how she normally woke up in her own place, it still felt unusual here. It shouldn't be possible that she missed CJ already, but she did.

For a few moments, she lay there reliving not the Christmas morning her mom had left and not every painful Christmas call with her father in the last decade. For the first time in…well, forever—she had happy memories.

Everything about last night had been magical. The sleigh ride down the middle of Firestone, handing out presents as Jingles—coming home with CJ and falling into bed with him…

It was perfect. Too perfect, almost. There was such a sense of joy and peace surrounding her and CJ and this time that it felt dangerous.

Last night, he'd made her feel special and wonderful. He'd lavished affection upon her—God, she'd never known sex could be *that* good.

She'd never been in love. Honestly, it scared her a little bit. She wasn't good enough for him. But, CJ being CJ, he made her think that maybe…

What was she doing? It was Christmas morning! Full of hope and happiness and excitement! She might only ever get one shot at a perfect Christmas morning with a perfect cowboy and she wasn't about to waste it lounging alone in bed. Besides, CJ was right—there was no future and no past. There was just today.

And today—like yesterday and last night—was going to be a gift. One she would treasure for the rest of her days.

Downstairs, she found CJ in the kitchen, sipping coffee. His cheeks were red and he had a strange smile on his face, one she couldn't interpret.

"Hi," she said.

"Merry Christmas," he said as he pulled her into his arms and kissed her fiercely.

She sank into his kiss. In the here and now, at least, she had this and by God, she wouldn't ruin it.

"I think Santa brought you something," CJ said when the kiss finally ended.

Natalie shot him a questioning look, but he didn't elaborate. Instead, he put his hand on her lower back and guided her toward the living room. He'd already plugged in the lights and he'd gotten a fire going. Natalie prayed for more than just a little snow.

She wasn't sure she ever wanted to leave. Not this place and not CJ.

"How long have you been up?" she asked, marveling at the scene before her.

For there, underneath the tree, was something small and golden. It hadn't been there yesterday.

"Go on," CJ said.

"But I didn't get you anything," she protested as she knelt and picked up the...

It was a star, a perfect golden star—the Christmas star. As she held it in her hands, her heart swelled. He had given her so much…but this? A gift under the tree for *her*?

Her eyes filled with tears. "It's beautiful," she told him, blinking as fast as she could. From this moment on, she would always have a tree and she would always hang the star on it, no matter what. "I don't deserve this."

"*You* are beautiful, and I think you do," he replied, crouching beside her and putting his arm around her shoulders. "Natalie, I know this hasn't been exactly normal, us getting to know each other, and I know you have to go back to your life in Denver, but…"

She stared at him. He was serious. Not only was he giving her the perfect Christmas, but he also wanted to see more of her.

Oh, God. She'd never fallen in love, never dreamed she could find someone who might possibly care for her in return—even a little bit.

But she was falling for him. He was good and kind and thoughtful and…

And she wasn't. She was still Natalie Baker, wasn't she? What if he put all this faith in her and believed that she was a good person and…

And she ruined it, just like she ruined everything?

"If you want to keep seeing each other…" he said, looking downright shy.

She should say no. She should end this while it was still perfect, before she did something that made him hate her. Because she would. That was who she was and she had promised not to lie to him. Not anymore.

But *no* was not what came out of her mouth. Maybe

she was weak. Maybe it was the fact that this was the best Christmas she could remember. Maybe she was just selfish.

Whatever it was, she said, "*Yes*. I want to keep doing this." All of it—not just Christmas. Riding out with him on his snowmobile. Feeding the horses. Snuggling under a blanket and watching movies. Even going to town and celebrating with all of his friends and neighbors—and especially coming home and going to bed with him. She wanted it all.

She'd always wanted things she knew she couldn't have—a happy family, friends who cared, a man she could love. He made everything feel like it was *possible*.

She kissed him—hard. So hard, in fact, that she knocked him over. She pulled at his clothes and he stripped hers off in a frenzy. He wanted her. She didn't deserve him but she wanted him, too.

She wouldn't screw it up. He was the best gift she ever could have asked for.

They made love in front of the fire while the Christmas lights twinkled in the background. Afterward, they lay in each other's arms and, for the first time, talked about the future. He could come down and spend the night at her place and she could come up on the weekends when she was done taping her show.

Her show…

No. She pushed that note of panic away even as she knew she couldn't avoid harsh reality forever.

She tightened her arms around CJ's waist and forced her thoughts to focus on the good things. CJ wanted to keep seeing her. They'd be together.

Oh, yes—she wanted to keep doing *this*.

* * *

That glow only lasted for so long. By the time they finished watching *Miracle on 34th Street*, doubt had slithered back into her mind in full force.

It was Christmas day. The one day a year when she called her father.

For a moment, she almost decided she wouldn't do it. Why did she have to?

But it was Christmas and he was her father. At least he'd stuck around. So she sort of owed him.

"I'm going to call my dad to wish him merry Christmas," Natalie said but she couldn't even manage to sound excited about it.

CJ noticed. "Are you sure?"

Of course she wasn't sure. They had been having a wonderful Christmas and she didn't want something like reality barging in on it. Who knew how much more time they had in this protective little bubble?

"No," she admitted, shooting him a weak smile. "But I don't want to give up on him. He's all I've got." She leaned over to get her phone, which had spent most of the day on the middle of the coffee table, silent and black.

CJ pulled her back. "That's not true," he told her, cupping her cheek and looking her in the eye. "You have me."

God, how she wanted that to be true. "CJ…" she whispered, brushing her lips over his.

"Go," he told her. "Call your dad." Then he got up and headed toward the kitchen to give her some privacy.

She didn't call, not right away. She opened up the camera app and cropped the photo she'd taken of CJ in his Santa suit. She saved it as her home screen with a smile.

But then she couldn't put it off any longer. She'd said she'd call and so she would.

The phone rang. And rang. Just as she was moving the phone away from her ear to end the call, her dad's scratchy voice crackled over the line. "What do you want?"

"Daddy?"

"Who is this?"

"It's me," she said, dread rising up in her stomach. "Natalie." Silence. "Your daughter?"

"Yeah, so?"

She swallowed down against the rising tide of panic. Why did she do this? Why did she try, year after year?

But then she stared at the Christmas tree with the bright lights, at her golden star glowing right in the middle. This wasn't the normal way she spent Christmas, alone in her sterile condo. She wasn't her normal self, either. She was better now.

"I wanted to call and wish you a merry Christmas, Daddy."

There was a painful silence. "You just gotta rub it in my face, don't you? Every year, you gotta call and remind me that this is the day she left. And you know why?"

"Why?" she asked in a shaking voice, unable to blink fast enough. She tried to put his words into context. He was slurring. He'd probably been drinking. He was upset. He was...

He wasn't done yet.

"Because you ruined Christmas, girl. And every year, you gotta call me up and remind me that I wasn't enough for her because she couldn't deal with a spoiled brat like you."

And with that, he hung up.

Natalie sat there, pain blossoming in her chest until she was nothing but regret.

Of course she ruined everything. Always had, always would. See? She'd even ruined her own Christmas because she thought she was doing a nice thing by reaching out to her father.

She'd thought...

What a fool she'd been, she suddenly realized. She'd thought she could be someone else and why? Because CJ treated her like a decent human? Ha. She'd never change. Even her father said so.

She was a former runner-up beauty queen with fake boobs and more wrinkles than she could keep at bay. She had nothing but her show. No family. No friends.

She had CJ...

But did she, really? This had been a great week. A nice vacation. But when she went back to her soulless condo and her fake morning smiles and her battles with Kevin and Steve over ratings, would she really have CJ?

No. Their lives were too far apart. If she gave up everything for him, she'd be left with nothing.

She needed her show. It was all she had.

She opened the photo app and looked at CJ in his Santa suit. Insecurity clobbered her on the back of the head and almost knocked her flat. She couldn't breathe.

Everything was wrong.

But she knew one thing she could do to make things right.

Even as it occurred to her, her stomach turned, but

she didn't stop to think about how he was different, how he cared for her, how he trusted her...

He was the one thing that would keep her show going. The *only* thing.

She cropped the photo and uploaded it to Instagram. Guess who's behind the beard? she typed, then tagged her producer and hit Share.

But instead of the normal pop of excitement that normally went with posting, she felt sick to her stomach. So she turned off her phone. She didn't want to see the notifications.

Besides, it was Christmas. A Santa teaser was the perfect thing to post. It wasn't a big deal. No one would know it was him, anyway.

And she had to keep her show. It was all she had.

Natalie had been quiet ever since she'd called her dad. CJ had asked if everything was all right, but she'd just curled into his side and asked him to start another movie. So he'd loaded up *The Santa Clause* and they watched it in near silence.

It hurt him that her father had obviously wished Natalie anything but a merry Christmas. But she didn't want to talk about it, so he didn't push.

The movie was nearing the end when his phone buzzed. "It's probably my folks," he said, kissing her as he climbed off the couch.

"You want to pause the movie?" She gave him a smile that was almost convincing.

"No, you keep watching, babe. I'll be right back."

Except it wasn't his parents on the phone. "CJ?" It was his half brother, Zeb Richards.

"Is everything all right?" CJ asked automatically,

trying to figure out why Zeb was calling him. Maybe he wanted to wish him a merry Christmas?

But even as he thought it, CJ knew that wasn't it. They did not have what a reasonable person might consider a "close brotherly relationship." In fact, the only time they had communicated outside of the meeting Zeb had called months ago about his proposed takeover of the Beaumont Brewery had been the message CJ had sent a few days ago.

"Depends on your definition of 'all right,'" Zeb said. "It appears Natalie Baker has decided you are a story after all."

She had? This was news to him. "Are you sure? She's been with me for the last week. She got snowed in and I haven't been able to get her out."

True, he had stopped trying to get her out several days ago. But still—she'd been here.

"I'm sending you a link," Zeb said, tactfully ignoring the implications of CJ and Natalie being snowed in together. "Daniel is already writing a press release acknowledging that you are one of our brothers, but you value your privacy, et cetera, et cetera, et cetera. He didn't want to release it without your approval. I've also spoken with Chadwick. He told me that whatever you'd like to happen, you'll have his help. So if you want to be publicly announced as a Beaumont, we can make that happen. And if not, we'll do our best to bury the lede."

A link? And Zeb had been talking with Chadwick? Daniel had already worked up a press release? "You know it's Christmas, right?"

"Trust me, I know. I'm hiding in my study from my wife. She informed me that I was not allowed to work today—but," he continued, sighing heavily, "this is important. You're family." Before CJ could even process *that*, Zeb said, "I'm also supposed to tell you that next year, you're invited to Christmas dinner. Casey's a little miffed that we didn't have the entire family over, although I told her I wanted our first Christmas to be just us."

CJ couldn't think a year ahead. Right now, he couldn't even think a minute ahead. "Are you sure?"

About any of it? How would Natalie have even gotten the story out? He'd been sitting on her phone for days and they hadn't been apart since he'd given it back to her. The whole day, it'd been on the coffee table.

And it wasn't easy for him to think of the Beaumonts—even ones who didn't have the same last name—as family. He understood that they were blood relatives, but he wasn't sure he wanted to give up being a Wesley.

"You can let me know," Zeb said in the silence. "But we're going to have to have an official response in a day or so. Sooner would be better. Daniel believes we need to get out in front of this before it gets out of hand."

"Yeah," CJ said, feeling numb as he ended the call. It wasn't just that he didn't know how Natalie might've gotten the word out to anyone about him. It was that...

Well, he thought he'd changed her mind. It hadn't been an explicit goal, certainly not during the first few days they'd been stuck in the living room together. But she hadn't pried. She hadn't asked questions. She hadn't demanded answers. Instead, she'd been vulnerable and fragile but also tough and unflappable. She'd rolled with the changes and embraced his chores and his town's party. She'd embraced *him*.

Hadn't she?

Or had it all been an act?

Seconds later, his phone pinged with a link. Dread churning his stomach, he clicked on it.

"Who's behind the beard?" It was a talking head that CJ vaguely recognized as Kevin Durante, another morning regular on Natalie's station. "Next on a special edition of *A Good Morning with Natalie Baker.*" The show's theme music played as the graphics flashed across the screen. CJ felt sicker with each passing second.

Then the camera focused on the handsome man. "Good morning, Denver. I'm Kevin Durante, in for Natalie Baker, who is on assignment. Our top story— has the missing Beaumont bastard been found?"

CJ's stomach clenched at that—*on assignment. He* was her assignment. And there it was—a picture of CJ sitting on Santa's throne. He recognized himself instantly.

CJ just stared at his phone. When had she taken the photo? He tried to run through the evening. It'd been such a flood of kids and parents and people spiking their eggnog... Wait. There'd been a break. He'd given her the phone and then she'd gone to get something to drink. And he'd talked with Dale and Larry for a little bit. That had to have been it.

She'd taken that photo and uploaded it. Kevin showed the original Instagram post. Because he didn't have anything else to say, he also read through some of the comments. There were the same sort of comments CJ had seen the one time he'd looked at the notifications on her phone. The whole thing disgusted him.

Kevin kept talking. There were "reports" that the man behind the beard was CJ Wesley of Firestone,

Colorado. But no one could confirm or deny that fact. Due to the weather, he explained, no one had been able to get to Firestone and none of the Beaumonts were talking.

"We'll have more on this developing story soon," Kevin announced cheerfully.

It was all CJ could do to watch the clip again. This was it. The moment his world changed forever.

That feeling only got stronger when Natalie walked into the kitchen. She still looked upset. Well, she could just be upset. He didn't even know if she had actually called her dad or if she had just checked in with the station.

"Well?" He was real proud of the way he managed to say that without his voice shaking with anger.

She didn't answer. Instead, she came straight to his arms and buried her face against his chest. "The movie was fine," she said, her voice muffled. "But I wish I hadn't called my dad. I... I'm letting him ruin my day and I shouldn't. I shouldn't."

It galled him how upset she sounded. Worse, it galled him when his arms came around her without his permission and held her tight.

Had any of it been real? He had only asked her for two things. He had asked her not to pry into his life and he had asked her for the truth. And she hadn't been able to give him either.

Still, he clung to this moment because he knew that as soon as he pushed her away, it was all over. The bubble around them had burst and Christmas would be over in a few short hours and everything would go back to the way it had been before she'd arrived.

He would go back to being alone. To hiding himself

so that no one would know his secret. Well, it was all over. The horse was out of that barn and there was no shutting the door behind it.

She leaned back and looked up at him, her eyes watery. "How about you? How are your parents?"

For a little while, his fantasy girl had fit into his fantasy world. And now that while was over. "I wouldn't know."

She looked at him in confusion. "Then who called?"

"My brother." The word still felt awkward in his mouth, but he was going to have to get used to it now.

"Did he call to wish you a happy Christmas?"

CJ shook his head. Then he held up his phone and hit the play button.

It took all of three seconds for her to realize what she was watching—three of the longest seconds of his life. Then her gaze met his, her eyes so wide—and filled with something that looked a lot like fear.

"Turn it off."

"Why? This is why you came, isn't it?"

All the blood drained out of her face and she began to tremble. "No," she said. It came out as a plaintive wail. "It's not what I wanted."

He just shook his head. "You're on assignment. Your boy Kevin said so himself."

"No," she said with more force. "I didn't think... I assumed— They weren't supposed to do anything with the photo until I got back. It was just a teaser. And I was trying to figure out how I could... I don't know." She seemed at a loss. "How I could redirect the attention."

"Redirect it? Come on, Natalie," he scoffed. "You're *all* about the attention, aren't you? You actually like it when people say those horrible things to you, don't you?" He saw her throat work as she swallowed, but she didn't say anything. "Well," he said decisively, "you got what you came for. I'll see about getting you back to Denver tomorrow."

Tears leaked out the corners of her eyes, but he wasn't going to be moved by them. For all he knew, she could cry on demand.

He should walk away. He was done with her and he wasn't about to give her a single thing more that she or anyone else could use.

But, dammit, it hurt to stand there and watch her try to put on a brave face. She swallowed again. "That would be for the best. I'm sorry that I've intruded on your holiday."

Liar, he wanted to say. Because he knew her tell. He'd thought—for a little while—that he'd known *her*. "All I asked of you was to be honest."

"I was," she said with more force. "I *was*—except that I made a mistake. I called my dad and he was terrible and I—I panicked. I don't have anything but my show. Without it, I'm nothing."

CJ let out a bark of laughter. "A mistake is an accident, Natalie. You can't convince me that you *accidentally* took a photo and then *accidentally* uploaded it across social media and that your coworkers *accidentally* did a four-minute segment on me."

She squeezed her eyes shut. "It was a mistake," she whispered. "Finding you, coming here—I warned you. I'm nothing but a selfish, spoiled brat and I ruin *everything*."

The last time she'd said that, he'd disagreed with her. This time, though, he didn't. She hadn't swallowed. She wasn't lying.

She dropped her head into her hands and dug the heels of her palms into her eyes. "I wish you'd taken a hatchet to my phone. God, I wish you had destroyed the thing."

"So do I," he said bitterly. "So do I."

Twelve

The next twenty-four hours were some of the most miserable of Natalie's life. She slept in the guest room—alone, of course. CJ stopped talking to her completely. Not that she could blame him—she couldn't. But it was unnerving, the way he watched her. His eyes were cold and his expression was one step removed from a full-scale scowl—and it was directed at her at all times. She felt like a mouse with a hawk watching her.

She knew she had done this to herself. But she was also pissed off at her producer and at Kevin. They had taken *her* photo and made it *his* story. She had thought that Steve would have the decency to at least wait until she could make it back to the studio—but he hadn't. He hadn't even checked in with her before he had taken her story and run with it. She had been cut out almost completely.

The writing was on the wall. She was going to lose her show.

The whole reason she'd gone looking for CJ in the first place had been to save her show. She'd found him and yet she was going to lose her show anyway.

She had nothing.

One of the few things CJ said to her was that she had to dig out her car while he used his backhoe to plow the remaining snow off the drive. She didn't want to be in the house alone and obviously, CJ didn't want her in there, either. She had dressed in her own clothes that morning for the first time in days, but she put on the snowsuit and headed out. It was another warm day and everything was wet and slushy—which meant the snow was back-breakingly heavy. But she didn't mind. It took all of her concentration to excavate her tires and, when she'd done that, she started trying to dig tracks to a plowed section.

She had to leave. She knew that. But even as she hefted shovel after shovel of snow, she wished she didn't have to go. If only she'd held on to sanity through that moment of panic and insecurity. If only she'd had faith in CJ. If only...

If only she'd been someone else. Someone good enough for him.

But she wasn't, so she kept digging. Once she had unearthed her car and CJ had unearthed the road, he hitched her car to his tractor and pulled it out. It was the last time she was alone with him, riding in the cab of his backhoe as he towed her car to the county road. The tension was a living thing because she had to sit on his knee, basically, but he didn't want to touch her.

Once they were at the road, she stripped out of the

snowsuit and handed it back to him. Then she held out the star he'd made her. "Here—you keep this."

He looked offended. "I'm not taking it back. I gave it to you in good faith." Every word he said was another splinter in her skin because her faith had not been good. Not even close. "It's yours. Just don't put it on TV." He turned to go.

She couldn't let it end. Not like this. "CJ?"

He didn't look back. But he did stop. "What?"

She took a deep breath. "This was the best Christmas I've ever had."

"Sure it was." He started to walk.

She should just get in her car and drive off—but she couldn't. "CJ?" she called out after him.

"What, Natalie?" He turned, his hands on his hips, and glared at her.

"I'm sorry."

Something in his face changed, but at this distance, she couldn't make out what it was. Without another word, he turned and climbed into the backhoe.

She stood there and watched until he'd rumbled around a curve in the drive.

He didn't look back.

"Are you sure you're all right?" his mom asked for the thirtieth time. "We can come home. We can get through this together, sweetie."

CJ stifled a groan. He'd finally bitten the bullet and video-called to tell his parents that the cat was out of the bag. He loved his parents—he did—but he just wanted to brood in peace and quiet while he still could. Being fussed over by his mother wouldn't make anything better.

"I'm fine," he repeated. "Daniel Lee—remember him? One of my half brothers? He wrote the press release and he's handling it. I talked it over with him and we agreed it would be better if you guys stayed in Arizona until this blew over. If you come home now, it will only add fuel to the fire and everyone's going to want an interview."

He could see his mother physically recoil at the idea of doing interviews about Hardwick Beaumont and what had happened thirty-four years ago. She had lived as Bell Wesley for so long that everything that had come before Pat had happened to someone else, it seemed to CJ. And he couldn't blame her. Who the hell wanted to have to explain what they were doing when they'd had an affair decades ago? Hell, he shuddered at the thought of his college girlfriend—up until now, the only other person who knew about his connection with the Beaumonts—coming out of the woodwork and dishing on their relationship.

But he knew that his mother was hurting for him. And he hadn't even told his folks about how deep he'd gotten with Natalie—or how much he was paying for that mistake.

"Well…" she said hesitantly.

"Son," Dad said, crowding into the camera's window. "We'll do what you want. We trust your judgment on this and if you say that you and your half brothers have the situation under control, then we're going to take you at your word." His mother looked doubtful, but she didn't disagree. "In fact," Dad went on diplomatically, "we were talking about pulling up stakes with the motorhome and driving over to New Mexico for a little while. Your mother would like to see Santa Fe."

"That would be great," CJ said, hoping he hadn't forced the enthusiasm past the point of believability. His parents mostly wintered in Arizona, but every now and then they did make side trips. Everyone in Firestone had a general idea of where they were in Arizona—but if they were in New Mexico, they would be even more insulated from any fallout. "You guys go and have fun, okay?"

They said their goodbyes and CJ ended the call. Then he sat there in the silence of his big, empty house and *brooded*. He put the odds of his parents showing up at fifty percent. Sooner or later, his mother would demand that they come home and check on him.

He'd deal with that when he had to—there were more pressing concerns. Now that the road was clear into town, he needed to make a supply run. But he didn't want to. Because there would be questions and maybe even reporters. For a half second, CJ wondered if Natalie would still be in Firestone, digging up dirt and wielding her charms like a weapon.

He had been *such* an idiot. That was the only logical conclusion. He had known what she was. She had been right—she *had* warned him. But he had let himself get swept up in the holidays and in her big eyes and her soft body. He had let himself be convinced that Natalie the woman was distinctly separate from Natalie Baker, morning television host. He had always trusted his gut in these sorts of things—but this was the second time that his gut had let him down when it came to women.

All he'd ever wanted was to be a Wesley and the world simply wouldn't let him. It didn't matter that his dad was a good man or that CJ had done his best to follow his father's example. All that would ever matter was that once upon a time his mother had conceived him with Hardwick Beaumont.

He had even had a phone call from the patriarch of the Beaumont family, such as it was—Chadwick Beaumont himself, welcoming CJ to the family and reassuring him that, no matter what level of involvement he wanted, he had the full support of the Beaumonts. CJ had honestly told his oldest half brother that he still wasn't sure what he wanted from any of them.

What had happened next still had CJ's head spinning. Chadwick had apologized for not contacting CJ when he'd located him three years ago.

Chadwick had known where he was—*who* he was— for three years. The news had rocked CJ. He had lived his entire life under the impression that he was unfindable. Yes, his mother had prepared him for the day one of the Beaumonts might locate him and do apparently nefarious things—but he'd never actually believed that would happen.

But he'd been wrong. Because Chadwick and Zeb had located him—and so had Natalie. And if it hadn't been her...

Someone else would have come for him. It was clear now—his parentage had been a ticking time bomb. He was still trying to get his head around it.

And failing. He looked at his Christmas tree—the one he had gone out and cut for Natalie. He hadn't plugged in the lights and the whole thing looked sad and forlorn. Tomorrow, he'd take off all the decorations and carefully pack them away in the bins. Then he would take the tree outside and burn it.

And that would be the end of him and Natalie Baker.

* * *

"And stay tuned for *A Good Morning*, where there will be some shocking new revelations about the Beaumont family," the morning news lady said with a smile at the camera.

CJ groaned. He was torturing himself by watching Natalie's station. Yes, part of it was self-preservation. He needed to know what was being said about him. Was his sex life about to become common knowledge? Had she taken more pictures of him or of his house? Would she display the star he'd given her like a hunting trophy? Would his friends and neighbors show up on TV, talking about how they never would've guessed there was a Beaumont lurking in their midst?

Forewarned was forearmed. But it was also the highest form of masochism he could imagine.

It had been six days since he had literally dragged Natalie off of his property. Six long days that had been filled with a barrage of emails and phone calls. After he'd gotten her back to the county road, the temperatures had dropped and everything had iced over so, at the very least, he hadn't had visitors. The roads were still too tricky for a bunch of city slickers to make it out this far. But that would change soon, he knew.

God, look at that—he had his own damn graphic now. The Missing Beaumont Bastard flashed in gray and red—the brewery colors.

Jesus. This was beyond him, which really only left him one option. He picked up his phone and dialed Daniel Lee.

"I take it you saw the teaser?" Daniel said without any other introduction.

It didn't matter what time CJ called, Daniel always

answered on the first ring and always seemed to be watching the exact same thing.

"It's never going to end, is it?" Natalie had enough on him to stretch this out for months if she wanted to.

True, she hadn't exactly been forthcoming with the information on all the episodes he'd watched so far. But it was only a matter of time.

"It will, eventually," Daniel added. "You've only been in the public eye for less than a week. It's New Year's Eve—I guarantee that tonight, someone, somewhere will do something more interesting than you."

"You think?"

"I know. Personally? I've never met a man as boring as you are."

CJ had to laugh at that. "Thanks, I think."

"It's a good thing," Daniel reassured him. "You're not just the most boring Beaumont, you're boring, period. There's not a single exciting thing about you and the public craves excitement. You'll see. Another week or two and who knows."

CJ desperately wanted to believe that—but he couldn't. Natalie knew him too well. He was tired of waiting for the other shoe to drop. "You really think I should go public?" That was what Daniel had been arguing for the last week—if they trotted CJ out and demonstrated to the world exactly how boring he was, people would lose interest faster. The mystery would be gone and without that, there was nothing to tease.

"Absolutely. Why? You change your mind?"

"Yeah." It felt like a defeat—but he had been beaten the moment Natalie Baker and walked into the Firestone Grain and Feed. "What are the options?"

There was a pause. "There are three viable options—

although I'm open to suggestions. First, we hold a press conference."

"Like Zeb did on the steps of the Beaumont Brewery? No." He had absolutely no desire to parade himself before a pack of bloodthirsty reporters and wait for the body blows.

Daniel chuckled. "I didn't say it was the best idea. You can also come into town tonight and put in an appearance at a New Year's Eve party. I can think of three venues that would provide an appropriate amount of press coverage without leaving you exposed."

CJ scowled at the phone. "That doesn't seem like my style." Better than a press conference, but not by much. "What's the third option?"

"The Beaumont family is going to be hosting an Epiphany party—that's January sixth." CJ rolled his eyes. He knew when Epiphany was. "It will be mostly family along with close friends. We could invite one or two reporters, give them exclusive access. I would expect you to do a short interview and smile for a few pictures. The angle would be that we were all one big happy family, of course."

"I wouldn't be the focus?" Because he had no interest in being the center of a news story where the Beaumont family welcomed their long-lost half brothers into the fold.

"I believe there would be some other announcements at this party as well. So I don't believe you would be the focus for long."

CJ thought about it. Assuming the roads were clear, he could do that. Finally, after all these years, he wouldn't run away from the idea of being a Beaumont. Instead, he was going to walk toward them. And hopefully be immediately overshadowed by some "other announcements." "All right."

There was another long pause before Daniel said, "Any idea what the shocking new revelation is going to be in ten minutes?"

CJ tried very hard not to groan out loud. His idea of hell was having his sex life discussed on TV. "No idea," he lied. But even as he did, he felt the muscle in his jaw twitch. And that made him think of Natalie all over again. Even his own mother had never figured out he had a tell. Natalie had *seen* him more than anyone else ever had. "Have you been able to contact her?"

That was one of the things Daniel was doing—talking to the media people and trying to, as Natalie had put it, *redirect* the attention. And Natalie was a media person.

"She's not taking my calls." That couldn't be good. "I tell you what, though—she's a hell of an investigative reporter."

"Yeah? Well, I guess so—she found me, after all." Although that wasn't quite as hard as CJ had once thought it would be, apparently.

"She didn't just find *you*," Daniel said. "She didn't start with you. She was digging in to me long before she tracked you down."

CJ frowned. She hadn't said anything about that to him. But then, she hadn't told him everything, had she? "Yeah? Did she find anything on you?"

"No. I've got too many firewalls. But she got close and she tripped some of my early warning systems." He whistled in low appreciation.

"What—are you in to her?"

His brother just chuckled. "No. Blondes aren't my

type. But there's a lot of political wisdom in keeping your friends close and your enemies closer. I'd hire her if I could. Her brains plus her looks—and her dedication? She could rob banks and get away with it scot-free."

CJ started to laugh.

"What?"

"I told her the same thing. I don't think she would take a job working for you, though. That show's the most important thing in the world to her." More important than he had been.

"Well, if you talk to her again, tell her I pay well." There was an ominous undertone to that statement, and CJ was reminded again that he did not know very much about Daniel. But then again, apparently neither did anyone else—what with all the firewalls and safety features and stuff.

He was probably overthinking it. Daniel was also the executive vice president at the Beaumont Brewery now. Having someone as high-profile as Natalie work for him would probably be a coup or something.

"Yeah, I don't think we're going to see each other again. But," he added, "if I do, I'll mention it."

"Thanks," Daniel said. "I'll get you the invitation to the party."

They ended the call just as the morning news anchor cut over to Natalie's show. The theme music and graphics played out over the screen and there she was, smiling at the camera just like she did every day. If CJ hadn't spent so much time with her, he wouldn't have noticed any difference—but now, he could.

Even though she was smiling and perky, her eyes had a dead look to them. Was that how she'd always looked on television? He was pretty sure—but it wasn't who she was. Because now he knew what she looked like when she was happy or upset or—God help him— aroused. He hated that he could tell the difference, but more than that, he hated that he cared. It wasn't his fault she had that look in her eyes. She had brought this upon both of them.

He didn't want to hear what she had to say but he couldn't look away.

"Good morning, Denver." She batted her eyelashes at the camera like she did every day, but something seemed off. She looked tense. Oh, God—was this it? Was his sex life about to become a lead story?

"This is going to be my last morning with you here on *A Good Morning*. I've decided to step away from television. Recently, I compromised not only my journalistic credibility, but also my personal code of honor. I took a picture of someone I care for and uploaded it to the internet without his permission. Here at *A Good Morning*, we pride ourselves on a higher standard of behavior. I wanted to take this time to thank each and every one of you for tuning in and for following me on social media. I'm going to be pulling back my online presence as well, but when I'm ready for something new—" she swallowed "—I will be sure and let my fans know."

"Liar," he muttered at the TV. She was seriously doing this? Was she seriously quitting live on the air? Because...of what? Because of *him*?

His heart began to pound wildly in his chest. She was. He was afraid that he might be hallucinating this—it was all wishful thinking after his conversation with Daniel. But then she looked at the camera and said, "To CJ Wes-

ley and the people of Firestone, I apologize. I confused
'likes' and 'shares' with hope and happiness. My mistake
was valuing comments and reach more than I did family
and friends. So, as the station moves forward into the
New Year, this program will be moving forward with
the new host, a man you'll all enjoy spending time with,
Kevin Durante and—" he saw her swallow again "—I
think you're going to like it. Starting January first—
tomorrow—I hope you tune in for *A Great Morning with
Kevin Durante*. Thank you for making me a part of your
lives for the last seven years. And I hope each and every
one of you have a happy New Year."

The show cut to commercial, but CJ barely noticed.
That was *it*? That was the shocking announcement? Not
a discussion of his prowess in bed or interviews with
his old girlfriends?

Natalie had quit. Because of him. He hadn't asked
her to—he was sure about that.

His cell phone lit up. Good or bad? Daniel texted.

Good, I think, he texted back.

You sure you're not going to see her anymore?

I have no idea, CJ replied honestly. But he was thinking that maybe…

He just might be seeing her sooner than he had
planned.

Like now. Like right *now*. He could get his truck
and, assuming he didn't skate into a ditch in the next
fifteen miles, be in Denver within an hour. He ought
to be able to find directions to the studio online, right?
It would take her at least that long to get off the air and
pack up her desk, right?

If you do, my offer of a job for her stands. Put a good word in for me.

CJ didn't even bother to reply. He was already up and shoving his arms into his sheepskin coat. Keys. He needed the truck's keys. And dammit, it was supposed to start snowing anytime—but he didn't care. He had to get to downtown Denver *now*.

He threw open the front door and hit the porch at a dead run—only to come to a skidding halt. For there, coming down the driveway, was a red Mustang.

Thirteen

Natalie felt so weird right now. Seeing this place again—it was almost too much. It'd only been a week since she'd left but it felt like a lifetime ago.

She had no idea if she was doing the right thing. Part of her was nearly paralyzed with fear. She had quit. And by now, the show had aired and there would be no going back. No doubt people were going to rake her over the coals. Only this time, she wouldn't be there to watch it unfold in real time.

But the other part? She rounded the bend and CJ's house came into view. The rest of her was anything but panicked. She didn't care what anyone thought. She really only cared what one person thought—CJ. She had hurt him and she was hoping that she could make it right—but she didn't know if that was possible. Still, knowing that she was here for him, instead of for ratings or reach, was freeing.

As she got closer to the house, she saw the front door fly open and CJ come running out. He looked half-crazed and for a second, she considered putting the car in Reverse and bailing. This was not a good idea in a long string of bad ideas. She shouldn't have come. She was crazy to think that he might accept her apology. She was crazy to think that he might want her back.

But if that made her nuts, so be it.

When he saw her, he came to a screeching halt and just stared as she got out of the car. For a long moment, neither of them said anything. Which, in the grand scheme of things, was probably progress. At the very least, he wasn't telling her to go to hell, so that had to count for something, right?

"You're here," he said in a strangled voice. "I thought you were at the studio—your show?"

"We taped it two days ago." She'd spent the last two days wondering if she should go back and un-resign. If the segment hadn't aired, had she really quit?

But Steve wouldn't have taken her back, anyway. Kevin had a shiny new show and Steve was happy for a chance to take another crack at the ratings and…

And they wouldn't miss her. But that wasn't the important thing, she'd discovered.

No, the more important thing was that *she* wouldn't miss *them*. What a revelation that had been—and she never would have had it without the man before her.

She had missed CJ. All she could do was hope that he had missed her, too. "I, um, I brought you a Christmas present." She took a deep breath and braced for the worst. If he were going to tell her to get the hell off of his property, now would probably be when it happened.

"It's not Christmas anymore," he said, staring at her as if she were a ghost.

"I know." She pulled her phone out of her pocket and held it out for him. "Here."

He looked down at the red bow she tied around the middle of it. But the bow wasn't big enough to hide the shattered screen. "What the hell happened to your phone?"

It was important to keep breathing. It would be silly if she passed out now. "I took a hatchet to it. After I deleted all my social media accounts. Aside from a few photos, there wasn't anything on there that I wanted to keep."

"I didn't ask you to delete your accounts. You didn't have to do that for me."

"I didn't." She took a deep breath. "I needed to do it for me. I might go back online, but it'll be on my terms this time. I need to... I don't know. I need to keep the negative out and that was so wrapped up with who I was that I just had to burn it down and start over."

His mouth was open and he was staring at her, and then her phone, and then back at her. It was a hard thing to watch, so she dropped her gaze. "What about your phone numbers? Your contacts?"

She shrugged. "I quit. My job, that is."

He took a step toward her. "So I saw. I saw your apology, too."

"I meant it. I made a mistake, CJ. I let a moment of panic overrule my judgment. I should've had faith in you. Because you're real. You are a real, honest, decent man and... And I don't know very many people like you. So I didn't know how to act around you."

When he didn't say anything, she looked up at him.

He managed to get his mouth closed, but his head was tilted to the side and he stared at her in open confusion. "I just did what anyone would do."

"No, you didn't—don't you see? I've never known *anyone* like you. You don't know how special you are and…" She squeezed her eyes shut so that she wouldn't do anything ridiculous, like start crying. "And I let you down. I ruined everything."

His face hardened. "Who said that to you?"

"What?"

"Who told you that you ruined everything?"

She blushed from the tips of her ears to her toes. This was one of her most painful memories. "My mom." If he had been anyone else in the world, she wouldn't have told him. But he had asked for honesty and she had absolutely nothing left to give him except the truth. "I was six, I think, and I didn't get what I wanted from Santa so I threw a fit and she told me that I was a spoiled brat and I ruined everything and I always had and I always would. Her body, her marriage, her career—*Christmas*. I ruined Christmas." She wrapped her arms around her waist, trying to ease the tightness there. "And then she left. She left and I've never seen her again."

His mouth flopped open again. No, he didn't know how special he was—how lucky he was to have two parents who loved him and protected him. "And your dad?"

She shrugged. "I ruined Christmas. So we stopped having one. I don't think he ever forgave me or her." She straightened up, turned on a brave face. "I did not save his phone number to my new phone. Every year I try to call him and every year, it hurts more. I'm going to stop trying to please other people. It doesn't matter."

"It does," he told her. "You were six—that matters."

He took another step closer to her—close enough now that she could feel the warmth from his body. "And you don't ruin everything, Natalie. I don't ever want to hear you say that again."

She closed her eyes again. "I ruined *us*. You gave me my phone back and I immediately took a photo. I didn't plan on uploading it. I didn't. I just wanted something to remind me of the best week of my life when it ended. And then my dad told me I'd ruined his Christmas again and told me to leave him alone and…and I panicked. I had this moment where I felt like I was nothing all over again and I was going to lose my show and without that, who am I?"

"Natalie…"

She shook her head. "I'm not telling you this to make you feel sorry for me. I just want you to understand that I was trying to find a compromise between what you wanted and what I thought I wanted and a semi-random Santa photo seemed the safest way to make our two worlds meet. But I was wrong about that. And I'm sorry."

The next thing she knew, she was folded into his arms. She didn't want to hug him back—she didn't want him to think that she needed this. Even if she did, just a little.

"My mom lives in fear of the Beaumonts," he said softly. "I always knew that Hardwick was my birth father because she told me that he might come for me one day and that if anyone named Beaumont ever showed up, I should run the other way or hide or scream. Beaumonts were dangerous and I had to be protected from them."

She leaned back in his arms and looked at him. "Really? I mean, I guess that makes sense—he usually kept the children in the divorces. But he was never married to your mother."

"Trust me, I know."

She was having trouble thinking with his arms around her, so she stepped away from him. "And Hardwick is dead, anyway."

For the first time, he smiled. "I knew that—but I don't think I understood it. Does that make sense? It was so ingrained in me to be afraid of the Beaumonts that, even after he was dead, I didn't stop hiding. But they're just people." He reached up and brushed a strand of hair away from her cheek. "I'm going to go to an Epiphany party with them on the sixth. I'll talk to a couple of reporters and be as boring as possible and then wait for the story to die."

She gasped at him. "You'll *what*?"

He shot her a crooked grin. "It's still going to upset my mother. She made a good life for herself and for me and she doesn't want anyone to think about a mistake that she might have made a long time ago. But I don't have to hide. I don't have to be afraid of who I might be." He stared down at her. "We all make mistakes, Natalie. It's how we make up for them that counts."

This time, she was the one who hugged him. "I—I don't know if I should apologize for finding you or not. If I hadn't, nothing would've changed. I would still be doing a job that made me sick, and you…"

"And I would be alone," he said into her hair.

She didn't know how long they stood there like that, but finally, the cold began to catch up with her. She had dressed better today—her own jeans and boots and a chunky turtleneck sweater. But they were still standing outside and the temperature was dropping. So, even though she didn't want to, she pulled herself out of his arms. "So."

His grin got slightly less crooked. "So," he agreed. She hadn't realized she was still holding her dead phone until he plucked it from her hands. He looked down at it as if he couldn't believe she had really smashed the damn thing, and then he reared back and threw it. "What are you going to do now?"

"Honestly? I'm not sure. I'm unemployed and I think I'm going to sell my condo. It's Natalie Baker's condo—and I don't feel like that person anymore. But I don't know how to do anything else. My whole life has been one long con game of trying to convince people I'm something that I'm not and now that I'm not going to do that anymore..." She shrugged. "I'm at a loss." His eyebrows jumped up and he looked like he was going to say something—so she hurried to cut him off. "I didn't come out here to ask if I could stay. I just wanted to apologize, CJ."

He mulled this over. "Apology accepted. And I wanted to say that I'm sorry, too."

Now was her turn to stare at him. "What? *Why?* You didn't do anything wrong. I was the one at fault."

"I don't think it's such a bad thing, being a Beaumont. Suddenly, I've gone from being an only child to having all these brothers and sisters who want to meet me. I'm not going to pretend I'm going to like all of them, but..." He shrugged. "It was always this terrible thing in my mind and I don't think it is so terrible in reality. So when I found out that you'd taken that picture, I was still acting like you had ruined my life. And

I'm not proud of how I treated you. But I don't think you ruined anything."

Unexpectedly, her throat closed up. It was sweet of him to say that, but they both knew the truth. "I'm glad to hear that." She may not have ruined his life, but she didn't think there was any hope for the two of them.

She should leave, she decided, and as she turned away a snowflake landed on her cheek. She looked up at the sky. It wasn't a rolling wall of clouds barreling down on her—but it was beginning to snow.

"Where are you going?" CJ asked, stepping to the side and blocking her path back to her car.

"I should leave before the weather gets really bad."

"Don't."

"What?"

He stared at her, his jaw tightening. "Don't leave. I want you to stay. It's New Year's Eve." He took a deep breath and then reached out a hand toward her. "I want you to stay with me."

"CJ, you can't be serious." Could he? Now that she thought about it, had he ever *not* been serious? He did what he said and he said what he did. There were no games when it came to CJ Wesley. "I screwed up! I took that picture of you and I posted it, remember?"

He looked off in the distance, where, maybe twenty or thirty feet away, her phone had met its final end. "Yeah, okay—you did. But I'm not going to think about what you did anymore. Instead, I'm going to think about what you didn't do. You didn't run back to Denver and broadcast all of my secrets. You didn't kiss and tell. Hell, except for that one photo, you didn't even say anything about my town."

"But that's not the end of it. Other people are talking, and other reporters will keep digging—and that's my fault."

He shrugged as if this were seriously no big deal. "This, too, shall pass. It's not just me against the Beaumonts. It's the Beaumonts against the world. I've got a family who's going to stand beside me and that's something I only have because of you, Natalie." He grinned and brushed another snowflake off her cheek. "Besides, I have a job for you."

She looked at him hard, trying to ignore the way his touch warmed her skin. "A job? Are you serious?"

"You talk about yourself as if you're useless—a talking head. But that's not what I see. I see someone who's intelligent and beautiful and whose capacity for kindness is there." She rolled her eyes, and he added, "It hasn't been nurtured properly, but it's there. And you did something that very few people have done—you found me."

"But that doesn't mean I'm qualified for a ranch job." Because if he were asking her to stay...

Well, it would be tempting. When they had been snowed in, she had wanted nothing more than for that time to never end.

But she wasn't a ranch wife. She didn't really cook. The only thing she had that would recommend her to that position was the fact that she was used to getting up early, but that wasn't enough.

"You're a little too shy around horses to be a good ranch hand," he said with a chuckle. "No, Daniel Lee has offered to hire you. He knows exactly how far you got trying to dig up information on him and he was impressed. And according to him, you're brilliant—and more tenacious than a private eye. Plus, you know how to handle the media. If you're interested, I could call him right now."

Her mouth dropped open as she stared at him. "You're lying." But even as she said it, she knew he wasn't. Not a single muscle in his jaw had twitched.

"Hand to God," he said, grinning wildly.

More snow fell from the sky. They were working their way close to full-on flurries. His hair was turning white and his beard was catching flakes. Soon the roads would get slick and her Mustang was not any better equipped for that than it had been two weeks ago.

"You know what else I'm not lying about?" he asked, stepping into her again and dusting snow off of her shoulders. "I'm not lying when I say that I want you to stay. You made me feel like it was okay that I was a Beaumont *and* a Wesley. You knew my deepest secret—but for the most part, it didn't matter."

"But it did, don't you see? I ruined—"

"No, you didn't. You *changed* things, Natalie—things that, in retrospect, needed to be changed." He leaned down and touched his forehead to hers. "You changed me for the better."

"How can you say that?" Because it didn't make any sense. She had hurt him—she knew she had. And anyone else would have held that against her. Including her own parents. Especially her own parents.

"Because it's the truth, babe. I accept your apology. I forgive you. And I hope you can forgive me for overreacting."

She couldn't stop the tears this time. Forgiveness? She'd come out here with the intent to apologize—and that was it. Forgiveness was such a foreign concept to her it hadn't even occurred to her as an option.

But she saw that he was right. She'd only been a little girl when she threw a temper tantrum. Probably every kid did that at some point—even him. It wasn't her fault that her mother had walked out. Her parents were messed up if they couldn't even forgive a little kid for doing something that all little kids did.

"Of course I do," she said, her voice trembling. She wrapped her arms around his waist and held him tight. "I'm not any good at this. I'm trying so hard, CJ. But I'm going to screw things up. Things that you think anyone would do? It's all new to me. But I want…"

She wanted it all and, no matter what he said, she wasn't sure she deserved it.

He tilted her head back and looked her in the eyes. He was only a breath away. "Just be honest, Natalie. The truth—that's all I've ever wanted from you."

"You changed me, too. You made me realize that I could be worth something to someone. You made me want to be good enough for you."

"You are. You're good for me. And I want you to stay. Stay for the New Year." His lips brushed against her, damp from the snow. "Stay forever."

She jolted in his arms. *"What?"*

"I love you," he said, and damn if he didn't sound completely serious. "Let's get married, Natalie."

She cupped his face in her hands. "You want to marry *me*?"

"I do. I trust my gut." Not a single muscle in his face moved—except for that smile. Oh, that grin of his warmed her heart—and a few other places. "And you? Is that what you want?"

"Yes," she whispered.

Just then, the snow began to fall in earnest. CJ swept

her up and spun her around, kissing her like she was worth something. She *was*. It would take some work, but this was New Year's Eve—a time for starting over, a time for hope. And, maybe for the first time, she dared to hope.

CJ looked up at the sky. "We might be snowed in for a little bit..."

"After last time, I resolved that I wouldn't go anywhere without a week's worth of clothes in the car."

CJ laughed and Natalie laughed with him. "Come on," he said, opening the door to her car so she could snag the duffel bag. "Let's ring in the New Year properly."

"Promise me," she said, leaning into him as they walked up to the house, "that we will always celebrate Christmas."

He turned and pulled her into a fierce kiss. "Always," he whispered against her lips.

For the rest of their lives, they would keep Christmas in their hearts.

* * * * *

They were both masked and they could pretend...

God, she needed to pretend. "Kiss me."

Cal couldn't see Quinn's expression beneath his mask, and it was too dark to see the emotion in his eyes. She felt his hesitation and worried that he would back off, that he'd yank them back to reality, to their lives. When his mouth softened, she knew that he was as tempted as she was.

He finally ducked his head and his mouth hovered over hers, teasing.

Minutes, hours, eons later, he lowered his head and his mouth brushed hers. His fingertips dug into the bare skin at her waist, and by their own volition her hands parted his jacket to touch the muscles at his waist, to echo his hold on her.

As he kissed her, as she lost herself in him, the world faded away, melting in the joy his mouth created. In this moment, as his mouth invaded hers, she wasn't the good girl, the do-gooder with the sterling reputation.

She was Cal, and Quinn holding her was all that was important.

* * *

Married to the Maverick Millionaire
is part of the From Mavericks to Married series—
Three superfine hockey players
finally meet their matches!

MARRIED TO THE MAVERICK MILLIONAIRE

BY
JOSS WOOD

® and ™ are trademarks owned and used by the trademark owner and/or its licensee. Trademarks marked with ® are registered with the United Kingdom Patent Office and/or the Office for Harmonisation in the Internal Market and in other countries.

First Published in Great Britain 2016
By Mills & Boon, an imprint of HarperCollins*Publishers*
1 London Bridge Street, London, SE1 9GF

© 2016 Joss Wood

ISBN: 978-0-263-91889-2

51-1216

Our policy is to use papers that are natural, renewable and recyclable products and made from wood grown in sustainable forests. The logging and manufacturing processes conform to the legal environmental regulations of the country of origin.

Printed and bound in Spain
by CPI, Barcelona

Joss Wood's passion for putting black letters on a white screen is matched only by her love of books and traveling (especially to the wild places of southern Africa) and, possibly, by her hatred of ironing and making school lunches.

Joss has written over sixteen books for Mills & Boon.

After a career in business lobbying and local economic development, Joss now writes full-time. She lives in KwaZulu-Natal, South Africa, with her husband and two teenage children, surrounded by family, friends, animals and a ridiculous amount of books.

Joss is a member of the RWA (Romance Writers of America) and ROSA (Romance Writers of South Africa).

This book is dedicated to my own Cal,
the port I run to in any storm.
I am so grateful to have you in my life.

One

Quinn Rayne flew across the parking lot on the Coal Harbour promenade, his feet slapping an easy but fast rhythm as he dodged both tourists and residents taking a late afternoon stroll on the paved and pretty walking and biking path next to the marina. The earbuds in his ears and his dark sunglasses were an excellent excuse to ignore the calls of recognition, the pointed fingers.

Even after a decade of being in the spotlight, he still wasn't used to being an object of curious, sometimes disapproving, fascination. Surely the residents of Vancouver could find someone new to discuss? There had to be someone in the city who was a bigger badass than he was reputed to be.

As he approached the marina, he slowed his sprint to a jog and then to a walk, fingers against the pulse point in his neck and his eyes on his watch. After two minutes he nodded, satisfied. He might not be playing professional ice hockey anymore, but he was as fit as he'd ever been. He'd see whether his players, when they returned to practice next week, had also maintained their fitness. For their sakes, he hoped so.

Quinn walked to the access gate to his wharf. He punched in his code to open the gate and jogged down to where his yacht was berthed. Because he owned one of the prime sites, he had unobstructed views of Burrard Inlet, with Stanley Park to his left and Grouse Mountain in front of him. Living on the water was more adventurous than living in a house and God knew how much he craved adventure.

Quinn stepped onto the *Red Delicious* and quickly ran up the steps to the main deck, the quickest way to access the living area. He slid open the door, pulled his earbuds from his neck and tossed them, his cap and his sunglasses onto the sleek table to his right. He glanced at his watch and wondered if he had time for a shower before Mac and Kade arrived to report back on a meeting they'd attended earlier with Warren Bayliss, their partner and investor.

Bayliss was an essential part of the ongoing process to buy the Mavericks franchise from the current owner, Myra Hasselback, who was also considering selling out to a Russian billionaire who owned a string of boring sports franchises. Quinn didn't need his brother's string of degrees to know that when he, a full Mavericks partner, was excluded from the meeting Warren called, then there was trouble in paradise.

And that it had his name on it.

Quinn walked into the massive open-plan living area and immediately noticed the small form tucked into the corner of his oversized sofa, a cup of coffee in her hand, staring out of the floor-to-ceiling glass windows. One foot was tucked up under her butt; her other—long, slim and sexy—was bent. She'd been sitting like that on the beach at Sandy Cove the first day he'd met her, gap-toothed and grinning, a six-year-old dynamo. She was his girl-next-door or, to be technical, the girl from three houses down. His childhood companion and his teenage confidante.

Sensing his presence, she turned her head, deep-red curls bouncing. Freckles splattered across her nose and onto her cheeks, each one perfect. God, he loved her freckles, had missed those freckles, her face.

He slapped his hands on his hips, not sure if he was just imagining her or if she was really sitting there, bright hair and makeup-free but so damn real he could barely breathe.

"*Red.* What the hell are you doing here?"

Her smile slammed into his sternum and Quinn's heart bounced off his rib cage. Callahan's deep, dark eyes danced as she jumped to her feet and Quinn found himself smiling, properly smiling, for the first time that day. He reached out, grabbed her and swept her into his arms. She weighed less than a feather and he easily whirled her around. The scent of wildflowers hovered around her. It was in the hair he buried his face into, on the warm, smooth skin he could feel beneath the barrier of her shirt. Her laugh rumbled through her and instantly lightened his mood. She'd always had the naughtiest, dirtiest laugh.

Cal Adam was back and his world made a little more sense.

Her feet still off the ground, Cal placed her hands on his shoulders and pushed away from him, her eyes clashing with his. "Hi."

"Hi back."

"You always had the prettiest eyes," Cal said, the tips of her fingers coming to rest on his cheekbone. "Ice green with a ring of emerald." She patted his cheek and rubbed her hand through his too-long, overly full beard. "Not sure about this, though. You're hiding that sexy face."

Quinn tightened his arms, his lower body responding as she wound her legs around his waist. A picture of her wet and naked, in exactly this position, appeared on his internal big screen, but he brushed it away. This was Cal, his oldest friend, his best friend—having lascivious thoughts about her was weird. And wrong.

He patted her small, tight butt. "Glad to see that you've picked up a bit of weight since the last time I saw you." It had been nearly two years ago and she'd been in hospital with a stomach bug she'd caught in Panama. Cal had looked almost skeletal. Always petite, at least she now looked on the healthy side of slim.

Cal smiled again, dropped a quick kiss on his lips, a kiss that had Quinn wanting more, needing to find out whether her lips were as soft as they appeared, whether that mouth that looked like it had been made for sin could, actually, sin. What was his problem? Was he now such a player that it was a habit to take every encounter with every woman to the bedroom? Even Cal?

Cal wiggled, her feet dropped to the maple floor and Quinn released her. She stepped back and pushed a curl behind her ear.

"*Red Delicious*, Q? That's an odd name for a boat." Cal made a production of fluttering her eyelashes. "Or did you name it after me?"

He grinned. "You wish I did. Nope, it was pure coincidence."

"Honestly, she's stunning," Cal stated, looking around.

Quinn followed her gaze. The sleek lines of the sixty-five-meter yacht were echoed in the minimalist furniture and cool white, grey and beige. Sometimes he thought it a little stark...

"It needs some color. Some bold prints, some bright cushions," Cal said, echoing his thoughts. Despite their long time apart, they still thought along the same lines.

"She's beautiful and bigger than your last yacht. How many does she sleep?"

"Ten on the lower deck. The master cabin is aft with a walk-in wardrobe and spa bath and there's another full cabin forward. Two small cabins midship There's another smaller, cozier lounge...that's where I watch TV, wind down. Two decks, one off the main bedroom and another entertainment deck with a Jacuzzi."

"Impressive. I want to see it all. When did you acquire her?"

"About a year back." Quinn ran a hand down Cal's hair and her curls wound around his knuckle. The smell of her shampoo wafted over to him and he wondered when Cal's hair had turned so soft and silky. So damned girly. Cal shoved her hands into the back pockets of her skinny jeans and arched her back. The white silk T-shirt pulled against her chest and Quinn noticed her small, perky breasts and that she was wearing a lacy, barely-there push-up bra.

He rolled his shoulders, uncomfortable. *Right. Enough with that, Rayne.*

Quinn rubbed the back of his neck as he walked across the living area to the kitchen. He opened the double-door fridge and peered inside, hoping that the icy air would cool his lascivious thoughts.

"Water?" he asked, his words muffled.

Cal shook her head. "No, thanks."

He slammed the fridge door closed and cracked the lid on the water bottle before lifting it to his lips.

"How is your dad?" he asked, remembering why she was back in the city, back home.

"Okay. The triple heart bypass was successful. I went straight from the airport to the hospital and spent some time with him. He was awake and making plans so I suppose that's a good sign."

"I'm glad he's okay."

"He'll be fine. Stressing about when he can get back to work." He saw the worry in her eyes, heard fear in her flat tone. "The doctors said he won't be able to return to work for a couple of months and that sent him into a tailspin."

"He had the operation a few days ago. Maybe he should relax a little. The foundation won't grind to a stop because he isn't there."

The Adam Foundation was the wealthiest charitable organization in Canada, funded by the accumulated wealth of generations of her Adam ancestors. Money from the Adam Foundation allowed an ever-changing group of volunteers, and Cal, to travel the world to assist communities who needed grassroots help.

Cal bit the inside of her lip and her arched eyebrows pulled together. "He'll need somebody to run it until he's back on his feet."

"Is that person you?" he asked, annoyed by the spurt of excitement he felt. God, he and Cal hadn't lived in the same city for ages and having her around would be a very nice change.

"Maybe," Cal replied, unenthusiastic. "We'll talk about it later."

Quinn frowned as he tried to work out why Cal felt so ambivalent toward the city they'd been raised in. It was beautiful, interesting and eclectic, but Cal only came home when she absolutely had to. Maybe it had something to do with the fact that her husband had been killed when the light aircraft he'd been piloting crashed into a mountain to the north of the city around four...no, it had to be five years ago now.

She'd married the same week she turned twenty-four and, thanks to their massive argument about her nuptials—Quinn had loudly and vociferously told her that she'd lost her mind—he'd missed both her birthday and her wedding that year.

"Does the press corps know you are home?" Quinn asked, changing the subject. Like him, Cal had a hate-hate affair with the press.

"Everyone knows. They were at the airport and at the hospital."

"Remind me again where you flew in from?" It had been a couple of months since they last spoke and, while they exchanged emails regularly, he couldn't recall where her last project had been. Then again, Cal—as the troubleshooter for her family's foundation—jumped from project to project, country to country, going where she was needed to ensure everything ran smoothly. She could be in Latin America one week and in the Far East the next. Cal collected frequent-flier miles like politicians collected votes.

"Africa. Lesotho, to be precise. I was working on a project to counter soil erosion." Cal nodded toward the center island of the kitchen, to his landline and cell phone. "Your cell rang and then your phone. Mac left a voicemail saying that he and Wren and Kade were on the way over to discuss today's train wreck." She tipped her head and narrowed her amazing, blue-black eyes. "What trouble have you landed yourself in now, Q?"

Quinn heard Mac's and Kade's heavy footsteps on

the outside stairs and lifted a shoulder. "You know what they say, Red—the trouble with trouble is that it starts off as fun."

After greeting his best friends—who were also his partners, his colleagues—and Wren, the Mavericks' PR guru, he gestured for them all to take a seat and offered drinks. While he made coffee, Cal was hugged and kissed by his friends and asked how she'd been. It didn't matter how infrequently they saw her, Quinn mused, she automatically slotted back into his life and was immediately accepted because Mac and Kade understood that, just like they did, Cal had his back.

Quinn delivered mugs of coffee and sighed at their doom-and-gloom faces. He could deal with their anxiety—Mac and Kade constantly worried that he'd kill himself chasing his need for adrenaline—but he didn't like their frustration and, yeah, their anger. His teammates and their head of publicity were pissed. Again. Not necessarily at him but at the situation he'd found himself in.

He tended to find himself in a lot of *situations*.

Hell, Quinn thought as he pushed his fingers through his sweat-dampened hair and gathered it into a knot at the back of his head, *here we go again*.

"Make yourself some coffee, bro. You're going to need it," Mac suggested, leaning back and placing his booted foot on his opposite knee.

"I'll do it," Cal offered.

Though he appreciated her offer, Quinn shook his head. "Thanks, Red, but I've got it."

Quinn ran his hand over his thick beard as he walked around the island into the kitchen to where his coffee machine stood. He picked up his favorite mug, placed it under the spout and pushed the button for a shot of espresso. The machine gurgled, dispensed the caffeine and Quinn hit the button again. He wanted whiskey, but he supposed that a double espresso would have to do.

"So how did the meeting with Warren go?" he asked as he turned around.

Mac, as forthright as ever, gestured to Cal. "Maybe we should do this in private."

Cal immediately stood up and Quinn shook his head. "You know that you can talk in front of Cal. What I know she can know. I trust her."

Mac nodded and rubbed his jaw as Cal sat down again. "Your choice."

"Warren is less than happy with you and he's considering pulling out of the deal."

Quinn gripped the granite island to keep his balance, feeling like a forty-foot wave had passed under the bow of the yacht. "*What?*"

"And why?" Cal demanded, his shock echoed on her face. "What has Quinn done?"

"Is this about the interview Storm gave?" Quinn asked.

"Partly," Kade replied.

Quinn took a sip of his coffee, planted his feet apart and looked out to the water. Earlier in the week he'd woken up to the news that his three-week stand had, a month after he ended it, decided to share the intimate, ugly details of their affair and final breakup. Storm tearfully told the world, on an extremely popular morning breakfast show, that Quinn was emotionally unavailable, that he constantly and consistently cheated on her. For those reasons, she now needed intensive therapy.

None of it was true, but she'd sounded damn convincing.

He'd been played; the world was still being played. He'd made it very clear to her that he wasn't looking for a relationship—and three weeks did not constitute a relationship!—but she'd turned their brief and, to be honest, forgettable affair into a drama. Storm's interview was a massive publicity stunt, the next installment in keeping her admittedly gorgeous face in the news.

"Come and sit down, Quinn," Kade said, gesturing to a chair with his foot. Quinn dropped his long frame into the chair and rested his head on the padded back. His eyes darted from Kade's and Mac's faces to Cal's. Her deep, dark eyes—the exact color of his midnight-blue superbike—reflected worry and concern.

"It's just the latest episode in a series of bad press you've received and Warren is concerned that this is an ongoing trend. He told us, flat out, the Mavericks can't afford any more bad press and that you are the source."

"Does he want me out of the partnership?" Quinn demanded, his heart in his throat.

"He's hinting at it."

Quinn muttered an obscenity. The Mavericks—being Mac and Kade's partner—was what he did and a large part of who he was. Coaching the team was his solace, his hobby and, yeah, his career. He freakin' loved what he did.

But to own and grow the franchise, they needed Bayliss. Bayliss was their link to bigger and better sponsorship deals. He had media connections they could only dream about, connections they needed to grow the Mavericks franchise. But their investor thought Quinn was the weak link.

Craphelldammit.

Quinn looked at Cal and she slid off the barstool to sit on his chair, her arm loosely draped around his shoulders. Damn, he was glad she was back in town, glad she was here. He rarely needed anyone, but right now he needed her.

Her unconditional support, her humor, her solidity.

He looked at Wren, their PR guru. "Is he right? Am I damaging the Mavericks' brand?" he asked, his normally deep voice extra raspy with stress.

Wren flicked her eyes toward the pile of newspapers beside her. "Well, you're certainly not enhancing it." She linked her hands together on the table and leaned forward, her expression intense. "Basically, all the reports about you lately have followed the same theme and, like a bunch of rabid wolves, the journos are ganging up on you."

Quinn frowned. "Brilliant."

"Unfortunately, they have no reason to treat you kindly. You did nearly run that photographer over a couple of weeks back," Wren said.

Quinn held up his hands. "That was an accident." Sort of.

"And you called the press a collective boil on the ass of humanity during that radio interview."

Well, they were.

Wren continued. "Basically, their theme is that it's time you grew up and that your—let's call them exploits—are getting old and, worse, tiresome. That seeing you with a different woman every month is boring and a cliché. Some journalists are taking this a step further, saying, since Kade and Mac have settled and started families, when are you going to do the same? That what was funny and interesting in your early twenties is now just self-indulgent."

Quinn grimaced. Ouch. Harsh.

Not as harsh as knowing that he'd never be able to have what they had, his own family, but still…

Seriously, Rayne, this *again? For the last five years, you've known about and accepted your infertility! A family is not what you want, remember? Stop thinking about it and move on!*

Kade picked up a paper and Quinn could see that someone, probably Wren, had highlighted some text.

Kade read the damaging words out loud. "Our sources tell us that the deal to buy the Mavericks franchise by Rayne, Kade Webb and Mac McCaskill, and their investor—the conservative billionaire industrialist Warren Bayliss—is about to be finalized. You would think that Rayne would make an effort to keep his nose clean. Maybe his partners should tell him that while he might be a brilliant and successful coach, he is a shocking example to his players and his personal life is a joke."

Kade and Mac held his gaze and he respected them for not dropping their eyes and looking away.

"Is that something you want to tell me?" he demanded, his voice rough.

Kade exchanged a look with Mac and Mac gestured for Kade to speak. "The last year has been stressful, for all of us. So much has happened—Vernon's death, our partnership with Bayliss, buying the franchise."

"Falling in love, becoming fathers," Wren added.

Kade nodded his agreement. "You generating bad publicity is complicating the situation. We, specifically the Mavericks, need you to clean up your act."

Quinn tipped his head back to look at the ceiling. He wanted to argue, wanted to rage against the unfair accusations, wanted to shout his denials. Instead, he dropped his head and looked at Cal, who still sat on the arm of the chair looking thoughtful.

"You've been very quiet, Red. What do you think?"

Cal bit her bottom lip, her eyes troubled. She dropped

her head to the side and released a long sigh. "I know how important buying the franchise is and I'd think that you'd want to do whatever you could to make sure that happens." She wrinkled her nose at him. "Maybe you do need to calm down, Q. Stop the serial dating, watch your mouth, stop dueling with death sports—"

The loud jangle of a cell phone interrupted her sentence and Cal hopped up. "Sorry, that's mine. It might be the hospital."

Quinn nodded. Cal bent over to pick up her bag and Quinn blinked as the denim fabric stretched across her perfect, heart-shaped ass. He wiped a hand over his face and swallowed, desperately trying to moisten his mouth. All the blood in his head travelled south to create some action in his pants.

Quinn rubbed the back of his neck. Instead of thinking about Red and her very nice butt, he should be directing his attention to his career. He needed to convince Bayliss he was a necessary and valuable component of the team and not a risk factor. To do that, he had to get the media off his back or, at the very least, get them to focus on something positive about him and his career with the Mavericks. Easy to think; not so easy to do.

As Cal slipped out the glass door onto the smaller deck, he acknowledged that his sudden attraction to Red was a complication that he definitely could do without.

"Callahan Adam-Carter? Please hold for Mr. Graeme Moore."

Cal frowned, wondered who Graeme Moore was and looked into the lounge behind her, thinking that the three Mavericks men were incredibly sexy. Fit, ripped, cosmopolitan. And since Quinn was the only one who was still single, she wasn't surprised that the press's attention was on him. Breakfast was not breakfast in the city without coffee and the latest gossip about the city's favorite sons.

Over the years his bright blond hair had deepened to the color of rich toffee, but those eyes—those brilliant, ice-green eyes—were exactly the same, edged by long, dark lashes and strong brows. She wasn't crazy about his too-long, dirty-blond beard and his shoulder-length hair, but she could understand why the female population of Vancouver liked his appearance. He looked hard and hot and, as always, very, very masculine. With an edge of danger that immediately had female ovaries twitching. After a lifetime of watching women making fools of themselves over him—tongues dropping, walking into poles, stuttering, stammering, offering to have his babies—she understood that he was a grade-A hottie.

When she was wrapped around him earlier she'd felt her heart rate climb and that special spot between her legs throb. Mmm, interesting. After five years of feeling numb, five years without feeling remotely attracted to anyone, her sexuality was finally creeping back. She'd started to notice men again and she supposed that her reaction to Quinn had everything to do with the fact that it had been a very long time since she'd been up close and personal with a hot man. With any man.

It didn't mean anything. He was Quinn, for God's sake! *Quinn!* This was the same guy who had tried to raise frogs in the family bath, who had teased her mercilessly and defended her from school-yard bullies. To her, he wasn't the youngest but best hockey coach in the NHL, the wild and woolly adrenaline junkie who provided grist for the tabloids, or the ripped bad boy who dated supermodels and publicity-seeking actresses.

He was just Quinn, her closest friend for the best part of twenty years.

Well, eighteen years, to be precise. They hadn't spoken to each other for six months before her wedding or at any time during her marriage. It was only after Toby's death that they'd reconnected.

"Mrs. Carter, I'm glad I've finally reached you."

Mrs. Carter? Cal's stomach contracted and her coffee made its way back up her throat. She swallowed and swallowed again.

"I've sent numerous messages to your email address at Carter International, but you have yet to respond," Moore continued. "I heard you were back in the country so I finally tracked down your cell number."

Cal shrugged. Her life had stopped the day Toby died and she seldom—okay, never—paid attention to messages sent to that address.

"I'm sorry. Who are you?"

"Toby Carter's lawyer and I'm calling about his estate."

"I don't understand why, since Toby's estate was settled years ago," Cal said, frowning.

Moore remained silent for a long time and he eventually spoke again. "I read his will after the funeral, Mrs. Carter. Do you remember that day?"

No, not really. Her memory of Toby's death and burial was shrouded in a mist she couldn't—didn't want to—penetrate.

"I handed you a folder, asked you to read the will again when you felt stronger," Moore continued when she failed to answer him. "You didn't do that, did you?"

Cal pushed away the nauseating emotions that swirled to the surface whenever she thought or talked about Toby and forced herself to think. And no, she hadn't read the will again. She didn't even remember the folder. It was probably where she left it, in the study at Toby's still-unoccupied house.

"Why are you calling me, Mr. Moore?"

"This is a reminder that Mr. Carter's estate has been in abeyance for the last five years. Mr. Carter wanted you to inherit, but he didn't want to share his wealth with your future spouse. His will states that if you have not remarried five years after his death, you inherit his estate."

"What?"

"His estate includes his numerous bank accounts, his properties—both here and overseas—and his shares in Carter International. Also included are his art, furniture and gemstone collections. The estate is valued in the region of $200 million."

"I don't want it. I don't want anything! Give it to his sons."

"The will cannot be changed and his assets cannot be transferred. If you remarry before the anniversary of his death, then you will no longer be a beneficiary of Mr. Carter's will and only then will his estate be split evenly between his two sons."

Toby, you scumbag. "So I have to marry within four months to make sure that his sons inherit what they are— morally and ethically—entitled to?" Cal demanded, feeling her heart thud against her rib cage.

"Exactly."

"Do you know how nuts this is?"

After begging her to read his emails, Moore ended the call. Cal closed her eyes and pulled in deep breaths, flooding her lungs with air in order to push back the panic. Everything Toby owned was tainted, covered with the same deep, dark, controlling and possessive energy that he'd concealed beneath the charming, urbane, kind personality he showed the world.

Cal scrunched her eyelids closed, trying not to remember the vicious taunting, her confusion, the desperation. He was five years dead and he could still make her panic, make her doubt herself, turn her hard-fought independence into insecurity. She couldn't be his heir. She didn't want to own anything of his. She never wanted to be linked to him again.

To remain mentally and emotionally free of her husband, she couldn't be tied to anything he owned. She'd marry the first man she could to rid herself of his contaminated legacy.

Cal turned as she heard the door to the lounge slide open and saw Quinn standing there. She pulled a smile onto her face and hoped that Quinn was too involved in his own drama to notice that she'd taken a starring role in one of her own.

Quinn frowned at her, obviously seeing something on her face or in her eyes to make him pause. "Everything okay?" he asked as he gestured her inside.

Cal nodded as she walked back into the lounge.

"Apart from the fact that I need a husband, I'm good." Cal saw the shocked expressions that followed and waved her comment away. "Bad joke. Ignore me. So, have you found a solution to your problem? Any ideas on how to get Quinn some good press?"

Wren leaned forward and crossed her legs, linking her hands over her knees, her expression thoughtful. "I wish you weren't joking, Cal. Quinn marrying you would be excellent PR for him."

Mac and Kade laughed, Quinn spluttered, but Cal just lifted her eyebrows in a tell-me-more expression.

"You're PR gold, Callahan. You are the only child of a fairy-tale romance between your superrich father and Rachel Thomas, the principal soloist with the Royal Canadian Ballet Company, who is considered one of the world's best ballerinas. You married Toby Carter, the most elusive and eligible of Vancouver's bachelors until these three knuckleheads came along. The public loves you to distraction, despite the fact that you are seldom in the city."

Could she? Did she dare? It would be a quick, convenient solution.

Cal gathered her courage, pulled on her brightest smile and turned to Quinn. "So, what do you think? Want to get married?"

Two

Cal called a final good-bye to Quinn's friends and closed the sliding door behind them. She walked through the main salon, passed the large dining table and hesitated at the steps that would take her belowdecks to the sleeping cabins below. Quinn had hurried down those stairs after she'd dropped her bombshell but not before telling her that her suggestion that they marry was deeply unamusing and wildly inappropriate.

She hadn't been joking and the urge to run downstairs and explain was strong. But Cal knew Quinn, knew that he needed some time alone to work through his temper, to gather his thoughts. She did too. To give them both a little time, she walked back into the kitchen and snagged a microbrew from his stash in the fridge. Twisting the top off, she took a swallow straight from the bottle. She'd been back in Vancouver for less than a day and she already felt like the city had a feather pillow over her face.

Being back in Vancouver always did that to her; the city she'd loved as a child, a teenager and a young woman now felt like it was trying to smother her.

Cal pulled a face. As pretty as Quinn's new yacht was, she didn't want to be here. A square inch of her heart—the inch that was pure bitch—resented having to come back here, resented leaving the anonymity of the life she'd created after Toby. But her father needed her here and since he was the only family she had left, she'd caught the first flight home.

Cal ran the cold bottle over her cheek and closed her eyes. When she was away from Vancouver, she was Cal Adam and she had little connection to Callahan Adam-Carter, Toby's young, socially connected, perfectly pedigreed bride. Despite the fact that she stood to inherit her father's wealth, she was as far removed from the wife she'd been as politicians were from the truth. The residents of her hometown would be shocked to realize that she was now as normal as any single, almost-thirty-year-old widowed woman who'd grown up in the public eye could be.

She'd worked hard to chase her freedom, to live independently, to find her individuality. It hadn't always been easy. She was the only child of one of the country's richest men, the widow of another rich, wildly popular man and the daughter of a beloved icon of the dance world. Her best friend was also the city's favorite bad boy.

To whom, on a spur-of-the-moment suggestion, she'd just proposed marriage. Crazy!

Yet…yet in a small, pure part of her brain, it made complete sense on a number of levels and in the last few years she'd learned to listen to that insistent voice.

First, and most important, marrying her would be a good move for Quinn. She was reasonably pretty, socially connected and the reporters and photographers loved her.

She was also so rarely in the city that whatever she did, or said, was guaranteed to garner coverage. In a nutshell, she sold newspapers, online or print. Being linked with her, being *married* to her, would send a very strong message that Quinn was turning his life around.

Because nobody—not even Quinn Rayne, legendary bad boy—would play games with Callahan Adam-Carter. And, as a bonus, her father and Warren Bayliss did a lot of business together, so Bayliss wouldn't dare try excluding Cauley's son-in-law from any deal involving the other two Mavericks.

Yeah, marrying her would be a very good move on Quinn's part.

As for her...

If she wanted no part of Toby's inheritance, then she needed to marry. That was nonnegotiable. And in order to protect herself, to protect her freedom and independence, she needed to marry a man who was safe, someone she could be honest with. She knew Quinn and trusted him. He lived life on his own terms and, since he hated restrictions, he was a live-and-let-live type of guy. Just the type of man—*the only type of man*—she could ever consider marrying.

Quinn wouldn't rock her emotional boat. She'd known him all her life, and never thought of him in any way but as her friend. The little spark she'd felt earlier was an aberration and not worth considering, so marrying him would be an easy way out of her sticky situation. No mess, no fuss.

And if she took over the management of the foundation for a while and found herself back in the social swirl, being Quinn's wife would assuage some highbrow curiosity about her change from an insecure, meek, jump-at-shadows girl to the stronger, assertive, more confident woman she now was. Nobody would expect Quinn—the Mavericks' Bad Boy—to have a mousy wife.

This marriage—presuming she could get Quinn to agree—would be in name only. Nothing between them would change. It would be a marriage of convenience, a way to help to free herself from Toby's tainted legacy.

It would be a ruse, a temporary solution to both their problems. It would be an illusion, a show, a production—but the heart of their friendship, of who they were, would stay the same.

It had to. Anything else would be unacceptable.

Provided, of course, that she could get Quinn to agree.

Was she out of her mind? Had she left the working part of her brain in... God, where had she been? Some tiny, landlocked African country he couldn't remember the name of. No matter—what the hell was Cal thinking?

Quinn had been so discombobulated by her prosaic, seemingly serious proposal that he'd shouted at her to stop joking around and told his mates that he was going to take a shower, hoping that some time alone under the powerful sprays of his double-head shower would calm him down.

It was the most relaxing shower system in the world, his architect had promised him. Well, relaxing, his ass.

He simply wasn't marriage and family material. God, he was barely part of the family he grew up within, and now Cal was suggesting that they make one together?

Cal had definitely taken her seat on the crazy train.

But if she was, if the notion was so alien to him, why did his stomach twitch with excitement at the thought? Why did he sometimes—when he felt tired or stressed— wish he had someone to come home to, a family to distract him from the stresses of being the youngest, least experienced head coach in the league? And, worst of all, why, when he saw Kade and Mac with their women, did he feel, well, squirrelly, like something, maybe, possibly, was missing from his life?

Nah, it was gas or indigestion or an approaching heart attack—he couldn't possibly be jealous of the happiness he saw in their eyes... Besides, Cal had only suggested marriage, not the added extras.

It was a normal reaction to not wanting to be alone, he decided, reaching for the shampoo and savagely dumping far too much in his open palm, cursing when most of it fell to the floor. He viciously rubbed what was left over his long hair and his beard and swore when some suds burned his eyes. Turning the jets as far as they could go, he ducked and allowed the water to pummel his head, his face, his shoulders. Marriage, family, kids—all impossible. Seven years ago, during a routine team checkup, he'd been told by the team doctor and a specialist that his blood tests indicated there was a 95 percent chance he was infertile. Further tests were suggested, but Quinn, not particularly fazed, hadn't bothered. He'd quickly moved on from the news and that was what he needed to do again. *Like, right now. Is it time for you to grow up, Rayne?*

His friends' lives were changing and because of that, his should too. Quinn swore, his curses bouncing off the bathroom walls. But, unfair or not, the fact was that his liaison with Storm, his daredevil stunts, his laissez-faire attitude to everything but his coaching and training of the team, had tarnished the image of the Mavericks and Bayliss didn't want him to be part of the deal. If Kade and Mac decided to side with him and ditch Bayliss as an investor, there was a very real chance that the Widow Hasselback would sell the franchise to Chenko. And that would be on Quinn's head.

His teammates, his friends, his brothers didn't deserve that.

He didn't have a choice. He'd sacrifice his free-wheelin' lifestyle, clean up his mouth, tone down the crazy stunts, exhibit some patience and stop giving the press enough rope to hang him. Mac and Kade, his players, the fans—everyone needed him to pull a rabbit out of his hat and that's what he would do. But how long would it take for the press to get off his ass? Three months? Six? He could behave himself for as long as he needed to, but it would mean no stunts, no women...

No women. After Storm's crazy-as-hell behavior, he was happy to date himself for a while. And the new season was about to start. With draft picks and fitness assessments and training, he wouldn't have that much spare time. Yeah, he could take a break from the sweeter-smelling species for a while, easily.

What he wouldn't do is get married. That was crazy talk. Besides, Cal had been joking. She had a weird, off-beat sense of humor.

Quinn shut off the jets, grabbed a towel and wound it around his hips. He walked out of his bathroom and braked the moment he saw Cal sitting on the edge of his king-sized bed, a beer bottle in her hand.

"Just make yourself at home, sunshine," he drawled, sarcasm oozing from every clean pore.

"We should get married," she told him, a light of determination in her eyes.

He recognized that look. Cal had her serious-as-hell face on. "God, Cal! Have you lost your mind?"

Possibly.

Cal watched as Quinn disappeared into his walk-in closet and slammed the door behind him. She eyed the closed door and waited for him to reemerge, knowing that she needed to make eye contact with Quinn to make him realize how desperately serious she was.

Dear Lord, the man had a six-pack that could make a woman weep. Callahan Adam, get a grip! You've seen Quinn in just a towel before. Hell, you've seen him naked before! This should not—he should not—be able to distract you!

Right. Focus.

Them getting married was a temporary, brilliant solution to both their problems, but she'd have to coax, persuade and maybe bully him into tying the knot with her. If she and Quinn married, she would be killing a flock of pesky pigeons with one supercharged, magic stone. She just needed Quinn to see the big picture…

The door to the closet opened and Quinn walked out, now dressed in a pair of straight-legged track pants and a long-sleeved T-shirt, the arms pushed up to reveal the muscles in his forearms. He'd brushed his hair off his face, but his scowl remained.

Cal sat cross-legged in the middle of the bed and patted the comforter next to her. "Let's chat."

"Let's not if you're going to mention the word *marriage*." Quinn scowled and sat on the edge of the bucket chair in the corner, his elbows on his knees and his expression as dark as the night falling outside. Oh, she recognized the stubbornness in his eyes. He wasn't in any mood to discuss her on-the-fly proposal. If she pushed him now, he'd dig in his heels and she'd end up inheriting Toby's tainted $200 million.

Being a little stubborn herself, she knew that the best way to handle Quinn was to back off and approach the problem from another angle.

Cal rubbed her eyes with her fist. "It's been a really

crazy afternoon. And a less-than-wonderful day. I spoke to my dad's doctor about fifteen minutes ago."

Quinn's demeanor immediately changed from irritation to concern. He leaned forward, his concentration immediately, absolutely, focused on her. It was one of his most endearing traits. If you were his friend and he cared about you and you said that you were in trouble that was all that was important. "And? Is he okay?"

"He looked awful, so very old," Cal said, placing her beer bottle on his bedside table. Her father would be okay, she reminded herself as panic climbed up her throat. The triple heart bypass had been successful and he just needed time to recover.

"The doctor says he needs to take three months off. He needs to be stress-free for that time. He's recommended my father book into a private, very exclusive recovery center in Switzerland."

"But?"

"According to the doc, Dad is worried about the foundation. Apparently, there are loads of fund-raisers soon—the annual masked ball, the half-marathon, the art auction. The doctor said that if I want my father to make a full recovery, I'll have to find someone to take over his responsibilities."

"There's only one person he'd allow to step into his shoes," Quinn stated, stretching out his legs and leaning back in his chair.

"Me."

"You're an Adam, Red, and your father has always held the view that the foundation needs an Adam face. I remember him giving you a thirty-minute monologue over dinner about how the contributors and the grant recipients valued that personal connection. How old were we? Fifteen?"

Cal smiled. "Fourteen."

"So are you going to run the foundation for him?"

"How can I not?" Cal replied. "It's three months. I spent three months building houses in Costa Rica, in Haiti after their earthquake, in that refugee camp in Sudan. I say yes to helping strangers all the time. I want to say yes to helping my father, but I don't want to stay in Vancouver. I want be anywhere but here. But if I do stay here, then I can help you, Q. Marrying me will help you rehab your reputation."

If this wasn't so damn serious, then she'd be tempted to laugh at his horrified expression.

"I'm not interested in using my association with you, sullying my friendship with you, to improve my PR," Quinn told her in his take-no-prisoners voice.

And there was that streak of honor so few people saw but was a fundamental part of Quinn. He did his own thing, but he made sure his actions didn't impact anyone else. His integrity—his honor—was why she couldn't believe a word his psycho ex spouted about their relationship. Quinn didn't play games, didn't obfuscate, didn't lie. And he never, ever, made promises he couldn't keep.

"I can rehabilitate my own reputation without help from you or anyone else."

Cal didn't disagree with him; Quinn could do anything he set his mind to. "Of course you can, but it would be a lot quicker if you let me help you. The reality is that, according to the world, I am the good girl and you're the bad boy. I don't drink, party or get caught with my panties down." God, she sounded so boring, so blah. "I am seen to be living a productive and meaningful life. I am the poster girl for how filthy-rich heiresses should behave."

"Bully for you," Quinn muttered, looking unimpressed.

"I know—I sound awful, don't I?" Cal wrinkled her nose. "But my rep, or the lack of it, can work for you, if you let it. Being seen with me, spending time with me will go a long way to restoring your reputation and, right now, it needs some polishing. The Mavericks are in sensitive discussions around the future of the team and, from what I can gather, your position within the organization is unstable. Your fans are jittery. You're about to start a new season and, as the coach, you need them behind you and you need them to trust you. They probably don't at the moment."

A muscle ticked in his jaw. She was hurting him, and she was sorry for that. His job—his career—was everything to him and her words were like digging a knife into a bullet wound.

"If we're married, the world will look at you and think, 'Hey, he's with Callahan, and we all know that she has her feet on the ground. Maybe we've been a bit tough on him.' Or maybe they'll think that your exploits couldn't have been that bad if I'm prepared to be with you. Whatever they interpret from the two of us being together, it should be positive."

"I cannot believe that we are still discussing this, but—" Quinn frowned "—why marriage? Why would we have to go that far? Why couldn't we just be in a relationship?"

Cal took a minute to come up with a response that made sense. "Because if we just pretend to have a relationship, then it could be interpreted as me being another notch on your belt, another of your bang-her-'til-you're-bored women. No, you have to be taken seriously and what's more serious than marriage?"

Quinn frowned at her. "Death? Or isn't that the same thing?"

"I'm not suggesting a life sentence, Quinn."

"And would this be a fake marriage or a let's-get-the-legal-system-involved marriage?"

Cal considered his question. "It would be easier if it was fake, but some intrepid journalist would check and if they find out we're trying to snow them, they'll go ballistic. If we do this, then we have to do it properly."

"I'm over the moon with excitement."

Cal ignored his sarcasm. "I'm thinking that we stay married for about a year, maybe eighteen months. We act, when we're out in public, like this is the real deal. Behind closed doors we'll be who we always are, best friends. After the furor has died down, after the Mavericks purchase is complete, we'll start to go our own ways and, after a while, we'll separate. Then we'll have a quick and quiet divorce, saying that we are better off as friends and that we still love each other, all of which will be true."

Quinn narrowed his eyes at her. "That's a hell of a plan, Red. And why do you want to do this?"

And that's where this got tricky, Cal thought. Without a detailed explanation, he wouldn't understand her wish to walk away from so much money. She'd have to explain that accepting Toby's money would stain her soul and Quinn would demand to know why. She couldn't tell him that the debonair, sophisticated, charming and besotted-by-his-new-bride Toby turned into a psycho behind closed doors.

She simply couldn't tell anyone. Some topics, she was convinced, never needed to see the light of day.

"Being part of a couple provides me with a barrier to hide behind when the demands of my father's high-society world become too much. I need to be able to refuse invitations to cocktail parties and events, to not go to dinner with eligible men, to do the minimal amount of socializing that is required of me. In order to get away with that without offending anyone, I need a good excuse." Her mouth widened into a smile. "My brand-new husband would be an excellent excuse."

Quinn closed his eyes. "You're asking me to marry you so you can duck your social obligations? Do you know how lame that sounds?"

It did sound lame, even to her. "Sure, but it will stop me from going nuts."

"The press will be all over us like a rash." Quinn said.

"Yeah, but, after a couple of weeks, they will move on to something else and will, hopefully, leave us alone."

Quinn didn't look convinced and stared at the carpet beneath his feet. "What happens if we do get married and you meet someone who you want to spend the rest of your life with?"

Jeez, she was never getting married—in the real sense—ever again. She'd never hand a man that much control over her, allow him to have that much input into how she lived her life. She'd been burned once, scorched, *incinerated*—there was no way she'd play with fire again. Marrying Quinn was just a smoke screen and nothing would change, not really. They had everything to gain and little to lose.

"Don't worry about that. Look, all I'm asking is for you to provide me with a shield between my father's world and the pound of flesh they want from me," Cal stated. "It's taking the lemons life gives you—"

"If you say anything about making lemonade, I might strangle you," Quinn warned her in his super-growly, super-sexy voice.

Cal grinned. "Hell, no! When life gives me lemons, I slice those suckers up, haul out the salt and tequila and do shots." She stretched out her legs. "So, are we going to get married or what, Rayne?"

He stood up and stretched, and the hem of his shirt pulled up to reveal furrows of hard stomach muscle and a hint of those long, vertical muscles over his hips that made woman say—and do—stupid things. Like taking a nip right there, heading lower to take his...

Cal slammed her eyes shut and hauled in some much-needed air. Had she really fantasized about kissing Quinn...*there*? She waited for the wave of shame, but nothing happened. Well, she was still wondering how good those muscles and his masculine skin would feel under her hands, on her tongue.

She had to get out of his bedroom. *Now.* Before she did something stupid like slapping her mouth on his. Her libido wasn't gently creeping back; it was galloping in on a white stallion, naked and howling.

Maybe getting hitched wasn't the brightest idea she'd ever had. She should backtrack, tell Quinn that this was a crazy-bad idea, that she'd changed her mind.

"Okay, let's do it," Quinn said. "Let's get hitched."
Oh, damn. Too late.

Three

Three weeks later...

Cal, yawning, stumbled up the stairs, her eyes half closed and her brain still in sleep mode. A cool wind from an open door whirled around her and she rubbed her hands over her arms, thinking that she should've pulled a robe over her skimpy camisole and boy shorts. Coffee time, she decided.

Cal looked to her right, her attention caught by the silver-pink sheen as the sun danced on the sea. Maybe she wouldn't go back to bed. Maybe she'd go up onto the deck and watch the sun wake up and a new day bloom.

"Morning."

Cal screeched, whirled around and slapped her hand on her chest. Quinn stood in the galley kitchen, a pair of low-slung boxers hanging off his slim hips, long hair pulled into a tail at the back of his neck. Oh, God, he was practically naked and her eyes skimmed over the acre of male muscles. His shoulders seemed broader this morning, his arms bigger, that six-pack more defined. She—slowly, it had to be said—lifted her eyes to his face. Her heart bounced off her rib cage when she realized his eyes were on her bare legs and were moving, ever so slowly, north. She felt her internal temperature rocket up and her nipples pucker when his eyes lingered on her chest. When their eyes met, she thought she saw desire—hot and hard—flicker in his eyes and across his face. But it came and went so quickly that she doubted herself; after all, it wasn't like she'd had a lot of experience with men and attraction lately. Lately, as in the past five years.

Her libido had picked a fine time to get with the program, she decided, deeply disgusted. It was a special type of hell being attracted to your fake husband.

"Do you want coffee?" Quinn said as he turned his back to her. Cal heard an extra rasp in his voice that raised goosebumps on her skin. His back view was almost as good as the front view—an amazing butt, defined and muscular shoulders, a straight spine. There was also a solid inch of white skin between his tanned back and the band of his plain black boxers.

Cal placed her hand on her forehead as she tried to convince herself that she wasn't attracted to him, that she was being ridiculous. She forced herself to remember that she'd seen him eat week-old pizza, that he was revolting when he was hungover and he sounded like he was killing a cat when he sang. She told herself that she'd never felt even marginally attracted to him so whatever she was feeling was flu or pneumonia or typhoid.

Her libido just laughed at her.

"Red, coffee?"

Quinn's question jolted her back and she managed to push a *yes* through her lips. Cal crossed her arms over her chest and felt her hard nipples pressing into her fisted hands. Dammit, she needed to cover up. She couldn't walk around half-dressed. Cal looked toward the salon and saw a light throw lying across the back of one couch. She quickly walked across the room to wrap it around her shoulders and instantly felt calmer, more in control.

Less likely to strip and jump him in the kitchen...

"Here you go."

Cal turned and smiled her thanks as Quinn placed a coffee mug on the island counter. Keeping the ends of the throw gathered at her chest, she walked toward him and pushed her other hand through the opening to pick up her cup. She took a grateful sip and sighed. Great coffee.

"I'm surprised to see you up and about so early," Quinn said, turning away to fix his own cup.

"Couldn't sleep," Cal replied.

Quinn lifted his mug to his mouth and gestured to the short flight of stairs that led to the upper deck. "Let's go up. It's a nice place to start the day."

On the deck Cal sat down on the closest blocky settee, placed her coffee cup on the wooden deck and wrapped her arms around her bent legs. She turned and watched as Quinn walked up the stairs, cup and an apple in his hands. He'd pulled on a black hooded sweatshirt and disappointment warred with relief.

Quinn sat down next to her, put his mug next to hers and took a big bite from his apple. They didn't speak for a while, happy to watch the sun strengthen, bouncing off the tip of the mountains on one side and the skyscrapers on the other.

She'd forgotten how truly beautiful Vancouver could be. And sitting here, feeling the heat radiating off Quinn's big body, she enjoyed the quiet. When they decided to marry, they'd stepped into a whirlwind of their own creation. Between dealing with the press, her responsibilities to the foundation and the beginning of the new hockey season for him, they had barely touched base since their quick Vegas wedding. And, despite her moving into the guest cabin downstairs, she hardly saw him.

That could be because he was already gone when she woke up and the nights when she knew he was in, she made a concerted effort to be somewhere else.

Cal had the sneaking suspicion that he was also avoiding her and wondered why. She knew what her reasons were—she'd prefer that he didn't realize that she lusted after him, that she spent many nights in her cabin imagining what making love with him would be like. She didn't want to complicate this situation, make it any more uncomfortable than it already was and, man, it was complicated enough already.

Cal lifted her cup to her mouth, the diamond in her engagement ring flashing despite the still-low light. Then again, at ten carats, the ring could be seen from space.

"How are things?" Cal asked Quinn, noting his tired eyes. "I haven't seen you since we attended that art exhibition two nights ago."

"Where we spoke to the press more than we spoke to each other," Quinn said, his expression enigmatic.

Cal shook her head, disgusted. "I expected some interest around my return, but this is ridiculous. And, if I'm out alone, they're always asking where you are."

"How do you answer?"

"I say that you're at home, naked, waiting for me to ravish you," Cal joked, but, instead of laughing something indefinable flashed in his eyes. Cal felt her mouth dry up. She waved her coffee cup and brushed the flash of whatever that was away. "I tell them that we both have very busy lives, that you're working."

"Well, that's the truth. I do little else but work. It's the start of the season and I have a young team who need extra practice."

"I saw that you have some new players on board. They any good?"

"If they weren't, they wouldn't be there," Quinn replied. "I might not take much seriously, but I don't mess around with the team."

Cal lifted her eyebrows at his touchy tone. Quinn was normally easygoing, tolerant and charming. Hearing him snap was always a surprise. She understood his frustration. Quinn didn't function well when he was bound by rules, when he felt like he had clipped wings. Wren, the Mavericks' PR whiz, had carefully choreographed every aspect of their fake marriage, from the leaked photographs of their quickie wedding to their appearances on the social scene. Someone having that much control of his personal life would rub Quinn raw.

Their marriage grounded him, but Quinn desperately needed to fly. Unfortunately, he'd been flying too close to the sun for far too long. "It's not forever, Quinn. You'll be rid of me before you know it."

Beneath his beard, Quinn's white teeth flashed. "Honey, I saw more of you via Skype when you were halfway across the world than I do now and you're living on my damn yacht. Though, in some ways, that's not a bad thing."

Okay, she was not touching that cryptic statement with a barge pole. "Maybe you and I need to reconnect, *as friends*. We need to remember that before we were caught up in this craziness, we enjoyed each other's company. Let's make some time try to be who we always were."

And if they managed to reconnect as friends, maybe

this ridiculous need to touch him, to taste him would disappear. God, she could only hope. "When are you free?"

Quinn frowned, thinking. "Tonight I have plans. Tomorrow night I'm having drinks with some potential sponsors. Thursday is poker night."

Once-a-month poker night with Kade and Mac was sacrosanct. Even Brodie, Kade's fiancée, was under strict instructions to not go into labor until Friday morning.

Boys.

"Friday?" Quinn asked, lifting his startling eyes back to her face. God, she loved his eyes.

Friday? *Really?* "That would work except for one little thing."

"What?"

"Friday is the Adam Foundation Masked Ball. It's only the most important social event on the city's calendar."

Quinn pulled a face. "And I suppose I *have* to be there?"

"Q, I'm the official host and you're my husband!"

"I'll be masked. How will they even know that I'm there? I could be anyone," Quinn protested.

"Yeah, there will be so many six-foot-three ripped men there with long blond hair and beards. C'mon, Quinn, you *knew* about this. I sent you an email about it last week."

"Ugh."

"Have you got a mask yet?"

Quinn sent her a get-real look and Cal sighed. Of course he hadn't; he'd heard the words *mask* and *ball* and tuned out. "Leave it to me."

"Plain black, as small as possible," Quinn growled. "Do not make me look like an idiot."

"The point of the masked ball is to be masked, as much as possible. Not knowing who is behind the mask is part of the fun," Cal protested. Knowing that choosing a mask would be pure torture for him, she'd already purchased a plain black affair that covered three quarters of his face. It was, she and Wren agreed, as fussy as Quinn would tolerate. "Relax. Plain black tuxedo, black tie and the mask. That's it."

Quinn made a sound in the back of his throat that sounded like a rhino going into labor. She patted his shoulder and smiled. "Quinn, it's a masked ball, not a root canal."

Quinn reached out and tugged her ponytail. "So what are you wearing?"

Cal looked down into her empty coffee cup, wondering if she should tell him about the dress she'd found in a tiny boutique in Gastown. Maybe not, because she still wasn't sure whether she'd have the guts to wear it. It was a kick-ass dress and not something her husband's friends and acquaintances would expect her to wear.

It would make heads turn and tongues wag and probably not in a good way. But no one would mistake her message: Callahan Adam-Carter had died with her husband, but Cal Adam—or Cal Adam-Rayne to be precise—was back in town. "I'm not sure yet," she hedged.

"Whatever you wear, I know you'll look fantastic. You always do."

Cal tipped her head and flushed at his words. It wasn't an empty compliment or a line. Quinn said the words easily and with conviction. He genuinely believed them. God, it was such a silly thing, but such easy acceptance meant the world to her.

"So what time do you want to leave for the ball?" Quinn asked.

Cal lifted her wrist to look at the face of his high-tech watch. She was going to be late for her early meeting if she didn't get cracking. "I'll find you there, somewhere. I have to be there early to check on everything, so you can get there later. Or come with Mac and Kade. Anyway, I have to go," Cal told him, leaning sideways to place a kiss on his cheek.

She inhaled his scent and instantly felt calmer, his arm under her fingers tight with muscle. God, her best friend—her fake husband—was all heat and harnessed power. Their eyes clashed and an emotion she didn't recognize flashed between them. Quinn's eyes dropped to her mouth and she touched her top lip with the tip of her tongue.

Quinn lifted his hand, bent his head and for one brief, red-hot second Cal thought that he would, finally, give her the kiss she was aching for. She waited, but Quinn just sucked in a harsh-sounding breath, pulled back and abruptly stood up.

Cal bent over to pick up both their cups, stood and walked to the stairs. "I'll see you at the ball, okay?" she said, her voice wobbly as she tossed the words over her shoulder.

"Sure," Quinn answered, sounding absolutely normal. So why did she sense—wish—that he was looking at her butt as she walked away?

It was later in the morning and Mac warbled a horrible version of the "Wedding March" tune as Quinn walked into the conference room at the Mavericks' headquarters. He handed Mac a sour look and frowned at Kade.

"What?" Kade asked, looking confused. "What did I do?"

"You instituted the ban on getting physical anywhere other than the ice or the gym," Quinn complained, dropping his helmet onto the seat of an empty chair. "If it wasn't for you, then I could shut him up."

"You really should see someone about those delusions, dude." Mac smiled.

Standing opposite Mac, Quinn placed his hands flat on the table, leaned across it and got up in his face. "And I swear, if I hear that stupid song one more time, I will rip you a new one, Kade's ban be damned."

Mac just laughed at him. "You can try, bro, you can try. So how is married life?"

Quinn pulled back, blew out his breath and tried to hold onto his temper. He had this conversation at least once a day and he was thoroughly sick of it. *What type of question was that anyway?* he silently fumed. What he and Cal got up to behind closed doors—which was nothing that would make a nun blush—was nobody's business but their own. Yet their marriage fascinated everybody, from his friends to the general public.

And why was Mac asking? He knew that their marriage was as fake as the tooth fairy. Quinn sent Mac an assessing look and decided to play him at his own game. "Actually, Cal and I had hot sex on the deck in the moonlight."

"Seriously?" Mac's face lit up with amusement.

"No, butthead, we didn't." Quinn looked at his helmet and wondered if he could use it to bash some sense into Mac's thick skull. He dropped into a chair, placed his elbows on the table and shoveled his hands into his hair. *"Dude,"* he moaned, feeling a headache brewing, "I don't know how else to explain this to you… Cal and I have been friends since we were in kindergarten. We are not going to sleep together. This is a sham marriage, one we entered to achieve a very specific objective. Remember?"

"What's the point of being hitched if you don't, at the very least, get some fun out of it? And by fun I mean sex."

Quinn didn't respond, knowing that Mac was just looking for a reaction. And they had the temerity to tell him that *he* needed to grow up?

"The point of their marriage was to rehab his reputation and that is going exceptionally well." Wren's cool voice brought a measure of intelligence to their conversation and Quinn could've kissed her.

"Really?" he asked.

Wren sent him a sympathetic smile. "Really. The press has definitely warmed up to you and Bayliss doesn't think you are the spawn of Satan anymore."

"Yay," Quinn said, hiding his relief under sarcasm.

Once he agreed to sell his soul to the devil—aka Wren and her publicity machine—he'd placed his life into Wren's very capable hands. She'd organized every detail of their wedding and made it look like a hasty, romantic, impulsive affair. The woman was damn good. No one suspected that it was a highly orchestrated con.

"And, despite some initial reservations about you and Cal, and how good you will be for her, the public sees your marriage as a positive thing." Wren's eyes left his face and dropped to the sheaf of papers on the table in front of her and Quinn knew there was more she wanted to say and she was debating whether she should or not.

Quinn rubbed the space between his eyebrows. "What, Wren?"

Wren lifted one shoulder in a shrug. "A good portion of the public is just waiting for you to mess it up."

Quinn threw his hands up in the air. "What can I mess up? You've banned me from doing anything that might raise an eyebrow. I'm married so I can't date." Quinn shook his head and looked at the broad band on his left hand. "That sounds insane."

"You do have a knack of complicating the hell out of your life, Rayne," Kade agreed.

That was the thing. He really didn't. His life, as he saw it, was uncomplicated: he went to work, coached the hell out of the Mavericks and got results that nobody expected from a young coach with little experience. So why couldn't they keep their hands, and their opinions, off his personal life? He kept it simple there too: he did what he wanted, when he wanted.

Well, except for this episode of his life. He really hadn't wanted to get married...

You're temporarily *hitched,* temporarily *grounded and for a damn good reason.* When he remembered what was at risk, he would stay married and well-behaved forever if that was what was required of him.

He would not be the reason the deal with Widow Hasselback failed. He would not give Bayliss a reason to pull out of the deal. He'd protect his team, his players, the brand. He'd protect the Mavericks with everything he had.

Because this place, this team, these men were his home. Yeah, technically, he had a family, but he hadn't spoken to any of them for years. A lack of understanding, communication and, okay, kindness had forced him to distance himself from them and it was a decision he did not regret. Kade and Mac, as annoying as they could be, were now his brothers and he would, at some point— *soon!*—go back to thinking of Cal as the sister he'd never had.

Cal, Mac and Kade were all the family he needed— the only family he'd ever have. He wasn't going to risk Cal not being part of his clan, part of his life, by acting on what was a frequent and annoying fantasy of stripping her naked and making her scream.

Quinn scowled up at the ceiling. His simmering attraction to Cal was unexplainable and ludicrous and it would pass—he just had to keep avoiding her as much as possible until it did—and their friendship would survive. This craziness would pass. Everything always did.

Quinn rolled his shoulders and felt like the walls were closing in on him. He imagined himself on his bike, leaning into a corner, the wind blowing his restlessness away.

"Oh, crap, he has that faraway look in his eyes. The one he gets when he's feeling caged in."

Mac's words penetrated Quinn's fog and he snapped his head up to glare at his friend. "What are you talking about?"

"It's one of your tells," Mac informed him. "You get glassy-eyed and we know that you're considering doing something crazy."

"I'm not going to do anything." Quinn pushed the words out. He wanted to. He wanted to burn some of this excess energy off. But he wouldn't. Not today anyway.

"Don't mess up, Rayne. Please don't jeopardize our hard work." Kade's words felt like bullets from a machine gun.

Ben is studying, Quinn. Don't disturb Jack.

Try to be more considerate, Quinn.

Why can't you toe the line, Quinn? Be more like your brothers, Quinn? Why do you have to be so much trouble, Quinn?

It was stupid and crazy and childish, but statements like *don't rock the boat, Quinn* and *be good, Quinn* just made him want to do the opposite. He loathed being told what to do. Quinn bit the inside of his lip and jammed his hands into the pockets of his leather jacket so his friends couldn't see his clenched fists.

He wasn't in control of his own life and he despised it and, yes, Kade was right—he did want to run.

It's not for long, Quinn told himself for the umpteenth time. In six months he could start, to a certain extent, living life on his own terms again.

"Sit your ass down, Rayne, and let's get to work," Kade told him and it took Quinn a moment, or twenty, to obey.

The Adam Foundation's masquerade ball was touted as "A sexy, masked Venetian affair" and Quinn thought most of the guests were taking the suggestion that they come disguised a little too far.

Elaborate wigs and masks effectively hid identities, allowing their wearers the anonymous freedom to indulge in some hard-core flirting and, if they wanted to, to go beyond flirting in the dark corners of the lamp-lit room.

It was behavior he excelled at, reveled in. Behavior he couldn't indulge in because, hell, he was *married*. And finding his wife in this packed ballroom was like looking for a particular piece of hay in a haystack. Full-face masks were the norm and he hoped that Cal hadn't bothered with a wig. Her red hair would be a great way to identify her. Damn, he thought as he turned in a slow circle, he should've insisted on knowing exactly what she intended to wear.

But, in his defense, he was still amazed that he'd been able to carry on any type of conversation that morning on the deck. Cal's tiny barely there shirt and tight shorts just skimming the top of her thighs put his brain in neutral. He'd removed every type of lingerie imaginable—from silky negligees to crotchless panties—from a lot willing female bodies, and her plain, white pajamas hadn't been anything extraordinary. But her in them? *Dynamite*.

Quinn shook his head. This was *Cal* he was thinking about. *Stop it!*

You're only thinking about her, like that, Quinn rationalized, *because you're a red-blooded man and she was wearing next to nothing. And, because you haven't been laid for nearly six weeks, pretty much any woman will do. Even Cal. It's normal. It didn't mean anything.* He had a fake wife; their marriage was a con they were pulling on the world. Nothing between them would change.

Ever.

Quinn adjusted his mask and did another scan of the ballroom. With so many people here, he'd probably only find Cal after they were allowed to remove their masks around midnight. Quinn looked at his watch. Two and a half hours to go.

Hell.

He noticed a bar at the far end of the room and was about to head in that direction when he saw two of his favorite women standing to the left of him. Rory's mask barely covered her eyes and Brodie's huge stomach made identifying them easy.

Making his excuses, he walked over and quickly dropped a kiss on each of their cheeks and he briefly touched Brodie's pronounced baby bump.

"Ladies, you both are looking spectacular," he said, his compliment absolutely heartfelt. He genuinely liked the women his friends were in love with.

"How is my favorite girl?" he asked Rory.

Rory smiled, her eyes softening. Both she and Mac doted on their baby daughter, Rosie, as did they all. "She's fine, at home. Troy is babysitting."

"Good man, Troy," Quinn said, meaning it. He really liked Rory's best friend and the fact that a super-qualified nurse was looking after their precious Rosie made them all feel more at ease. He turned to Brodie and looked down at her bump.

"You look like you've swallowed a bowling ball, Brodes."

"I feel like I've swallowed a bowling ball," Brodie replied, reaching up to touch his smooth jaw. She lifted his mask and sighed before dropping the mask back onto his face. "But let's talk about you, sexy guy. We didn't recognize you until you spoke. Looking hot, Quinn. I very much like the new look."

Oh, yeah, that. Cutting his hair and shaving off his beard had been an impulsive decision. There was a salon next to his dry cleaners and when he'd picked up his tux, he'd popped his head in and saw that the place was empty. He'd intended to trim his hair, shorten his beard, but the stylist, who turned out to be young, pretty and very persuasive, charmed him into going short. He'd agreed, partly because she was cute but also because everything else seemed to be changing in his life so he thought he might as well change his looks too.

In for a penny and all that.

"What prompted the makeover?" Rory asked.

Quinn frowned at her. A makeover? He'd had a haircut and shaved his beard off. Why was she busting his chops? She'd obviously been hanging around Mac for far too long. "It's *not* a makeover."

"It's a dramatic change—long hair to short and spiky, no beard. When you end up looking ten times better—which, I have to point out, should be illegal in your case—it's a makeover." Rory started to lift his mask again, but Quinn gently pushed her hand away. "Those lips, that jaw."

"Those eyes," Brodie added.

Quinn felt the tips of his ears growing hot. He ran a

finger around the edge of his collar. "Will you two stop? Please?" he begged.

"Yeah, please stop," Mac said as he joined them, his arms instantly going around Rory's waist. "I think I might gag."

"He just looks so different," Rory explained. "This new you is, well, hot." She fanned herself.

"Okay, honey, enough now," Mac said, an edge creeping into his voice.

Kade walked up to them with three glasses of champagne and ignored Brodie's dark look when he handed Rory and Kade a glass each and kept one for himself. "Hi, Quinn. Sorry, I didn't know you were here. I've ordered you a sparkling water, honey."

Brodie's frown deepened. "Oh, joy. Can I have a sip of champagne, at least?"

Quinn hid his smile as Kade monitored just how big a sip of alcohol Brodie was taking. When she went in for a second sip, Kade yanked the glass away. "That's enough."

Quinn smiled at Kade's protectiveness. His friends adored their women and Quinn was thrilled that they were so happy. Yet he also felt a little like a third wheel, a thought that would horrify them all. But it wasn't an unfamiliar feeling. In his parents' house he'd always felt on the outside looking in. Despite his ability to shoot the breeze, to charm blood out of a rock, or the panties off nuns, he'd seldom connected on an emotional level with people and shared very little of himself, even with his friends. Not because he didn't trust them—he did—it was just a habit he'd cultivated when he was a kid and one that still served him well.

He wasn't a talker, preferring to work his inner world out on his own. Cal was only the person he'd opened up to as a kid...

Quinn felt the energy in the room change, heard the low buzz of voices that indicated something was happening. He slowly turned and looked toward the door to see a woman walking into the ballroom.

Her dress left him—and every other male in the room—in no doubt as to how close to perfect her body was. If he could actually call what she was wearing a dress. The word *dress* implied fabric and there was little of that. It could only be designer and, like three quarters of the dresses in the room, it was black. Unlike the other dresses, it was ridiculously sexy.

The best way Quinn could think to describe it was that someone had painted her torso with fabric swirls. One started at her neck and covered a breast, while another ran under her arm and across her other breast and covered some of her stomach, meeting in a perfect point at her hip. A slit revealed a long, toned leg ending in a strappy, sky-high black-and-silver sandal. Quinn forced his eyes up and took in the blunt-cut, chin-length, jet-black bob. He could see little of her face beneath the complex gold mask made from feathers, chains, beads and fake gemstones. Gorgeous skin, a pointed chin and lips painted a bright, siren, sexy red completed the picture.

She was exactly his type: sophisticated, sexy, mysterious. Hot enough to melt glass. Yet, she was missing... *something*.

Quinn looked at Mac and then at Kade, deeply amused that their mouths were open and that their eyes had glazed over. He watched, laughing quietly, as Brodie and Rory exchanged eye rolls.

He understood, intellectually, that she was the sexiest thing on two feet and, yeah, if he was single and acting like himself, he definitely would not say no if she suggested a little bed-based fun, but...

The memory of Cal, dressed in her simple white pajamas, sporting a messy head of red curls and sleepy, dark eyes, was infinitely more tempting and so much sexier than the smokin' body in a barely-there dress.

It was official—along with his long hair and his beard, he'd also lost his mind. No, Cal was *not* sexier than this babe. Cal was *not* sexy at all. She was his friend! Friends and sexy did *not* go together.

"I so need a drink," Quinn muttered. Or a brain transplant.

He barely felt Brodie's hand on his arm, didn't realize that she was trying to get his attention until her nails dug into his skin.

"I wanted to tell you how much I enjoyed meeting Callahan," Brodie said, her expression sincere. "She's so down-to-earth."

Oh, yeah, right. He remembered hearing something about Rory and Brodie inviting Cal to lunch last week. Quinn flicked another glance at the hot woman—she was definitely worth another look—before answering. "She always has been. Despite their wealth, her parents are too. Well, her dad is. Her mom passed away a long time ago."

"And you've known each other all your lives?" Rory asked.

Quinn nodded. "I met her when I was eight. She lived a few doors down from me. For the next decade I treated her home like mine."

Rory sipped her wine, interested. She looked around, made sure that no one outside the group could hear her question. "And there's never been anything between you?"

Quinn tossed his hands up, frustrated. "You've definitely been living with Mac for too long. We're friends. We've always been friends. Why does everyone keep asking that?"

Rory, the meddler, just smiled at his heated response. "Maybe, my darling Quinn, it's because it's a question that always gets a heated reaction from you."

"I *definitely* need a drink," Quinn growled. He leaned forward and dropped his voice. "Fake marriage. Friends. Nothing has changed. Status quo. What else can I say to convince you? Should I go over and flirt with Miss Swirls over there to prove it to you?"

Quinn flicked a look across the room and noticed that her back was to him. That view was almost as luscious as the front, just acres of creamy skin from the base of her neck to low on her buttocks. Whoever designed that dress had to have a degree in engineering because Quinn hadn't the foggiest idea how it was attached to her body. When he went over to talk to her, to flirt with her—he was still allowed to flirt, wasn't he?—he'd try to work out how it all stayed tidy.

Kade's laugh rolled over him. "Sure, go ahead if that's what you want to do. But maybe, *possibly*, it's not *us* you're trying to convince."

Four

Her *husband* had stood her up, Cal realized, standing in the shadows on the terrace, taking a break from the busy ballroom. It was past eleven and she'd yet to find Quinn.

Okay, there were two hundred men at the ball, but it wasn't like Quinn, masked or not, would be hard to find. Long hair, heavy beard, taller and broader than most. She hoped he made an appearance by midnight. People would be expecting him to stand at her side when she thanked her guests for attending, when she called for their masks to be removed. If he wasn't, then there would be questions—questions neither of them needed, especially since the world seemed to be buying their fake marriage and the interest in their personal lives seemed to be waning.

From the shadows, Cal had an unrestricted view of the ballroom and she scanned the room, idly noticing that the dance floor was packed. Nope, couldn't see him... *Dammit, Rayne!*

She did another slow scan of the room, ostensibly to look for Quinn but knowing that she wouldn't mind taking another long look at the guy she'd been trading glances with all evening. She first noticed him early in the evening, soon after she arrived, and while she couldn't really make out his features—*damn these masks!*—she instinctively knew that he was six foot something of coiled power, radiating testosterone, heat and… God, sex.

Hot, messy, slow, dirty, *sexy* sex.

The kind of sex she'd never experienced since all her lovers had been more of the this-is-about-me-not-you type. And Toby had been their king.

Jerk…

Anyway, she was just so grateful that she felt sexually attracted to someone besides Quinn. That proved to her that her long dormant libido had come out of hibernation and she was attracted to good-looking men in general and not Quinn in particular. Her lust wasn't directed at Quinn specifically so that was a relief.

Such a relief.

Cal inhaled the gently fragranced night air. She'd escaped to the balcony partly because she needed a time-out but mostly because she'd felt Hot Guy's eyes on her at various times during the evening. It started with a prickle between her shoulder blades and then heat traveled from her coccyx up her spine and she knew that HG was looking at her, that he was the reason for the sudden bump of her heart, the fact that the air had disappeared from the room. She'd turn and, yeah, as she suspected, he'd been looking at her. Yet he never made a move to approach her; he'd just kept his brooding, intense gaze on her.

Animal magnetism—she suddenly understood that concept. Totally, absolutely, innately. It didn't matter that she hadn't seen his face, heard him speak—those details were inconsequential. All she knew was that she wanted to get her hands on that body, to explore that wide chest, those big shoulders, the muscles of those long, long legs.

Her attraction to him and, she supposed, to Quinn made her feel happy. The throb between her legs and the flutter in her stomach made her feel normal again. For the first time in Vancouver, in nearly a decade, she felt strong and confident and in control. During her marriage, events like this had felt like minefields and she'd tiptoed her way through the evening, fumbling her way to the end. She constantly monitored her words, checked her responses, made sure that nothing she did or said could cause offense.

Amazing what a few years and being Toby-free could do, Cal thought. She was wearing a dress that Toby would never have allowed her to wear, had slapped on siren-red lipstick that he would've hated and she'd spent the evening gently flirting with every man who'd approached her. She'd had *fun*.

Cal heard the beat from the band and as the vocalist belted out the first line of a new song, she shimmied her hips, lifting her shoulders in a sensuous roll.

Dancing alone, in the moonlight, Callahan?

She heard Toby's sneering voice in her head and smiled as she raised her arms over her head and did a slow, sexy, shimmery twirl.

Yep. It's my ball and I can dance if I want to...

Big hands landed on her waist and spun her around. She sucked in an astounded breath but didn't resist when Hot Guy walked backward, stopping when her back rested against the cool wall behind her.

Cal's eyes widened as his long form pushed her into the stone and blocked out all the light in this already dark corner. She could taste his breath—whiskey and peppermint—and her heart threatened to climb out of her chest. She should be scared, she thought, but she wasn't. She was just utterly, comprehensively turned on.

"You smell like wildflowers...*ah, crap*!"

God, she recognized that voice; she knew that voice as well as she knew her own. *"Quinn?"*

So Hot Guy was Quinn and her libido, dammit, was still only attracted to one guy, the *wrong* guy.

Quinn's curse flew over her head, but she didn't care. She didn't want to think about who he was, *what* he was. His hands on her hips made her heart race; his thigh between her legs made her hot. She'd never wanted anyone's lips over hers as much as she wanted his, here on this terrace with four hundred people inside dancing and chatting.

The moment hung, heavy with expectation, vibrating with intensity. Caught up in passion and in the fantasy of the moment, she put her fingers on his lips and shook her head, not wanting the fantasy to evaporate.

They were both masked and they could pretend... God, she needed to pretend.

"Kiss me."

Cal couldn't see his expression beneath his mask and it was too dark to see the emotion in his eyes. She felt his hesitation and worried that he would back off, that he'd yank them back to reality, to their lives. When his mouth softened and his thumb drifted over her ribs, she knew that he was as tempted as she was, that she wasn't the only one wanting to visit Fantasy Land.

He finally ducked his head and his mouth hovered over hers, teasing, tempting. She waited, knowing he would get to it, in his own time. He wasn't a man who could be rushed and she didn't want him to. She wanted the anticipation, the headiness, the bubble, the fizz. She wanted it all.

Minutes, hours, eons later, he lowered his head and his mouth brushed hers. Her hands trembled as she pushed her fingers into his hair. His fingertips dug into the bare skin at her waist, and by their own volition her hands parted his jacket to touch the muscles at his waist, to echo his hold on her.

As he kissed her, as she lost herself in him, the world faded away, melting in the joy his mouth created. In this moment, as his mouth invaded hers, she wasn't the good girl, Cauley's daughter, the do-gooder with the sterling reputation. She wasn't the heiress, the widow, the fake wife, the princess.

She was Cal. Quinn holding her was all that was important. When they kissed, her world, for the first time in far too long, made sense. Here in this moment, there was perfect clarity, absolute understanding...of everything.

Then the universe shifted as he pushed his hips into hers, rocking his long erection into her stomach. Now his kisses weren't enough and she made a sound of desperation deep in her throat, groaning as his hand left her hip to cover her breast, his thumb finding her nipple and teasing it to a point that was almost painful. In response she dropped her hand and tried to encircle him, frustrated by the barrier of his pants.

Quinn murmured something, his words too low to make out, but she knew they were hot and encouraging so she fumbled for the zipper of his fly as he pushed away the clingy fabric covering her right breast to reveal her bare skin. Then his amazing lips sucked her bottom lip into his mouth and she stumbled on her heels, utterly off balance. A broad hand on her butt kept her upright and his other hand dipped into the slit high on her thigh, found the tiny triangle of her thong and pushed the silk aside. As he touched her intimately, knowingly, she found him, long and hot and jerking with need. She rubbed his tip and he stroked her clit and she started to free-fall…

"Please, please, please. Don't stop," she begged, arching her back as he pulled her nipple against the roof of his mouth. She needed him to push her over the edge, needed him to take her there…to that magical place that had always, always been just out of her reach. "That feels so damn amazing. God…"

It took Cal a little while to realize that he had, in fact, stopped, that he was statue-still, that his fingers had stopped creating magic and that his mouth had left her breast. It was a couple more seconds before it sank in that his fingers were leaving her body, that he'd—

That he'd stopped at a crucial point. He was going to leave her high and dry and throbbing with need.

What? Why? What had happened? Cal sucked in air, trying to get her bearings, trying to get her noodle-like knees to lock.

When she thought she could put words together, she looked up at him, adjusting her mask so she could see through the slit-like holes. "Why did you stop?"

"Because making love to my best friend up against a wall just outside a ballroom with her guests inside was never part of the freakin' deal!"

Twenty seconds ago he'd had Cal's nipple in his mouth, his fingers on her—oh, God, he couldn't go there. He'd been a minute away from pushing her dress up to her hips and sliding home. He'd been lost, in the best way possible, in the heat of her—deaf, dumb, blind and crazy with lust…

For Cal!

For his best friend!

Quinn stepped away from Cal, zipped up his pants and pulled his stupid mask from his face, throwing it onto the floor at their feet. He heard Cal's gasp and looked at her through narrowed eyes. She'd pushed her mask up into her wig and he saw desire blazing from her eyes.

He felt the jerk in his pants and closed his eyes. He still wanted her, still wanted to take the…the…*situation* to its natural conclusion. Judging by her rapid breathing and her squirming, so did she.

He was not about to take Callahan up against a wall. He wanted to, but he wouldn't.

And the frustrations just kept rolling in, Quinn thought, pushing his fingers through his short hair. He walked away to grip the edge of the balcony, trying to get his labored breathing under control. He was only out here because he was annoyed at not finding Callahan in the ballroom, frustrated because he wanted to see her, talk to her, laugh with her.

Bothered because his thoughts kept wandering to his fake wife, and wondering where she was, he'd deliberately turned his attention to Swirls and, admittedly, that hadn't been a hardship. He'd hoped that she'd distract him from his current obsession with his fake wife.

She hadn't, so, needing a break from the perfume-scented air inside, he'd wandered onto the balcony. When he saw Swirls swaying in the moonlight, he'd stepped up to her, thinking he'd dance with her, needing distraction from the bubbling sexual tension and frustration living with Red caused.

Then all hell broke loose…

"You shaved your beard, cut your hair," Cal whispered, her fingers against her mouth. "I didn't recognize you."

Quinn placed his hands behind his head and stomped down the terrace, staring into space. He didn't like feeling so off balance so he took refuge in an emotion he did understand: angry frustration. He spun around and glared at her. "So you allowed a stranger to put his hands on you? Do you know how dangerous that is? God, I could've been anyone! A predator! A rapist!"

Cal's mouth fell open. "Are you seriously lecturing me? Right now?"

Quinn was about to respond when he realized that her right breast—her perfect, perfect breast—was still on show, the fabric of her dress pulled to the side. He dropped his hands and waved his hand in the general direction of her torso. "Will you please cover up?"

Cal looked down and gasped. She hastily pulled the fabric back in place and he almost groaned in disappointment.

"You don't need to be such a jerk," Cal muttered.

"You don't need to be so damn tempting," Quinn retorted without thinking. He closed his eyes and tipped his head back, praying for sanity. Or a lightning strike. Or a time machine to roll them back to an hour ago, to earlier in the evening, to birth.

Except that he couldn't quite regret kissing Callahan. Kissing Cal had been...man, so wonderful. Even worse was the fact that he wanted to do it again, and so much more. God, he was in trouble.

"Let's take a couple of breaths and calm down." Quinn rolled his head in order to release the knots of tension in his neck and when he felt marginally calmer, he spoke again.

"Look, Red—" he deliberately used his childhood nickname for her "—the fact remains that you're you and this was...wrong."

Well, not wrong per se but wrong for them. They were best friends. He didn't want to lose her. Lose that.

"Wrong?"

Quinn ran a finger around the edge of his collar and wondered where all the air had gone. Damn, if this was anyone else, he'd have managed to charm his way out of this situation, but she wasn't a stranger and he was living with her, *married to her*. Fake married but still...

"Well, not wrong but...weird."

"Weird?"

Why did she keep throwing his words back in his face?

Quinn shook his head and prayed for patience. He was trying to think, dammit! But his brain refused to work properly because it was still processing how Cal felt, tasted...

He took a step forward, wanting to kiss her again and abruptly stopped. Closing his eyes, Quinn told his libido that finishing what they'd started would be a very bad idea.

Very, very crazy-bad idea.

Sleeping with her would be the equivalent of dousing the friendship bridge with napalm before igniting it with a surface-to-missile rocket.

Best friend, living together, fake wife. The complications were crazy.

He needed to fix this, now, immediately. And to do that he'd have to stay calm—and keep his hands off her—because the situation was amped enough without any more drama.

He needed a joke. He and Cal had always been able to laugh together. It would be a way to lighten the mood.

Except that he couldn't think of anything remotely funny to say. And God, this silence was becoming even more awkward. And tense. And...hot. Cal gnawed her bottom lip and placed her hand behind her back and inadvertently lifted her chest and he wished that she hadn't covered up.

Okay, he *had* to get them back on track. "Look, I don't want this to cause awkwardness between us."

"I think we are way beyond awkward, Quinn."

"I'm sorry." It was all he could think of to say.

Cal drilled him with an intense look. "What, exactly, are you sorry for?"

Quinn covered his eyes with a hand and rubbed his eyes. "Why can't you see that I'm just trying to not make the biggest mistake of my life, Cal?"

He dropped his hand, blinked and his heart felt like it was in free fall as he waited for her response. And when she spoke again, she sliced his heart in two. "Of all the mistakes you've made, and you've got to admit that there have been some zingers, I'm devastated that you think that almost making love to me was your biggest."

Quinn watched Cal walk away and wished he could find the words to explain that his friendship with her was, possibly, the only thing he'd ever done right. That was the reason why making love to her would be such a mistake. He couldn't risk losing the best, purest relationship he had in his life for a quick orgasm.

Orgasms were easy to find; somebody who understood him wasn't.

Cal kept a healthy distance between her and Quinn as they walked down the dock toward his yacht. Cal looked to her left and saw that Quinn was staring straight ahead, his jaw tight.

They hadn't exchanged a word since leaving the ballroom and the silence between them was heavy and saturated with tension. They'd had their fights before—all friends did—but this situation wasn't that simple.

It wasn't simple at all.

She'd had her hand around his… Cal lifted her hands and rubbed them over her face, no longer concerned about dislodging her wig or smearing her makeup. She'd had her hand in his pants…

Cal shivered again and this time it wasn't from humiliation; it was because she wanted to touch him again. That and more. She wanted to kiss him, needed to feel his mouth on her breasts, needed to feel that pulsing build between her legs. She wanted him to take her over the edge, to make her scream as he filled her, stretched her.

Cal groaned and stumbled. Quinn grabbed her bare elbow and his fingers dug into her skin and Cal just managed to keep her frustrated moan behind her teeth. She stopped walking and stared at the ground, not wanting him to see her face because if he did, he would know how much she still wanted him, how close she was to begging—*begging!*—him to finish what he started.

"Are you okay?" Quinn, asked, his voice low.

Cal nodded, conscious that his hand was still holding her arm and sending sparks through her. "Fine."

"You're cold." Quinn placed his hands on her bare upper arms and rubbed her skin and Cal had to stop herself from purring. "Where is your coat?"

She had no idea. In his car? At the ball? Who knew? "Uh…"

Quinn shrugged out of his tuxedo jacket and draped it around her shoulders. Cal pulled her wig off, handed it to Quinn and pushed her arms into the sleeves of his jacket, still warm from his body. His scent—sandalwood and citrus—mingled with the smell of the sea and she felt that buzz in her womb again, was conscious of the beat of butterfly wings in her stomach. God, she was definitely going off the deep end.

She heard Quinn's heavy sigh. "Let's get home, Red. It's been a hell of an evening."

It really had. Cal folded her arms across her chest, bunching the fabric of his beautifully tailored, designer jacket. They continued in silence, climbed the steps to the main deck and Cal waited while Quinn unlocked the sliding doors and flipped on some lights. She stepped inside and shrugged off her shoes. She slipped off his jacket and handed it to him, aware that his eyes seemed to be taking a long time to move off her chest. She looked down and was thankful to see that everything was properly covered up.

But Quinn still seemed fascinated by her dress.

"That dress. It's a damned miracle I can string a sentence together," Quinn drawled, his eyes hot but his expression rueful as he dropped his jacket on top of her mask and wig. "There were more than a few eyebrows raised when your guests realized that you were behind that getup."

"I assumed there would be," Cal told him, heading for the kitchen. Leaving the lights off, she opened the fridge and pulled out a bottle of water and lifted it up in a silent offer. Quinn nodded and she pulled out another one, handed it to him. Quinn, always a gentleman, cracked the lid, handed the bottle back to her before opening his own. Cal sipped and looked at the inky water outside, lights from skyscrapers behind them tossing golden ribbons across the water.

"Want to explain that?" Quinn asked, taking a seat across the island from her, his elbows on the granite.

In the light spilling from a lamp she took her first long look at Quinn, clean-shaven and sexy. His beard was no longer a distraction; she could see the line of his strong jaw, the smooth skin of his neck, the tiny dimple in his right cheek, the scar on his top lip. She'd given him that scar, she remembered. She'd smacked him with a metal photo frame for dismembering four of her favorite Barbie dolls.

It had taken three weeks for her to talk to him again. At seven, she'd been more stubborn than most.

"By the way, I like seeing your face." She tipped her head. "But you'd look better with some stubble."

That was the type of comment Cal-his-friend would make, the Cal she was trying to be.

Quinn ran his hand over his smooth jaw. "Thanks. It's a change. And why do I suspect that you are trying to change the subject?"

Cal sighed. She'd forgotten that Quinn wasn't that easily distracted. "Back to my dress, huh?"

"Would you prefer to talk about what happened on the terrace?" Quinn asked, his voice low but resolute.

Cal scrunched her nose. "No," she admitted. She wanted to do it again, but she most certainly did not want to talk about it.

"Then back to the dress," Quinn told her, looking determined. And remote and nothing like the crazy-with-need man who'd kissed her with such skill on the terrace. Where had he gone? She'd like him back.

"Though we will have to discuss what happened between us at some point."

"Does never work for you?" Cal asked, feeling the heat rise up her neck.

Quinn just sent her a steady look and her shoulders slumped.

"You were never very good at being an ostrich," Cal complained. "Sometimes you've just got to shove your head in the sand and wait for the storm to pass over."

"Not the way I work, Red," Quinn said. "So, your dress. I think you wore it to make a statement."

"And what statement might that be?" Cal demanded.

He was perceptive and so damn smart. Oh, she knew he didn't think so; he'd been compared to his brilliant brothers all his life and that made him think that he was less than. Unlike them, he wasn't a genius, but he had something his brothers didn't: the ability to read people, to look below the surface and work out what made people tick. Quinn was intelligent, but, more than that, he was street-smart.

"Your dress was a declaration of independence, a way to tell the world that you are your own person, fully adult and fully responsible. That you are, finally, making your own choices."

Yeah, *that*. Her dress had also been a silent way for her to send a message to Toby's world that she wasn't the polite, meek pushover she once was. It was her act of rebellion, years overdue, and she didn't regret her choice.

Dancing in the dark, allowing a stranger to put his hands on her, had been another little rebellion, her way to walk on the wild side. Except that the stranger wasn't a stranger...

Cal placed her elbows on the cool granite of the island and massaged her temples with the tips of her fingers. Why couldn't she stop thinking about his lips on hers, the way he tasted—sexy, dark, sinful?

"God, Cal, don't look at me like that," Quinn begged, his fists clenched at his sides. "This is hard enough as it is."

"I've never been attracted to you in my life. Why now?" Cal moaned.

"I'm choosing to believe that it was because it was a masked ball and because everyone is encouraged to misbehave," Quinn replied, his voice sounding strangled.

Cal lifted her head and met his eyes. "So if I walk around the island and kiss you, you're going to push me away and tell me that the attraction only lasted as long as we were masked and in the dark?"

Quinn stared at her and she saw the thin line of his lips, watched his eyes narrow. She knew that he was considering whether to lie to her, to tell her exactly that. He opened his mouth and the lie hovered between them, silent but powerful. Then his shoulders slumped and he rubbed his big hand over his face.

"I want to say that," he admitted, his voice rough. "But I've never lied to you and I won't start now."

"And?"

Quinn stared up at the ceiling. "I want you, but I don't want to want you. So what are we going to do about this, Callahan?"

Well, frankly, she'd like to get naked and hit the nearest horizontal surface and let him rocket her to an orgasm. She'd been so close on the terrace and she still felt unsettled, grumpy… She sighed. Unfulfilled. Horny.

Cal wanted to suggest one night—one crazy, hot, steamy, uninhibited night of passion. They had a few hours until the sun came up, before life intruded and they could spend that time exploring their attraction, giving and taking pleasure. They could step out of their friendship and pretend the past and the future didn't exist, live entirely for the moment. Wasn't that what you were supposed to do? Carpe diem and all that? The past was gone and the future was still on its way…

They could start off with her sitting on this island and then they could move onto that blocky couch. After that they could shower together; she'd seen his massive shower—all sorts of things could happen in that oversized space. Then they could nap before he woke her up for round three, or four…

"I think we should go to bed, separately, and get our heads on straight. Forget this ever happened."

Cal's eyebrows slowly pulled together as she made sense of his words. That sounded suspiciously like she wasn't going to get lucky. Not tonight or anytime soon. There would be no couch or shower or nakedness and definitely no orgasms.

Forget this happened? How was she supposed to do that? He'd had his hand between her legs, for God's sake!

"Sex is easy, Cal. Friendship is not. I'm not tossing a lifetime of memories away because we want to scratch an itch. This stops here, tonight. We are friends and we are not going to color outside the lines."

Cal blinked. She definitely wasn't getting lucky tonight, dammit.

"Uh…okay?" It definitely wasn't okay! There was nothing remotely okay about this stupid situation!

"We're going to forget this ever happened. We're going to wake up tomorrow morning and we're going back to being friends, easy with each other, the way we've been for the last twenty years. Clear?"

Cal glared at him. "Stop being bossy. I heard you the first time. You don't want me and we're going back to being friends."

"I never said I didn't want you!" Quinn threw up his hands and climbed off his stool, slapping his hands on his waist before dropping his head to stare at the floor. He always did that when he thought that his temper was slipping away, when he felt like he was losing control of the situation. Good, she wanted him to lose control. She wanted his reassurance that she wasn't the only one whose world had been rocked by their kiss, by the passion that had flared—unexpectedly but white-hot—between them.

"Go to bed, Cal," Quinn said. "Please. I don't want us to do something we'll regret. Sex has a way of changing everything, of complicating lives. My life is complicated enough and I'm trying to do the right thing here. Please, I'm begging you, go to bed."

Her libido, long neglected, whimpered in protest, but her brain, slowly regaining control, insisted that he was right, that she had to be sensible. Cal pursed her lips, hitched up her skirt and walked away. Being sensible, she decided, was no fun at all.

Five

Quinn watched Callahan run down the stairs to the lower deck and when he heard her bedroom door slam shut, he grabbed his jacket and slipped into the night. He walked to the promenade, the popular walkway empty at this late hour. Most of the boats were dark, he noticed as he shoved his hands into the pockets of his pants. Ignoring the bite of the wind and the mist brushing his face with wet fingers, he walked to the nearest pier. At the end of the pier he rested his arms on the railing and took a deep breath of the cold, briny air. Three in the morning, the loneliest, most honest hour of the day, he thought.

Situation report, Quinn decided. He'd friend-zoned Callahan. He'd said no to some hot, bedroom-based fun with the woman he liked best in the world. He was as proud of himself as he was pissed off. Was he out of his mind? Or was he, for once, thinking with his big brain?

A little of both, he admitted, staring at the awesome

views of the Vancouver skyline. He had the same views from his yacht, but because he didn't trust himself not to run down to her room and sneak into bed with her and lose himself in the wonder that was Callahan, he was standing on a dock freezing his ass off instead.

Resigned to the fact that he was going to be cold for a little while still, Quinn watched the lights reflecting off the water and tried to make sense of the evening, trying not to imagine how it would feel to explore that luscious mouth, how she would look after he peeled that sinful dress off her equally sinful body...

Quinn's groan bounced off the water and he gripped the railing, dropping his head between his taut arms. He couldn't, shouldn't, wouldn't. Apart from what he had with Mac and Kade, his friendship with Callahan was the only relationship in his life that was pure, uncomplicated, based entirely on who he was as a person and not on who people expected him to be.

The rest of the world saw the pieces of him he allowed them to see. Depending on whom he was with, he could be the charming rogue, the life and soul of the party, the daredevil adventurer, the tough and focused coach.

Cal saw the big picture of who he was and he, in turn, knew what made her tick, understood what drove her. Well, he had up until she got engaged to her now-dead husband.

Quinn's hands tightened on the railing. He still had no idea why she'd married Carter and why she still, to this day, refused to discuss him. Carter was firmly off-limits and Quinn wondered why. It wasn't like Cal to keep things to herself.

Then again, Carter had always been a touchy subject between them. From the first moment Quinn heard she was dating the forty-year-old businessman, he'd mishandled his reaction. He'd told her, in fairly salty language, that Carter was an idiot and that she needed to have her head examined. Cal had told him to keep his opinions to himself. He'd tried, but when they announced their engagement, he'd told her, stupidly, that he wouldn't watch her throw her life away and that if she married Carter, he was walking out of her life. In his youth and arrogance he'd thought that nothing could come between them, that their friendship was that solid, that important.

She'd married Carter anyway.

Carter, her marriage and his death were still taboo subjects. Was it because the pain ran too deep? Because Carter was—God forbid—her one true love, someone who couldn't be replaced? Quinn hoped not. Unlike him, she wasn't cut out to be alone, to flit from casual affair to casual affair, from bed to bed.

Hearing that it was extremely unlikely that he'd ever be able to father a child—amazing what routine blood tests could kick up!—just cemented his resolve to be alone, to choose when and how he interacted with people, with women. He'd trained himself not to think about what he couldn't have—a wife, a family—and he'd never allowed himself to take a relationship further than a brief affair. What was the point? It couldn't go anywhere…

But being attracted to someone who knew him so well scared him.

Cal was an essential part of his ragtag, cobbled-together family and you did not mess with family. She was his best friend and you did not try and play games with something that had worked so well for so long. You did not break what worked…

It did not matter if she had a body to die for and a mouth made for sin. It didn't matter that their kiss had been hotter than hell, that he'd been rocked to the soles of his feet. That he'd never felt so...

Quinn closed his eyes. He'd never felt so out of touch with himself, so caught up in the moment. A bomb could've dropped next to him and he wouldn't have noticed and that...well...freaked him out. Callahan—dark eyes and a steaming-hot body, the only woman he'd ever kissed who made him forget who he was, who made the world recede, caused his brain to shut down as soon as their lips met—was an impulse he could not act on, a risk he could not take. Because he could not, *would not* mess with the only family he had...especially when he'd never been part of the one he'd originally been given and he was unable to create his own.

Fact number one: Quinn was a good-looking guy.

Fact number two: he was a superbly talented kisser.

Fact number three: he was her best friend.

Fact number four: she'd acted like an idiot last night. Worse, she'd acted like a desperate puckbunny who'd throw her mother under a bus to get it on with a Maverick.

She was mortified.

Cal wiped the perspiration off her face with the back off her wrist and waited for her heart rate to drop. She'd pushed herself jogging this morning, trying to outrun her embarrassment. It hadn't worked. Now she had to face the music. Frankly, she'd rather have her eyes pecked out by a starving vulture.

If she was really, really lucky, then Quinn would've left the yacht already to do whatever he did on Saturday mornings and she could delay the inevitable for twelve or fourteen hours or so.

Cal heard the hiss of the coffeemaker, the bang of a cupboard door and realized that bitch Luck was laughing at her. Maybe if Cal slipped her trainers off, she could sneak past him...

Cal sighed. Running away from a situation—or running into another situation because she was running away from another—was how she made things worse. She was a grown-up, and she faced life head-on. She took responsibility for her actions, for her choices, for her life.

But she just didn't want to, not this morning. Cal lifted her foot to take off her trainers.

"Avoiding me, Red?"

Busted. Cal stared down at her multicolored trainers and eventually lifted her eyes to meet his. He was wearing his inscrutable mask, but his eyes expressed his wariness and more than a little confusion.

"Morning. How did you sleep?" Cal asked with false cheeriness.

Quinn lifted one mocking eyebrow. "About as well as you did."

Which would be not at all. If she had the same blue stripes under her eyes as Quinn did, then there wasn't enough makeup in the world that could do damage control.

"Coffee?" Quinn asked.

"Please."

Cal walked over to the window and placed her hand on the glass, looking at the low, gray clouds. The wind whipped up little peaks of white on the waves and, under her feet, the yacht rocked. She longed for a day of pure sunshine and she felt a sudden longing for a clear, hot day in Africa, the sun beating down on her shoulders, the shocking blue sky.

Quinn cleared his throat and she turned to see him holding out a mug. Cal took it and her eyes widened when a zing of pleasure shot through her as their fingers connected.

Their attraction hadn't dissipated in the cold light of morning.

Dammit.

Quinn leaned his shoulder into the glass and stared broodingly out of the window, his mouth a grim line. "We have a problem."

Of course they did.

Cal took a large sip of coffee before wrapping her hands around the mug. "What now?"

Quinn gestured to his tablet on the island. "Your dress caused a stir with the press."

Oh, that. Cal looked at the large clock on the wall behind him. "I haven't even had breakfast yet and you've been online already?"

Quinn snorted. "As if. No, Wren emailed me the highlights. That woman is a machine."

"I'd say," Cal replied. "So, what are they saying about my dress?"

"A lot. Some columnists said it was good to see you pushing the envelope. Others said it was too much. One suggested it was a dress more suited for a…" Quinn's words trailed off and he looked uncomfortable.

Ah, she'd expected that too. "A hooker?"

"A high-class one," Quinn clarified.

Like that made a difference.

"It was on the Celeb Chaser blog. Don't read the article—it was vicious."

"Give me the highlights," Cal demanded, her coffee sloshing in her stomach.

"You looked like a slut. Carter would be so embarrassed to see you like that. You're a disgrace to his name." Quinn scowled. "It also mentioned your dress is the first indication that my dissolute lifestyle is rubbing off on you."

Come on, how could anyone be rude enough to write that? "Moron," Cal stated, rolling her eyes.

"I'll get my lawyers to demand they write a retraction," Quinn told her, his lips thin with displeasure.

"I appreciate the gesture, but it's not worth the time or the effort," Cal said. "Were you embarrassed by what I wore?"

She didn't give a damn about Toby and his opinions—being dead, he had no say in anything she did or thought anymore. But she did care what Quinn thought. She'd always trusted his judgment. Had she gone a little overboard in an effort to assert her independence?

Quinn looked puzzled. "Are you really asking me if I was embarrassed to be seen with you wearing that dress?"

Well, yes. Cal nodded, hesitant.

"Why the hell would I be? Yeah, it was—let's call it minimalist—but you looked incredibly sexy." Quinn's mouth tipped up at the corners. "Hence me kissing the hell out of you on the terrace. I just wanted to get you out of it."

Cal waved his words away. "Okay, I get that, but was it too much?" She took a deep breath. "Did I look, well, tarty?"

Quinn's smile was a delicious mixture of reassurance and male appreciation. "Red, you don't have a tarty bone in your body. You are all class, no matter what you wear."

Something hot and wicked arced between them and Cal found herself looking at his mouth, licking her lips. His eyes turned a deeper green, heated by desire, and she knew he was mentally stripping her, his hands on her skin, his mouth tasting her. God, she wanted him. Quinn broke their stare and she heard his long, frustrated sigh.

"Something else caught the press's attention last

night," Quinn said. His worried voice broke the tense, sexually charged silence between them.

In the past eight hours, she'd kissed and groped her best friend and they'd upset the apple cart that was their relationship. She'd had no sleep and she wasn't sure how much more she could take.

Cal hauled in a deep breath and rolled her hand. "Hit me."

"Some reports are questioning whether there is trouble in paradise."

"Our paradise? Meaning our marriage?" Cal clarified. Of course there was trouble in paradise but nobody should realize that but them. "Did they catch us groping on the terrace?"

"There's nothing too unusual about a man and wife getting hot and heavy, Callahan. If anything, that would've reinforced the fact that we are crazy about each other."

Oh. True. Cal wrinkled her nose, puzzled. "Then what?"

"I didn't join you on the stage when you gave your thank-you speech. When you told the guests that they could take their masks off, I was, apparently, scowling at you and looking less than happy. And we didn't dance and weren't as affectionate as we usually are toward each other."

Cal thought back and realized the reporters were right. She and Quinn usually had no problem touching each other. They'd always been affectionate. It meant nothing for her to hold his hand, for him to put his arm around her waist, to tuck her into his side. They enjoyed each other's company and the world noticed that. Toby had certainly noticed and he'd loathed her friendship with Quinn.

Last night, she and Quinn—after leaving the terrace with the memory of what they'd done fresh in their minds—hadn't known how to act around each other. She'd been both angry and turned on, both discombobulated and annoyed, and she knew Quinn well enough to know that, behind his cool facade, he was as unsettled as she was. The easiest course of action—the only way to get through the rest of the evening—was to ignore each other, to pretend they hadn't just tried to swallow each other whole.

"We have no choice but to ride the storm. And, according to Wren, that means arranging another outing to show the world that we are happy and in love and that all is well with our world," Quinn stated quietly.

A raindrop hit the window and Cal watched it run down the glass. "Except it's not."

"Yeah, but nobody knows that but us," Quinn stated. "We have to do this, Cal. We can't back out now."

She had to ask, she had to find out where they stood. "And what about last night? What do we do about what happened on the terrace?"

"That," Quinn said behind gritted teeth. "Now *that* we are going to simply ignore."

Quinn sat on the corner of Wren's desk, picked up her pen and twisted it through his fingers as Wren typed. After five minutes, she leaned back in her chair and crossed her legs.

"They can take potshots at me, Wren, but saying that Cal looked like a hooker is not, and never will be, acceptable," Quinn stated, still fuming despite the fact that it was Monday and he'd had the weekend to work through his anger. "I want them to write a retraction or else I will sue them for libel."

Wren placed her hand on his knee and gave it a reassuring squeeze. "Hon, you know that won't work and that it will just add fuel to the fire. Let it go."

He couldn't. He'd seen the worry in Cal's eyes when she'd asked him whether her dress had been inappropriate, had seen that she was questioning her taste, her own judgment. He was so angry that one article—two hundred badly written words—had caused her to question herself.

"Trust me, there's nothing you can do and you reacting to it is exactly what they want you to do." Wren patted his knee again.

Quinn knew she was right and that still irritated the hell out of him. He wasn't the type to walk away. He always preferred action to negotiation, doing to thinking. "Do you know who this Celeb Chaser is?" he asked, still not ready to let it go.

Wren didn't answer him. "Do you want what's best for Cal?" she demanded, her feminine face turning tough.

What kind of question was that? She knew he did.

"Not responding, in any way, to this article is what's best for Cal," Wren told him. "And that's not negotiable."

Wren just cocked her head when his curse bounced off the wall. Quinn swiped his palm across his face and sent her an apologetic look. "Sorry. Frustrated."

"Sure you are, but I don't think it's the article that's the true source of your frustration."

When he didn't ask her what she was implying, Wren shrugged. "So, I made reservations at Sylvie's for eight tonight for you and Cal. After Sylvie's, you are going dancing at Beat. Try to look like you are having fun, like you are in love. We need the press to believe that."

Beat? He'd never heard of it and he thought he knew all of the trendiest clubs in the city. "Is that the new club we invested in, the one in Sandy Cove?"

Wren shook her head. "That's Cue, as in billiards.

No, Beat isn't a club. I suppose it's more of an old-fashioned dance hall, sexy music, low lighting… It's very romantic."

Yay, romance. Exactly what they needed because they weren't sexually frustrated enough already.

Oh, this just got better and better. Quinn rubbed the back of his neck. He understood Wren's need to do some damage control after the ball—he and Cal had looked like anything but the newly married, blissfully happy couple they were supposed to be—but was a romantic dinner and dancing really necessary? Surely they could just hit a club, let the press take a couple of photos of them looking happy and the balance of the universe would be restored. If they went to a club, then they wouldn't have to talk much and that could only be a good thing because talking to Cal had suddenly become hard work.

For twenty-plus years conversation had flowed between them easily. One kiss and a hot grope and they were tongue-tied, desperately awkward.

He hated it. They needed to resolve it, and quickly. He couldn't imagine going through the rest of his life, this marriage, this *week* not being able to talk to Cal. Cal was his sounding board, his moral compass, his reality check. Although she was living in his house, it felt like she was back in Africa and they had no means to communicate.

And when he wasn't thinking about all the things he wanted to discuss with her, then he was thinking about their kiss, the way she tasted, the softness and scent of her endlessly creamy skin. He wanted to kiss every freckle on her face, wanted to see if her ridiculously long eyelashes could tickle his cheek, how her hands felt wrapped around his…

"You two need to look like you're in love. Sylvie's is

romantic and Beat is a sexy, sexy place." Wren's cool voice interrupted his little fantasy.

"I've given a few of my more trustworthy press contacts the details. They'll be there to snap you looking hot and happy. Do not mess it up," she warned, drilling a finger into his thigh.

"Why do you automatically assume that I'm the one who'll muck it up?" Quinn grumbled.

"The best predictor of future behavior is past behavior," Wren replied, her voice tart. "You threw the first punch in that bar two years ago. You BASE jumped off that building and got arrested for trespassing because you had no right to be there. You were caught flying down the highway on your Ducati. You—"

Quinn held up his hand. "Okay, point made. I will be a good boy and act like a besotted fool."

Wren cocked her head and frowned at him. "Is that what you think love is? Foolish?"

Quinn looked at her, caught off guard by her question. "Sorry?"

"I'm just curious as to why you think that love is foolish. You make it sound like a waste of time, like it's boring, almost annoying."

"You get all that from one word?" Quinn lifted an eyebrow, hoping that his expression would dissuade her from pursuing the subject. Unfortunately Wren wasn't, and never had been, intimidated by him.

"The definition of *foolish* is *lacking good sense or judgment*. Pretty fitting coming from the man who has sold a million papers thanks to his lack of judgment. I find it interesting that you'll take physical risks but you won't risk your heart. That you think bailing off a building with just a parachute to break your fall is acceptable but falling in love is dangerous."

"I never said it was dangerous. I said it was foolish."

Wren snorted. "Because it's dangerous. Because your heart could get hurt."

"This is a ridiculous conversation," Quinn muttered, standing up. "And it's over. Will you email Cal the details about tonight or should I?"

"It's your date. You do it." Wren crossed her legs and smiled. "Feeling a bit hot under the collar because I mentioned love, Rayne? It's not so bad, you know—your buds seem to be stupidly happy as they go about creating their families."

Creating their families... Quinn hauled in a deep breath, hoping the air would blow away his resentment. He couldn't have what everyone else did—not in the way they had it—and he was trying to do the best he could with what he did have. Why couldn't anyone see that?

Ah, maybe because you've never told a soul about what you're missing?

"Are you done?" he asked Wren, his voice tight with annoyance.

"I just want you to be happy, Quinn," Wren told him, her voice soft but sincere.

Quinn stood up and jammed his hands into the back pockets of his jeans. "The thing is, Wren, I am happy."

"Could've fooled me," Wren muttered as he left the room.

Six

Sylvie's was a luxurious, upmarket restaurant serving traditional Italian cuisine in the fashionable Gastown area of Vancouver. It had been a while since she'd eaten at the award-winning restaurant and on any other night she would be looking forward to the evening in the steel-and-glass, exposed-brick restaurant with its incredible wine selection and innovative dishes.

Before the ball, Quinn would've been her favorite person to dine with. They would spend ages discussing the menu and deciding what they would eat, arguing about who ordered what because they would, inevitably, end up swapping dishes halfway through. Or she would eat a third of her meal and Quinn would polish off the rest. But that would be dining with the old Quinn, her best friend, not the Quinn who'd pinned her to a wall and kissed the hell out of her, who'd stroked her to the point of overheating and then backed away.

The Quinn she still wanted and couldn't have.

Cal, dressed in a thong and a tiny strapless bra, glared at her bed and the pile of clothes she'd tossed onto it. What was she supposed to wear on a date that wasn't a date with a husband who wasn't actually a husband, with a man who was your best friend but whom you really wanted to get naked with?

Did that make any sense at all?

Cal placed her hand behind her head and groaned. Should she wear the fire-red shift dress with cowboy boots for a country-chic look? Or should she pair it with heels for an urban-chic look? But the long sleeves might be too hot for dancing. Designer jeans and a bustier? Nah, too sexy. Maybe the halter-neck, vintage 1950s, black-and-white, floral dress with her cherry-red stilettos? She had to make up her mind sometime soon—Quinn would be knocking on her door and she still had to do her makeup and her hair.

All she wanted to do was pull on a pair of yoga shorts, her Feed Me Ice Cream T-shirt and veg in front of the TV, eating pizza and drinking red wine. She wanted to watch a horror movie with Quinn, both of them mocking the special effects and providing commentary throughout. She wanted to put her head on his shoulder, or her feet in his lap, have him swipe the half-eaten piece of pizza from her hand.

She wanted him to pick her up and lay her on her back, lean over her and slide his mouth over hers, have his hand drift up her waist and encounter her breast, his thumb swiping her nipple. Cal closed her eyes, imagining him pushing her pants over her hips, exposing her to his hot gaze. His finger sliding over her, testing her, groaning when he realized she wanted him as much as he wanted her...

"Red, have you seen my wallet?"

Cal's head snapped up as her door opened. It took her a moment to realize the object of her fantasies was standing in her doorway, athletic shorts riding low on his hips, his broad chest glistening with perspiration. He'd been for a run, Cal remembered. They'd passed each other on the dock as she'd arrived home. He'd been wearing a shirt then and hadn't bothered to talk to her except to snap out a brief "See you soon."

Cal bit her bottom lip, her eyes traveling over those long, muscled, hair-roughened thighs; up and over that ridiculously defined abdominal pack; across his broad chest. God, he was hot. When she reached his face, she realized his eyes were still south of the border. Cal lifted her hand to touch her chest and encountered the soft lace of her strapless bra, the warmth of her breast spilling over the top.

She wasn't exactly wearing much, just a brief pair of panties that matched her bra. And Quinn seemed to like what he was looking at. Should she pick up her dress and cover herself or just stand there? Before their kiss, before the madness, she would've mocked him, told him that he looked like a goldfish with his open mouth and sent him on his way.

The only place she wanted to send him was into her bed, to get naked under her covers.

God, she was in so much trouble.

Cal watched as Quinn placed his hands on his hips and closed his eyes. Her eyes looked south again and, yes, there was a ridge in his pants that hadn't been there before. "God. This, you…"

Cal cocked her head, intrigued. Quinn was never disconcerted, was never at a loss for words. He always had a witty comeback, a way to diffuse tension, a smart-aleck comment. Right now he looked as flustered and, judging by the steel pipe in his pants, as turned on as she was.

"Uh… I'll find my wallet and I'll see you downstairs."

Cal released the breath she was holding as he spun around and walked away. She forced her legs to move across the pale floor to shut the door he'd left open.

When she'd proposed this marriage, she'd thought Quinn to be a safe bet, someone who wouldn't disturb her calm, orderly life. How could she have been so wrong? He was supposed to be the one man in her life, the one relationship that was stable, solid and unchangeable. Platonic, dammit.

She'd never believed that she would spend her nights— and a good part of her days—flipping between imagining what making love to Quinn would feel like and reminding herself that sleeping with Quinn would not be a good idea.

Having sex with Quinn would make their situation even more complicated; it would be another layer to disassemble when they split up. They were risking their friendship, something that was incredibly important to both of them.

When she felt brave enough to be very honest, she knew she was also terrified that if she slept with Quinn, she could open the portal to feeling something deeper and more intense than she did right now. Those emotions had the potential to be too powerful and if she surrendered to them, she felt like she was granting someone else— Quinn—control over her heart, her life.

She couldn't do that, not again. Not ever. No one would have control over her again.

Until something changed, until they managed to navigate their way back to friendship, they were caught in sexual purgatory, Cal realized. Unable to be lovers but definitely more than friends. It was, she noted, a very short walk from purgatory to hell.

"Let's talk about us sleeping together."

Cal had been concentrating on her *fritto misto di mare*, thinking that the food at Sylvie's was utterly delightful, when Quinn dropped his bombshell statement. She swallowed her half-chewed prawn, washed it down with a sip of fruity white wine and leaned back in her chair. Quinn carried on eating, slicing into his roasted monk fish and lifting his fork to his mouth. He chewed, looked pensive and went back to his dish to prepare another bite.

"After an hour of laborious conversation, how can you toss that across the table and then continue eating?"

Quinn shrugged. "I've tried ignoring it, but it isn't going away so we need to discuss it. And I'm still hungry. And this fish is delicious."

Cal leaned across the table and kept her voice low, not wanting to take the chance that there was someone in the restaurant who had brilliant hearing. "*It?* Are we talking about sex in general or you and me in particular?"

"Both." Quinn gestured to her plate and leaned across, jabbing his fork into a piece of her squid. "Your food is getting cold." He ate her squid and pointed his fork to her plate. "Damn, that's good. Do you want to swap plates?"

"No, I want you to explain your comment."

Quinn reached for his wine and wrapped his big hand around the bowl of the glass. Candlelight cast shadows across his face and turned his hair to gold, his eyes to a deeper shade of green. The skin of his throat and his forearms, exposed by his open-collar gray shirt and rolled-back sleeves, was tan. He looked fantastic and she wanted to jump him...

The urge just kept growing in intensity.

"What we did, that kiss…it's changed us," Quinn quietly said.

She couldn't argue with that. Of course it had.

"The question is, what are we going to do about it?" Quinn took a sip of his wine. "Are we going to do what we're both thinking about?"

Cal felt the need to protest, to hold her ground. "What makes you think I'm thinking about sex with you?"

"The fact that you stare at me like you want to climb all over me and do what comes naturally." Quinn looked impatient. "C'mon, Red, we've always been honest with each other, brutally so. Let's carry on doing that, okay?"

Cal wiggled in her chair, ashamed. "I know. Sorry." She bit her bottom lip and placed her forearms on the table. "I've always known that you were a good-looking guy. I've known that since you were thirteen and Nelly Porter grabbed you and dragged you behind the gym to kiss you senseless."

Quinn smiled. "She shoved her tongue in my mouth and I nearly had heart failure. She was my first older woman."

"She was thirteen and a half." Cal's smiled died. "But the point is that I know that women like you, that they are attracted to you, that you're hot. Intellectually, I understood it, but it never translated."

"Translated?" Quinn frowned.

Cal tapped her temple. "I got it here, but lately—" she placed a hand on her sternum and stumbled over her words "—I get it, physically." Cal dropped her head and felt the heat creep up her neck, into her cheeks. "I never expected to be attracted to you, to feel that way about you."

"I didn't either, Red, and it's growing bigger and bolder. I don't think we can carry on the way we have been living. It's driving me crazy." Quinn tugged on the open collar of his shirt. "I keep telling myself that you are my best friend and that our friendship is too important to mess up. But you have no idea how close I came to tossing you on the bed tonight when I saw you in your sexy lingerie."

Cal saw the heat in his eyes, the desire. Nothing more or less, just pure attraction untainted by manipulation or punishment. "But how could one kiss, one grope change everything?"

"Who knows?" Quinn drained his glass. "But I know that I've relived that kiss a million times, wanting and *needing* more.

"Aren't you curious?" he asked after a short silence. "If that kiss was so good, don't you wonder how good we'd be in bed?"

Cal felt hot…everywhere. The heat pooled between her legs. "I'm crazy-curious," she admitted.

"Of course, that could be because I haven't had sex since Toby," she added. Oh, how she wished she could blame her current obsession with Quinn's body—with Quinn—on the fact that she'd been in a long, dry spell.

It took a moment for those words to sink in. "You haven't had sex in five years?" he clarified.

Okay, he didn't need to look so horrified. "No. Anyway, let's change the subject."

"Let's not." Quinn lifted their joined hands and nudged her chin so she had to look at him. "Five years since you last had sex tells me that you could take or leave it. That suggests your experiences in the bedroom weren't that great. Not surprising since you were married to the biggest asshat on the west coast."

"It's not nice to speak ill of the dead," Cal told him, eyes flashing.

"I spoke ill of him when he was alive so I can when he's dead. So, am I right? Okay, I know you won't answer that, but I'll take your nonanswer as a yes." Quinn shook his head. "What an idiot."

"Can we go back to talking about risking our friendship for sex?"

"And it is a risk," Quinn said, his chest rising as he pulled in a huge breath. "I want you, but every time I think about losing you because of sex, I start backpedaling like crazy. I want a guarantee that if we sleep together, we won't let our friendship get weird."

"It's weird right now, and we haven't even slept together," Cal pointed out.

Quinn leaned back in his chair and looked stubborn. "I want the sex and I want my friend."

"There is only one thing I'm sure of when it comes to relationships, Quinn, and that's there are no guarantees. It is never how you think it's going to be."

"Is that what happened with your marriage, Cal? Did it not turn out to be as great as you expected?"

Cal forced herself to meet his eyes.

"Every time I refer to Carter or your marriage, you shut me down. You don't talk about it and you talk about everything. Especially to me. Which means that you're either still mourning him because you were crazy in love with him or you had a really bad marriage."

Cal couldn't help the shudder and she winced when Quinn's eyes sharpened. "That's it. It was bad, wasn't it?"

Oh, he saw too much, knew her too well. "Maybe I don't talk about it because I know you never liked him, because you never wanted me to marry him," Cal protested, voicing the first excuse she thought of.

"Rubbish! I never wanted you to work overseas, in dangerous countries and situations, but you did and we still talk about your work. Your marriage is over. Your husband died. Okay, so it wasn't great, but why won't you talk about it? It's not like you're the first person in the world to make a mistake."

Because she still, years later, felt like an idiot. Because she'd found herself—a strong, independent woman—in an abusive relationship and not sure how she was going to get out of it. Toby had brainwashed her into thinking she couldn't make it in the world alone. Up until the day he died and she had to make it on her own. And then she proved him wrong by surviving and then flourishing.

She'd never allow a man to do that again, to climb so far inside her head to control how she felt about herself. To control anything she did or thought. No matter how much she wanted Quinn, she'd never let him control her, dominate her. And wasn't sex a manifestation of dominance?

Or was she just projecting her memories of Toby and sex onto Quinn?

Cal tapped her finger on the stem of her wineglass, deep in thought. Quinn had never, not once, tried to control her, dominate her or manipulate her, so why did she assume he would be like that in bed? Quinn wasn't Toby...

Quinn. Was. Not. Toby. And she was not the woman she'd been with Toby. *Everything* was in her control. She could choose whether or not to have sex, how much to give or take, how much to allow. This was her life, her body.

Her heart...

She could do this.

"Talk me through it, Quinn. Sleeping with you, I mean." Her heart knew that sex with Quinn would not be like sex with Toby but her brain still needed a little convincing.

Quinn pushed his plate away and reached for the wine bottle, dumping a healthy amount in both their glasses. He smiled and it was a potent mixture of slow and sexy. "I could make it good for you, Cal... No, I would make it amazing. You need amazing. You'd leave my bed bone-less, satisfied, happy. I'm a good lover."

She didn't doubt it.

"And that's not because I'm experienced but because it's important to me that my lovers enjoy it as much as I do. And you are a hundred times more important to me than anyone I've ever taken to my bed before."

Cal heard his sincerity, his growly voice sparking a firestorm over her skin.

"Sex, to me, is about so much more than my orgasm." Quinn's eyes on hers dried up all the moisture in her mouth. "It's about discovering the exact texture of your skin. Is it as creamy, everywhere, as it looks? I've always loved your freckles and I need to know if you have freck-les in unusual places."

His voice was grumbly and so freakin' sexy as he con-tinued. "I want to feel your hair tickle my stomach. I want to know whether you smell of wildflowers between your legs. I want to drown in the heat of your mouth. You have the sexiest mouth. I bet you don't know that."

He was killing her, Cal decided. Her hands and panties both felt damp with excitement. "I want to hear your moans, your breathy voice in my ear tell-ing me what you like. I want to hold you as you shud-der, feel you as you go over the edge. I want to find out what it's like making love to you, with you, Cal."

She couldn't stay here, not for one more minute. His voice had whipped her up until all she could think about was allowing him to do everything he mentioned and anything else he thought of.

"So let's find out."

Hunger, hot and hard, flared in his eyes. He stood up and reached for his wallet. "Yeah, let's."

She pushed her chair back and tossed her napkin on the table as she stood up. She looked up at him and nodded once, slowly. This was about sex, about physical relief, nothing more. She could do this...

This wasn't about control or deeper feelings or the future. Or her past. This was about walking on the wild side, tasting the storm, riding the wind. This was about Quinn.

This was about tonight. The future could look after itself.

Quinn whipped open the sliding door and placed a hand on Cal's back, urging her inside. He slammed the door shut behind him, wincing as she jumped. If she changed her mind, he'd cry like a little girl. He needed this...

He needed her.

Please don't let her change her mind.

Quinn stepped toward her, searching her face. In her eyes he saw a bit of what-the-hell-are-we-doing but nothing else that would make him back off. She wanted this, wanted him, and his heart swelled.

Quinn put his hands on her hips, swallowing a relieved sigh when her breasts flattened against his chest, when her hands slid over his pecs to his shoulders and up to his neck. He kissed her, slid his tongue into her open mouth and resisted the urge to squeeze her tighter, to suck her into him. Cal's hand dropped down his back and yanked his shirt up, trying to find the skin of his lower back. Impatient, he grabbed the back of his collar and pulled his shirt off in one vicious yank. He heard Cal suck in a hard breath and a second later her mouth was on his chest, tasting his skin above his heart with the tip of her tongue.

Such a small gesture, he thought, closing his eyes. Yet it sent a spark of pure light straight to his groin. Quinn took her face in his hands, bending his head to kiss her. He devoured her, pouring the frustration of the last few weeks of wanting her into his kiss. Cal moaned in his mouth and Quinn thought he was feeling far too much fabric and not enough skin.

He walked her backward until the back of her calves hit the sofa. "I wish I had the patience to slowly undress you, but I don't," Quinn said, his mouth against her neck. "Get naked, as quickly as possible."

Quinn yanked off his shoes as she stepped out of her heels and when his hands went to unsnap his pants, she released the ties holding up the bodice of her dress and then pushed the fabric down her hips. Her sexy dress dropped to the floor and she stood in front of him, pink lingerie and most of her endlessly creamy skin on display.

"I don't see any freckles," he murmured, his finger sliding across the tops of her round breasts.

"You're not looking closely enough," Cal replied. She nodded to his still-buttoned pants. "Need some help getting those off?"

"I can manage." Quinn smiled as he pushed his pants and boxers over his hips revealing himself to her curious gaze. Her eyes deepened to black and her body flushed.

With need. For him. Quinn felt a hundred feet tall, Hercules-strong. Unable to wait any longer, he unsnapped her bra and her breasts fell into his hands. Quinn skimmed over her breasts, across her nipples, his eyes falling to her flat stomach. He smiled when he saw her belly button ring. He dropped his hand and touched it, rolling the small diamond between his fingers.

"I remember when you got this. You were sixteen and mad at your mom because she wouldn't let you get a tattoo," he whispered.

Cal smiled. "And you bought me a chocolate milk shake and told me jokes to stop my tears." She touched his cheek and then his chin. "You hated it when I cried."

"I still hate it when you cry," Quinn told her, kissing the fingers that drifted over his lips.

Cal sucked in her bottom lip. "Please don't let this be a mistake, Quinn."

Quinn's hand lay flat across her lower stomach, warm and solid. "No matter what, Red, we'll always be friends. Nothing and nobody, not time and not this, will change that."

"Promise?"

"Promise. And I promise that I'll make this good for you."

"It's already amazing," Cal stated as his fingers slid under the lace of her panties and touched the most feminine part of her.

Man, she felt marvelous. Wet, hot, girly. God, he was rock-hard and he wanted nothing more than to slide into her, feel her engulf him, hot and ready. But this wasn't about him; this was about Cal. He'd promised to make sex wonderful for her, to allow her to feel what she never had before. He wanted to make this special, to build her up, to let her experience the magic that was fantastic sex. It felt right that he was sharing this with her, that he was showing her how hot, dirty, crazy and wonderful sex could be. They'd done so much else together, had experienced so many firsts, that it seemed, well, fitting that he should show her how amazing sex could be.

Reminding himself to go slowly, he pushed her panties down her smooth thighs and gently lowered her to the couch. He bent down, dragged his wallet out of his pants pocket and found his emergency condom. He ripped the packaging open, slid the latex on and turned to face Cal, lying on the couch, open to his gaze. With her red curls, dark blue eyes, luscious skin and that made-to-sin-with-him mouth, she was the most beautiful woman he'd seen in his life.

"God, Cal," he whispered and then moaned when her thighs opened as he settled on top of her, his erection finding her hot, secret, girly opening.

"You haven't found any more freckles yet and you don't know if I smell like wildflowers," Cal whispered into his ear as her nails dug into the skin of his butt and she lifted her hips in that age-old invitation to come on in.

"I'll do that later," Quinn promised. He needed all of her, as much as he could get, so his tongue invaded her mouth and his cock pushed into her, finding her soft and hot and silky and perfect.

Cal wrenched her mouth away and whimpered. He stopped, looking down at her in concern. "You okay?"

A strand of red hair covered her cheek and her eyes blazed up at him. "Just don't stop. Please!"

Quinn wanted to reassure her, but he couldn't—it was all too much. He felt both honored and terrified that she needed him as much as he needed her. She was too much. So responsive, so sensitive.

Quinn pumped his hips, Cal moaned and he never wanted to stop. "Quinn! Please..."

Quinn pushed himself up on one hand and reached between them to touch her, his fingers immediately finding her special place. She bucked, moaned and her internal muscles clenched around him. She bowed her back and slammed her hips up, taking him deeper. He felt her vibrate, felt her release and, having no willpower left, let go, pulsing into her.

Quinn felt her hands running up his butt and his back. He listened to her breathing. Instead of rolling right off as he usually he did, he took the moment to inhale her sex-and-flowers scent, enjoying the feel of her lips as she dropped tiny kisses on his jaw, her soft hands roaming his body.

When he finally lifted his head to look at her, her eyes were languid and soft and oh-so-satisfied.

"Well, that was fun. Want to do it again?" she asked with a husky laugh.

Hell yes.

Seven

Quinn looked across the picnic area at Ferguson Point in Stanley Park and noticed that Cal was surrounded by kids. She had a toddler leaning against her shoulder, another in her lap and an older girl had a slim arm around her neck. Six or seven kids, all of different ages, were sitting on the grass in front of her, fascinated by whatever she was saying.

This event—a picnic for children who'd survived a life-threatening illness—was another of the foundation's annual events. Quinn didn't mind joining her and supporting the event. He believed in what they were trying to achieve. And spending the day sitting in the sun and eating junk food in Stanley Park was good for anyone's soul, sick or not.

Kade and Brodie sat on a park bench with him, watching the activity. Some of the older kids were throwing a Frisbee. There were kids on the swings. Toddlers were chasing bubbles and squealing.

"What is she doing?" Quinn asked Brodie, gently nudging her with his elbow, wincing when he connected with little Cody's foot instead of Brodie's side. Her and Kade's brand-new son was asleep in her arms. "Sorry, sorry... Did I wake him?"

"It would take a bomb to wake Cody," Kade replied. He sat on the other side of Brodie, his arm around her shoulder. "And, from what I gathered when I walked past, Cal is telling them a story, something to do with the animals in the forest."

"She's really good with kids," Brodie said, twisting to put Cody into Kade's spare arm and snuggling into her husband's side. Cody's eyes flicked open as he was resettled, looked up at his dad and fell back asleep, utterly content.

Kade was a good dad, Quinn realized and his heart bumped. He looked across at Mac who was talking to Wren, his arm across Rosie's small chest, holding her between his legs, her back to his stomach. He was oblivious to the fact that his daughter was drooling over his hand. Kade and Mac had made the transition from bachelors to husbands to fathers easily and happily, taking the added responsibility in stride.

Quinn was proud of them for stepping up to the plate, for putting their women and their children first, for making them a priority in their lives. They'd embraced love and this new stage of their lives with enthusiasm and joy and Quinn was happy for them.

He would never make that transition, would never have to rearrange his life to make room for a family and he was okay with that. Wasn't he?

Of course you are! And really, why do you want to borrow trouble thinking like that? Don't you have enough problems dealing with your attraction to your temporary wife and best friend?

Quinn pulled his gaze off Cal to look at the panoramic view of English Bay. Yet the amazing scenery was no competition for the woman sitting on the grass, her bright hair in a long braid, freckles scattered across her nose and cheeks. God, he loved her freckles, loved that lush mouth, the fascinating dark blue of her eyes. The gorgeous dip of her back above her butt cheeks, her elegant toes, the perfection of her breasts, her pretty—

"So, is there any chance of making this fake marriage real?"

Quinn's head snapped around and he looked across the empty space where Brodie had been sitting. He'd been so focused on watching Cal he hadn't noticed Brodie leaving the bench.

His frustration with himself, and his discomfort over the fact that Cal had him under her spell, made him scowl. "What?"

"You and Cal."

"What about me and Cal?"

"You look good together, you enjoy each other's company and you're more real with her than you've ever been with any of your previous women—"

"*Real?* What does that mean?"

Kade didn't react to Quinn's hot tone; he just kept his steady gaze on Quinn's face. He tried not to squirm. "With her, you're you. The real you."

"I'm exactly the same person whomever I'm with," Quinn protested.

"You are degrees of you," Kade replied, tipping his head. "You can be charming, the life and soul of the party, a daredevil, all determination and hotheadedness. You are also a don't-give-a-toss bad boy."

Quinn thought about arguing and then realized that he couldn't think of anything to say that would counter Kade's argument.

"When you are relaxed, quieter, not trying so hard to show everyone that you're such a bad ass—that's who you are when you are with us, when you are with Cal. The real Quinn."

Right now he was the wanting-to-punch-Kade version of himself. The truth always hurts, he realized. He did use different elements of his personality to navigate different areas of his life, but that didn't mean he liked to be called on it.

"Doesn't everybody pull on different sides of their personality to get through the day? To get them through life?"

Kade nodded as his finger slid down Cody's nose, his expression contemplative. "Sure. But it's important to have a person you can relax with, who you can drop the pretense with. Cal is your person."

No, she wasn't. Not like that. Well, maybe like that but not in a happy-ever-after way. She was his best friend and the person he was sleeping with. He was temporarily, legally bound to her and when they were done being married, they'd still be best friends.

They had to be. It was what they'd promised.

"It isn't like that," Quinn protested.

"It's like that," Kade insisted. "Why won't you see it?"

Everything was changing, Quinn thought, ignoring Kade's question. A few short months ago his life made sense. He'd been wild and free, but he was now married and sleeping with his best friend. He'd spent more time thinking about kids and families in the past weeks than he had all his life.

His world had shifted off its axis and he didn't know

how to move it back, or if he even wanted to. Being a husband, having a family wasn't something he could wrap his head around, but, somewhere and somehow, he'd stopped dismissing the notion for the nonsense he'd always thought it to be.

Irritated with himself, he watched as Cal stood up. His heart stumbled as she scooped up the smallest toddler and easily settled the dark-haired boy on her hip. The child dropped his head onto her shoulder and shoved his thumb into his mouth. Cal patted heads, squeezed shoulders and started to walk toward Quinn, her cheek against that small, dark head.

God, she'd be a good mom. Even if he could imagine a life with her, he could never give her children. He'd want to give her children. Kids, for Cal, would be a deal-breaker. He knew Cal wanted a big family one day and he would never be able to give her what she truly deserved.

Sometimes he thought that he should tell her, just blurt it out and get it done. Didn't she deserve to know? He should have told her years ago, as his best friend. Then again, he hadn't told Mac or Kade. He hadn't told anyone…

Sometimes, like now, he felt like he wanted to tell Cal. That could be because he was feeling connected to her, dammit—*emotionally* connected. Great sex had the ability to create those connections and usually, when that happened, he distanced himself from the source of the connection. That couldn't happen with Cal thanks to their friendship and the wedding band on his finger.

Quinn wiped his hand across his forehead. He was being too introspective; he was overthinking and overanalyzing. *Take a step back and pull yourself together, Rayne.*

He and Cal were friends who were having sex. It wasn't something to fret over. And his secret was his to keep...

"Hi," Cal said as she approached them and patted a chubby leg. "Meet Lee, who is a cutie-pie." She flashed a smile at Kade and looked down at Cody. "God, he's gorgeous, Kade."

Kade's smile was pure pride. "Isn't he? I do really good work."

Cal grinned. "I think Brodie might have helped a bit."

Kade patted the seat beside him and stood up. "Have a seat. I'm going to put my guy in his stroller and then I might start a game of soccer." He looked in Quinn's direction. "Do you want to play?"

Quinn shook his head. "Maybe later."

Quinn watched Kade walk off and then stretched out his long legs and tipped his face to the sun. "You've had a good turnout. There are a lot of kids here."

"Yeah." Cal sat down and the little boy curled up against her chest. "My mom started this event a couple of years before she was diagnosed. She loved kids."

"As you do," Quinn said. He half turned in his seat and gripped the end of her braid between his thumb and index finger. "During your marriage, I kept expecting to hear that you were pregnant."

Distaste flashed across Cal's face and Quinn frowned, puzzled. "You didn't want kids?"

"Not then," Cal muttered. She shuddered and her arms tightened around Lee's small body. Quinn looked down and saw the child's eyes had closed. He'd stopped sucking his thumb.

Quinn ran his finger down her cheekbone, along her jaw. "I'm presuming that you'd like a family one day?"

More family talk? There was definitely something

wrong with him. Quinn watched as Cal captured her bottom lip between her teeth and nodded. "Yeah, I really, really would."

He pushed the words past that expanding ball in his throat. "Then, after we're done, you're going have to marry again, find a good guy who will give you a kid or three or four."

Cal rolled her eyes. "C'mon, Quinn, since when do I need to marry to have kids? Hell, I don't even need a man to have a baby. Have you heard of sperm banks?"

Quinn looked at her horrified. "Are you insane? You can't pick the father of your children out of a database!"

"Why not?"

"Because he could be a psycho?"

"I'm sure they weed out the psychos in their screening process."

Quinn wasn't sure if she was yanking his chain or not. "No sperm banks, Cal. Seriously."

"Well, what are my other choices?" Cal demanded, leaning into his shoulder. "I suppose I could have a series of one-night stands with men I think would be good genetic material but that seems, well, tacky."

Okay, that sounded even worse than the sperm banks. The thought of another man's hands on her body made Quinn want to punch someone. "No one-night stands, Callahan."

"Well, I'm not going to fall pregnant by wind pollination, Rayne. Anyway, I'm not nearly ready to have a kid and when I am, I'll make a plan. I might even ask my best friend to donate some of his boys. He's my favorite person, is stunningly good-looking, smart as a whip and I like him. But don't tell him that."

Quinn stared at her. He blinked, trying to make sense of her words. There was no way she could possibly be asking him for the one thing he couldn't give her. No way, no how.

Life couldn't possibly be that much of a bitch.

"Take a breath before you pass out, Rayne. Jeez," Cal said, patting his thigh with his free hand. "It was just an idea that popped into my head."

"Cal—"

Cal's fingernails pushed through his jeans and dug into the skin of his thigh. "Okay, I get it, that's a solid hell no."

Hurt flashed across her face and dropped into her eyes. Her chin wobbled and Quinn felt like a toad. He pushed the words up his throat. "I'm sorry, Cal, but I could never do that."

Quinn looked at her profile and sighed. He had to tell her, had to give her the reason for his refusal. Besides, if there was anyone whom he would share this secret with, it was Cal. He might be stupidly, crazily attracted to her, but she was still his best friend. Her friendship was still more important to him than the fantastic sex. He liked and respected her. She'd trusted him to show her how amazing sex could be; he could trust her with his biggest, darkest secret.

He took a deep breath and forced the words out. "There's little I wouldn't give you, Red, but I can't give you—what did you call them?—my boys."

"I get it. You don't want to be a dad, have a family, be tied down."

Quinn pinched the bridge of his nose with his thumb and forefinger. "God, Cal, shut up a sec. Okay?"

Cal jerked her chin up, but she stopped talking and Quinn sighed. The best way to say this was just to get it out as quickly and painlessly as possible. "I can't have kids, Cal. I'm infertile."

Cal frowned. "No, you're not."

"Yeah, I am. Every couple of years the Mavericks players have a full medical, where the team docs check us out from tip to toe. The results indicated that I am infertile."

"Did they do a sperm test?"

"No, just a blood test. Apparently it's quite a rare condition, but I've got it."

"What's the condition called?"

Quinn shrugged his shoulders. "Hell if I can remember."

Cal's fist thumped his thigh. "When did you find out and why didn't you tell me?"

Quinn covered her fist with his hand. "They told me a couple of weeks before your wedding. I picked up the phone to call you, but then I remembered that you weren't talking to me." He looked at her distraught face and sighed. "Look, Cal, this isn't a big deal—not to me anyway. I've never wanted kids, never wanted the whole picket fence deal."

Cal leaned sideways and dropped a kiss on his shoulder. He felt the heat of her lips through the fabric of his hunter-green T-shirt. "I'm so sorry about that whole no-talking thing. That was my fault and it was wrong of me."

"I did call your husband a first-class moron and threatened to kidnap you to stop you from marrying him," Quinn conceded.

Cal kept her lips against his shoulder and her words whispered up to him. "Sometimes I wish you had." Before he could ask her to explain her cryptic statement, she pulled away and spoke again. "I understand why you don't want kids and marriage, Quinn."

He lifted his eyebrows. "You do?"

"It's not quantum physics. You were hurt and ignored as a child and you're scared of being hurt again. Because your parents let you down, you are reluctant to take another chance on being loved."

"Whatever," Quinn growled, hating that she was right, that she'd put his deepest fears into words and made him face them. "My not being able to have kids is not a big deal, Cal."

He wasn't sure who he was trying to convince. Himself or her?

"It is, to me," Cal stated, her tone fierce. "It's a big deal because I think you would be an amazing dad, an amazing husband. If you dropped that shield, that fear of being hurt, and allowed yourself to love, you'd be a wonderful family man."

Cal lifted her hand from his thigh and rubbed the back of her neck, her eyes on his face. "Look at you, all puzzled and weird, thinking I've lost my mind. I haven't. I just know you, Quinn, better than anybody. *I. Know. You.* You're a wonderful friend and you'd be a great husband.

"Listen," she continued, "you need to investigate this condition, find out what you can do. There are other options for you to have a family. Adoption, surrogate sperm—"

"Cal, enough!" The words shot out like bullets. He shook his head and lifted his hands. "I'm good. This is my life. I'm okay with not being able to have kids. I always have been."

Cal shook her head. "I don't buy it. You could have it all, Quinn."

Quinn shook his head and gripped her chin in his hand. "Don't you dare feel sorry for me, Red."

"This so-called infertility is just another excuse for

you not to commit, not to get involved," Cal said, her expression mulish.

Okay, he wasn't going to waste his time trying to convince her. "That's your perception, Callahan. Discussion closed."

"No, it's not."

"Let's talk about Carter, your marriage and his death."

Her face closed up and her eyes turn cool. "Let's not. Ever."

"Why won't you—"

Cal stood up and the child in her arms opened his eyes and blinked at the sudden movement. "Don't do this, Quinn."

"Why are you allowed to prod and pry, but I'm not? Why don't you trust me with the truth?" Quinn demanded, following her to his feet and pushing his hands through his hair. Why did he need to know about Cal's life with Carter? The man was long dead and he didn't affect Cal's life anymore, so why did her secrets about him bother Quinn so much?

God, this was confusing and annoying. This never happened when he slept with women he didn't talk to. Quinn jammed his hands into the pockets of his jeans and rocked on his heels, frustrated. She might trust him with her body, but she didn't trust him with her past.

And that stung.

Conversations like this—hell, any conversation with Cal lately—made him feel like he was standing in a basin on six-meter swells, desperately trying to keep his balance. Too much was happening, all at the same time. He was married, living with and making love to his best friend. His marriage would end at some point in the near future and, he assumed, sex as well. Would their friendship also end?

And if it didn't, could he still be her friend without remembering the spectacular sex? Could he forget that she had three freckles on the inside of her thigh, would the memory of her breathy moans fade?

He'd said that sleeping together would cause difficulties, but he'd underestimated how many and he certainly hadn't realized the degree to which the sex would mess with his head.

Cal was now, without doubt, his biggest complication.

"Coffee."

Cal buried her head in her pillow and felt Quinn's eyes on her. She was lying on her stomach, naked, the white cotton sheet skimming the top of her butt. She felt him rolling to his side and she turned her head sideways. He was supporting himself on a bent arm and his other hand played his favorite game, joining the dots on her shoulders. He loved her freckles as much as she hated them.

"Where's my coffee?" Cal whined and he laughed.

"Good morning to you too, Red." Quinn skimmed his hand down her back and over her butt. "Did you sleep well?"

"No, because you kept waking me up," Cal muttered, squinting up at him. He had a crease in his face from the pillow, hectic stubble and bed hair and he'd never looked more beautiful.

"If I recall, you woke me up the last time." Quinn pushed a strand of hair out of her eyes and off her forehead.

She blushed and Quinn laughed. "Don't feel embarrassed, Red. Not with me."

Cal closed her eyes, turned her face back into the pillow and let out a long groan. She couldn't help it. She became an uninhibited, wild woman with him, happy to go wherever he led her. It was the only place where she allowed Quinn a measure of control over her. In every other sphere they were absolute equals.

He never questioned where she was or what she was doing and when she did explain, he listened to her activities with interest and trusted that she'd been where she said, doing what she said. He allowed her, without any fuss, to contribute to the expenses living on the boat and when she'd purchased some jewel-toned cushions to add color to the neutral palette, it had taken him three days to notice. He told her he loved whatever she was wearing but insisted he loved her birthday suit best.

He was easy to live with, but their friendship had always come easy.

Cal rolled over, pulled the sheet up to cover her breasts and pushed her hair off her face. "This is weird. Don't you think this is weird? When do you think it'll stop being weird?"

"What is weird, exactly?"

"You and I naked. Together. Friends don't get naked."

"We have, we do," Quinn replied. "Don't overthink this, Cal. We're lovers in the bedroom, friends outside of it. It doesn't have to be more complicated than that."

Cal tipped her head and seemed to consider his words. Simple, no drama. So refreshing. She yawned and when she lifted her arm he traced the words of her white-ink tattoo across her rib cage.

"'She flies by her own wings,'" Quinn read the words aloud. "Why that phrase, Red?"

It was a statement of her independence, but, like so much else, she couldn't find the words to explain.

"When did you get the tattoo, Red?"

"About a year after Toby died."

There, she'd said his name out loud. It was, she supposed, some sort of progress.

"I like the white ink," Quinn commentated. "It's feminine, pretty."

She still found it difficult to talk about her past, so she lowered her eyes and sent him a hot look, dropping her gaze to his biceps and then his chest. "You are the baddest bad boy around and, sadly, the only one without any ink. How can you still be scared of needles?" she teased.

"I'm not scared," Quinn shot back. "I just don't see the point."

Cal rolled her eyes. "I was there the night you tried to get your first tattoo, Quinn. You passed out when the guy sat down next to you and lifted the tattoo machine. Wuss. Repeat after me, I'm a scaredy-cat." Cal sang the last word in an effort to distract him.

Quinn didn't take the bait. "Why those words, Cal?"

Aargh! Stubborn man!

"I have another one."

"You're avoiding the subject and I'll let you, for now. But at some point, sometime soon, I want to know why. So… Where? I thought I'd explored every inch of your body."

Quinn pulled down the sheet and his eyes skimmed over her torso, down her belly. Her heart thumped and her skin prickled. Occasionally she forgot that he was her oldest friend. Sometimes he felt like a tantalizing mixture of new and old, of excitement and comfort.

"Where's the second tattoo?"

"Here." Cal lifted a slender foot and twisted her ankle so he could see the tiny feather on the instep of her foot. It was beautifully rendered, a subtle white and silver shot through with gentle pinks.

Quinn cupped her foot in his hand and swiped his

thumb across the tattoo. "It's in memory of your mom. She always picked up feathers, wherever she went."

Cal bit her bottom lip, touched that he'd remembered. "She said they were messages from angels. I've started looking for feathers now too."

Their eyes met and, through them, their souls connected. "And do you find them?"

Cal smiled. "Yeah, I do. All the time. I choose to believe they are my mom's way of telling me she is still around, watching over me." She pulled her foot from his hand and wriggled, suddenly uncomfortable. "I suppose you think that's silly."

"Why would I?"

"Because the dead are supposed to be dead, gone." Cal spat out the words like they were bitter on her tongue.

Quinn rolled off the bed, stood up and grabbed a pair of jeans from the back of the chair in the corner. He pulled them on, left the buttons undone and walked over to a chest of drawers, pulling out a T-shirt for Cal to wear. He handed it to her and Cal pulled it over her head, the soft blue cotton swallowing her smaller frame. She'd never quite realized how much bigger than her he was until they'd started sleeping together.

Big but gentle, in control of his strength.

Quinn lifted his shoulders to his ears before dropping them abruptly. "I think you are mentally, and spiritually, tougher than anybody I know. Anybody who lost their mother and husband within the space of two years and managed to keep going, to keep it together, has to be. And if finding feathers gives you comfort, then who am I to judge?"

Cal knew she shouldn't compare, but if this had been a conversation with Toby, then she would've been ridiculed and mocked, disparaged and called a child. God, Quinn was Toby's exact opposite.

"I'm not sure the feathers are a message from your mom, but I know how much your mom loved you, so if finding feathers makes you feel close to her, then I'm not going to judge that, Red. I have no right to."

Cal's eyes filled with tears and she felt comfortable showing him her pain. "I miss her so much, Quinn. Still."

"I know, Red. I do too."

Cal knew that to be the truth. Her mom had been his because his own mother had been so bad at the job. Rachel had celebrated his achievements with him, the sports awards, the very-impressive-but-not-brilliant report cards. She'd accompanied Cal to watch his hockey games. She'd attended his graduation. She'd been a strong and loving presence his whole life and Cal knew he flat-out missed her too.

"What do you think she'd think about this?" Quinn asked, his voice sounding strangled. "Would she approve of you and I doing this?"

Cal took a moment to respond. "I'm not sure. I mean, she loved you, but she might think it was strange, like I sometimes do. Don't you ever look at me and wonder what we are doing?'

"All the time." Quinn scratched the back of his head. "Do you want to stop?"

Hell, no! Cal dropped her head, inspected her nails and when she lifted her head again she grinned. "It's not *that* strange."

Quinn laughed and dropped a hard kiss on her mouth. "Talking about strange… My mother left a snotty voice message saying they'd expected us to visit by now, to explain why we eloped, why there wasn't a wedding, why they had to read about my marriage in the press."

Cal frowned. "You didn't tell them? Quinn! It's been nearly three months. What were you thinking?"

"I was thinking that, since I haven't spoken to my parents or my brothers for years, I didn't need to tell them anything," Quinn replied, defensive.

"Why haven't you spoken to them?" Cal asked, swinging her legs so she sat on the edge of the bed. "Did you have another fight?"

Cal remembered their last major dustup—they'd objected to his career as a professional hockey player and he'd told them he no longer gave a damn what they thought—and after that fight, she knew his relationship with his parents and, consequently, his brothers had cooled.

"Nope. We just faded away." Quinn shrugged. "Anyway, they suggested that we have supper. To be honest, I think they want to see you, not me."

"Why? Your parents never had much time for me."

"They never had much time for anybody who didn't have an IQ of 150 or above, so don't take it personally." Quinn pushed a hand through his hair. "And I have no idea what's behind the invite. I gave up trying to figure out my family a long time ago."

"Do you want to go?"

Quinn gave her his are-you-mad look and Cal wrinkled her nose at him. "I think we should go."

Her mom was dead and her father had nearly died; family was important!

"God." He sighed and scrubbed his face with his hands. "I am quite certain I was swapped at birth. You're going to be stubborn about this, aren't you?"

"Yep."

"I'll see when we can go over," Quinn capitulated and she smiled.

Cal shook her head. "Let's not eat there. You know your mother burns water. Why don't you invite them here and I'll cook?"

"You can't cook either," Quinn pointed out. "And grilled cheese sandwiches don't count."

"Hey, I happen to be a very good cook...now."

"Then why haven't you cooked for me, *wife*?"

Cal mock-scowled at him. "Because we're frequently not home to eat. And when we are, you bring food home. Or we eat at Mac's or Kade's."

"When did you learn to cook?" he asked, obviously curious.

Cal dropped her head and her hair hid her face. Cooking had been another of Toby's efforts to turn her into the perfect wife. "Toby sent me on a couple of cooking courses." And that was all she was saying on *that* subject!

Before he could ask her to elaborate, Cal stood up and walked over to the en suite bathroom, putting a little extra sway in her hips, hoping to move him off the topic. His eyes, as she'd hoped, moved to her chest and then headed south.

"I'm going to take a shower," Cal told him. "Call your folks, your brothers, invite them to dinner. It'll be fine."

"Ack. That's too much wishful thinking for so early in the morning," Quinn grumbled.

"Right now, I'm also wishfully thinking about coffee," Cal said from the doorway of the bathroom. "Feel free to make my wishes come true."

Quinn grinned at her. "I thought I did, last night."

Yeah, he had and did. Every night.

Cal shut the bathroom door behind her, caught a glance of the happy-looking woman in the mirror and did a double take. She barely recognized her bright eyes, her naughty smile, the sheer contentment on her face. *Don't do this, Cal*, she warned herself.

Don't set yourself up for a fall.

Quinn was temporary, their marriage was temporary—it was all so very temporary. Being with Quinn, being happy like this was a wonderful treat.

But it wasn't real life and it would end.

Happiness always did.

Eight

When Quinn returned from walking his family back to the promenade, he stepped into the main salon and dropped his head to bang it against the glass door.

"I think you're right. I think you were swapped at birth," Cal said, standing next to the dining table and looking at the remains of the meal she'd spent hours preparing. The filet of beef was virtually untouched, the blueberry cheesecake was intact and there was still half a dish of rosemary-and-garlic-roasted potatoes. "Could they not have told you they are now all vegetarians? That three of them are on a raw food diet?"

Quinn stepped away from the door. "On the plus side, they did polish off the steamed vegetables."

"And a bottle of ten-year-old whiskey and three bottles of your best red wine." Cal sniffed, thoroughly annoyed.

It had been over twelve years since she'd shared any time with the Rayne family, but Cal soon remembered why she and Quinn had spent most of her childhood hanging out at her house. His relatives were, quite simply, hard work and after an interminable evening Cal understood Quinn's need to keep his distance.

Why couldn't they see the man she did? The smart, funny, successful man who would love them, spoil them, if they gave him half the chance. He didn't need to be a genius. Being Quinn—loyal, funny, responsible and mentally tough—should be enough.

"Jeez, why did they bother to come to dinner?" Cal demanded, stacking the dirty dinner plates and taking them to the kitchen. "They spent most of the time talking to each other and barely spoke to us."

Quinn picked up the dirty wineglasses and placed them on the counter next to the dishwasher. "Ah, but they did express their reservations about our marriage and Ben did tell me that I am flaunting my wealth because I'm living on a yacht."

"Ben is still the idiot I remember." Cal rolled her eyes.

Quinn did another trip to clear the dining table and after placing some serving dishes in the dishwasher, he leaned against a counter and frowned. "Jack was more reserved than normal."

Cal bit the inside of her lip and wondered whether she should express her opinion of his brother's relationship with his long-term partner. Maybe she should just let sleeping dogs lie...

"He and Rob want to get married," Quinn told her, pouring wine into two clean glasses. Cal took the glass he held out to her and smiled her thanks. Jack and Rob marrying would be a very bad idea, especially for Jack.

"Cal? Have you got something you want to share with me?"

Dammit. The man had a master's degree in reading

her body language. Cal slowly turned around, still not sure whether she had a right to say anything.

"Spit it out, Red," Quinn commanded.

She'd never told anyone about the reality of her marriage to Toby and if she didn't shut down this conversation, she'd end up telling Quinn her dirty little secret.

This wasn't a conversation she could dip her toe into and back out of when the water got a bit chilly. This was sink or swim. She didn't want to do either.

Why couldn't she keep her big mouth shut around Quinn? Surely, by now, she would've learned to? "Cal, talk to me."

"I think Jack is being abused, possibly physically, definitely verbally by Rob," Cal quietly stated.

"What?"

"You heard me," Cal replied, crossing her arms.

"Why do you think that?" Quinn asked. Cal could see he was caught between denial and disbelief. "I thought Rob was the most reasonable, rational person at the table tonight. Apart from you and me, naturally."

Cal tapped her finger against her wineglass. "He's charming, I agree, and he made an effort to talk to us, to you," Cal replied. "He was civil and we needed civil tonight to balance out the crazy."

"Then why would you think he's beating up on my brother?" Quinn asked, genuinely confused. "Either physically or verbally?"

Cal looked around the kitchen and sighed. She didn't have the energy to tidy up, but, unfortunately, the kitchen elves were on strike. And her pride wouldn't let her leave it for Quinn's cleaning lady to sort out in the morning. She put down her glass and started to rinse the dirty plates so she could place them in the dishwasher.

"I agree that nothing about Rob's behavior suggests

that he's an abuser, but everything about Jack's behavior does," Cal said, keeping her voice low. God, why had she even opened up this can of rotten worms?

She was okay. She could still walk away from this subject. She *would* walk away if it got too intense. Talking about abuse made her heart race and it made her remember why she never wanted to be embroiled in a relationship again.

You're in a relationship with Quinn...

No, she wasn't, not really. They were legally married, friends outside the bedroom and lovers within it.

She'd only married Quinn to sever the last cords tying her and Toby together. But talking about abuse felt like she was surrendering a little of the confidence she'd fought so hard to regain. She was overreacting. This was Quinn! The only person she could trust with this information. He was, first and most importantly, her friend. Her oldest, and best, *friend*.

Quinn flipped open the dishwasher and held out his hand for the wet plate. Quinn still looked expectant and Cal knew he wasn't waiting for another dish. "Jack looked at Rob every time he voiced his opinion, wanting his approval. He served Rob his food, kept asking if he needed anything. Agreed with everything he said."

"Jack's always been needy, a fusser," Quinn stated.

"This goes deeper than that. He was nervous, constantly looking for Rob's approval."

"Isn't it natural to want approval from the people we love and who love us?" Quinn asked, confused.

Cal sighed. She understood that it was difficult to accept that his tall brother was being abused by the much shorter, less bulky Rob, but she also knew that abuse had nothing to with size. Like Toby, Rob needed to have the upper hand, needed to be in control, and he knew exactly what buttons to push to get Jack to dance to his tune.

"Beneath the facade of charm, I heard Rob's patronizing condescension, the I'm-not-entirely-sure-why-I-put-up-with-him attitude. I wanted to lean across the table and smack his smarmy face," Cal said. "Trust me, Rob's a snake."

"You don't have to like him, Red, but it's a big jump from being a jerk to being an abuser."

"It's not as far as you think," Cal muttered, not entirely under her breath.

Back off, Cal. Now!

Quinn frowned at her. "Sorry, what?"

Cal shook her head and waved her words away. "Trust me on this, Quinn. Your brother is in an abusive relationship." She closed the dishwasher and, hoping to move off the subject, she nodded toward the cheesecake. "Do you want a piece?"

Quinn laid a hand on his heart and tapped his chest. "God, yes. It looks fantastic."

Cal opened the drawer to take out a knife. Cal cut two slices and placed them on a plate. He took the fork she held out and dug in.

"Poor Ben. I saw him eyeing the filet. The guy is jonesing for a steak and fries." Cal scooped up her cheesecake and slipped it into her mouth, the tart berries a perfect complement to the creamy filling and the sweet base. "Damn, that's good."

"I would never have believed that you made this if I hadn't seen you whipping it up earlier," Quinn admitted, going back for a bigger forkful.

"I'm a girl of many talents."

"You so are." Quinn looked at her and her stomach

did that swirly, jumpy, bats-on-speed spin it always did when Quinn looked at her that way.

Quinn took another bite of cheesecake and frowned at the rest of the dirty dishes. "Leave the mess. Let's take the cheesecake and wine up onto the deck."

Cal followed Quinn up the stairs as he walked toward the large, square ottomans next to the Jacuzzi. Sitting down, he patted the cushion next to him. Cal sat, tucking her feet under her bottom and resting her glass on her knee.

"Jack's an idiot if he's being abused," Quinn stated as he put the plates on the coffee table in front of them. "Seriously, one slap and he should lay charges."

He made it sound so easy, Cal thought. So black and white. He had no idea how words could be twisted and used as weapons, how cruel loved ones could really be. Abusers could win acting awards, easily able to play the victim, always stating that they couldn't understand why they were so badly treated when they loved so much. Few people understood what it felt like to live with the fear, the crazy scenarios, the accusations and the recriminations.

By the time Toby started slapping her, her confidence had been smashed to smithereens. Regaining her sense of worth and finding herself again had been a battle of epic proportions.

"I just don't understand how someone can put up with that crap," Quinn said, leaning back and lifting a forkful of cheesecake to his mouth. "It doesn't make sense to me."

It never made sense to anyone until they were walking through the sludge of an abusive relationship, not sure how they got into this swamp and having no way to get out. And to Quinn, who was so self-reliant and confident in who and what he was, it was an anathema.

Quinn waved his fork in her direction. "So, tell me why you think Rob is abusing Jack."

Cal looked into her wineglass, thinking furiously. This was a watershed moment and she had to decide whether to own it. She either had to tell Quinn about her rotten marriage and her abusive husband or she had to shove it back in the corner and pretend it had never happened. She either had to trust him with all of the truth or nothing at all.

Quinn would…what? Hit her? Disparage her? Mock her? Of course he wouldn't. Quinn wasn't that type of man. Hadn't she told him that she knew him? And she did. Quinn wouldn't lose his temper. He'd control his reaction and she'd be safe.

Of course he would—this was *Quinn*.

Besides, telling Quinn wasn't about how he'd react but about whether she had the strength to do this, the courage to face her past. She'd grown so much in the past five years and she was a new Cal, a better version of the girl she'd been before she'd met Toby.

Telling somebody, telling Quinn, meant freedom. She would be shining a light on her dark past.

Releasing her pain would heal her. It would give her closure.

Didn't she deserve that? Cal finally acknowledged that maybe she did.

Her decision made, Cal lifted her eyes. "Before I go into that, I need to tell you something…and it's linked, in a roundabout way, to your question about Jack."

Quinn looked puzzled. "Okay."

"I asked you to marry me for a reason."

Quinn frowned, confused. "Yeah, I needed to look

better in the press and you needed some distance from the social swirl."

Cal shook her head. "All true, but there was another reason, one I haven't told you."

"Okay, that sounds ominous. What?"

Cal explained about the inheritance, told him how she needed to be free of Toby. "I don't need his money. My mom left me a trust fund and I stand to inherit a bundle from my dad."

Quinn looked astounded. "You walked away from $200 million?"

"I couldn't take his money. It was…" Cal hesitated. "It was tainted. I'll explain why, but let me go back to my comment about Rob's abuse of Jack." Cal sucked in a deep breath, looking for her courage. "The thing is, Quinn, I can recognize controlling behavior from a hundred yards away. I was married to a man who controlled everything I did, everything I said."

Quinn cocked his head. It would take a moment for the truth to sink in—it always did.

"I was Toby's possession, just like Jack is Rob's," Cal continued.

Cal watched as his protective instincts kicked in and anger jumped into his eyes. "Go on," he said, his jaw tight.

"In hindsight, there were subtle hints of his controlling streak when we were engaged, but I thought he was just trying to protect me. After we married it got progressively worse."

Quinn bounded to his feet and loomed over her, his hands on his hips and his face suffused with anger. Cal felt a touch of panic, but she pushed the feeling away and pulled in a deep breath. This was Quinn. Quinn would *never* hurt her.

"Why the hell did you stay with him? Why didn't you divorce him? Why didn't you walk?"

He made it sound so simple; yet, at the time, it hadn't been.

Quinn looked down at her, now bewildered as well as furious. "Why didn't you call me? Jesus, Cal, why the hell didn't you tell me about this? I would've—"

"You would've punched him and caused a scene," Cal told him, her voice firm. "Then he would've pressed charges and you'd have ended up in jail, convicted for aggravated assault. I couldn't do that. I couldn't allow you to destroy your career."

"My career isn't that fragile."

Toby had ruined so much that she hadn't been prepared to take the chance.

Quinn pushed his fingertips into his forehead, upset and angry about something that had happened years ago. Cal reminded herself that he wasn't angry with her but at what had happened to her. He had such a good heart and he was incredibly protective of the people he allowed into his life. She loved that about him. She loved him…

Cal felt fear roll over her, hot and terrifying. She couldn't love Quinn—that wasn't part of the deal. Anything other than being part time lovers and full time friends wasn't part of the plan. She couldn't love Quinn. It wasn't safe to love Quinn.

She couldn't think of that now. Maybe she wouldn't think about it again at all.

She had to tell him the rest of her story or she never would.

"He was also physically abusive."

It would take a moment for the truth to sink in.

"What did you say?"

"Toby liked to use force to get his point across."

"Carter hurt you?" Quinn's roar was louder this time and Cal winced. Oh, God, he was losing it. Anger, dark and dangerous, sparked in his eyes and every single muscle in his body was taut. She had to bring him down; she had to diffuse the situation.

"It wasn't that bad, Quinn." Cal placed a hand on his arm. "He slapped me a couple of times. It was mainly verbal—"

"Don't you dare defend him!" Quinn linked his hands behind his head, incandescently angry. "He raised his hand to you—there is no excuse!"

It was important for her to keep calm. Arguing with him wouldn't help.

"I'm not defending him, Quinn, I'm trying to explain what happened."

"When did he start hitting you?" Quinn demanded, the cords in his neck tight.

Dammit, he would have to ask that question. "About six months after we married," Cal admitted.

"And you stayed with him for another year?" Quinn shouted. "I don't understand this, you! Why didn't you bail?"

"Because, by then, I had no self-confidence. He told me he would destroy me and my father if I walked out on him."

"And you believed him? Come on, Red, you are smarter than that!"

Cal wrapped her arms around her bent knees and tried not to feel hurt. Quinn didn't understand. "I used to judge women who stayed in abusive relationships too. It's easy to stand on that pedestal, but Toby knocked me off it with a single slap."

Her gentle rebuke hit its mark. The fire went out of

Quinn's eyes, but the tension in his body remained. He pulled in a deep breath and then expelled the air and rolled his head. After a few minutes he walked back to the daybed and sat down next to her.

Quinn picked up her hand and threaded his fingers between hers. The anger was still there, but it was under control. "So, explain it to me. Why did you stay with him, Cal? I can't understand why you didn't leave the first time he hurt you. You know, you *knew*, better than that."

Shame and embarrassment rolled through her. "I told myself I didn't want my big, fancy, expensive wedding to be a waste of money—a stupid reason—and I didn't want to admit that I'd made a huge mistake. Pride and stubbornness played a part."

"Oh, Cal."

"Mostly, I didn't want to look like a fool," Cal admitted and wrinkled her nose.

"Did you ever think about leaving him?"

"I was leaving him," Cal said. "The day before the accident I told him that I was filing for divorce. We had a huge fight and he told me he would destroy me. Destroy my father. Then he punched me, really hard, in the ribs."

She saw anger roll through him again, hot and powerful. "God, I so want to find Carter's grave, dig him up and beat him back to death."

"He broke three ribs. After his death, the press reports said that I was too shocked to cry, that I was beyond tears. All I could think about was that he couldn't hurt me again. I wouldn't have to deal with a messy divorce, with the drama that would follow. I felt like I'd received a get-out-of-jail-free card." Cal looked at him with wide eyes. "Is that wrong?"

Quinn shrugged. "Not from where I'm sitting." He

squeezed her hand. "You could've called me, Cal. I would've helped."

"I know, but I felt…"

"Like a fool?"

"Yeah. I thought that since I'd gotten myself into the situation I needed to get myself out." Cal pulled their joined hands into her lap and leaned against his shoulder. "I was very young and very dumb. I was grieving my mom's death and he made me feel bright and beautiful and, I guess, safe. Protected."

"I was also there. Didn't I make you feel like that?" Quinn demanded,

Cal shook her head. "Toby spoiled me. You've never done that. You treat me like an equal, like an adult. Toby promised that my life would be drama-free with him. After Mom died, I wanted that."

"Life is never drama-free."

"I know that now," Cal said. "I'm sorry I didn't tell you, didn't ask for your help, that I haven't told you about this before. It was my ugly little secret."

"We all have secrets, Cal, but nothing about you—not even your secrets—can ever be ugly." Quinn turned toward her and placed his hand on her cheek. The tenderness and regret in his eyes made her heart trip. "I wish you'd come to me."

Cal tasted tears in the back of her throat. "I do too. I know now you would've been there for me, Quinn, just like I know that you would be there for Jack if he allowed you to be." Cal mimicked Quinn's action and put her hand on his rough, stubbled jaw. "You're such a good man, Q, even if you don't believe it half the time."

"Not so good," Quinn said, his voice rough with emotion.

Cal shook her head. "You'll never convince me of

that. You are both tender and strong and that combination floors me."

Tenderness flared in Quinn's light eyes, along with desire and protectiveness.

She couldn't resist him.

Nine

"Red—God, why can't I resist you?"

His eyes roamed over her face, looking at her like he was seeing her for the first time. And Cal knew that, even if it was just temporary, their friendship had retreated to make room for a blazing love affair.

It might only last the night or it might be strong enough to withstand the passage of time. No matter how long it lasted, she would enjoy him, as much as she could.

"I need you. I need to love you right here, right now, in the dark, in the cold night air," Quinn told her, his hands reaching for the belt that held her rich purple wraparound jersey together. His hands pulled the fabric apart and he skimmed her torso, cupped her breasts while his tongue invaded her mouth, sliding against hers in a dance that was as exciting as it had been the first time he kissed her on the terrace at the masked ball.

"You taste so good." He broke the contact with her mouth to murmur the words.

Cal moaned and her hands slid over his chest, down his waist to grip his hips. He hadn't bothered with a coat so she had easy access to the buttons on his shirt and she went to work on them. She soon felt the contrast of the chilly night air and his superhot skin. Cal felt his hand under the cup of her bra and she shivered, excitement skittering over her. These were hands that knew her, knew what she liked, knew how to touch her.

Quinn pushed Cal's shirt down and off her arms and he groaned when he pulled his head back to look at her lacy bra barely covering her creamy breasts. He dropped his head to pull her nipple into his mouth, tasting her through the barrier of the lace. Cal linked both arms around his head and held him to her. She needed this, needed him to need her, to crave her. She felt powerful and feminine, confident and sexy. Strong.

God, she felt strong.

Quinn's hands dropped to her stomach, fumbling as he tried to open the buttons on her jeans. He cursed, sounding uncharacteristically impatient. "I need you. I need to be inside you, loving you."

Quinn groaned, his mouth on hers as he pushed her jeans and thong down her legs. She kicked the garments off and moaned when his fingers stroked her with exquisite care. "So hot, so warm. Mine."

God, she was. *His, only his.*

Cal snapped open the button to his jeans, tugged down his fly and Quinn sighed when her hand found him, long, strong and so hard. She couldn't wait, couldn't cope with his drive-her-crazy foreplay tonight. She just wanted him inside her. Completing her.

Quinn shucked his clothes and pushed her down onto the ottoman. With his hands on her thighs, he gently pushed her legs apart. He leaned over her, his expression hot and hard and intense and, with a lot of passion and little finesse, he entered her with one long, fluid, desperate stroke. She was wet and ready for him. He stopped for a moment, his arms straight out as he hovered above her, her astonishment at how in sync they were reflected in his eyes. He was rock-hard and ready and she was very, very willing.

She could feel every luscious inch of him, skin on skin, her wet warmth coating him, his head nudging her womb. He felt amazing and... *God!*

"Quinn!" Cal smacked his shoulder with her fist and he pulled his head back to look down into her face.

"What? What's wrong?" he demanded, his voice hoarse with need.

"Condom! You're not wearing one."

Quinn pushed himself up on his hands to hover over her. She really didn't want him to pull out. She loved the intimacy of making love to him without a barrier. It felt real...

"I'm clean and I'm—" he choked on the words "—you know...a genetic dead end." He supported himself on one hand and she saw the muscles in his shoulders and biceps bunch as he lifted his thumb to caress her cheekbone. "If I have to run downstairs for a condom, I will, crying all the way. But I've always used a condom and I was tested last month. I'm clean, there's no chance of you falling pregnant and I just want to make love to you, feel every inch of you, with no barriers between us. Because, God, you feel amazing."

She clenched her internal muscles, involuntarily responding to the emotional plea beneath his words. His jaw was rigid and she could see he was using every speck of willpower he had to stop himself from plunging into her.

"Okay, yes," Cal said and her hands flew over his ribs, down his hips and over his butt, pulling him deeper into her. "Move, Quinn, I need you."

"Not as much as I need you, baby," Quinn growled as he forced himself to keep the pace slow. Cal whimpered with need, slammed her hips up, driving him deeper inside.

"Harder, deeper, faster," Cal chanted.

Quinn had no problem obeying that particular order and he pistoned into her, his hand under her hips to tilt her pelvis up so she could take him deeper. She suspected he was a knife's edge away from losing it and she wanted him sharing this with her.

Cal lifted her hands between their bodies to hold his face. She stared into his eyes, blue clashing with green, and smiled. "Let's fly together, Quinn."

Quinn nodded. "Now?"

"Now."

Cal let herself dissolve around Quinn, her body shaking with her intense orgasm. Love, hot and powerful, roared through her as Quinn groaned and threw his head back. She felt him come deep inside her.

His, Cal decided. Only his.

Cal rolled over and, not finding Quinn, put her hand out to pat his side of the bed. Frowning, she opened her eyes. Hearing the sound of water running, she looked at the closed bathroom door. Cal sat up, grateful for a moment alone, a little time to think.

Last night she suspected that she might be in love with Quinn. In the cold light of morning she knew it to be true. She'd fallen head over heels in love with her oldest friend.

Idiot.

Had she really been stupid enough to think he was

a safe bet, to think she'd be immune to his charm, his quirky sense of humor, to that luscious body and to-hell-with-you attitude? He was the least safe person in the world to love. Yet here she was, feeling all those crazy emotions she'd swore she'd never feel again. She wasn't supposed to be thinking of him in terms of commitment and forever. Quinn didn't do commitment and he had no concept of forever. He married her because he needed an out, a way to mend some fences. He married her because he trusted her to not make waves, to not make demands on him that he wouldn't be able to meet.

Quinn wasn't perfect, but she didn't need him to be. He was perfect for her. He was strong enough to allow her to be strong. They argued, but he didn't overpower her. He didn't force his opinion on her. He trusted her to be the best version of herself, was strong enough to deal with the broken bits of her, adult enough to know that everyone had their quirks.

He knew her, flaws and all. Better than that, he accepted her, flaws and all.

For that reason, and a million others, she loved him. In a soul-mates, be-mine-forever way.

The way he'd made love to her last night, both on the deck and later in this bed—the way he'd held her like she was precious and perfect—gave her hope. She felt excitement bubble and pop in her stomach. Maybe they had a shot...

"You're looking a bit dopey, Red."

Cal jerked her head up. Quinn's shoulder pressed into the door frame and a white towel around his hips was a perfect contrast to his tanned skin. He looked as gorgeous as ever—and as remote as the International Space Station. Unlike her, Quinn wasn't having a warm and fuzzy, I-love-you moment.

"Hi."

Quinn lifted an inquiring eyebrow. "What's up?" he asked, stalking into the room. "You have your thinking face on."

Damn, he knew her so well.

"You might as well spit it out, Red. You know you want to."

She did. She wanted to tell him how she felt, wanted to admit to him—and to herself—that she wanted a real marriage between them, something that would see them through to the end of their lives. She wanted to be the brave, strong, confident woman she'd worked hard to be and ask him if he felt the same, ask him whether he could love her like she needed to be loved.

Cal wrapped her arms around her knees, biting down on her bottom lip. "I could tell you, but I don't know if you want to hear what I have to say."

Quinn's eyes hardened and turned bleak. "Are you going to tell me something else about Carter that I won't like?"

"No. I told you about the abuse and the inheritance and that's it," Cal replied.

"Then what is it?" Quinn asked, looking at his watch. "And, sorry, I don't mean to rush you, but I need to get to headquarters for a strategy meeting with Mac and Kade."

She couldn't just blurt this out on the fly. They needed time to talk about it. Cal blew air into her cheeks. "Leave it. We can talk later."

Quinn gripped the bridge of his nose, obviously frustrated. "Cal, just say it."

Well, okay then. Cal kept her eyes on his as she spoke her truth, her voice shaking. "I'm in love with you and I want to spend the rest of my life with you. I want this marriage. I want you."

Happiness flared in his eyes but quickly died as confusion and fear stomped over that fragile emotion. Quinn rubbed his hand over his jaw and then moved it to rub the back of his neck. "God, Cal. That was not what I expected to hear."

"Yeah, I figured."

"I'm not sure what you want me to say…"

Cal pushed her curls off her face. "It's not about what I *want* you to say, Quinn. I'd just like to know if you think it's a possibility…whether you might, someday, feel the same."

Quinn disappeared into his walk-in closet and when he reappeared five minutes later, he was dressed in track pants and a Mavericks hoodie. He carried his shoes to the bed, sat down on the edge and slowly pulled on his socks.

Cal waited for him to speak and when he did, his words were precise and deliberate. "I think this is all going a bit fast. Last night was emotional and I realize that talking about Carter was difficult for you. The floodgates opened and you released a lot of feelings and I think you might be confusing that release with love. Could that be possible?"

Cal considered his words. Nope, she decided. She was definitely in love with him. "Sorry, that's not it."

Quinn bent over and stared at his sneakers before tying the laces. "The sex between us is amazing, Red, and we're good friends. That doesn't mean we are in love." Quinn sat up and looked at her, his expression determined. "*If* this is happening, then we need to take a step back, figure out what the hell we're doing before we make plans and promises that will blow up in our faces."

Cal nodded, conscious of the slow bruise forming on

her heart. "You still haven't told me if you love me or not."

Quinn stood up and slapped his hands on his hips. He didn't speak and when Cal finally looked up, she saw fear and confusion in his eyes. "I don't know, Cal. I don't know what I feel. This—*you*—it's all a bit too much." He glanced at his watch and grimaced. "Let's think about this, step away from the emotion and consider what we're doing. What we're risking."

Cal clearly heard what he wanted to say but couldn't because he didn't want to hurt her: *What you're doing, what you're risking.*

He was giving her an out, a way to go back to sex without the messy complication of love.

Quinn picked up his wallet and cell phone and jammed them into the pockets of his hoodie. "I have a…thing… this evening. You?"

Cal lifted her chin, knowing damn well he didn't have plans since they'd discussed seeing a movie tonight. But her pride wouldn't let him see her disappointment, wouldn't permit her to ask for anything more. "I have a *thing* too."

Quinn nodded and walked to the side of the bed. Cal kept her face tipped, waiting for his customary see-you-later, open-mouth kiss, but he kissed the top of her head instead.

It was the age-old, you're-looking-for-more-than-I-can-give-you brush-off.

Message received, Quinn. Message received.

A week passed and Cal wasn't sure why she was at the Mavericks arena midmorning, especially since she had work piling up on her desk back at the foundation. If pressed, she supposed she could say she'd come to talk to Quinn about their upcoming schedules, whether he could attend a theater production with her later in the month. There were a dozen questions she could ask, but nothing that couldn't be resolved during a two-minute phone call or later that day when they touched base back at home...

Home. It might be a good idea if she stopped thinking of the yacht in those terms.

Coming to the arena had been an impulsive decision but one that was rooted in her need to see Quinn. She wanted to talk him into having lunch with her, to try and push past the barrier her impulsive declaration of love had created between them a week ago. They were still living together, still sleeping in the same bed, still making love. But they weren't communicating. They were two people who were sharing his space and their bodies and nothing else. She didn't think she could live like this for much longer. She was back in purgatory, except this time they were lovers but not friends. She felt angry and sad and, yes, disappointed.

They were acting exactly how they'd said they never would and they were hurting each other. They needed to break this impasse. One of them had to be brave enough to walk away before they destroyed their friendship. She'd raised the subject of love; she'd changed the parameters of their marriage by uttering the *L* word so it was her responsibility to fix what was broken.

While she waited for Quinn to call an end to the practice session, she thought how much she loved to watch him skate. Cal propped her feet up onto the boards that lined the rink. He was poetry in motion, at home on the ice just as he was on land. Dressed in jeans and a long-sleeved T-shirt with a sleeveless jacket over his broad chest, he looked bold and determined.

And utterly in charge.

His players took his direction easily and quickly and, while they respected him, they certainly weren't scared of him. It was obvious they gave him a thousand percent all the time. You didn't work that hard for someone unless you were inspired to do so.

He pulled no punches. No one was spared his praise or his sharp tongue. Even Mac, his partner, was treated exactly the same as the rest of the players. On the ice there was only one boss and Quinn was it. That amount of intensity, that power was…well, it made her panties heat up.

Cal, digging into a bag of chips, looked up when she heard the click-clack of heels. She smiled at Wren, who was making her way to her seat in the first row back from the rink. On the ice, Quinn was barking orders to his squad, short blond hair glinting in the overhead lights.

"I heard you were here," Wren said, bending down to kiss her cheek before dunking her hand in the bag of chips.

"Sneaky thief," Cal muttered as Wren settled into the chair next to her.

"You can't eat a mega-sized bag of chips by yourself. You'll get fat," Wren told her. "I'm just being a good friend, helping you out."

"Yeah, yeah," Cal replied and placed the bag between them. She nodded to the thick envelope on Wren's knees. "And that?"

Wren patted the envelope and popped another chip in her mouth. After swallowing, she passed the envelope to Cal and smiled. "That, my darling, is the measure of our success. You actually did it."

"Did what?" Cal asked, opening the envelope and pulling out a sheaf of papers.

"The rehabilitation of Rayne. Those are the photocopies of every article mentioning you or Quinn over the past month and every single one is positive. Quinn is redeemed. By the love of a good woman."

Cal started flipping through the papers, stopping now and again to read a headline, to look at a photograph. There was one of them kissing outside the coffee shop close to her office, another of them in Stanley Park at the picnic, walking hand in hand and laughing. Old Friends, New Lovers read one headline. Are Quinn and Cal Vancouver's Most Romantic Couple? Is It True Love?

"The Mavericks brand is stronger than ever and trust in Quinn, as a person and as a coach, has been restored. Instead of baying for his blood, the press is now baying for babies." Wren's hand dipped into the bag again and she stood. "I'll leave you to take a look through those. Thanks, Cal. I could never have whipped him into shape on my own."

Baying for babies? Cal felt her heart tighten. That was never going to happen and it made her feel sad, a little sick.

If Quinn wanted a family or marriage, if he wanted *her*, he would've initiated a discussion about their future. He would've asked to talk about her ill-timed and unwelcome declaration seven days ago.

His silence on the subject said everything she needed to hear: he absolutely wasn't interested in anything more than what they had.

He'd married her for a reason and since that goal had been achieved, there was no rationale for staying married. It was time to cut her losses and try to move on.

Cal tipped her head to look up into Wren's lovely face. "Does this mean we can start, uh, dialing it down?"

"Sorry?" Wren asked, confused.

Cal shoved her fingers into her hair, lifting and pushing the curls back. "That was the plan—we make it look good and then we start drifting apart."

Wren waved at the papers in Cal's lap. "If you faked everything, then I commend you on your magnificent acting." Wren placed her hands on her hips and scowled. "But I've been doing this for a long time and I know fake when I see it. This isn't one of those times."

"We're friends."

"Pffft. You are so much more than that. You are good together. Damn, girl, you are the best thing that's happened to that man in a very long time. You don't seem unhappy either, so why on earth do you want it to end?"

She didn't, but what she wanted was beside the point. "It will end, Wren."

"Then you are both idiots," Wren told her before bending down and kissing Cal's cheek. "I hope you both change your minds because yours could be an amazing love story."

Wren touched Cal's shoulder and gave her a sad smile before walking away. Cal gathered the articles together and pushed the papers back into the envelope and laid it face down on her lap.

She had to start controlling her attraction to Quinn instead of letting attraction control her. If she didn't, she would find herself in the same situation she'd been in years ago, hopelessly in love with a man who didn't love her, without any emotional protection or power.

Oh, wait…that horse had already bolted from the stable; she already loved Quinn. She loved him like a friend; she loved him as a lover. She simply, deeply, profoundly loved him, in every way a woman could.

Okay… She loved him, but that didn't mean she couldn't protect herself. She was not prepared to let all rational thought disappear and capriciousness rule. She'd learned her lesson well.

Unlike her younger self, she could now look at relationships, and men, and see them clearly. Quinn didn't love her, not romantically in a I-want-to-spend-the-next-sixty-years-with-you type of way. He loved making love to her. Maybe because she was handy and she was the only person he could—without making waves and headlines—have sex with. Quinn was also exceptionally good at separating his emotions from, well, anything and she knew he could easily separate their friendship from making love.

She didn't have any desire to change Quinn. Yeah, her goal had been to rehabilitate his reputation, but she had no desire to rehabilitate him. She'd always loved him for who he was, the adrenaline junkie who'd jump off buildings with a parachute strapped to his back, who laughed like a maniac on roller-coaster rides, who leaped from one crazy stunt to another in order to feel alive. Because he'd spent his childhood hoping to be noticed, and she understood his need to feel alive, to feel free. She understood what motivated his crazy...

She loved him. She understood him. She would feel like she'd had her limb amputated when they parted, but they had to end this. Her heart was already battered and bruised, but that was better than having her psyche and her soul decimated.

She and Quinn needed to have a serious talk about splitting up. They needed to come up with a plan for how to navigate the next couple of months. They had to start winding down their relationship, start spending some public and private time apart. They had to be strategic in how they drifted away from each other.

She didn't want the public to blame Quinn. She didn't

want to reverse the current wave of good press he was receiving. Her father wanted to return to work and so could she; there were problems with the projects in Botswana, India and Belize she needed to attend to. They could blame her work, distance and time apart for the breakup of their marriage. Everyone understood that long-distance relationships never worked...

Cal pulled a bottle of water from her bag and twisted the cap. She took a long swallow and replaced the cap as Quinn called a break.

Quinn's eyes met hers across the ice and he lifted a finger to tell her he'd be with her shortly. Happy to wait, Cal watched as the players glided across the ice, most of them in her direction. As they removed their helmets, she recognized some faces from the barbecue on Quinn's yacht last weekend.

"Hey, Cal."

Cal dropped her feet and leaned forward, smiling. "Hey Matt, Jude. Beckett."

Beckett sent her a bold smile. "*Mrs.* Boss Lady."

Cal leaned back and crossed her legs, amused when six eyes followed the very prosaic movement of her denim-covered legs tucked into knee-high leather boots. God, they looked so young, so fresh-faced. Compared to Quinn, they looked like boys. These boys still had a lot of living to do. They needed to experience a little trouble, needed to have their hearts broken and learn a couple of life lessons. Then their pretty-boy faces would become truly attractive.

Cal jerked her attention from her thoughts to their conversation.

"So, what are we doing tonight?" Beckett demanded, sliding guards onto the blades of his skates before swinging open the door that would take him off the ice. He walked between Cal and the boards and dropped into the chair next to her, sending her an easy, confident grin. "FOMO's, Up Close or Bottoms Up?"

"What's FOMO's?" Cal asked, interested. She knew that Up Close was a club and that Bottoms Up was a sports bar owned by Kade, Mac and Quinn.

Beckett stretched out his arms and his hand brushed Cal's shoulder as he rested it against the back of her chair. Not wanting to give him any ideas—he was far too slick for his age—Cal leaned forward and rested her elbows on her knees.

"It's a place downtown," Beckett replied. "Want to come?"

Matt flicked a glance toward Quinn and shook his head. "Uh, Beck, not a great idea. Boss man wouldn't like it."

Cal frowned. The comment sliced a bit too close to the bone. "Last time I checked, I was a grown-up and I make my own decisions. Quinn doesn't do that for me."

Jude pinched the bridge of his nose. "Seriously, Cal, he really won't like you…"

Beckett's laugh was rich. "If she wants to come, let her. We'll be there from around ten."

Who went out at ten? Ten was when most people were thinking about bed, or sitting in their pj's eating ice cream. "Ten?"

Beckett picked up the end of her braid and rolled it in his fingers. "Maybe you are too old to party with us." Cal almost didn't notice the sly look he sent Quinn, the smirk to his fallen-angel mouth. "Maybe you should just be a good wife and stay in. Quinn *definitely* won't like it."

She knew she was being played, but she couldn't bear the thought of this young whippersnapper thinking anyone had control over her.

Cal jerked her braid out of his fingers. "For your information, Quinn has no say about what I do or who I do it with."

Beckett lifted an amused eyebrow. "Okay then, *Mrs. Rayne.* FOMO's, at ten. Do you want us to collect you?"

"I think I can get there under my own steam," Cal told him, her tone slightly acidic.

"Get where?"

She hadn't heard Quinn's silent approach, but Matt and Jude's tense body language should've given her a hint. Beckett's sly smirk deepened and Quinn's fierce frown didn't intimidate him in the least. "Hey, boss. Just to let you know, Callahan is joining us at FOMO's tonight, if you want to hang out."

Quinn's eyebrows nearly disappeared into his hairline. "At FOMO's?" He folded his arms across his chest and scowled. "No, she's not."

Beckett stood up and shrugged. "I told her you wouldn't like it, but she said you're not the boss of her."

"Hey, I'm right here!" Cal stated.

"You are *not* going to FOMO's."

Cal tilted her head. Right, this was just one small reminder as to why she shouldn't want to stay married. Nobody was allowed to make decisions about any aspect of her life but her. "I am. And you are not going to stop me."

Cal stood up as Beckett, Jude and Matt made a tactical retreat.

Quinn looked like he was making an effort to hold on to his temper. "Cal, listen to me. FOMO's—"

"You can't tell me what to do, Rayne! We're sleeping together and that's it." Cal pulled her bag over her shoulder. "You are never going to control me, tell me what to do or how to do it. I will never allow a man that measure of control again."

"I'm not trying to control you! I'm trying to tell you that FOMO's is—"

"Save it! I'm not going to listen!" Cal wasn't interested in anything more he had to say, her temper now on a low simmer. What was it about men and their need to control the situation, control how their women acted? Was it ego? Stupidity? A rush of blood to the head? Whatever it was, she wasn't going to play his game. She might like his bossy ways in the bedroom, but everything else—her money, her clothes, what she did and how she did it—was strictly off-limits.

She loved him and he didn't love her. It was that simple. But even if he did fall to the floor and beg her to spend the next sixty years with him, she would never grant him the right to dictate her actions.

"I'm done with this conversation," Cal told him, her voice quiet and cold. She picked up the envelope and slapped it against his chest. "Wren dropped these off. When you see them, maybe you'll agree that we need to talk. We need to start thinking about dialing this down."

"What are you talking about?" Quinn raised his voice as she started to walk up the stairs to the exit. "Come back here, I need you to understand why I won't allow you to go to FOMO's."

Cal half turned and raised one shoulder, her face flushed with anger. Did he really use the word *allow*? After everything she'd told him? Seriously? "*Allow?* You won't allow me to go? Who the hell do you think you are? I don't answer to you, Rayne. I am not one of your players or one of your bimbo girlfriends who will roll over at your command!"

"Callahan!" Quinn growled.

Cal just kept on walking.

Yeah, they really needed to put some distance between them.

Ten

Black and pink and purple, Cal thought as she walked into FOMO's. Lots of black and pink and purple. Not her favorite color combination. Cal slid into a small space near two guys standing at the bar. Between attempts to catch the eye of a bartender, she looked around for Beckett or any of the Mavericks players. She couldn't see them and she wondered, not for the first time, what she was doing here.

Clubs weren't her scene; the repetitive thumping of the music gave her an earache and the flashing neon lasers gave her a headache. The smell of liquor and cologne and perfume clogged her nose and she felt claustrophobic from the bodies pressing her against the bar.

"What can I get you?" the barman shouted at her, his white teeth flashing and his dreadlocks bobbing in time to the beat.

A taxi? An oxygen mask? "A club soda and lime. Hey, have you seen the Mavericks players in here tonight?"

His hands deftly assembled her drink, but his eyes gave her an up-and-down look. "Honey, you're a little old and a lot overdressed to catch their eye."

"Thanks," Cal said, her tone dry. "Have you seen them?"

He nodded toward a floating staircase in the corner. "They are upstairs." He slid the glass toward her. "You look really familiar. Do I know you?"

"No," Cal quickly answered, but she didn't kid herself that she wouldn't be recognized sometime soon. Not everyone in the club was drunk or stoned and she could guarantee that the vast majority of those who were still sober were Mavericks fans.

"I have that type of face," Cal told him. She reached into the pocket of her tight skinny jeans and pulled out a bill. Before she could hand it over, she felt a hard body press her into the bar and a hand shot past her face, strong fingers holding a twenty-dollar bill.

Cal sighed when the bartender took the man's money and not hers. She frowned, waving her money at him. "I want to pay for my own drink. No offense intended."

"I've been offended all damn day," the familiar voice growled in her ear. "I was offended when you flounced away, when you wouldn't answer any of the ten calls I made to you, when you didn't come home before coming here."

Dammit. Quinn had tracked her down and he was here, stalking her. Not that his presence was too much of a surprise. Quinn wasn't one to walk away from a fight.

"Quinn and his missus!" The bartender held up his knuckles for Quinn to bump. "Haven't seen you in here for ages, man!"

"Yeah, wives tend to frown on their husbands visiting FOMO's, Galen."

"That's the truth, dude."

He knew the bartender, which meant he was very familiar with this club. Cal looked at the raised dance floor to the right of the bar and sighed at the skimpily clad women—girls—writhing and grinding. It was probably one of his favorite hunting grounds.

"What are you doing here, man? And why did you bring your woman?"

"Cal and I were on our way to dinner and I wanted to stop in and check on my boys. They behaving themselves?" Quinn asked.

Galen nodded to the floating staircase. "They're upstairs, blowing off some steam. No paparazzi up there, no dealers, just some of their regular girls."

Quinn nodded. "Let me know if that changes."

"Will do, boss man."

Galen passed Quinn a beer and he wrapped his fingers around the neck of the bottle and the other hand around her wrist. She tugged at his hold and he bent his head toward hers. She was sure that anyone watching him would think he was whispering something sexy in her ear, but his words were anything but. "You. Stay."

"I am not a dog! You don't get to tell me to sit and stay!" Cal shot back, wondering how she could be so annoyed with someone who smelled so good and turned her insides to mush.

"Callahan, I am on the edge of losing my temper with you and you won't like it when I do. Do not push me."

Cal bit her lip and looked up at him, suddenly, inexplicably, scared. Toby always used the same words—*do not push me*—before his hand shot out, sometimes stopping and sometimes connecting. Sometimes the slap turned into a punch, sometimes a tap; once or twice his palm left finger marks on her cheek. Even worse was when the slap morphed into a caress, into foreplay, into sex she didn't want to have.

Cal bit her bottom lip and tried to get her racing heart under control. Quinn wasn't Toby; he would never, ever hurt her. So then why did she feel like she was being controlled by a bigger, stronger personality than herself?

Oh, God, this had little to do with Toby and everything to do with Quinn and the fact that she'd allowed herself to be vulnerable again. Once again she'd handed over her love, her most precious gift, and once again it had been rejected. Everything she'd worked for—her independence, her sense of self—was slipping away... It felt like *she* was fading away.

She couldn't control the sudden surge of overwhelming anxiety. Feeling like she couldn't get any air, she lifted her hand to her throat and patted her skin, trying to tell herself to breathe. But it was too hot in the club, too noisy and her heart was pounding so hard she felt like it was going to jump out of her chest.

Panic attack. She hadn't had many—she'd started having them in the month before Toby died—but she instantly knew what was happening. Dizziness, a tingling body and ice running through her veins. She wanted to run away from Quinn, this place, her life, but she couldn't. She held onto Quinn's arm, hoping his heat and warmth would pull her back from that dark, horrible place.

"What the—" she heard Quinn's words from a place far away and felt her knees buckling. Then Quinn's arm was around her waist and he pulled her into his embrace, his hand holding her head to his neck, his voice in her ear.

"I've got you, Red. Just breathe. C'mon, baby, just breathe, in and out."

Cal concentrated on his soothing voice, on his

strength, on the warmth of his body, his smell. His heat. She pulled in air, slowly, as he suggested, and the ice in her blood melted and the world stopped whirling. She managed to move her arms so she held his hard waist, her hand clutching the fabric of his black button-down shirt. His fingers in her hair massaged her scalp.

"C'mon, Red, get it together. I'm here and you are fine. You just need to breathe, suck in the disgusting air."

His words caused her to let out a snort of laughter and Quinn's arm around her hips tightened a fraction. "There we go. You're getting there."

Cal pulled in a deep breath, felt her head clearing and nodded, her nose bumping into his jaw.

"If I put you down, will you be able to stand?" Quinn demanded, his lips on her cheek.

"Yeah."

Cal wobbled when her heels hit the floor, but Quinn stabilized her. She stared at the open patch of tanned skin revealed by the collar of his shirt and struggled to make sense of what had just happened. Oh, God, if this wasn't another sign that she had to put some emotional distance between her and Quinn, then she didn't know what was. She couldn't be in a relationship with him, with anybody. If just a couple of words could send her into a tailspin, and his touch could bring her back from the edge, then she needed to get out.

He made her want what she couldn't have, what she wasn't prepared to give. She didn't want to cede that much control over her heart, her thoughts, her life. A relationship meant sacrifice; it meant losing control. It meant bouncing between love and trepidation, between hope and despair.

Love meant being vulnerable.

"Let's get you out of here." Quinn cradled her head

between his hands and rested his forehead on hers. She felt his breath, minty fresh, on her cheeks, her nose, whispering across her forehead. "God, Red, what's happening to us?"

Back on the *Red Delicious*, Quinn watched Cal as she carefully sat down on the edge of the sofa's square cushions and stared at the maple floor beneath her feet. They needed to talk, but was she up to it?

He'd always prided himself on being forthright and honest, but this week he'd been anything but. He knew, better than most, how under-the-surface emotions could fester. He'd seen the looks Cal had sent him, the confusion on her face when he made love to her and then emotionally retreated. He was being unfair, but he wasn't sure how to resolve their stalemate.

"I'm going up onto the deck. I need some air."

Quinn nodded and went into the kitchen to pull two wineglasses from the cabinet. He dropped to his haunches and quickly scanned his wine collection before deciding on a robust red. As he reached for the corkscrew, he noticed the thick envelope he'd tossed onto the counter earlier. He'd been so angry with Cal that he hadn't bothered to look inside, but now he was curious. Putting the corkscrew down, he opened the flap and spread the papers on the counter. He sucked in his breath at the photographic documentation of the past few months with Cal.

God, they looked happy, in love, crazy about each other.

There was a photo of him watching her at that art exhibition and he saw love and lust, pride and affection written all over his face. In every photo, the world could see their crazy chemistry, knew their thoughts weren't far away from the bedroom. Some of the photos managed to capture their genuine liking for each other, their trust in each other. He could easily see why the city assumed they were in love.

A camera had flashed in the club earlier, capturing him holding Cal's face in his hands. When that photo appeared online or in tomorrow's social column, they would see a man looking at his woman, adoration on his face.

Because he did adore her—he loved her—but did he love her like *that*? Did he love her enough to walk away from the safety of his lone-wolf lifestyle, enough to give her what she deserved, what she craved? A home, a family—through surrogacy, through adoption, through some nontraditional way—and the love and commitment and fidelity she deserved? Could he put her first, forever and always? Could he build the family he now knew he wanted with her? Could he trust her to put him first, to be the rock he wanted to lean on?

It would be easier to walk away from her right now, tonight, to let whatever they had die a natural death. But if they ended it now, it would take months or years for their friendship to recover, if it ever did. Could he risk that? Could he risk losing her to keep his heart safe?

He didn't know...

Quinn picked up the wine bottle and glasses and took them up to the deck. Cal stood at the railing looking up at the skyscrapers of downtown Vancouver. He loved the deck at night, dark and quiet despite the hectic light show above and behind them.

Cal kicked off her shoes and his eyes traveled along her legs in those tight jeans to her tiny waist, displayed by her snug coat. He put the glasses and wine down and walked toward her, placing his front to her back, pulling aside her hair to place a hot kiss on her elegant neck.

He knew they needed to talk, but he wanted this first, the magic and wonder of her under him. He wasn't sure where they were going, but he needed to love her one more time before words got in the way.

Because words always did.

Early the next morning Cal felt Quinn's kiss on her neck, heard him pull in a deep breath as if he were trying to inhale her. His arm was tight around her; his thigh was flung over hers as if he were trying to hold her in place. It meant nothing, Cal reminded herself; him holding her was a conditioned response.

Cal opened her eyes as Quinn rolled away from her, leaving the bed without speaking to visit the bathroom. She hoped he'd come back to bed, but she didn't really expect him to. Her instinct was proven correct when he walked over to the large window and placed his arm on the glass above his head, his expression disconsolate.

"What caused your panic attack last night?" Quinn asked, without turning around.

Cal didn't bother to pretend that she was asleep. Neither of them had slept and, instead of talking, they'd reached for each other time and time again, as if they knew this conversation would change everything between them. Well, dawn was breaking and the night was over...

Cal pushed back the covers and stood up. She pulled a T-shirt from the pile of laundry on his chair and pulled it over her head. She walked over to the large porthole to stand next to Quinn. He'd pulled on a pair of sleeping shorts and a T-shirt while he was in the bathroom and Cal was grateful. She didn't think they could have this conversation naked.

"You told me you were on the edge of losing your temper," Cal replied, placing her hand on the glass.

She felt Quinn's penetrating look. "And you took that to mean...what? That I would hurt you?"

She lifted a shoulder. "Intellectually, no. Emotionally, I rolled back in time. I have issues about being controlled."

"Because of Carter." Quinn rubbed his hand over his jaw. "But you do know I would never, ever lay a finger on you?"

"I know that, Quinn, I do." Cal looked at him, so big and bold and so very pissed off. "I don't respond well to orders anymore and I didn't like you telling me what to do."

Quinn linked his hands behind his neck, his biceps bulging. "And I had a damn good reason for that. You didn't know what you were walking into last night," Quinn snapped. "FOMO's is, on the surface, a pretty normal club."

"Then why did you have a problem with me going there?" Cal demanded, sitting on the side of the bed, surprised when Quinn sat down next to her, his thigh pressing into hers.

"I said that it's normal on the surface. Girls looking for rich guys, guys looking for pretty girls. I'm on good terms with the bartender, as I am with at least ten others throughout the city, because I pay them to keep an eye on my players, especially the younger ones."

Cal frowned at him. "What? You pay them to spy on your players?"

"I pay them to keep me informed. There are lots of temptations out there for young kids with too much talent and money. Those bartenders and bouncers tell me when they think a player might be in danger of going over the edge. I try to stop it before it gets that far."

"How?"

Quinn looked grim. "Suspension, random drug tests, threats, bribery, coercion. I'm not scared to use what works. I will not let them throw their talent away, throw their future away because they are young and dumb."

"Oh." Cal turned his words over. That was so like Quinn, deeply honorable and innately protective. "Your players were upstairs...so what's upstairs?"

"Strip joint, men and women. Lap dances. Men on men, women on women and any combination thereof. It's a cool place to hang out, to show that you have no issue with your sexuality. I don't care who does what to whom, but the drugs flow through there like water through taps," Quinn stated in a flat voice. "If you had gone up there, on your own, without me, and you were photographed, it would've gone viral."

"I was on my way up there," Cal admitted.

"Yeah, I know. We ducked a bullet. It would've been pretty hard to explain why you were in a strip joint when we are so happily married," Quinn said.

"Except that we are not happily married. Or even properly married."

"No, we're not." Quinn rested his forearms on his thighs, his hands linked. "I looked at the photos, the articles. It seems as if we've done a great job of convincing the public that we are in love."

"But we're not, are we?" Cal asked, her heart in her throat. Well, she might be, but he wasn't.

Quinn pushed an agitated hand through his hair. "It's become complicated, exactly what we didn't want it to be."

He was looking at her as if he expected her to drop another conversational atomic bomb. She could see the trepidation in his eyes, the tension in his hard jaw. He was bracing himself for begging and tears.

She wouldn't do that, Cal decided. She wasn't going to beg him to love her. She'd rolled that die already and lost. She wasn't going to do it again.

But, God, it hurt. Cal sucked some much needed air and looked for a little bit of courage.

For the first time she made the conscious decision to lie to him. It was, she rationalized, for their greater good.

"I love you. I always have. But I won't let myself be in love with anybody, Quinn, not even you." She couldn't keep sleeping with him, couldn't keep up the pretense. Because she knew with every day she spent with him, every night she slept in his arms, she would fall deeper in love with him and leaving him would become impossible. She needed to save herself and to do that she had to leave. Now.

"Maybe we should—" Cal stopped. She didn't want to say the words because once they were said, she couldn't take them back. Nothing would ever be the same between them again. If she said what she needed to, she'd lose him, lose what little of his love she had. God, she'd had no clue this conversation would be so difficult.

Quinn moved so he sat on his haunches in front of her, his arm on his knee, his fingers encircling her ankle. "Maybe we should stop, Cal. We absolutely should play it safe, be sensible. Sleeping together complicated what was supposed to be a simple arrangement."

And so it starts...

No, don't think about how much it hurts. You can fall apart later. When you are alone. You've been through worse than this, Callahan. You can cope with a little heartbreak.

Focus on the practicalities. They still had a role to play, a marriage to act out.

"And the press? How do we handle them?"

"We don't do so many public appearances together and when we do, we make sure that we aren't acting so affectionate," Quinn suggested, his voice rough with an emotion she couldn't identify.

Cal tucked her legs under her bottom and pulled his shirt over her knees. "It might be easier if I left...the city, the country."

Besides, being away from him would give her the distance she needed to patch her heart back together.

Shock and denial flashed across his face and Cal lifted a shoulder. "That would be the best option, Quinn. The easiest way to do this."

Quinn muttered a curse and drummed his fingers on his thigh, obviously upset. "Okay, tell me what you're thinking."

"My dad is bored with being idle. He's itching to come back to work and if I give him the smallest excuse, he'll be home in a flash."

"Is he well enough to work?"

"It's been three months so I think so." Cal raked her hair back with her fingers and twisted it into a loose knot at the back of her neck. "And I should get back to my own work. There are problems everywhere that I need to sort out, some I can only fix by being on the ground." Cal nodded as a plan started to form in her head. "I suggest we issue a press statement, saying that I need to return to work, that we're going to do the long-distance marriage thing until I wrap up some projects. Except that the projects take longer than expected and, as a result, we start drifting apart."

Quinn's face gave nothing away and Cal had no idea what he was thinking. Damn, she'd always been able to read him, had always known what he was thinking until recently, when he kept his thoughts hidden from her. She hated it. Despite their best efforts, the last three months had changed their friendship.

They'd chosen the situation; they'd known the risk. Now they had to deal with the fallout.

"That could work," Quinn agreed. "When will you—"

"Go?" Cal finished his sentence. She didn't think she could live with Quinn and not touch him, not make love to him. If she moved anywhere else, then a lot of questions would be asked. The best solution was to leave, as soon as possible.

She just needed to find the courage to walk away, to do what was necessary. For both their sakes.

"ASAP, Quinn. I don't want to draw this out, make it harder than it needs to be." Cal dropped her gaze so he couldn't see how close she was to losing it.

Quinn's arm around her shoulders, him hauling her into his side, told her he'd already noticed. He kissed her temple and rested his head on hers. "We really should've kept this simple, Red."

Cal placed her arm around his neck and closed her eyes, feeling his heat, his hard body and ignoring the throb between her legs, her blood roaring through her veins. "Yeah, we really should've. We weren't very smart, Quinn."

It was the second game of the season and Quinn stood in their newly acquired owners' box in the Mavericks arena looking down at the rink. The seats were starting to fill and there was a buzz in the air.

The fans were excited and he could understand why. Yesterday he, Mac and Kade had signed the final papers giving them a majority ownership of the Mavericks and fulfilling their biggest dream.

Kade and Quinn stood next to him and he saw, and ignored, the long look they exchanged. He took a sip from his coffee cup. He grimaced. The coffee, like everything else over the past month, tasted like crap.

"We are now the official majority owners of the Mavericks," Kade said, a goofy-looking grin on his face. He bumped fists with Mac, who was also wearing a stupid-ass grin. They were still on a high from yesterday, still assimilating the knowledge that the deal was, finally, done.

The Mavericks, as they'd planned ten years ago, was theirs. They'd worked like crazy, taking financial risks, pouring their hearts and souls into the team and it had finally, finally, paid off. Quinn part-owned a professional hockey team, the *only* hockey team.

He should feel happier.

Mac's fist plowed into his shoulder. "I've seen you more excited over a pizza, dude."

Quinn looked across the ice, guilt closing his throat. This was a turning point, a major achievement, and he was sucking the life out of the party. Normally, he'd be the one celebrating the hardest, but little was normal since Cal left.

Everything felt strange, out of place. It was as if his life was now one of those fun-house mirrors, everything distorted, unfocused. But that wasn't his friends' fault; it wasn't anyone's fault but his. He made his choices and was living with the very crappy consequences.

Suck it up, Rayne. He dragged a smile onto his face and lifted his cup in a salute. "Here's to us. We kicked ass."

Kade's small smile acknowledged Quinn's effort to get into the swing of things. "Good try, but your level of enthusiasm still sucks. So, let's talk about it."

"Might as well," Mac agreed.

Oh, God. What was with his friends and their desire

to talk things through? They were guys. Guys didn't talk stuff to death.

"Nothing to talk about," Quinn snapped and frowned at Mac. "And we need to get down to the locker room."

"We have time," Mac replied.

Kade removed a stick of gum from his pocket, unwrapped the paper, keeping his eyes on Quinn. "Nothing to talk about? Really? Except Callahan, that is. How is she?"

So it looked like they were going to discuss Quinn's absent wife and his nonmarriage. "She arrived safely in Lesotho. I haven't spoken to her recently."

"Why not?" Kade asked.

"She's in a mountainous region with a bad signal," Quinn snapped.

"Wren manages to talk to her every couple of days, so do Brodie and Rory," Mac commented, his face and tone bland.

Busted. How could he worm his way out of this? What excuse could he use? Quinn rubbed his temple and decided he was too tired to look for one. Besides, these were his best friends, his safety net.

"It's just easier not to talk to her." Quinn took another sip of coffee and grimaced. He placed the mug on a high table and pushed it away.

"You miss her."

Miss her? That was such a stupid, tame, word for what he felt. He couldn't sleep, couldn't concentrate, couldn't think for missing her.

He absolutely missed his lover, missed his friend. "Yeah, I miss her."

"Why did she leave again?" Mac asked.

Quinn rubbed the back of his neck. "We decided that the...situation was getting out of control."

"Out of control how?"

Kade looked at Mac; Mac shook his head and echoed Kade's look of confusion. Really, was Quinn going to have to draw them a picture? "Neither of us wanted a happily-ever-after deal. Neither of us wanted to commit so we dialed it down before we…before we found ourselves doing that."

Kade tried to contain his mirth, but Mac just let it rip, his laughter rumbling over them. Quinn felt his fist clench and wondered if he would be forgiven for punching his best friend shortly after they realized their biggest professional and business triumph. And before a game.

Probably not.

"Glad that I amuse you. Moving the hell on—"

"How can you not realize that you and Cal are in a committed relationship, that you have been for years?" Kade asked, bemused.

"What are you talking about?" Quinn demanded.

"Moron, you've been friends for twenty years. That's commitment right there. Easy, natural, something that just is."

He'd try to keep this simple and maybe they'd understand. "Yeah, we were committed to a friendship, not a love affair."

"You worked to keep your friendship alive. You wanted to keep that connection. It was very damn important to you. And to her. You've been more committed to each other than anybody else in your lives. Your commitment to each other is longer than our friendship, longer than your career with the Mavericks, so much more meaningful than your relationship with your family. And you're both wusses, running away from each other," Mac bluntly said.

Oh…hell. Quinn wanted to deny his words, wanted

to argue, but he couldn't find anything to say. There were reasons why he couldn't have a be-mine relationship with Cal.

"It's not as simple as that," Quinn croaked the words out.

Two sets of eyebrows lifted. God, he'd never felt so exposed, so completely vulnerable. How could he tell them, these two masculine, *virile* men...

He rubbed his temple and when he looked up at them, his eyes reflected his anguish. "Cal wants kids. I can't give her any."

Kade and Mac stared at him for a long time and while he saw sympathy on their faces, he didn't see pity. Thank God. If he had, he would've handed in his man card. Kade tapped his fingers on the table, a sure sign that he was thinking. "Why do you think that?"

Quinn explained and they listened intently. Kade frowned and shook his head. "You need to get a second opinion. I don't think you can rely on one blood test years ago as a definitive diagnosis."

Mac nodded. "And, if it turns out you can't have kids, then there are other options. Adoption, surrogacy, sperm banks. Hell, I'll even donate some of my magnificent boys to the cause."

Kade choked on his beer and Quinn's mouth dropped open. Then humor—unexpected but welcome—bubbled to the surface. He shook his head. "It's bad enough working with you, training you—having to raise a mini-you would do my head in."

"The point is, there are options. But—" Kade sent him a hard, cool, assessing look "—before you get there you have to decide whether you want Cal in your life or not. Separate and apart from the giving-her-kids issue."

"Which he does," Mac interjected.

Which Quinn did. More than he wanted to keep working, coaching, *breathing*. His life without her in it had no meaning, no color, absolutely no direction. And even less joy. Kade was right: he'd never been able to commit to anyone because he'd always—even if it was only on a subconscious level—been committed to Callahan. He loved her. He'd always loved her. His subconscious knew what it wanted and it had been waiting a damn long time for his body and his brain to catch up.

"Yep, he's getting there." Mac gripped Quinn's shoulder, their equivalent of a girly hug.

Quinn felt he should say something, should express his gratitude that he had these two guys solidly in his corner. But hell, what could he say that didn't make him sound like he'd grown a pair of ovaries?

"Thanks," he eventually muttered.

Mac grinned. "Well, you know that we'd take a bullet for you. Not in the head, or in the heart, but maybe like in the ass…or the big toe."

Quinn, for the first time that night, for the first time in a month, laughed. As his laughter rumbled out, he felt his mobile vibrate. He pulled it out and swiped the screen with his thumb.

His laughter died and something that felt like hope took its place. "I need to go."

Mac snatched the mobile from his hand, read the message and handed the phone to Kade. Quinn was too shocked to object to them reading his messages. All he cared about was going home.

Kade slapped the phone back into Quinn's hand.

"I have to do this," he said, hoping they'd understand. "Cal and I need to talk."

Neither Mac nor Kade said anything for a while and Quinn's heart sank. He understood their reluctance, he was, after, running out on his responsibilities. The Mavericks, the game...they were important, sure, but Cal was his *life*.

Then they grinned and he knew that they'd been messing with him. Jerks.

"Go, we'll handle your responsibilities here," Kade told him. He grinned. "I mean, really, how difficult can coaching be?"

Quinn shoved a hand through his hair and narrowed his eyes at Kade. At the door he turned and sent Kade a withering glare. "Payback is a bitch, Webb."

Kade just laughed. "Get the hell out of here, Rayne, before we change our minds."

Quinn bolted.

Eleven

Living her life without Quinn was like trying to make the world spin in another direction. It simply didn't work. It made her feel dizzy and ditzy and…sad. Bereft. Alone.

She'd tried. She'd given it her best shot and, after a month, she was over living on the other side of the world, trying to remember why it was better that she and Quinn were apart. The only thing that was true, real, important was that they stay linked, that he remain a part of her life, in any way she could get him.

She didn't know how that would work, what role she was going to play, but they could work it out. They *would* work it out. He'd been the biggest part of her life for most of her life, the person she'd loved best all these years, and while she loved him, fiercely, she'd take him any way she could get him.

Cal opened the door to Quinn's home and dropped her overnight bag to the floor. Although she knew Quinn would be at the arena, preparing for a Mavericks game, she tipped her head, listening for movement, hoping she'd hear him upstairs. Hoping she could see him, drink him in.

Cal played with her cell phone as she walked toward the huge windows. She placed her shoulder against the glass and stared out at the water; she'd missed this view, missed his home.

Missed him with every atom of her being.

She'd always thought that love was something ethereal, an emotion that made you happier, prettier, smarter, more worthwhile. She'd dived into a marriage with Toby in order to feel safe and protected, in the hope that he'd take her to a place where grief didn't exist, where nothing could hurt her. She'd miscalculated there. Toby had hurt her and she'd been slapped in the face with everything she'd been running from.

His death had released her and, instead of trying to work through her issues with men, commitment and marriage, she'd dismissed both the species and the tradition, choosing to go it alone.

Only to find all she wanted and needed in the man who'd always been her rock, who made her laugh, who'd always encouraged her to fly but who would catch her if she crashed.

Because love wasn't perfection. It wasn't big houses and gourmet meals, designer clothes and fake smiles. Love wasn't the storybook kiss in the rain. It wasn't red roses or deep, soulful conversations.

Love was messy. Love was imperfect. Love was sarcastic text messages and two-minute phone calls, buying takeout and eating it on the bed before making love. Love was arguing and sharing the shower, stealing his cup of coffee when you were running out the door, morn-

ing kisses before teeth were brushed. Love was a friendship set on fire. Love was not running when things got
tough; it was having the courage to reach out for more.

Love was traveling across an ocean from one continent
to another to tell her best friend, the man she loved best,
that she wanted everything he could give her, whether
that was a little or a lot.

Cal took a deep breath, felt her heart kick up. She
couldn't call him. He was preparing for a game and he
wouldn't answer. Quinn had tunnel vision when he was
in the zone and he was never more in the zone than when
he was preparing for a Mavericks game. But she could
send him a text. He'd get it when the game was over and
that would give her some time to think about what to
say to him.

For the first time ever, she couldn't find her words
with Quinn, couldn't explain what she was thinking and
feeling. Maybe it was because this time the words she
needed to say were too important, the feelings too scary.
She typed and erased four messages and cursed herself.

Keep it simple.

Hi, I wanted to tell you that I miss you, that I miss us.
Maybe you can give me a call and we can chat about
us, our marriage? Please?

Cal pushed the send button on her phone and bit her
bottom lip. What if he didn't reply? What if he came
home and was upset to see her back? Oh, God, what if
he'd moved on? What if he came home with a puckbunny
groupie on his arm?

Maybe coming back to Vancouver was a bad move,
she thought, staring at the ocean, fighting back her tears.

Maybe she should leave. Go back to Africa and then onto India, bury herself in her work.

Except she'd done that, had tried to push him away, had tried to forget him, but she'd failed spectacularly. No, she wouldn't run. She'd wait, talk to him, repair whatever she could of their friendship.

She realized that he would never love her, not the way she wanted him to, but they could be friends and maybe that would be enough.

So she'd stay here and wait.

Thank God he was one of the bosses because blowing off an important game, leaving the stadium before his team was about to go on the ice, would get his ass canned if he were an employee, Quinn thought as he swung his Ducati in and out of traffic. As soon as he got to the yacht, he'd call Cal back, find out where she was. Then he'd call the team's pilot and tell him to file a flight plan for their company jet.

He needed to grab some gear and his passport—God, he couldn't forget his passport. Quinn steered his bike into his parking spot at the marina, ripped off his helmet, shoved it under his arm and started jogging toward the access gate and the *Red Delicious*. As he ran, he looked down at his cell, his thumb hovering over the green button to call Cal back. What would he say? How could he express everything that was in his heart?

Why did this have to be so damn difficult? He didn't want to spill his soul on a telephone or via an internet connection. Nope, if he was going to make an idiot of himself, then he was going do it properly, face-to-face.

And if that meant flying halfway around the world, then that was what he would do. Besides, he knew he could persuade her to his way of thinking—a proper marriage, love, staying together, being together—by kissing her, helping her get naked. Hey, a guy had to use whatever worked.

Quinn stormed onto the yacht, belted up the stairs and whipped open the door. He threw his helmet onto the chair at the door and thundered down the stairs to his cabin. He pushed the green button and the call rang as he yanked open the door to his walk-in closet. Stepping inside he grabbed some T-shirts and tucked them under his arm.

One ring, two, three, four—God, she had to answer.

He tossed the shirts onto his bed and dropped to his haunches next to his nightstand. He stared at the small wall safe in the table and couldn't remember the code. What if she didn't answer? What if he couldn't get ahold of her? What would he do? Where would he go?

"Hello?"

Quinn stood up abruptly, swore and rubbed the back of his neck. "Hi, sorry. I didn't think you were going to answer." He spat the words out, hardly able to hear his own voice above the thundering of his heart.

"Hi. Shouldn't you be at the game?"

"I should. I'm not." Just hearing her voice made sense. *She made sense.* "Where are you?"

"Why?"

"Because wherever you are, I'm on my way there." God, he sounded like an idiot. "I mean, I'll get there. Give me some time. You're right—we need to talk."

"You're coming to me?"

He thought he heard amusement in her voice but dismissed it as a figment of his imagination. It wasn't like he was thinking straight at the moment. "Yeah, the company jet is at my disposal. It'll get me where I need to go. So, can you text me directions?"

"I can do that. But it's pretty simple, I can tell you over the phone."

"God, Red, I can't think straight, and I definitely won't remember anything you say. Just text me. I'll get to wherever I need to be as soon as I can." And he prayed it wouldn't take more than a day or two.

"Okay, um, great. See you soon." Cal disconnected and Quinn stared at his blank screen, a frown on his face. Dammit, that was it? That was all she had for him? He was flying out to see a woman he loved and all she could say was *see you soon*? God, she was the most infuriating, crazy, annoying brat he'd ever laid eyes on. The only woman he'd ever loved, would ever love.

And, yeah, two days was better than two weeks, two months, two years, never. So he'd be a man and suck it up...

His phone flashed and Quinn swiped his thumb across the screen. He read the message, frowned and read it again.

At your bedroom door, turn right. Walk up the stairs and look for the girl holding the bottle of wine and two glasses.

Holy, holy, *holy* crap.

Quinn thundered back up the stairs, skidded into the lounge and stopped by the cream-colored sofa, his hands gripping its back with white-knuckled fingers. Cal noticed that his chest was heaving and his breathing was erratic. She was amazed, thrilled, that her presence could raise the heartbeat of this superfit man.

Her man. Maybe...

She looked for something to say, some witty comment

to break their charged silence, something to slice through the tension. She had nothing so she lifted her half-full glass of wine. "Want some?"

"Wine? No." Quinn's voice, deep and dark, rumbled across her skin as he walked toward her, his eyes a little wild and a lot determined. Her throat closed up as he narrowed the distance between them and she allowed him to pull the glass from her hand, watching as he placed it on the coffee table in front of her. "That's not what I want."

"What do you want?" Cal asked, tipping her head back to look at him, wishing he would touch her, kiss her.

"You. Any damn way I can get you." Quinn's gaze dropped from her eyes to her mouth, where he lingered as if he was fighting the urge to kiss her. Cal sighed when his hand cupped her shoulder, skimmed up her throat, her jaw, stopping when his palm rested on her cheek, his fingers in her hair.

Cal needed to touch him so she placed her hand on his chest. "Your heart is racing," she murmured.

The corners of Quinn's mouth kicked up. "Yeah, it started doing that when I saw your name on my screen and it went into overdrive when I realized you are here, in my home, and not a continent away. Why are you here, Cal?"

She tried to tell him why, but the words wouldn't come. Instead of telling him that she loved him, that she wanted a lifetime with him, she bit her lip.

"Why were you going to hijack the company jet to come to me?" she whispered, hoping he was braver than her.

"I was going to fly over there and beg you to come home. To me." Quinn's voice was saturated with emotion. "My life…is not that exciting anymore. Not without you in it."

She needed clarity, needed to know what he meant by that statement. "As a friend? As a lover?"

"As my everything," Quinn whispered the words against her lips and the last, tiny kernel of fear dissolved. "You're the only woman I've ever loved, the only person I fully trust."

"Quinn." Cal bunched the fabric of his shirt in her hand, closing her eyes when his lips touched her temple, her cheekbone, the lids of her eyes.

"Nothing gives me as much of a thrill as I get when I wake up with you in my arms, when I come home and you're here. Nothing gets my heart racing like making love to you. Nothing feels as good as watching you shatter when I'm inside you. You are my highest peak, my biggest wave, my fastest ride."

Cal linked her arms around his neck and stood on her tiptoes to brush her lips against his mouth, to push her breasts into his chest, her hips into his. If she could climb inside him, she would. "Quinn."

Quinn kissed her and she felt his love in his lips, in the way he tasted her. His lips sipped at her; his tongue traced the fullness of her bottom lip, the edges of her teeth, before it slid inside to tangle with her tongue. It was a kiss that promised, that soothed, that excited. It told the story of their past and painted a picture for the future, of a friendship set on fire.

Then his kiss slowed, he hesitated and pulled back to look at her, a question in his eyes.

"Why did you come back?" he asked, his hands on her hips, the tips of his fingers digging into her skin. Cal touched his cheek and realized there was doubt in his eyes, and fear. Fear that he was the only one feeling this way...

Cal swallowed, humbled by the fact that this strong, brave man was insecure, that he needed her reassurance, that he wasn't the only one who was risking his heart. "I came home because you are, simply, my home. You have always been my deepest connection, my best friend. You bring out the best in me. You make me want to be better, do better."

Quinn's eyes softened, turned a brighter green. "Are we saying that we love each other?"

Cal nodded her agreement but didn't drop her eyes from his. He just looked at her, waiting for her to verbalize her thoughts, to make them real. "I do love you." But she'd always loved him, so she thought clarity was needed. "I am so *in love* with you."

"As I am with you," Quinn replied, resting his temple against the top of her head, hugging her to him. "God, baby, I've missed you so much."

"I've missed you too. I never knew how long nights could be without you beside me," Cal said, snuggling in as her tension drained away. "I didn't think you could love me, but I knew I had to be near you, if only as a friend."

Quinn's hand squeezed her butt in a way that was anything but friendly. "Like we could be in the same room without wanting to get each other naked. Talking about getting naked..."

"Were we? I thought we were going to spend the next couple of hours being all mushy," Cal teased him, not quite able to imagine her adrenaline-seeking man being ridiculously romantic.

"I do my best romancing naked," Quinn assured her,

his hand tugging on the hem of her flowing, rust-colored sweater.

Cal lifted her arms and he pulled the sweater over her head and tossed it to the floor. Instead of reaching for her, Quinn held her away from him, his face questioning. "Is that what you need from me, romance?"

Cal cocked her head. "Would you give it to me?"

"I will try to give you whatever you need to make you happy. Fidelity, respect, love—that's a given. I'm not a romantic guy, but if that's what you need to feel secure, I'll try."

His sincerity hit her in the gut and her jumpy heart settled, sighed. "I don't need the gestures of romance, Quinn. I just need you. The Quinn I've always known is the Quinn I want in my life. I just need you to tell me you love me occasionally and to get me naked as often as possible, and I'm grand."

"I have no problem with telling you I love you. I always have and it seems to be as natural as breathing."

"Me too."

Sadness dimmed the happiness in his eyes. "What about kids, Cal? I can't give you kids."

Cal hastened to assure him that her love wasn't conditional. "I'm still not convinced about that, but we'll work it out. You and I, we can work anything out, as long as we do it together."

Cal's eyes drank him in. His beautiful eyes, his jaw rough with stubble, his relaxed mouth. His hair was longer and not so spiky and...

Cal laughed and she lifted her hand to a spot just above his ear.

Quinn raised an eyebrow. "What?"

Cal tugged the white feather out of his hair and held it up for him to see. "I think my mom approves."

Quinn touched the feather with his index finger before pulling Cal into his arms and dropping his face into her neck. "I do love you, Red."

Cal felt his heart thudding under her hand and knew her happy-ever-after had arrived. Their life together, she decided, was going to be an amazing ride.

Epilogue

Three months later...

"Now tell me this wasn't a grand idea," Mac demanded, lifting a champagne bottle to refresh Brodie's and Rory's champagne flutes. The six of them, with Rosie and Cody, were sitting on the veranda, having just come back to the luxury house after an afternoon spent on the beach.

Cal had no problem telling Mac that his impetuous decision that they spend a week at the house they jointly owned in Puerto Rico was a fine idea and she lifted her untouched glass in his direction. "Fantastic idea, Mac."

"Wait until you live through a hurricane here," Rory muttered, but her eyes laughed at her husband.

Mac took his toddler daughter from Rory and dropped a kiss on her puckered lips. "It was just a little wind, Rorks, and you took shelter in my big, brawny arms."

"Well, one arm. The other was fairly useless at the

time," Rory corrected him. "God, you were a terrible patient."

Their friends laughed when Mac scowled at her. Cal leaned back in her chair and picked her feet up to tuck her heels on the edge of the chair, thinking that it wouldn't be long before she wouldn't be able to sit like this. She was surprised Quinn hadn't noticed her rounder shape.

For the last day or so, since they'd left Vancouver, she'd been wondering how to tell him he was going to be a dad, probably in around thirty weeks or so. He'd be surprised and, she hoped, ecstatically happy. Even happier than they presently were...if that was even possible.

Quinn, sitting next to Kade, picked up Cody's foot and bent his head to gently nibble the baby's arch, causing Cody to chuckle heartily every time. They'd been playing this game for ten minutes and neither of them was bored with it yet. Cal felt her eyes fill with tears and after she'd blinked them away, she caught Kade's gaze and saw him tip his head, his eyes quizzical.

Kade always seemed to sense a secret just as it was ready to be divulged. And what was she waiting for? These were Quinn's best friends—her best friends— their family. Quinn wouldn't care how he heard that he was going to be a dad, and they'd get a kick out of seeing his happiness.

Cal flicked her eyes to Cody, gave Kade the tiniest nod and his eyes flashed with understanding and joy.

"Quinn—" she started to speak, but her words drained away. She bit her lip, her mind a blank. It was such good news, crazy-good news, but her throat had closed from too much emotion.

"Hey, butthead—" Kade jumped into her silence, winking at Cal "—did you ever go back to the doctor to redo those fertility tests?"

Quinn looked up at him and scowled. "I'm playing a rather excellent game with your son and you have to spoil the moment by raising *that* subject? Thanks, Webb."

Kade wasn't remotely chastised. "Well, did you?"

Quinn reached out and took Cal's hand in his and she felt the tension in his fingers. "Cal and I decided that we'd do it when the season ended, when we had a moment to breathe. We're taking a little time for ourselves before we go down that road."

"But you do want kids?" Kade demanded.

Cal saw Quinn's Adam's apple bob and the slow, definite nod of his head. "I want whatever we can have. As long as Cal is at the center of our family, I'm good."

Tears, silent and powerful, rolled down Cal's face. Her small sob had Quinn whipping his head around to look at her and his eyes widened in shock. "Crap! What did I say? Red, don't cry—jeez! I'm sorry, I know it's a sensitive subject and Kade is a moron for bringing it up."

"I agree with that," Mac chimed in.

Cal let out a laugh and placed her hand on Quinn's cheek, pulling his frowning face back to hers. "Stop looking at Kade like you want to thump him, darling. He's actually being a good guy, trying to help me out here."

"Told you so," Kade said with a smirk, rubbing his unshaven chin across Cody's fuzzy head.

Quinn frowned. "What do you mean?"

Cal blinked away her tears and smiled. She reached past Quinn and tapped Cody's foot. "We're going to have one of these." She looked at Rosie, who was dipping her fingers into Mac's beer glass and shoving her wet digits into her mouth. "Or maybe a pink one, like Rosie. Um…maybe you should move your beer glass out of your daughter's reach, Mac."

Mac picked up his drink and Rosie let out a yell of protest.

Rory covered her eyes with her hand. "Oh, God, she's definitely a Maverick. Heaven help me."

Quinn shook his head, still confused. "I don't understand. What are you trying to say, Red?"

Cal smiled and pulled his hand to her stomach. "Do you remember I asked you for some of your boys?"

He was still confused. "Yeah, and I told you that I don't have any."

Cal laughed. "Four pregnancy tests and a scan the day before yesterday says you do, my darling. So, do you want to come on an adventure with me, Q? You, me and our munchkin?"

Quinn lowered his forehead to hers, his eyes glistening with hope, excitement and undiluted joy. "Red, I love you to distraction and you should know by now that I would go anywhere with you. You, and them—" he jerked a thumb toward his friends "—are my family, but I'm thrilled, ecstatic, that we're making it bigger."

"We're halfway to having our own junior Mavericks team, men," Mac drawled. "Another from each of us and we can put a team on the ice. But, really, to make an impact, we'd need a couple more…"

* * * * *

*If you liked this novel, pick up these other sexy,
fun reads from Joss Wood*

TAKING THE BOSS TO BED
ONE NIGHT, TWO CONSEQUENCES
THE HONEYMOON ARRANGEMENT

and the first two books in
FROM MAVERICKS TO MARRIED

Mac's story
TRAPPED WITH THE MAVERICK MILLIONAIRE

and Kade's story
PREGNANT BY THE MAVERICK MILLIONAIRE

All available now from Mills & Boon Desire!

* * *

MILLS & BOON®

PASSIONATE AND DRAMATIC LOVE STORIES

sneak peek at next month's titles...

In stores from 15th December 2016:

One Baby, Two Secrets – Barbara Dunlop *and*
The Rancher's Nanny Bargain – Sara Orwig

The Tycoon's Secret Child – Maureen Child *and*
Single Mum, Billionaire Boss – Sheri WhiteFeather

An Heir for the Texan – Kristi Gold *and*
The Best Man's Baby – Karen Booth

Just can't wait?
Buy our books online a month before they hit the shops!
www.millsandboon.co.uk

Also available as eBooks.

MILLS & BOON®

EXCLUSIVE EXTRACT

Saoirse Murphy's proposal of a 'convenient'
arrangement with paramedic Santiago Valentino
soon ignites a very inconvenient passion...

Read on for a sneak preview of
SANTIAGO'S CONVENIENT FIANCÉE
by Annie O'Neil

Saoirse went up on tiptoe and kissed him.

From the moment her lips touched Santiago's she
didn't have a single lucid thought. Her brain all but
exploded in a vain attempt to unravel the quick-fire
sensations. Heat, passion, need, longing, sweet and tangy
all jumbled together in one beautiful confirmation that
his lips were every bit as kissable as she'd thought they
might be.

Snippets of what was actually happening were hitting
her in blips of delayed replay.

Her fingers tangled in his silky, soft hair. Santi's wide
hands tugged her in tight, right at the small of her back.
There was no doubting his body's response to her now.
The heated pleasure she felt when one of his hands
slipped under her T-shirt elicited an undiluted moan of
pleasure. He matched her move for move as if they had
been made for one another. Her body's reaction to his
felt akin to hitting all hundred watts her body was capable
of for the very first time.

She wanted more.

No.

'Oh, I doubt it,' Noah interrupted, but he still didn't sound entirely happy about the idea, which surprised her. Perhaps she'd misread his flirting earlier. Maybe he really was like that with everyone and, now the reality of having to spend time with her had set in, he was less keen on the idea. 'Melissa has quite the packed schedule for the wedding party, you know. She's right—you're going to have to find someone to take over most of your job here.'

Eloise sighed. She *did* know. She'd helped Laurel plan it, after all.

And, now she thought about it, every last bit of the schedule involved the maid of honour and the best man being together.

Noah smiled, a hint of the charm he'd exhibited earlier showing through despite the frown, and Eloise's heart beat twice in one moment as she accepted the inevitable.

She was doomed.

She had the most ridiculous crush on a man who clearly found her a minor inconvenience.

And—even worse—the whole world was going to be watching, laughing at her pretending that she could live in this world of celebrities, mocking her for thinking she could ever be pretty enough, funny enough…just *enough* for Noah Cross.

Don't miss
SLOW DANCE WITH THE BEST MAN
by Sophie Pembroke

Available January 2017
www.millsandboon.co.uk